Advance Pr

"The latest miracle from the master of supernatural suspense, where the grace of the prose is so measured and the charm of the characters so magical that it takes some time to notice that the stiletto of dread has already slid between your ribs."

— Peter Atkins, author of the novels *Morningstar, Big Thunder,* and *Moontown*, and the screenplays *Hellraiser II, Hellraiser III, Hellraiser IV,* and *Wishmaster*

"Hirshberg knows all the pressure points of the human soul. With a poet's prose and a storyteller's keen eye for detail, he tells a heartfelt and heartbreaking story about the way we find the most precious things in life, and the way we lose them, no matter how tightly we try to hang on."

— Ian Rogers, author of *Every House is Haunted*

"Glen Hirshberg asks what is lost to humanity when imagination is left to be exploited by those more interested in destruction than creation, and what will become of what remains. *Infinity Dreams* is a puzzle of sorts, a quest, an unraveling, a love story, a warning. A beautifully written talisman to be treasured."

— Mary Rickert, author of *The Shipbuilder of Bellfairie* and *You Have Never Been Here*

"Glen Hirshberg is one of the best the horror genre has to offer. His Bradbury-haunted prose is elegant, sophisticated, and always utterly chilling. Read his work, and thank me later."

— Christopher Golden, *New York Times* bestselling author of *Road of Bones, Ararat, Snowblind,* and *Red Hands*

INFINITY DREAMS

The Nadine and Normal Adventure

GLEN HIRSHBERG

CEMETERY DANCE PUBLICATIONS

Baltimore

❖ 2021 ❖

Cemetery Dance Publications
132B Industry Lane, Unit #7
Forest Hill, MD 21050
www.cemeterydance.com

First Cemetery Dance Printing

ISBN: 978-1-58767-811-0

For Jeff, who found me the Moonstone, then Worse Things Waiting, way back when finding was hard.

For my dad, who always took me with him.

And for Kim and Kate and Sid, who keep coming up with new things worth finding, and showing me how.

HOME

"My *favorite* story?" Nadine says, glancing over her shoulder toward the almost silent hallway. The Collector is back there, shuffling in and out of the bedroom or maybe leaning in the doorframe in the shadows to listen. She's sure—almost—that he knows someone's here. Possibly, that's why he acts this way on the rare, rare days they have visitors. Possibly, in some walled-off corner of what's left of that brain, he imagines he's standing guard. Looking out for her. As if he was ever much use at that. Quietly, without gesture or sound, she lets her heart break a little more.

"Any that come to mind," the young journalist says. He has perched himself in the room's lone armchair, which was their friend Tony's chair once. It is, still, if Tony ever somehow finds his way back and claims it. No matter how hard or how often Nadine cleans it, his smell—pot, garden mulch, Dentine, sourdough, mostly pot—clings to every crack in the mottled, maroon leather. She could have the cracks repaired, has occasionally considered it. But then it wouldn't be Tony's chair anymore, and no longer of use to them or him. No good for anything except sitting on. Barely chair at all as far as she is concerned.

The journalist is too tall and young and blond for this room. He makes the house small. Most days, especially misty ones when it's just her and her murmuring man, this place can still feel like a world. Their world.

Out the floor-to-ceiling windows, late afternoon shadows slide down the hillsides with the marine layer, obscuring the edges of the lawn she hand-mows every Thursday morning. The wind has kicked up, too, chasing still more shadows out of the sycamores ringing the 1200 square-foot A-frame she used to consider more houseboat than house. The place they slept, poached eggs, fought for each other's distracted attention, stored the very little they kept. Sometimes made love. Their own private way-station on their way to more elsewheres.

These days, it's a house, for better and worse. Not just moored, but dry docked.

The Collector has emerged from the hall. He's over in the kitchen, in plain view, picking up pans, putting them down. Murmuring. Possibly, he's talking to the eggs he no longer remembers how to make. He laughs once. That rare, sudden, barking laugh. Joy grenade, Nadine used to call it. Maybe somewhere down deep, wherever he is in there, he's joyful, still.

She has been silent too long. *And why are her eyes closed*?

She opens them. The young journalist has unfolded his writing case on his lap. At first, she'd taken the case for some hyper-hipster hold-all for his laptop. The perfect accessory for the millennial wordsmith dabbling at or more kindly clutching for a profession that had once relied on in-person, conversation-based relationships instead of text messaging and digital brand management. A collectible.

But now she thinks it could be a memento from a grandparent. Certainly, it's the real thing. Its leather covering is dark, tessellated, pulling back from the frame at every corner like skin off a skull. But its custom-sized paper has been stacked neatly in its slot, its blotting pad properly anchored, its pen tray filled not with quills but everyday G-2s. The whole thing really does look prepped for practical use, a tool for engagement rather than enshrinement, and therefore resistant to collectors.

Unless they're the proper sort. Hers and Normal's.

"Sorry," she says. "What?"

In the kitchen, the Collector drops a pan. It bangs off the counter, peals like a bell as it falls to the floor. He doesn't pick it up, wanders around the counter and across the living room, between Nadine and the young journalist to the glass front door. He doesn't linger there the way they used to together, as though at the prow of a ship, occasionally but not usually touching. Sharing moments of experience, the *experience* of experiencing. Staring side by side into the mist.

Not through it, they used to tell each other, standing there. *Into it. To see what's in it.*

To Nadine, part of what was in that mist was home. This one, but also her first, a continent and ocean away. She always imagined the mist *coming* from there, yet another wave of ghost-emigrants fleeing famine, Troubles, drunken fathers, peat smoke, to pour into this clearing and sing her the old songs. The greatest songs.

Oh, It's a long way.

Don't work on the railroad.

Come home.

The young journalist is watching Normal, not the windows or mist. There's something in the way he watches that surprises Nadine; it also calms her, strangely. The only thing moving is that gaze. He doesn't produce a camera or iPhone from a pocket and snap a picture. The pen he clicks open isn't poised over paper, has settled back into the webbing between thumb and forefinger. It doesn't tap.

He's just looking at her man.

To see what's in him.

"Normal," she calls, though she's feeling more protective than nervous. Not like she has been all week, anticipating this visit, trying to imagine what this young journalist thought he'd find here, and who could possibly care. "Come away, now." She starts to stand. "Come on, I'll make you…"

He's already moving, though. He never completely stopped. He no longer looks through or into anything; he's just circling. Back he goes behind Tony's chair, down the hall toward the book-lined den where he'll stand a while by the shelves or file drawers packed with handwritten (his) and typed (hers) pages he no longer reads. He melts into his own shadow.

"You're not what I expected," the journalist says, after an appropriate interval. Nadine lets herself settle back onto the couch, into this room. This person actually speaking *to* her. She eyes the journalist's flaxen hair, strange eyes. Bright blue, with lighter blue ringing them. Even at rest, his limbs stay cocked like a grasshopper's.

"Same to yourself," she says. Then, "How so?"

The journalist's smile is impish. *Good God, flirty*?

And is this her smiling back, now?

"Both more and less banshee," he says.

Nadine snorts. Her first good one in ages. First of this whole, cursed year. "Let's start with the more."

"Your hair," he says.

To her amazement, Nadine flushes. She'd known the journalist was coming, prepared for it. She'd changed her sweatshirt, hadn't she? But it's as if she has only now remembered she *has* hair. Can feel the weight of all that black-and-white beating down her back, pooling on and spilling over her shoulders.

"Eyes, too," says the journalist. "That's some blue."

Flirting. Jaysus. Doing it well, too, or else she's even lonelier than she knew.

He isn't just young and handsome, either. Fucking prepossessed, this one. Not how she used to like them. But apparently, now...

"How about the less?" she snaps.

He shrugs. "Well, you're not keening. You haven't howled me from your house."

"Early days. I hardly know you." She puts a hand to her chin, taps her cheek with her thumb. Her old, unconscious thinking/researching gesture from back when she was still her. When she and the Collector were what they'd been. Not so long ago.

Less than eighteen months. How can that be?

Her eyes narrow. "They say I keen?"

Again with the shrug. Also the grin. "They call you banshee."

"That's because I'm Irish. And a woman, and a collector, and I know what the fuck I'm doing. Most men, let's face it, the terminology's limited. Only so many words you lot understand. Heel. Stay. Banshee."

Up on the wall, the wishing-tree clock blows its kiss to the quarter-hour. It rustles on its wooden base, the not-quite-golden pendulum catching and flashing a sliver of light from somewhere. The young journalist laughs at the clock or her, and Nadine lets her eyes close once more, makes her usual wish. Once upon a time, she'd had dozens, although they were more yearnings, every one of them something she acted upon.

"You were going to tell me a story," the journalist says, and Nadine opens her eyes.

"I was?"

"If I can find the magic words. With my limited terminology." His smile flashes again. Just the right width, right duration.

Like smile projected on rock, she thinks, folds her arms instinctively across her chest, then shakes her head. Really, she's going to have to find ways to get out of this house and away from this clearing occasionally. Do the shopping, maybe, instead of having it delivered. Find mah-jongg partners, people who understand how to wash tiles. She opens her mouth to answer, but what come out is another question.

"Which publication did you say you're from, again?"

The young journalist's hands rise from his lap, palms up, as though she'd pulled a gun on him. He even leaves the pen on the writing case. "You caught me. I didn't."

Nadine's shudder is at least partly satisfaction. Her own little wishing-clock kiss. Apparently, at least a few of her instincts are still functioning. Spider-senses intact. Except…

Alarmed? *Should she be?* Is *she?*

In the den, a file drawer slides open, slides shut. No bang, just noise. Nadine stares at the journalist. He's still got his hands up. Is positively beaming.

"What on earth are you doing here, then?" she says.

Slowly, he lowers his hands. That pen clicks open. He leans forward in his chair like a horse straining at a bit. Or a cat coiling to pounce. Or a kid with a head full of stories.

"The Squad sent me," he says.

Way back in her own head, Nadine actually hears her brain grinding awake. Unused and unoiled gears clanking, pistons lurching into motion.

Well, hello, self. What's the craic?

She slides forward, too, lowering her stare directly into the young journalist's. "The *Flying* Squad?"

Oh, yes, she's awake. The journalist's startled jaw-drop makes her laugh out loud.

"You know what that was?"

"Is. Apparently. And now that's *you*, blushing." *Oh, yes,* she thinks, *I really should wake up more often*. She lowers her arms, folds her hands together, watches her visitor regain himself.

"You know what the Squad is?"

"They warned you I was a banshee."

Later, she will remember what he didn't say next. The confirmation he didn't offer. In the moment, though, she's too busy being proud of herself for being herself.

"What's the point of a group like that, now, though?" she asks. She has even forgotten her original question—the one about why this man has come—and the reason she asked it; as ever, or at least as it was, she's gotten too curious now. Interested, in the way she used to be almost every minute of her life. "I mean, with internet, eblasts, text notifications, instant verification…why would Southeby's or Christie's or whichever house you're from even need you? Wasn't the whole point of the Squad that it would zap in unannounced at a moment's notice, show up at some overlooked little estate or bankruptcy sale and identify one or five actually valuable items, set up their own event on the spot, and sell dear and quickly? Something like that?"

"Something like that," the journalist says. Watching her. "I…we're just acquirers, now. *Seekers*, if you will. Like you two..."

...were.

He doesn't say that. Was about to. If he'd smiled, she really might have commenced keening. Thrown him out. But he's too canny. Or maybe kind. Or just controlled. He doesn't even shrug.

"We're like you. And as you know, for exactly the reasons you say and more, it's tough to get to the really good things first anymore. The rare and beautiful and valuable things. But that's the point. That's why they need us. Precisely because it's harder every day to secure properties of quality before your competitors know they're out there. Have your likely bidders on immediate alert. Pull off and insure a 100 percent white glove sale, with no costly site or equipment rentals, no overhead, no warehousing. No *catalogue raisonne* nor staff to write and produce one. These days, the gold standard is *simple.* Clean. Quick. Maximum return on investment."

There it is, Nadine thinks, controlling her grimace. *The Houses. Their ethos and ambiance and language and intentions suffusing everything they say, everyone who works with, buys from, or sells to them. As rigid and monolithic and boring as the FBI, no matter how modernized their methods.*

There's a familiarity to it, though. A comfort in knowing that the Houses she and Normal have scorned all their lives remain as they were.

Except that if the Houses have heard of she and Normal—and why wouldn't they have, of course they have—then they have to know there's nothing for them here. Certainly nothing she would sell. Not to them.

"Aye. So. You or your boss woman got onto us, somehow. Heard we were a bit..." She avoids glancing toward the hall but can't help hearing the Collector shuffling around. Touching book spines. Whistling tunes all jumbled together, seemingly all at once. A walking "Unanswered Question," except most of his songs are hers, from her childhood. County Clare wandering songs. "Rambling Boys of Pleasure." "Flower of Finae."

"...hampered," she murmurs. She doesn't bother controlling her sigh.

The journalist cocks his head, waves one hand in a gesture clearly meant to seem kind. Or *be* kind. Why wouldn't he be? "Not currently trading. Perhaps in a bit of need." He doesn't gesture at anything, point at the wishing-tree clock or tap Tony's chair, nothing so gauche or graceless. "And as you said, there really aren't so many unexplored attics anymore, are there? Untapped reservoirs? Undiscovered treasured caves, with dragon or without?"

This time, his smile is both smooth and genuine. House he may be. But he loves what he does. So much that he glows. "You guys really are legends, you know."

Snort number two erupts from Nadine's mouth and nostrils. "Jaysus, who's *your* friend circle, then?"

"One that overlaps yours."

"Unlikely." Impossible, in fact. Almost. Given that she and the Collector have no circle—their clientele came because what they collected had no market, no *catalogue raisonne* or dedicated swapping website or even competitor bidders, usually—and even fewer friends. Other than each other.

And yet. The Houses have so many resources. So much money. This guy seems exactly the sort the big players have always hired. Smart and fast. Cunning and charming. Determined as fuck. It doesn't seem so unlikely that he and they have gotten wind of at least a few of the things and people and places she and Normal have rooted out.

They could easily have heard of or done business with The Strip Mall of the Gods guys, just for example. The Clockmaker and Mr. Map both.

The Hamtramck baker, sure.

The entire town of Jolene, assuming the Houses could find it.

Even so. "No," she says. "Just doesn't seem likely."

"I'm here, aren't I? How do you think that happened?"

"If you'd actually talked to anyone about us—anyone who actually knows us—you'd know there's nothing for you here. We don't collect."

"The Collector doesn't collect?"

"That's right."

"I beg to differ."

"Have a gander, then. Wander the grounds. Closing time's six o'clock, because I have to get his dinner." Again, she stands.

"Stories," the young not-journalist says, stops her in the instant of turning away. "Seems to me there are a few of those lying around."

She doesn't sit back down. She's too out of sorts, too, and also tingly. Most likely just from having someone else in her house for the first time in so very long. It annoys her. When, exactly, had she gotten scared of people?

"What would the House want with stories?" she murmurs.

"What does the House always want?"

"Aye, so. But how would you convert what I say into—"

The bang from down the hall shivers her in place, and rockets the young journalist—not-journalist—off Tony's chair. He quivers before her on his grasshopper legs. But he keeps his eyes on her, not down the hall.

Nadine steps around him. "Normal?" she calls.

For answer, she gets the Collector's grenade laugh. Then a second bang. The file cabinet, she realizes. Drawers he can slide open, slam shut. Such a satisfying sound. Like pealing a bell with a hammer.

Just the toy for what's left of her man.

"I'm not selling," she says, dead flat, pleased to sound that way. She returns her attention to the not-journalist, but keeps herself positioned between him and the hall. Him and Normal. No matter what, she doesn't want to talk about what she's lost. Not today.

The banging stops.

"Not selling," says the not-journalist. "How about sharing, then? Just one story. For a colleague. A novice, still just learning. You can tell, I think, that I genuinely want to hear. Excuse me for saying so, but it also seems like you kind of want to tell."

With an effort, Nadine directs her rising hand back to her chin. Away from her eyes. If she touches her eyes, she'll start crying. "Kind of."

"Well, then. Come on. Your favorite."

She shakes her head. To her surprise, she realizes she's no longer resisting. She's just stumped. The stories, all the stuff they've found and places their searches have taken them…once upon a time, she'd gladly have fanned them out in her memory. Picked over and selected just the one for this moment. Back when she'd believed the point of the hunt was the finding. Or even after that, when she'd thought the point was the hunting.

Before she'd truly understood what collecting meant to her, and what she collected.

"I don't have favorites, I'm afraid. It's just not how I work."

"How about *his* favorite, then?"

Before she realizes she's doing it—as though he really has found the magic words—her mouth falls open, and out spills a fucking ballad, fully formed, like it's been in there all this time. A story about songs. And Spook. Their night of songs.

HIS ONLY AUDIENCE

Around and beneath them, the houseboat thumped and shuddered, and as usual on their visits here, Nadine wished the Collector and Spook would just turn off the shortwave and sit a while. Maybe, instead of hunching forever at the wooden table in this windowless hold, they could try the deck in the starlight. Let the world bring wonders *to* them, for once. All those things down there in the bay, for instance, living or just floating beneath them. Knocking against hulls. Murmuring hello.

"Got one," Spook said, straightening in his chair as though called to attention. Out of the hiss and static, the spurts of Iranian classical music and snippets of BBC-wherever broadcasts, the dot-dash chirruping from ships so out of time that they still used Morse code as though anyone were out there to receive or translate it, a voice flared. Flickered out. Caught again as Spook worked the console knob, locked in on the signal, and held.

Ice-voice. The voice ice would speak in, if ice spoke. Female, if ice had gender.

"*Seven. Six. Eight. Five. Null.*" Crackle. Empty frequency. Then again. "*Seven. Six. Eight...*"

By the third repetition, as always, Nadine felt herself leaning forward, too. Forgetting the bay, she unfolded her arms, uncrossed her legs, and lowered her ear next to Normal's, aimed toward the receiver with its console knob and compass face, its warped and blistered wooden casing.

After a few seconds—as if she'd just popped up in the porthole through which he always viewed the world—he blinked at her.

"Come on, now," she half-whispered, batting her blues at him. "You can do it."

He didn't bat his browns, wouldn't have known how or what for. But he sure had them. Brown like the stirred up bottom of a bottomless pool.

"Hello," he said.

"There, so. Was that so hard?"

"*Six. Eight. Five. Null,*" said Spook's radio.

"A new one?" she asked, without taking her eyes off the Collector's.

Spook had already grabbed his newest notebook from the shelf behind him. He flipped fast through pages and pages and of charts. Lists, Nadine knew, of all the numbers stations he'd ever located in decades of scouring the bands. Usually, he could tell just by the voice whether he'd heard the signal before, though Nadine wasn't sure how, given that so many of them sounded identical, anonymous, which was exactly as intended. Such a strangely beautiful thing to collect: voices minus voice. Code minus meaning. Memory stripped of memory.

"Think so," Spook said.

She wondered if there'd been voice-training school for numbers broadcasters right after World War II, when these stations were apparently most in use, an essential Cold War communication tool. Then she amused herself trying to imagine the instructors' corrections ("Flatter, please. Less inflection"), then the instructors (Doorknobs with mouths? Fans with voice boxes?), then the classrooms (the windowless hold of an anonymous houseboat, say, lined all around with shelves full of notebooks full of numbers, inhabited by a man who called himself a ghost and his even more obsessive friend, who'd brought a date?). Had there been a Bletchley Park for blankness, where you learned to drain yourself entirely from your own speech?

What did it say about her that she definitely would have wanted to go there? To hear and see, anyway.

"You look happy," the Collector murmured, surprising her again. For the millionth time.

"Donkey's abortion," she muttered, and thought about kissing him. She let them both return their attention to the voice instead.

Just a recording, of course. A signal someone forgot to turn off. Probably. A long-forgotten automated messenger bleating code into the ether for absolutely no one.

When he'd reached the end of his most recent chart, Spook nodded. "Brand new." With his mechanical pencil, he noted down the number string.

"But not the one meant for your dad?" Nadine asked.

She'd said it so gently, but a shadow still swept over Spook's sun-seamed, friendly face. Only recently, after extensive covert research of her own, had Nadine realized what had originally inspired this collection. But it wasn't why Spook collected, or at least it wasn't now. If it had been, she wouldn't have asked.

"No," he said, and closed the notebook. He shook his head. The second time he did that, the shadow fell away. He glared at Nadine. Respectfully. "There I was wondering why they call *me* Spook."

Seven. Six. Eight…

"Huh," said the Collector, staring sidelong at her.

"Didn't mean to intrude," she said. "Got curious."

Spook tapped the notebook, shook his head. He even smiled. "No need."

Leaning back from the radio, the Collector tapped the back of his head with his spindly fingers. "You never actually *were* one, were you?" he asked, startling Nadine yet again. Here was her man asking an actual personal question. Interacting with a friend, participating in a moment, though his eyes remained riveted to the radio. He was cataloging, too, Nadine knew. Storing away information, though God knew into what sub-folder in which cabinet in which library in the memory palace that passed for his brain.

But he was also here. Present. That wasn't her training or impact, she wouldn't have claimed that.

It might have been his reason for *wanting* to be present, though. Probably was. So many days—most of their days—the fact that she knew that was more than enough.

Spook waved a callused hand through his own whitening hair. "Me? I'm a carpenter. Houseboat handyman. That's all I've ever been or wanted to be."

"Son of Spook," Nadine said. Lightly, lightly.

Spook laughed. "Roger that. Son of Spook. Hey, sorry. What are we drinking?"

"Something Belgian," blurted the Collector, as though beating a televised Jeopardy contestant to an answer.

Nadine rolled her eyes. "Wow, pulse-o'-my-heart. You're on fire tonight. Now let's try Something More Specific for $200?"

Then she grinned. These evenings, after all, were rare in their lives. Spook still technically qualified as a client. But unlike virtually everyone else who employed them, he didn't want to beat anybody to a rediscovery or horde anything esoteric. He simply wanted to hear, and maybe locate, these stations. Even more, though, Spook wanted like-minded company. And he served them Belgian beer every time they came, and sometimes warm Camembert. By the standards of her life with the Collector, these evenings were practically Gatsby parties. Couples Club.

"Rodenbach, I think," Spook said. "It's a Rodenbach night." He smiled at Nadine, the Collector, his radio—which, right, would have had to count as Spook's date for Couples Club, but still—and got up.

"Can I hunt a new one?" said the Collector, gesturing at the radio.

"Sure. Like this." Spook put his hand on the knob at the base of the compass face. Slowly, artfully, like a safe-cracker, he pushed it in, and rotated it. Spats of static filled the air. Boat-chirp. Guitar strum. The BBC again, then an Arabic voice, more static-spat.

"Wait," the Collector snapped. "Go back."

"Back where?"

But the Collector had seized the knob. His turns at it were jerkier, fumbling, though as always, he learned fast. When he'd finished futzing, he straightened and raised an eyebrow at Nadine.

Her smile bloomed from way down inside her. "I love this song."

"I know. Me, too."

"You love songs? There are songs you love? Or recognize as songs?" She was laughing, reaching for his hand when he burst out singing.

"She was gone when I first met her/couldn't even find the floor."

Nadine joined in. To her amazement, Spook did, too. *"I helped her out, I brought her down/but she wasn't there anymore."*

Belgian beer, she was thinking. *Group singalongs, to songs they all knew.* Maybe she still lived on this planet, after all. They were positively harmonizing as that exquisite last verse arced towards its conclusion, their voices hitting the rise right on time at *"Swept off down the..."*

Except the voice on the radio didn't rise. It plunged instead off that so-familiar melody down to a low, droning drawl, where it rooted furiously in a furrow of words Nadine had never heard before, gorgeous and wrong and strange. Something about "*mist in bones,*" about "*the heat under midnight.*" Then—like a rabbit chased from a garden—it skipped from the song entirely, and the music grooved out on a skewed, broken acoustic guitar arpeggio. The Collector swiveled the volume almost all the way to silent.

"You knew that was going to happen," Nadine said, her voice somewhere between amazed and accusatory.

"I thought it might." The Collector's fingers drummed the table. "Actually, I didn't really think so. I mean, frankly, I thought that particular search for that particular client was never going to...Spook, where's that signal coming from? Can we locate it?"

"You can if I'm involved," Spook said, beer and group singalong instantly discarded in favor of quest. Because he and the Collector were the exact same species, Nadine realized. And here she was edging forward on her bench. Watching what Spook did. Calling up from her own formidable memory everything she already knew about Robert William Guthrie, and pulling the laptop she never left home without from her nightpack. If she wasn't quite the same species, she was a related one. Had been long before *Bouquiniste* Day, when the world winked out or didn't, and Normal happened, and her life changed.

She thumbed her computer awake.

From the bookshelf above the galley sink, Spook took down some sort of cloth-bound reference volume. He started flipping pages, asking, "What band? Can you read the number off the dial? I need the whole set of digits."

But when the Collector told him, he stopped flipping, glanced up. "You sure?"

The Collector actually twitched in his impatience like a birddog with the scent in his nostrils, the leash all but strangling him.

"That's local," said Spook.

"How local?"

"Next door, practically. Right there." Spook gestured toward the front of the boat, the open water, as if pointing to a precise spot. "Hang on." He popped a latch on a gray metal container Nadine had always taken for a breadbox and withdrew an impressively ridiculous piece of machinery. Another radio-type thing with two mini dish-antennae on top, a square red light cube that looked like it should blink, and the words *Coast Guard Issue* stamped on the side. When he flicked a switch, the cube blinked.

"Ha," Nadine said. "You *are* a spook."

Spook swiveled another dial. The dish-antennae rotated. Rotated more. The red cube blinked. "Not even fifteen miles out. Straight toward the Farallons."

"We need a boat," said the Collector, standing. "How do we get a boat?"

Spook stared at him.

At least that meant he wasn't watching her, because Nadine realized she had exactly the same idiot thought. She caught the Collector's eye and grinned.

"You're telling us this thing actually floats?"

"What's the point of a houseboat that doesn't?" Spook snapped, jostling past, already up the little stairway onto deck with the Collector right behind him.

For one more moment, though, Nadine remained in the hold, with the Rodenbach forgotten in the fridge and Robert William Guthrie's greatest song still echoing in her head, but in her companions' voices.

"Having a house?" she murmured. To no one. In no tone. "To have friends over in? On a boat?"

Instead of more drinking and singing, she'd now be spending this evening chugging out to sea, following the only known Pacific migration path of the giant Great Whites but not seeing them, either. Nothing so earthly (or oceanly) for this crew. No. They'd be chasing a phantom signal, in the hopes of finding yet another lost phantom-thing somebody else who wasn't them wanted.

And that, she'd learned decades ago, was just how she liked it.

Grabbing her laptop off the table as the engines rumbled to life, she joined Spook and the Collector topside. The houseboat shrugged free of its moorings and slowly, cumbersomely—like a domesticated manatee, something a Farallon Great White would swallow without even slowing—shuddered out of its berth, out of the harbor into the open water of the Bay.

Earlier, on the long drive down the coast from their little redwoods-adjacent A-frame to the harbor, both she and the Collector had remarked on the unusual absence of fog. The hillsides and forests rolling down to the Eel and Russian rivers had glowed almost emerald where moon- and sunlight met. But now, the moment the houseboat cleared the harbor's headland with its automated light flashing clear and white into the dark, wisps of mist rose to shroud them. By the time they were three miles out, the continent had vanished, and the rumble of the boat's engines sank into itself as though swaddled in gauze.

This mist was neither thick nor cold. But Nadine could feel it wriggling along her skin and into her pores, familiar but no more pleasant for that. Like so many things here, it reminded her of Lissycasey, County Clare. One of those winter nights when the fog streamed down from Galway Bay and across the Burren into town, triggering in her and her mother alike this exact same nameless ache. This dry dampness. Even when she'd *been* home, this kind of mist had made her feel far from it. Her mother, too. Not just ghosts in their world, but guests.

Which is what they were, after all. What everyone was. Which was why, or some of why, the collectors she and Normal knew collected. Their objects were proof of passage, and reminder of it. Medicine for mist-ache.

Switching on an overhead floodlight, Spook cut the boat's speed, kept checking their course. Once, he sent the Collector below to make sure the signal he'd caught was still broadcasting. When the Collector assured him it was, he nodded.

"We'll be alongside him in twenty minutes. Maybe less. As long as we don't accidentally run him over."

Shaking out of her reverie, Nadine held up her laptop. "Anything I can poke around for? Want to tell me exactly what you think you heard?"

"Same thing you did," said the Collector, staring into the fog as though translating it.

"Yeah, okay. But it meant something else to you."

"To our client, not me."

"Grand. Are you really making me do this one question at a time? Is this those nights again?"

The Collector smiled. Distractedly. "Habit. Always fun hearing you get—"

"I thought we don't do music people."

"It's not that we don't do them. It's that we're rarely what they need. I mean, either they're hunting rare pressings or smuggled rehearsal tapes or whatever—and those aren't that hard to track, and then it's just a question of what someone's willing to pay, so, snore—or else they're hunting something they've heard about, or been told stories about. And those things almost always turn out to *be* stories. Apocryphal concerts, or mythical surprise shows no one actually saw but everyone somehow *knows* occurred. I really thought this was one of those. I mean, it's been years."

"At least twenty, right?"

That earned her an actual glance. A moment of distraction from his distraction. "How would you know that?"

Nadine sighed and smiled all at once. "Because I *don't* know about it. So your interaction with this person is pre-me. It's one of those clever markers I use."

"Oh, yeah." His grin was neither apology nor even acknowledgement. But there was love in it. Sometimes.

"Right, so," she prompted.

"You'd like this guy. Super-passionate Robert William Guthrie-freak."

"Which makes him pretty much like every other Robert William Guthrie freak on the face of the—"

"Yeah, yes, sure.. But this guy built a *tower* on top of his house."

"A what, now?"

"An actual turret, so he could go up and lock a trap door and be alone with the music. He calls it the Tower of Song."

"*Do dum dum dum, de doo dum dum,*" Nadine hummed, and when the Collector just stared, she smacked her free hand against her forehead and groaned. Naturally, Normal didn't know *that* song. Too much a favorite of too many other people's. Too many versions freely out there for people like her mom to sing to herself on mist-ache nights like this, with her husband long dead and her daughter on the other side of the world.

Something played on normal-wave radio. Barely collectible at all.

She wrapped her arms to her chest as tendrils of mist wriggled deeper. "Never mind, dear. Go on."

At the wheel, Spook stared straight ahead, looking impressively Captain-like. That was comforting, especially now that the water around them looked nowhere near green anymore, but black. Opaque. Probably, it was empty. Not full of monsters.

"Nadine, the way this guy talks about Robert William Guthrie performing…"

"Don't even his fans hate Robert William Guthrie performing? Doesn't he take some sort of pride in butchering his own tunes instead of singing them the way people love hearing them? That's what I've always heard."

"Right. But this guy claims most people just don't understand. He says Guthrie's on this eternal quest, because he knows there's a *right* way—and only one—to say or sing every single word, in every song, on any given night. The way those specific syllables, in that rhythm, to that melody, in Guthrie's voice, are meant to sound *that day*. But according to our client, catching all of that at the same time, in one performance, is like chasing a specific butterfly. Trying to get it to land on you. Most nights it's not even there. Others, it's there, for a single second, and then..."

The first bump against the bottom of the boat did little more than surprise them, knock Nadine sideways half a step and cause her to clutch her laptop. That turned out to be good, because the second bump rocked the ship sideways, dropped the Collector to one knee, and caused Spook to hiss in surprise.

"The hell..." he said, standing on tiptoes to peer over the bow. The Collector pulled himself to his feet. He looked so completely astonished—as though he'd only just remembered or maybe realized he was on a boat—that she relaxed a little.

"Was that a log?" she asked Spook. She didn't want even to say *shark*.

Instead of answering, he held the wheel, watched the water. Every few seconds, it bumped against them, sometimes hard but never as forcefully as that second time. Eventually, he shrugged. "Just water, I think. It's a little riled up out here."

Which couldn't be unusual, Nadine figured. Definitely wasn't, not out Farallons way, or in the middle of any other ocean. She did note the barely-there uncertainty in Spook's voice. It was possible, she realized, that she'd logged more actual sea-time in her life than he had.

"Should be there in five," Spook said. "Maybe less."

The boat thumped again. Not too hard.

"So, our man," Nadine prodded the Collector, at least partly to distract herself. "Mr. Tower of Guthrie."

The Collector blinked, nodded. "Well, like I said. No matter what you think of Guthrie, you'd love hearing our client talk. I'm not really a music-o, as you know, but this guy made me get it. He helped me understand. He talked about this one legendary version—the version we just heard, I'm pretty sure, with those extra verses—that Guthrie did of that song exactly once on some radio show when he was very young, and then discarded for some reason. It's never been heard since. By anyone. He says that when Guthrie gets it right, you can flat out *feel* the magic. And when you sit with this guy, our client, and you listen to him explain, you really can hear—"

"You can't, though," Nadine said.

The boat bumped, and Spook swore.

The Collector was neither surprised nor annoyed at her interruption. He also had no additional reaction to the possible Great White gnawing a hole in the hull. He just waited to hear, because he was much more interested in what she might say than whether they drowned. Which was why they really were a team as well as a couple.

Nadine went on. "You can't really hear it. Not like they do. I know those guys. They're all over Ireland. They explain it to you every night down the pub. They point out the moment. They get all excited. They get so excited, you think maybe you actually *do* hear something. But really, they just make you want to, because *they* want to so badly. But the magic in music...it's not just in the singer. Not any singer. Not in any one way of singing, on one night, for everyone. It can't be. That's too simple. But maybe—"

"There," said Spook, and right as he said it, the boat—as though shuddering down a launch into a pond—heaved sideways, then leveled, and the bumping stopped. Spook cut the motor. They drifted slowly and smoothly toward the sailboat just taking shape in the mist. Seemingly forming out of it.

It looked tiny, floating there, like some kid's toy sucked out to sea. So still it seemed becalmed. Or abandoned. Its deck empty and silent, mast disproportionately tall, green sail slumping in the absence of wind. As the mist closed around and behind them, blotting out the entire rest of the world, a shudder slid up Nadine's back. She felt more awe than anxiety, though. As though she were on the Ark, at the moment they spotted the olive tree sticking up from the deluge. Abruptly, she turned around. Between clouds of mist, she could see the water through which they'd come swelling and flattening and slapping over itself as it churned.

She gestured toward the sailboat. "Isn't that awfully small to be way out here?"

Spook kept glancing back and forth between the water ahead and the water around and behind. The glassiness, flat as an ice sheet, between houseboat and sailboat. The roil everywhere else.

"No," he said. "But I see what you mean."

"It's like a hurricane," said Nadine. "Like we've reached the eye of one."

"A hurricane *under* water?"

"I don't know. Can that happen?"

"Sssh," the Collector snapped.

Startled, they shushed. The houseboat drifted closer. Then she heard it, too. Somehow—carried on mist across black and motionless ocean—what reached Nadine's ears sounded almost exactly like the signals that had streamed from Spook's shortwave. Same tinny compression. Same sense of traveling unimaginable thousands of miles, even though it was coming from right in front of them.

Hands on the bow, head tilted forward to listen, Nadine let the music lap against her. Flow inside her. Her fingers tingled, then her spine. "That's Muddy Waters," she murmured. "Wow." She listened. "Really early Muddy Waters. God, so early. Do you hear? Is this…I had a boyfriend—"

"Kieran," the Collector murmured. Not like he cared particularly, or like he remembered what significance Kieran once had for her. For him, too, for that matter He was simply prodding her story forward. Seeing where it went.

"Him. So. He used to suck this down like air. This era. These guys. And I say this has got to be one of the first times with amps. One of the first times anyone, anywhere, heard that grimy, amazing…" She looked up, stared at the Collector. "Unless this *is* the first time. But that day's apocryphal, there wasn't any recording or…okay, whose boat is that?"

"Hallo, the ship," Spook called out.

Nadine hunched, awaiting rifle shots, Blind Pew and Israel Hands boiling out of the hold. When nothing happened, she scowled up at Spook. "*'Hallo the ship?'* People really say that?"

Spook's smile could be surprisingly shy, sometimes. It made him look forty years younger than he was. "I'm pretty sure *somebody* says it."

But nobody answered. In silence Spook's houseboat glided up to the little sailboat. With one more glance at Nadine—for approval, she realized, because like the Collector, he actually thought of her as Captain most of these nights—he clambered down to the deck, took up a coil of rope, tossed it over the sailboat's rail, and in a few efficient passes of his hands knotted the crafts together.

"What's next, then? *'Permission to come aboard?'*" Nadine murmured.

Spook shrugged. "Could try it. It's a little *Star Trek*."

"What's wrong with *Star Trek*?" said the Collector, and Nadine laughed, and Spook, too.

Then Spook actually yelled it out.

The music went silent. But only for a second, and only, it turned out, because a song had ended. Another one started. Some 1930s crooning thing, violins warbling, a moony voice floating up from the crackle to drift on the mist, hollow as mourning dove call.

Almost until the end of that song, they waited. The music set all three of them swaying on that still water. If they stayed here any longer, Nadine thought, the Collector might even ask her to dance.

Instead, he said, "I'm thinking permission granted."

"Normal..." Nadine warned, but he ignored her.

"In fact, I'd say we're *invited*."

With that, as the crooning song melted into whistling, he stepped over the houseboat rail onto the deck of the sailboat. Right as his foot found wood, a banjo broke out of wherever speakers were down in that hold, hurtling off at breakneck speed; the whistler bobbed around on its wake like a water-skier.

"Maybe it's all automated," Spook said.

Gripping the rail, Nadine nodded toward the Collector. "Maybe we should find out before your man there decides he can hornpipe." She watched Normal stumble over coiled ropes, a stack of lifejackets, making straight for the shadowed set of steps leading down into the sailboat's cabin. He was tapping his hands to the beat of the banjo. Or the thrum of the search.

Carefully, Nadine swung her own legs over the houseboat rail and onto the sailboat. Spook followed, and Nadine experienced a momentary but powerful misgiving. She almost asked him to go back, just in case the sailboat really was something pirate-y, or just stranger than it already seemed.

But in a different way than the Collector, Spook was in his element. He'd curled in a sneaking pose, and now he scuttled forward, his feet soundless on the nearly-dry deck.

Playing spook, Nadine realized. Being his dad.

Neither curled nor scuttling—but keeping quiet, all the same—Nadine joined her boys at the mouth of the stairwell. Whatever was down there, it was candlelit. The light looked warm and orange. It wavered like the voice of that crooner, melting constantly into itself.

"Do we go down?" the Collector whispered, as if he weren't already on the second step.

The voice from below boomed in the near-silence, as though they'd hit a depth charge. "Seems ridiculous to stop now."

Right, great evening, thanks for having us, Nadine thought, but didn't bother opening her mouth. The Collector had already skipped off down the stairs, pulling her with him without touching her or turning around.

Unless that was her own curiosity, pulling.

At a paint-spattered wooden table, behind a disappointingly Best Buy-looking set of broadcasting equipment and a cassette deck and a laptop and a lamp and one not-so-Best Buy reel-to-reel, sat a gray-haired black man in a white T-shirt. The shirt did indeed have a Jolly Roger on it. If the man cared at all who'd boarded his boat, he gave no indication.

"We did call out," the Collector said, moving toward the table. "Didn't you hear us?"

The man shrugged. "Knew you weren't the Coast Guard. Probably weren't a shark. Didn't see much point in breaking the flow of my show." He had thin shoulders and even thinner arms strung with veins that stretched like strings down guitar necks to surprisingly muscular wrists. Huge hands, though. Nadine watched them as they flicked over knobs, cued up a track on the laptop, set it playing. Some grimy, grinding mid-50s blues.

"They call me the Collector." Normal stuck out his hand, which struck Nadine as a dubious idea.

The man at the table hardly looked up. "Do they, now. Always happy to meet a brother."

"And you?"

"Me? I'm the pirate radio DJ of your dreams. If you have proper dreams, with music in them."

Everywhere Nadine looked—up the walls, in recessed spaces where storage cabinets and life-vest cubbies should have been—she saw narrow wooden shelves crammed to capacity with cassettes in clear cases. The cases had been labeled with identical strips of red tape that caught the flickers of light and glowed, faintly. Each strip had a black number string Sharpied or possibly even stenciled into them. *LA82235. BD112460.* Nadine glanced at Spook. He'd noticed, alright, was already leaning closer. Looking for strings or patterns he recognized. Yet again, that sea-damp sensation brushed over and through her. As though she herself were mist, and the air was moving through and reshaping her. It wasn't pleasant.

Reaching behind himself, Radio Man selected a case without seeming to look, popped out the cassette, and slid it into the deck. Spook—target acquired, reconnaissance apparently completed for the evening—had taken up post against the doorframe through which they'd entered. He looked antsy, disappointed. Behind him, light caught and flitted in the clear plastic cases. The Collector, meanwhile, plunked himself on the table's edge, gaze flashing everywhere: up the walls, over the broadcasting equipment, into the eyes of their host.

His eyes had leveled on the Collector's. Had not left his face.

From the speakers mounted into the wall, Fender Rhodes chords sounded. They sounded thick, brooding, strange, neither minor or major, their rhythm steady and slow, relentless as hammer-on-railroad-ties. The voice took too long to come in, was barely audible, as though the microphone had been set too far from his mouth.

Unmistakable, anyway. Wavery as the candlelight, cartoon-deep, swooning. Dracula minus fangs and even hypnotic power, lovelorn and hopeless and so much more seductive for that, at least to a dreaming, distracted Irish lass, attacked from all sides by pub versions of "The Fields of Athenry," out for a drive through the Burren moonscape with Kieran, the boy with the flecks in his eyes that suggested worlds and weren't.

"Holy shit, Blaine Fury," she murmured, then stopped. She leaned into the table, listening more closely.

Not a song she knew? There were *no Blaine Fury songs she didn't know. And that whistling in the background... not human whistling. Wind. Wind with snow. And no other instruments at all?*

Her mouth opened, just to breathe, not to speak. Then she spoke, too. "Blaine Fury in Montreaux."

For the first time since the Collector had introduced himself, Radio Man turned toward her. "Very, very good. *Not* home base for most of my listeners, I have to say..."

"1977," she said. "December? January?" Her eyes leapt to the cassette case face-down on the table. The red label and its numbers made total sense, now. *BF122677.* She did note, in some corner of her astonished brain, that the case no longer captured light, had gone about as reflective as the wooden tabletop. But she didn't process that then. "My god. December 26th? What is that, the week after Mick stole his wife? The *day* after? Jesus, I heard about this session. I read about it. Him bunged up in that castle with that guitar player he wouldn't even let in the studio, just playing and playing. Songs he'd half-finished, other people's songs. But...I read nothing got recorded. Not one note."

"Yes," said Radio Man. "That's what you've read." For the first time, he smiled. Strange smile. No glee in it. Not the kind you'd expect from a collecting man with a literal boatload of treasures thousands of people might have wept...paid...bled to get their hands or ears on.

There was pride in the smile, alright. But not the collecting sort.

Those specific syllables, she thought. *That particular tune, on any given day. Like chasing a butterfly...*

She stared up the shelves of plastic cases, their glows so faint. Like tea-lights. Something tickled inside her. "So, what you collect. What you play on your show...are *perfect* moments? There really is such a thing?"

Even before Radio Man spoke, the Collector started knocking knuckles on the table. Not in rhythm with the music, but he kept rapping, which drew Nadine's attention to his face. His eyes had narrowed, focusing over her shoulder toward the stairwell or maybe nowhere at all, and his lips were compressed, head half-tilted.

Because she'd missed something.

Radio Man pushed back from his broadcasting equipment, folded his veiny arms across his chest. Even sitting, he looked thin as a telephone pole.

And as dangerous to touch?

"Don't know about that," he said. "No, I think I'd call them...hmmm ...*awakenings*. How's that?"

"*First* moments," said the Collector. He rapped so hard on the table that even Spook, who'd been gazing upstairs at the mist and moonlight, glanced over.

Then Nadine had it, knew what was bothering her. That tea-light glow and flicker everywhere. But there were no tea lights down here. No candles, either. Her eyes flicked back to the Blaine Fury cassette case, which was plain plastic. Not glowing. Which meant that all this glow...that low, lovely, orangey light...

Radio Man's attention returned to the Collector. This time when he spoke, his voice swelled. Not so much in volume, but with a force that could have been joy. It approximated joy, Nadine thought, hand rising to her heart, which was doing its own rapping against her ribs. Also, absurdly, she seemed to be fighting back tears.

"I like that," he said. "First moments. That's good. And true. For them, yes. For each and every one. The first moment they..." He grunted. It could have been throat clearing but came out a giggle. "...*call up* what they have in them."

More tabletop-rapping. Hard. Arrhythmic. Annoying. Not like the Collector at all. With a sigh, he stopped, looked away from her and back to Radio Man. "What you gave them," he said.

For Nadine, three things happened at the same time: her mind went wild, conjuring hurricanes under water, moments like butterflies, gorgeous voices adrift in mist, the glow in this room; also, she started shivering deep under her ribs and couldn't get that to stop; and finally, she realized why the Collector was knocking, and why that wasn't working.

"Well, now," said Radio Man.

"Leaving only the question of what you ask in trade."

Their host laid his enormous palms on the table, fanned his fingers like a poker player calling a bet.

"Wow," said the Collector, and meant it. He'd stopped knocking; he was too busy being amazed. Head over heels for the thousandth time at the moment of discovery. Which always left him vulnerable.

"Normal," Nadine murmured, trying to get his attention despite knowing that was hopeless.

"Okay, wait. Let me get this straight. There really is a crossroads? I mean, is that what they do? Meet you at the crossroads, go down on their knees?"

"We can crossroads," Radio Man said. "I can come to your living room. Your rented castle in Montreux." He glanced at Nadine and winked. "Hell, we can meet at 7/11 if that's most convenient."

Carefully, slowly, Nadine edged forward. Her feet felt unsteady beneath her, and her heart thudded. But her eyes kept flying to the tapes.

The red glow radiating faintly from every single one of them. From the tapes themselves. From whatever it was this man had taken from all these people and threaded onto spools. She found herself studying the spines, the initials and dates, realized she could guess almost all of them. Because every person on these walls had become someone collected on walls. Every single one.

"And in return you get..." Even here, in dead calm in mid-ocean in mist, where it didn't seem so silly at all, the Collector almost laughed as he said it. "...their souls?"

Radio Man snorted. "I don't exactly *get* anything. I accept what they offer. I remove what they no longer need. Or can't have."

Nadine had reached the Collector's side. Casually, so casually, she let her arms dangle down the back of his chair. Unlike the Collector's, her taps barely qualified as sound. She didn't need them to be sound. She just needed him to register that they were there, and understand what he'd been doing wrong, so they could finish whatever the hell they'd started and get out of here. Preferably with as little as possible *removed.*

But of course, by this point the Collector had locked in on this conversation, and paid Nadine no attention whatsoever. "So, their souls. Like I said."

Radio Man rested his chin in those hands and pursed his lips. Eventually, he shook his head. "I don't think they'd say that. I think they'd say their *souls*—whatever you mean by that—are right there." He gestured not at the tapes but his speakers. The music streaming from them. "Wouldn't you?"

Partly to cover any noise from her taps, but also because a sudden and profound disappointment had welled up in her, Nadine said, "That can't be it."

When Radio Man swung her way, Nadine flinched. The guy had barely moved, and yet the movement surprised her, hadn't seemed predictable or even intentional, like the slither of a downed power line. At least he was watching her face, not her hands, and not the Collector's face at the moment he realized what she was doing. She felt that happen, too, in his spine. Meanwhile, another shiver shook her, and to her astonishment, as Radio Man watched, her eyes welled. *Beautiful Blaine Fury, alone and abandoned up there in his castle cold. The Heathcliff of her stupid, mist-draped, teenage dreams.*

"What can't be what, child?" The 'child' wasn't sarcastic, certainly not nasty. "And why can't it?"

"Music," she murmured. She made herself speak louder, because the Collector had returned his own hands to the table and started tapping again. But recognizably, now. In rhythm, just not song-rhythm. *Dot-dot-dash. Dot-dot-dot-dash.* She continued speaking, but felt Spook look up, knew he'd realized, too. Comprehended, at last, that the Collector was talking to them. "Inspiration. Every great note anyone's ever played. It can't just come from you. I don't believe it."

Cocking his veiny arms behind his head, Radio Man ground out a laugh. "Good. Because I never said it did. Who said anything about *all*? I'm just talking about these." He gestured up the walls.

Dot-dash-dash. Dot-dot-dot...

"The ones who want it so badly, it's like a whistling in their blood. Like teeth in their hearts. Bites them every single time they breathe. The ones who want it like that, and don't quite have it. Or they have too much of...hell, I don't know. Something else." There it was again. That smile. This time, Nadine pinpointed what it was that made it so unsettling. So *wrong*.

Not the pride in it. But the kindness, where no kindness should, or seemed, to be.

"These are my charges," Radio Man said, nodding at his tapes. "Children, almost." Abruptly, he snapped his eyes toward the Collector. Whether he'd understood or not, he'd registered all that knocking. And now it had stopped.

And because he was looking at the Collector, he didn't see—somehow missed—what Nadine glimpsed out of the farthest corner of her eye. The lightning snatch of Spook's fingers. The single cassette disappearing into the pocket of his coat.

"Souls. Again." said the Collector, fast.

He'd seen Spook, too. Was providing cover.

Leaning across his equipment, Radio Man half-rose, a panther coming out of its crouch. Nadine grabbed the Collector's arm to pull him away.

But the man didn't lunge. "That word again. I don't like that word."

"You have a better one?"

"I think we should go, now," Nadine murmured. Over her shoulder, to Spook, she added, "Want to go get the boat ready?"

"Sure," said Spook. "See ya." Quickly—though nowhere near quickly enough if Radio Man had cared—he scampered up the steps onto the deck of the sailboat.

Radio Man stayed where he was. He seemed to be thinking, still. "It's not like that at all. You've got it wrong." He waved his hands over his equipment. "*Soul.* No. It's more like an appendix. Like...an extra antenna. Or, not exactly extra. I mean, we're all mostly born with it. The thing that lets us... pick up signals, say. Yes. I like this." He was nodding, grinning. "The thing that pulls in signals from people around us. Lets us immerse in lives not our own. A valuable bit of ourselves, I admit, unlike an appendix.

"But. If what you want, in your very core..." He stopped grinning, then, pinned the Collector in place and Nadine, one foot already on the stairs, in hers. "...in your *soul*...If what you want is to draw the magic of being alive right down out of the air, and then broadcast that back *out* of yourself... well. That extra antenna can get in the way, don't you think? You can't shut it off. It's more like a nose than ears. Constantly pulling in all those ordinary, aggravating, everyday voices. All that chatter. Connecting you, whether you like it or not, to each bland, dull, daily passing moment, and therefore obscuring the ineffable. The sublime..."

The Collector was on his feet. On the radio, Fender chords hammered themselves into compressed flatness, then nothingness, leaving just the faraway whistle of the long-ago Montreux winter wind. Radio Man sat back down in his chair, hands flicking over the controls, cueing up another miraculous track. Nadine shot up the stairs, the Collector behind her. She resisted checking over her shoulder but held still in the starless, misty air just long enough to listen for trailing footsteps. She heard none.

"Hurry," she hissed, and was both relieved and amazed to see the Collector surge past her, for once.

"*You* hurry," he said, leaping across the little gap onto the houseboat as Spook worked furiously at the knot he'd made, swung the ropes free. The Collector offered Nadine his hand. She swatted it away as she jumped across and landed, skidding, beside him.

She grabbed his arm again. "You stole from that guy? You don't steal from anyone, ever, and you think *that guy's* an easy first mark to try?"

"I didn't steal. Spook did."

Nadine punched him in the shoulder as the houseboat shuddered back to life, the engines loud in the preternatural stillness, atop motionless water that didn't stir.

"*That's* what you two eejits decided with your feckin' knocking? Are you crazy? Are you both crazy?"

"Did you get it?" the Collector asked, half-dancing in his excitement. "Spook, you have it?"

"Right here," he said. "Morse code. Genius."

"Nadine's idea. I was just trying to get your attention."

Flashing a momentary grin toward her, he snatched the cassette case out of Spook's jacket pocket.

Nadine shook her head, shivered yet again. "What is your Robert William Guthrie fanatic paying you, anyway?"

"It's not for him," said the Collector, fumbling with the case, clicking it open. "I wouldn't have done it for him."

A tape slid into his hands. The red glow in its spools was faint, so faint, but there. The little throb occasional, even less perceptible than it had seemed on Radio Man's boat. Cupping his palm, the Collector cradled the cassette as though it were a bird-chick. Only after a long moment of staring at that did Nadine look up at his face. He was weeping.

"Normal, what the hell is—"

"He was one of the first clients who ever came to me, Nadine." He handed her the empty case. The initials on the spine were none she recognized. "One of the very first. I laughed at him. I remember laughing. He said he was looking for...himself. That he'd lost a piece to a collector. That if I ever saw it, I would know. And could I please bring it back. God, I don't even know where he is, or if he's still making records, or if he's even alive. But if he is, and I can bring him this—"

"I wouldn't, if I were you," boomed Radio Man.

Nadine whirled, expecting him already flying at her, outsized hands pouring out of the air like condor talons.

But he just stood on the deck of his own ship in the dead water, fully ten feet away already, and he kept those hands folded behind him. Like wings.

Spook gunned the engine. But the Collector said, "Stop."

"Stop?" Nadine snapped.

The Collector stepped to the rail of the houseboat. That was when Nadine noticed the mist. It seemed to slide down the air like raindrops on windowpane. Within it, Radio Man and his ship had begun to blur. Waver.

"Why not?" asked the Collector. "Why shouldn't I return this to the man you took it from?"

Possibly, the Radio Man shrugged. Already, it was hard to tell. "Accepted it from. But regardless. Just what do you think will happen when you do? When you return that mostly useless hyper-awareness of other people, plus all the ordinary, awful, beautiful, ravenous yearnings that come with it? The kind the rest of us feel so furiously when we're young? That's a whole lot of hope and hunger you're holding, friend. What you're *not* holding is the extra time, experiences, disappointments, and wisdom that would satisfy or lessen them, or at least make them bearable. Help you learn to live with them or let them go the way the rest of us do. You sure you want to give that back?"

One last time, as mist streamed around and over him, Radio Man flashed his smile. All that terrible, beautiful kindness.

"Is that the kind of gift you give your friends? Do you think, in the end, he'll say he preferred your gift to mine?"

The Collector started to answer. But the first slap of ordinary, churned up, open water banged into the hull, knocking them all off-balance, tilting them forward. By the time they'd righted themselves against the rail, there was only mist behind them. Maybe Radio Man's sailboat was still in it. But the music had gone.

Silently, Nadine handed the Collector the cassette case, watched him return the tape to it and the case to his pocket. He didn't speak. Spook aimed the houseboat toward shore. Water seemed to give way around them, rocking them as they moved, but gently, now. Sleepy nighttime ocean, seagulls above it. Monsters way down in it.

"What are you going to do?" Nadine touched his hand.

The Collector let her. He even squeezed back, once. "I think I'm going to go down and listen to the radio."

Nadine stayed on deck and let him. And that's where she found him once they'd moored back at Spook's berth: sitting by the shortwave, still tuned to the band where Radio Man's station had been, listening to spits of static on the empty air.

HOME

Disappointed, of course, Nadine thinks as she spoons tea, pours milk. He in her story, she in his reaction. But she'd known both would happen before she started.

For one moment, her eyes linger on the latest unopened tin to arrive from the Hamtramck baker, delivered just this afternoon. No note, as usual. No design on the tin except that familiar red star which she'd first assumed signified something from the baker's Solidarity-fueled Gdansk youth, but turned out to be the logo for Hamtramck's long defunct Negro league baseball team.

She allows herself a small smile. She could break out whatever was in there, after all. Offer her fervent young not-journalist that. He'd almost certainly appreciate it. Probably, he'd survive the experience.

But no. Whatever came from Hamtramck went to the Collector, first. Went to the Collector, period, most times. Safer that way. Unless there were *babki* involved. For *babki*, she'd risk it.

For now, she arranges bourbon creams and Rich Teas on a plate. Nothing rare or even homemade, simply correct. She checks the overhead cupboard for the cheap serving tray she is almost sure they still own. Mostly, she manages not to monitor her guest as he peruses the living room, eyes everything on the walls, glances down the hall toward wherever the Collector is now. He hasn't come to steal, she's all but certain of that. The Houses don't steal, don't need to. Not directly, anyway. Not with their hands. Besides, what would be worth it?

Whatever he came for, he's disappointed, though. Has to be. There's no prize here, no pot of gold to be bought or prized from the little cottage at the misty end of the rainbow he'd been so certain he'd discovered. Nothing to spirit off to his Squad to enshrine in catalogs, or use to entice rarified clientele or astound more experienced, worldly colleagues.

As for herself, what had she imagined? That he would gawk in wonder? Make some startling connection to someone else's story she hadn't yet heard? Shudder in empathy or understanding? Understanding of what, exactly?

Had she really expected him to be like Normal, in other words, and so make her less lonely for a few hours?

He has moved all the way across the room to the window. The wishing tree clock rustles as he passes, its not-quite-golden pendulum darkening with his shadow. It's not really rustling at him, of course. Just marking more empty minutes passing.

"Excuse me," she calls. "I'll just take himself his..."

Cup and saucer in hand, she hurries down the hall. She finds the Collector on their bed in their room with only the nightlight switched on. Not until she hands him his tea does she realize he is also holding Louisa the teddy-lizard. His friend Tony's lizard.

Briefly, Nadine stares down into its left pin-eye, watches her own shadow-self reflected (or trapped, or protected) there.

Poor Tony. Who'd wound up more like her man than she'd ever dreamed. The thought jars her, triggers a tsunami of sadness almost strong enough to rock her off her feet.

At least Normal isn't screaming. That seems to be the primary difference between he and his oldest friend these days. He's also grabbing for the bourbon creams, which means there's still some part of him in there.

"Here, so." She lifts Louisa gently from his other palm and settles the saucer and biscuits in his lap. Laying the lizard on their headboard, she gives it a single stroke with her thumb. "There, now."

"*I thought I stooped to kiss her*," the Collector sings out, almost like he knows that song. How often has she even hummed that one, anyway? Has she ever?

She hums it now as she returns to the living room, but stops at the edge of the hall. Her hands twist in the hem of her sweatshirt, and her eyes well.

She mouths but does not give voice or tune to the last words of the verse the Collector started.

"And I awoke in California, far, far from Spancil Hill..."

*God*damn*it,* she thinks. *How much of him* is *still him? How close is he to his own surface?* Sometimes, she could swear he's there, just under the skin. Right around the corner of his own eyes, lurking like some wily river trout drawn—almost—by her lure.

But other times...

"Can I see the cassette?" asks the young not-journalist.

The fact that he has stayed—is going to stay, has slipped off his coat and draped it on the back of Tony's chair—surprises Nadine. It also rankles her. She doesn't know why. Partly, it's the way he has laid the jacket.

Not obsessively, not even neatly. Casually. Like a university kid home to his mother's. Like he owns the chair.

"What do they call you, anyway?" Nadine says, returning to the kitchen to pour her own tea, get the biscuit plate. On impulse, she serves herself the remaining bourbon crèmes. This guy can have Rich Teas. Serve him right.

His smile radiates the same something as his discarded jacket. Not just sass, not quite flirting. *Insouciance*, she thinks, stirring milk. Not a word she has used or called up often in life. But here is its living, preening dictionary illustration photo.

"Didn't I say?" He perches on the arm of Tony's chair.

"Strangely, you did not."

She hands him his tea, arm's length. He doesn't brush her fingers, but he smiles in her face. Flecked eyes like kaleidoscopes. She imagines them spinning, mesmerizing her, like some off-his-nut supervillain's in a cartoon. Or a boy's she could have fallen for. Once.

Saucer in hand, still perched with one foot off the floor, he seems to consider.

She backs away, resettling into her own impression on the couch.

"Hard question, is it?"

After a sip of tea, he shrugs. "How about The Rev."

Automatically, Nadine snorts. "Brilliant. Why can't any of you lot just be called Bill?"

He laughs, at least. A real, honest laugh, and damn right. She watches him lift his cup. Out of politeness, for show. The foot that isn't propping him up taps at the air. Whatever he came here wanting, he still wants it.

"The Rev." She bites into a bourbon cream, tastes home. Peat-fire tang, sea wind through grass and the cracks in mud-molding between stones. "Suits you, I suppose. There's a fervor, all right."

Balancing cup and saucer, he doffs an imaginary cap. On an older (or less intense) person, the gesture might have looked graceful. Even gracious.

"Less sure I see holiness, though." She's half-teasing. half-probing, God knows for what. "Wisdom either."

For the first time all morning, he looks genuinely taken aback, even offended. The cup rattles in his lap as that twitching leg jerks to stillness. He's like an animal abruptly aware it's been seen.

Then he isn't. He smiles. Unless she's mistaken, he even blushes. "Oh," he says. "I see."

"You see?"

"Reverend. That's what you're assuming. Sure."

Sure?

"Now can I see that cassette?"

Nadine takes another swallow of tea, partly to wash down the biscuit, partly to buy time. She knew she'd fallen out of practice with people, especially smart and wily and perceptive ones. But this far? All morning, she has felt pitched from moment to moment, clinging to the conversation rather than reading or guiding it. Or just feckin' having it.

"What for?" she finally says.

"Are you saying no?"

"I'm saying…I'm trying to imagine the House catalog listing is all. *Old, clear c-22 cassette tape, in case. Like new, possibly never played. Glows a very little if looked at just so.*'

"How about the sound, though?" he murmurs. Fervently. "Have you composed our listing for that?"

Even as she answers—long before the Rev points it out—Nadine realizes what's strange. It hasn't seemed strange until this instant, and that may be the most disconcerting thing about the whole afternoon so far. Her voice comes out low.

"Never played it."

His stare and slight jaw-drop are exactly what she'd expect, precisely correct. And if they come a beat soon, or simply sooner than the rhythm of this conversation dictates—as though it's been scripted, practiced in advance—well, that makes sense, too, doesn't it? He's wily, and at least today, she's slow.

"Never?" he asks.

"Why would we?"

"Why *wouldn't* you? More importantly, how could you not?" He's got his lips still parted, head tilted, all civilized astonishment.

Also genuine astonishment. It's only his timing that's wrong. Feels wrong. Because, again, she has lost her sense of other people. Folded even further into herself and this house and the whistling, shrinking hours than she'd imagined.

The Rev senses her bemusement. His next question is surprisingly gentle, more drawing back a curtain than prodding her over an edge. "You never wanted to hear what it was you'd scored?"

"Rescued," Nadine snaps,

The Rev leans back on Tony's chair arm and nods. He's not only ceding her point but agreeing. "Rescued." He grins. "Stole. You're telling me that legendary you and the legendary Collector had no interest whatsoever?"

"It's not ours," she says.

"And yet you didn't return it, either."

She wants this kid to leave, now. More, she wants him to shut up. Stop stirring her. Because for the first time in ages—first time, period, somehow—she wants to hear that tape.

The Rev keeps at her. "You didn't give it back to your pirate radio man. Didn't send it to your original client. You know its value. You know its rareness. And you're honestly telling me you neither capitalized on it nor opened it up, slipped it in a player, and figured out once and for all what it was you'd liberated?"

"Liberated," she says, watching the Rev's eye-flecks, which don't actually whirl.

Laying cup and saucer on the coffee table, he straightens and folds his arms over his chest. Like a feckin' psychiatrist, now, at the moment he holds up the mirror. Reveals patient to self. "You stopped at having it, in other words. You're more plain old collectors than you think."

Her defense comes instantly, fiercely. "That's us, yeah. Have a gander." She waves at the almost bare walls, the den down the hall stocked with well-used books they've (or at least she's) actually read. "Hoarded treasures everywhere."

"No kidding," he says, startling her silent. "So I see."

The mist outside has drizzle in it, now. It taps against the windows as though it has grown nails. Lets loose mist-squirrels to scurry over the roof.

"You see what?"

"Treasures. Just like you said."

"Not your kind."

"But I also see collectors. Real and rare ones. People who know this isn't about hoarding, or even having."

Speaking of which, Nadine thinks abruptly. *When has the Collector himself last made a sound? Where is he at this moment?*

She knows, though. He's out of sight in the hall, in shadow, likely staring slantwise into a fingerprint he just made on the wall. Listening even as he mouths song lyrics, old client names, places they've been or heard about, whatever's beating its wings to get out of him today. Straining toward her voice like a kid underwater, as though they're playing a game. Her shouting, him trying to guess what she said.

It's instinct that keeps her from glancing that way, and thereby alerting the Rev to Normal's location.

It's also arseness. *Because he already knows.*

"What are you on about?" she tries.

He doesn't glance toward the hall or answer her question. He simply continues. "*Real* collecting...Collecting that matters..."

"Matters?"

"It's about uncovering, isn't it? Attuning ourselves to the power of wanting. The power *in* wanting. In touching and holding. In objects. In us. It's about *awakening.*"

"Jaysus, did I give *you* the bourbon crèmes by mistake?"

"Stop it," he says, more forcefully and fervently than he has said anything so far. Then, just a touch more softly, "Please. This is rare for me. A treat for me. Someone to really talk to. Isn't it for you?"

Suddenly, he's just a gangly, brainy, wacky kid perching there. Heart, brain, mouth, almost nothing else. Barely the skin to cover him. Buzzy little dragonfly gobbling up world, which isn't enough to sate him, isn't quite the world he'd heard about or dreamed. Is in fact a torture chamber too exquisite, too perfect, to have been conceived by god or man, because it's just that almost-bearable amount less than the creatures born into it imagine it should or could be.

A few of its creatures, anyway. Blaine Fury in his winter castle. Her ma, who will never admit it. Tony. The Ibis, and when's the last time Nadine has let herself think that name?

This radiant, revved-up kid. Normal and her.

Except for one thing, she realizes: she rarely feels tortured. She doesn't, now. Just lonely.

She can't help it; her eyes flick to the hall. "I'll get you more tea," she murmurs, starting to stand.

"I don't want tea," he snarls, freezing her in place.

She has one hand one-extended for his saucer, the other on her couch. *I have this wrong,* she thinks, but doesn't even know which *this* she's referring to.

"To the *moon,* Alice!" the Collector blurts from the hallway. It's the sound of his voice, as much as the absurdity of the outburst, which knocks Nadine loose. Frees her from whatever she got stuck in, there. He swings into the living room, looks at his hands, reverses, vanishes.

Mission accomplished? Does he still have missions?

Whatever his intention, she's laughing, now. The Rev, too, she's relieved to see.

He shakes his head. "Where'd that come from?"

"The more interesting question is how he even knows that line. How *I* know it. I don't think I've ever even seen that show, not really, and he… I mean, even before… he was never much of a one for shows."

"No," the Rev says. He stands, too. Taller than the Collector, and therefore tall, indeed. "I bet not."

There's a current in this room, Nadine realizes. It keeps dragging her towards this guy, or pushing her back, or both. An eddy, so. That's when she finally realizes who this guy reminds her of. Which explains at least some of his effect, surely.

"No more tea, then," she says. To cover. "What is it you do want?"

"Right now?" He smiles as though he has seen her thoughts, and whatever it is that's eddying here, it intensifies. "I want to hear how you two met."

THE FOSSILIST

Kieran. Sweet Jesus, Kieran. And being that kind of young.

When the bus had finally dropped her back in Lissycasey, Nadine trudged sopping and sobbing up the hill, through slanting evening sleet, opened the door to her house, and found her mother pouring custard sauce on an apple cake. For a long, shuddering breath, she just stood in the wet. Her mother went on pouring as though she hadn't heard the door or felt the draft.

For once, this time, her mother broke first. But only because glee overwhelmed her.

"You're inviting the rest of the gales, too, or just the one?"

"Ma. Tell me you didn't bake me a cake to celebrate my boyfriend leaving me."

"I baked *me* one. You're just company."

Fury helped, possibly in the exact way her mother intended. Stepping inside, Nadine shivered free of her overwhelmed mac and shook out her hair. She'd just turned to close the door when her mother called, "Wait, he's left *you*, too, the gowlbag? Not just Ireland?"

"At the airport," Nadine muttered. "After I gave him the backpack he'd had me carry all the way there for him. He said I knew how he gets when he gets lonely, and that it would kill him to hurt me."

"Which wouldn't be all bad, when he puts it that way."

Words bunched in Nadine's throat. Only a few of them were for her mother, and all of them fled when her mother clapped her hands.

"He really did. He left you, too. This calls for candles."

The apple cake, when Nadine finally gave up boycotting a few hours later and came out of her room and sat down at the table to eat it, tasted even better than usual. The sugarcoating cracked in her teeth, on her tongue, and the sponge and custard melted against the roof of her mouth and turned it smooth, warm, new.

"I feckin' found it for him, Ma," she said later, curled against her mother's shoulder over two a.m. tea and soda bread. "How stupid am I?"

"Not stupid. Just naïve enough to think everyone else is out there hunting their lives like you do, instead of just tumbling around."

"It was my idea. *Oh, Kieran, look, you could do this! Be a* bouquiniste. *Look, there's licenses available and everything. Take the pittance your shit dad left and just be in Paris and sit by the Seine and sell books and read them. I'll follow you there as soon as term's up.*"

"He won't even do it, you know. The *bouquiniste* bit. It'd take too much imagination. Too much actual work."

"He'd do it if I was with him."

"No. *You*'d do it, and he'd trail behind like one of those little dogs with the eyes."

"He's hurt, Ma. He's so sad in there."

"He's shite."

"He's depressed. He's got reason to be."

"Depressed. Shite. These things, my girl, are not mutually exclusive."

Only toward dawn, when her mother got up to reheat the kettle, did Nadine abruptly sit up straight, stare at her pale, shaky hands around her cold mug, and say, "That gobshite *dumped* me."

"That's my girl," her mother said.

Two weeks later, the letter came. The first four pages accused Nadine of pushing him away ever since she'd enrolled at UCG three years ago, and also treating him like he wasn't good enough for her, apparently by not responding to questions he'd never asked (*How's class, what are you studying, are you busy, etc.*).

You never once bothered to just be in my life with me, one line read.

"He's right about that," Nadine whispered to her mother, who'd simply sat across the kitchen table while Nadine reread the letter, resisted asking, and therefore lured Nadine into sharing it. "I was always bringing him my world. My music, my crazy dreamlands, my discoveries. I never just sat with him in his world."

"He'd have to have one, first," her mother said.

Even Nadine barely skimmed the next two pages, which were all one paragraph, largely devoid of punctuation. *You only saw me when you came home weekends you didn't want your new friends to see me you never ONCE invited me out with them.*

"Because you wouldn't have come," her mother snapped when Nadine showed her that part, thwacking the page so hard that she punched a fingernail through it. "Because you *said* you wouldn't come, you bastard. It was all too scary for you. Galway. University. Too many people actually trying to do something with their days. Too high a likelihood of seeing your girl you say you love happy without you, and then you might have had to try being happy alongside her, and then who would you even be?"

"Not helping," Nadine said, her reading slowing. Slowing.

Sorry, her mother didn't say.

On the top of the seventh page, alone in its own paragraph, in blue ink instead of black—the only thing in blue, he went right back to black for the rest of the letter—Kieran had written, *Please come. Please, Nadine.*

And then he wrote about Paris. Getting crepes from a stall and wandering nowhere, crossing *arrondissement* lines without even realizing, dropping down unexpected stairs into neighborhoods or parks and drifting under laundry strung off balconies, past statues and murmured conversations, through lives in other languages. Going to a midnight movie alone, not understanding a word, stepping out into bright moonlight to walk the cobblestones along the Seine with the city shadowlit and the water slapping lightly at its banks.

Not until her third rereading did Nadine recognize those words, remember that they were mostly hers. She'd used them to paint Kieran a picture of his possible new French life, just waiting for him to claim it. One of those worlds she'd dreamed.

She didn't mention that realization to her mother. But she did think maybe she wouldn't respond to Kieran's summons, after all.

In fact, she definitely wouldn't have, except for the newspaper clipping which he had folded into the letter.

She'd almost thrown it away right when she slit the envelope. It had fallen to the floor, and she hadn't even bothered picking it up. Finally, having read the whole letter twice, then somehow manufactured enough defiance to stare down her mother until her mother shook her head in disgust and got up to start the dishes, Nadine stood, too. Gathering pages and envelope in her fist to bin them, she stooped to collect the clipping. For no good reason, on her way to the trash can, she unfolded it. In mid-stride, in the middle of the floor, she stopped.

The article had been cut from the *International Herald-Tribune*. It wasn't even a whole article, ending mid-sentence where Kieran had snipped and folded it. Either because the clipping had been a lucky afterthought, or because he really was the devil, and knew precisely how to lure her.

Or because he knew and maybe loved her.

Even her mother wouldn't have suggested otherwise. Manic depressive, serial manipulator, and narcissist he may well have been. Was. But he'd also been her lover almost three years. He'd accompanied her—because she'd taken him, made him come—to the Giant's Causeway, and more than once. He'd seen the way she got when she was there, among those stones, beside that ocean. Whatever else he was or did, he knew her.

After 170 Years, the headline read.

Possibly more, the story started. Apparently, no one knew exactly how long that single battered, flaking, padlocked bookstall had been there, bolted to the rails among all the other weathered green *bouquiniste* bins that lined the Left Banke. It bore no markings, no sign that it had been touched at all except for the remarkably contemporary and sophisticated combination padlock hung on its original latch. No one could remember when that had appeared, either.

There were rules governing the *bouquiniste* trade, the article made clear, and those were strict, clear, non-negotiable, longstanding. Especially the one requiring all *bouquinistes* to open their stalls a minimum of four days a week, fifty-two weeks a year, without fail, or lose their licenses. Not only were the rules clear, they were enforced.

Except when it came to this one bin.

According to every single *bouquiniste* the journalist could find to talk to, that stall had not been opened in living memory. City officials, meanwhile, declined comment.

Soon, though, everyone would have answers. According to the multi-lingual green leaflets that had suddenly sprouted on railings between and behind bookstalls on both sides of the Seine like some rare vine that flowered once in a generation, that lone, long-shuttered stall would be opened, at a public ceremony, by a representative of its owner, on the evening of the—

That's where Kieran had cut the article. He hadn't even let her see the date. The fucker. It could have already happened, for all Nadine knew.

At some point, her mother had reappeared over her shoulder. Now, with surprising gentleness—or possibly caution—she laid a soapy hand on Nadine's arm.

"No," she said.

"Ma," said Nadine.

"Resist. I'm begging you."

"Who else would send me something like this? Who else would understand?"

"Nadine, he's a feckin' faery. *Come away, human child.* That's him."

It could be true. Probably was. Nadine could feel the pull of him, for sure. The danger there. Tears welled in her eyes. She turned away fast so her mother wouldn't see. "I thought *I* was the faery. *Your* faery."

"You're my faery chaser. And you're going to go, and you'll go too far, and you'll doom yourself."

Blowing out breath, Nadine turned and faced her mother square. The tears in her eyes didn't fall or even threaten to. She shook her head. "I like watching hurling with you too much," she snapped.

After a long time, her mother shrugged. "Hurling could save you."

In the 24 years since that moment, she'd seen her mother for exactly 41 days, total. Watched hurling with her once. She knew this because her mother kept a count, attaching it to the bottom of every one of her letters.

All Nadine wrote on the postcard she sent Kieran was, *Coming.* She didn't say when or how. Fair play, and serve him right. Having used the periodicals room at the UCG library to ascertain that the storied book bin wasn't going to be opened until late March—and wanting to defy Kieran because of the first two-thirds of that letter, and also show her mother she could—she held out until the Spring recess. She tided herself over by researching *bouquiniste* origin stories, which led her to better stories about the surprising and sustained connections between *bouquinistes* and spying or resistance during the Terror, the Napoleonic tyrannies, the Resistance. All of those stories, everyone acknowledged, could be apocryphal. But there were so many of them.

About the locked stall, though, she found next to nothing. To her relief, she thought as much about what it might contain, and about *bouquiniste* spies, as she did about her sweet, vindictive, wandering boy during those long weeks.

Not more, though. She wouldn't have admitted it to her mother; she didn't like acknowledging it to herself. But she could feel Kieran's perpetually cold, corpse-y hand in hers as she walked to and from campus through the sleet off the sea. Could imagine holding it, warming it while he leaned into her and let her buoy him, the same way he had so many rain-wracked, wind-whipped days, skirting the rubble-strewn lots and half-built track houses on the walk home from their respective schools, sharing squares of Cadbury Lime. The next time they walked together, they'd be sharing warm *pan au chocolate* by moonlight on a bench by a pond in the *Jardin du Luxembourg.* Ghosting over the world together, hunting its magic. He and she. Him safe from his demons, and her un-lonely.

She hardly slept. She got no additional missives from Kieran, and sent none.

On the day, her mother not only declined to accompany Nadine on the bus to Dublin or even to the bus stop but exited the house before dawn without saying goodbye. She left a loaf of still-warm soda bread, which meant she'd been up since three baking it, plus a note:

The world's so full of weeping. Why chase more? I miss you already. Don't say hi to Michael F-ing Furey for me.

Nadine's plan was just to show up. Knock on the door of Kieran's basement flat or be waiting on his steps if he was out, so she could watch his face unfold to her light. Then leap upon him and spirit him directly to bed or to crepes, depending. All during the bus ride down the gray-green, mist-wrapped country, she assumed that was still her plan. But at Shannon Airport, she found she couldn't help herself, and apparently hadn't expected to, because she also found her coat pocket full of coins, more than she ever carried, as though she'd wished them there. She located a phone, got an international operator, and pushed the coins through the slot.

She got no answer. Thought that best. Thought about Kieran's face at the moment of recognition—long nose, surprisingly full lips, cocked head on the long crane-neck she loved and could set shuddering simply by brushing it with her breath as the weight he always carried flew off him like dandelion seed—and dropped the coins back in her magic pocket. She practically skipped her way onto the plane, settled in her seat, and watched her Ireland life drop away through rain rattling against the window like thrown stones.

The landing at Charles De Gaulle—the City of Light bathed pale rose as they descended into it; the cathedrals and trees and Tower springing from the land as though out of a pop-up book; the seemingly sudden switch of every conversation around her into fluid, flowing French; and of course the call made moments after deplaning, having navigated payphone instructions with surprising ease as her single bag of books and clothes thudded against her hip with the beat of her heart—would strike Nadine, forever afterward, as something out of a movie. A bad one, a laughable rom-com without the com. In fact, the whole thing struck her that way even as it was happening.

She got an answer this time. A laughing girl who responded to Nadine's English in English, but with a pronounced and decidedly not-French accent. Too harsh. German, maybe? Swiss?

"Key-yan," the girl called—drunkenly, Nadine thought, but also happily—and then Kieran was in her ear, in her head, one last time.

The next words they spoke may as well have been scripted, didn't even need saying. Nadine said them anyway, for form's sake.

"I'm here. In Paris."

"You…what? What for?"

For a single moment, Nadine thought she might cry. For form's sake, again. She also considered hanging up, turning around and asking if this plane was returning to Shannon and whether she might slink right back on board and curl up on a jumpseat in the back where she wouldn't have to face anyone.

But then, to her own amazement, she laughed. "Bye, Kieran," she said. "Loved you."

"Nadine, wait—" she heard, thought she heard, didn't care if she heard.

Gone. Dandelion seed, indeed. Except streaming off her instead of him.

She went straight to the nearest kiosk, found a rack of Cadburys she'd never seen and hadn't known existed, and bought a Turkish Delight bar. It tasted like rancid soap, the sour goo seeping into the chocolate and souring that, too, turning it too soft. Nadine finished the bar anyway as she strode from the airport into a bus queue. At least Turkish Delight wasn't lime, which she'd also found disgusting, she realized now. Chocolate-covered tile cleanser to the Turkish Delight's soap. Maybe Cadbury had a whole line of bathroom-inspired flavors. Perfect for the Kierans of the world, so you could have pleasure and your mouth washed out for daring to all at the same time.

Not until she'd squirmed into the last free window seat on the bus did she remember her mother's soda bread. She ate that, forehead against the cracked and juddering glass, as Paris slowly unfolded itself and went on unfolding in a sprawl of alleys and traffic and exhaust and cigarette smoke and slow-melting twilight that guttered and flung like some magically suspended upside-down candle.

At no point did she sleep, but eventually—when the bread was finished, at the exact moment she licked the last crumbs off her salty, Turkish Delight-slimed fingers—Nadine realized she had nowhere to go, nowhere to be, no one waiting, and no idea where she was. Someone in the next row of seats said the words, "Saint-Germain," and without planning, without thinking anything except that she was here, Nadine stood and exited the bus and found herself standing, for the first time in her life, on stones that weren't Irish, adrift in the world she'd always heard and read and dreamed was out here.

She was free. Free as she had ever been or ever would be again. She knew this even in the instant, which felt every bit as lonely as she'd imagined. Every bit as wild, reckless, and sad. She'd never seen herself chasing Finn MacColl's gold at the mythical end of the Giant's Causeway, didn't even want it. She wanted the Causeway. Here it was.

Come away, she hummed. Heard her mother hum.

Here I go...

She would never even know how long she wandered. It felt like days but was probably less than two hours, because the *Jardin du Luxembourg* was still open when she turned a corner and found herself at its gates. At some point before that, confronted with a payphone suspended incongruously on a brick wall at the mouth of a silent alley, she called her mother collect. She could have used her coins but suspected she might need every one of those, now. For a brief, terrible moment, listening along with the international operator to the phone in her house ringing, she wondered if her mother might reject the charges.

But her mother didn't answer. And when the operator—in English, but with that sliding, serrated French buzz to her words—said, "Zere is no reply," Nadine said, "Yes. Okay. It's far."

As if that explained anything. As if she were not just on the other side of England but *elsewhere.* She hung up, resumed walking, and found herself at the *Luxembourg* gates.

"*Quinze minutes, quinze minutes,*" the gendarme at the entryway snapped, tapping his wristwatch as though waking something in it.

"*Oui, d'accord, bien sur,*" Nadine murmured awkwardly back, slipping past, staring down that perfect lane of just-budding trees, toward *that fountain* plashing far ahead. The actual fountain, the one from pictures, with the palace beyond it. The whole garden shimmered silver-gray in silvery moonlight blurred with shadow, like a sketch of itself. Like a sketch she was making, right that second. Tomorrow, in sunlight, it would be a painting. Maybe after that—someday soon—it would turn real. Become simply somewhere she went. Whenever she felt like it.

Pond, she thought, and lit out seeking one, and found it. The only people she passed were kissing, tucked back in tree shadows except for one teenaged boy pawing desperately, feverishly at another teenaged boy who was holding the hand of the statue by which they stood. That sight almost stopped Nadine dead, struck her as insanely sexy, and also sad, and also brand new. She forgot the pond and then remembered it and went there. For the last few minutes of her first *Jardin* night, she watched a single toy sailboat glide on the mirror-flat, depthless surface of the water. If that boat had an owner, Nadine never spotted her.

She exited the garden a few steps behind the kissing boys, who were no longer touching or even talking. Watching them, she experienced another shudder, but of familiarity this time; she wanted to wish them both *bon chance* and more kisses, because she suspected they wouldn't be having many more. Not until she had passed the gendarme, still tapping his watch but also clucking, now, did it occur to Nadine that she had nowhere to sleep. Also no idea where to look. She turned around.

"Hostel?" she asked the guard, blanching at his scowl and her own pronunciation. She wasn't even sure that was the right French word. "*Hoh-stel?*" she tried.

"*Hostile*?" the gendarme asked, eyes zeroing on some precise spot between Nadine's collar bones as though he'd spotted something crawling there.

"*Oui, oui, hostile.*"

"*Qui*?"

Nadine started to answer, wave a hand, felt her face flush as her complete cache of French words swept from her brain like sand off sea-rock. "Thank you," she muttered, "*merci*, no, never..."

She'd gotten halfway across the street when the gendarme called her back. This time when she turned, she found him laughing. He'd pulled his cap off his head, revealing a surprising cirrus cloud of whitening hair. When he saw her face, he laughed harder.

"*Ho*-tel," he said, punching a finger at the air with each syllable as though telegraphing the word to her. "*Hotel.*"

"No, *non*," Nadine said, resisting laughing back for whatever reason. Slumping, finally, beneath the not insignificant weight of the too many books and not enough clothes in her bag. "No hotel. No..." she fumbled at her jeans pockets, turned them out. "Hostel."

"*Si. Ho-tel.* Hostel."

Now Nadine did smile. She couldn't help it and no longer wanted to. "Oh. *Je comprends.*"

"*La.*" The gendarme pointed up the street, making to-the-left motions, saying more *La*s, as though he was singing.

She found the place he'd suggested, but they had no beds. The caretaker did suggest another hostel only a few blocks away, which she found easily enough. It also had no beds.

"Wow," Nadine said to the round-faced, white-whiskered woman at that establishment. "For the *bouquiniste*?"

"*Qua*?" said the woman, drawing back as though she thought Nadine might be stoned or drunk. With her shoulders up, she really did look like a cat.

"Is that why everything's full? Because of the... the..." Even in English, she didn't have words for whatever tomorrow might be. Assuming it was going to be anything other than a normal day around here. "The big bin opening?"

Been open-ing, the woman mouthed. Eventually, she seemed to decide Nadine was harmless, and shrugged. "Race," she said, and made chugging motions with her arms next to her hips. "Marathon."

Forgetting to solicit more hostel suggestions, Nadine returned to the street, wandered to her right. Even the cafes, mostly, had shuttered themselves now. She passed a series of taverns with pumping, disappointingly familiar music pouring out their open windows. "Like a Virgin." "Der Kommissar," to which she found herself automatically doing the shoulder dip she and her Junior Cycle friends had synchronized during tyke-nights at the Discos. "Ca Plane Pour Moi," quite possibly the only French song capable of making her feel like she hadn't even left the Emerald Isle.

There was a smell, though, underneath it all. Just city waterway, but without the Liffey's oilslick overlay or the Shannon's boggy, foggy undertones. This water smelled like cobblestones, cigarette smoke, streetlights and moonlight and old, old shadows. At least, those were the associations Nadine's brain clamped to it. She let herself drift in its general direction, toward what she was sure was the Seine. Maybe she'd just walk there all night, or find a bench, drop her bag, and sit and smell and watch the City of Light until daylight returned to it.

Just as she had that thought, in the middle of a block she was sure—almost sure—she'd never before traversed, she pulled up short. On her left, suspended chin-height, half-in half-out of the shadows of the building to which it was affixed, sat the payphone from which she'd tried calling her mother. She recognized it by the semi-circular gouge in the metal along the top, as though someone had taken an ice-cream scoop to it. Beyond it, she saw the same alley, silent, featureless, doorless.

Except for the door down at the end, on the right, which she hadn't noticed before. It even had a neon sign over it, so dim that it barely penetrated the shadows. As Nadine stared, it seemed to flare like a lightning bug, then wink almost all the way out.

Ho el.

It's a sign, she thought. Which was indisputably true, one way or another.

It's a phone, she thought, tapping the gouged metal payphone casing as she slipped past. *It's a shadow. It's my shadow on a wall. It's Paris.*

I'm in Paris.

Not just the door but the semi-detached building around it seemed wedged amongst these other buildings, several stories shorter and a darker stone, also a little turned sideways, as though it had just recently jostled in here. The door hung slanted, not quite true. Light snuck out the bottom left corner. The knob was brass. In it, she could see her hand, red, as she reached to turn it.

She stepped directly into some kind of den, no entryway. A fire blazed in the grate across the room, though it wasn't cold outside. At least, Nadine hadn't noticed the cold until this warmth washed over her. The thin, tatty carpet underfoot glowed orange as though heated. On the yellow, rumpled, feather-pillow couch along the left-hand wall, a portly man with a rudder for a nose sat and sweated with his legs folded underneath him and his shiny blue shirt billowing in some invisible breeze. Except for the sweat beading his bald pate and creeping through the shirt where it touched his skin, he looked positively serene, haloed by heat, on the verge of levitating.

Like the Buddha, Nadine thought, and then got a load of his son. It had to be his son, a near-exact replica except rail-thin, eight or nine years old, and with a full head of mussed, curling blond hair. Same nose, billowy blue shirt. Same Mediterranean-tinged skin that seemed to soak up firelight. Same eyes. *Those* were what identified them as family. *Aegean* is what popped into Nadine's head, the color of the sea in postcards of Crete. Which was ironic, considering that she'd learned in her last Classics class that ancient Greeks hadn't named that color, or at least hadn't called it *blue*. They'd called it dark, or *wine*-dark. Which it wasn't. And yet…

Team Buddha, Nadine thought. *Neither of them paying any attention to her.*

"Dead cats," the boy said, in no-accent English. English learned off audiocassettes, or maybe South African English. That was an accent Nadine could never place or characterize.

The girl by the fire—twitching in a long, threading sweater, pale, *not* Team Buddah—grinned at the boy. "Just one?"

The boy grinned back, leaning forward on his own crossed legs. The father made no move to hold or restrain or correct him.

So what made Nadine think he'd just done that?

"Just one," said the boy, but quietly this time.

"A skeleton cat? From the olden days? Or new dead cat? Are there secret catways? Secret cat tunnels underneath?"

The girl's accent was Scandinavian, maybe. Northern European, for sure. The boy might or might not have been a native English speaker, but this girl definitely wasn't. Now, with a flick of a gray-sweatered shoulder, she caught Nadine's eye.

"What is your thought, intruder who just walked in?"

Before Nadine had any idea how to answer or even what the question was, the Buddha—Buddha the Elder—held up his hand. "Shall I tell you what I think?" He gazed at the girl by the fire. *Kept* his gaze there, actually. Unless she'd missed it, he hadn't so much as glanced up to see who had stumbled in the door.

His door?

He kept a single finger in front of his face. "I think you are indeed a fine *imitateur*. Or *imposteur*."

In her holey jeans, bare feet, and threading gray sweater, the girl curtsied, then laughed.

Lowering his finger, the Buddha smiled. "So which is it, then?" Slowly, he turned in Nadine's direction.

"I did perform a most excellent *you* a few minutes ago," said the girl.

"Do her," said the Buddha, catching Nadine's gaze for the first time.

For no reason—unless exhaustion, loneliness, residual Kieran-fury, and having nowhere to sleep in a foreign country counted—Nadine shivered. She opened her mouth, and only then realized she wasn't at all certain this place was a hostel or even a business.

"*Sure, where am I*?" said the fireplace girl, in stunning Irish-ese. Dublin Irish-ese, not Clare, but still. "*Pardon, Sir. I'm a lost colleen, noo-where to goo.*"

"You're mixing whole counties, now," Nadine said.

The fireplace girl grinned. *"Seen my faerrrry anywhaerrrry*?"

Startled, Nadine edged toward the door. She felt exposed, naked, as though this girl could see right down inside her.

But that was ridiculous. She was just doing cartoon-Irish. Not cartoon-Nadine.

"I'm,..." Nadine stopped before actually saying *lost*. "Sorry," she tried instead. "I thought this was a hostel. For travelers."

"Come in, then," said the Buddha. "Warm yourself."

Once he finally looked away, Nadine eased her bag off her back. She rolled her head around the ache in her shoulders, then took a few uncertain steps toward the fire. Heat swaddled her, became uncomfortable almost immediately.

"It's going to be a cat," said the Buddha's son, rocking in his lotus pose.

"That is your final guess?" said the fireplace girl.

The Buddha sighed. "A wasted guess. Foolishness."

"What's yours, then, wise sweaty man?"

Nadine burst out laughing. Too late, she threw a hand over her mouth to stifle it, but the fireplace girl gave a sassy little hip wiggle and winked at her. Nadine laughed harder.

"What's yours?" said the Buddah. Serenely.

The fireplace girl kept smiling, but her voice came out quieter. "Hmm. Based on the very little you have told me..."

For some reason, in the ensuing pause, the Buddha sighed. He also looked confused, Nadine thought.

"I think it will be good," said the girl. "I predict amazement. I will guess...pages. Falling-apart pages from the original ship you say sank. From those books you have claimed are the very first books sold on the Left Banke."

Nadine felt her own mouth fall open in amazement. "Umm," she started. "Wait. Are you talking about—"

But the Buddha looked positively flummoxed, now. He rubbed sweaty fingers into his eyes. "So, from the smattering of apocrypha and embroidered legend I fed you, you cleverly extrapolated and came up with...the most obvious possible answer."

"The most *likely* one." The fireplace girl grinned. "Do you know more than has been said? If no, then we are guessing. I guess first books sold from sunken ships."

"Or, presumably, *not* sold," the Buddha muttered, sliding his hands into his pants pockets and slumping over his considerable gut. "Since they will still be in the bin."

"Saucy," said the fireplace girl.

Nadine still hadn't managed to get her mouth all the way closed. Sweat broke out on her own arms and down her chest, which made her feel as though her skin was melting into its own pores. Everything about the last few minutes seemed to be happening out of order or in reverse. Or in a dream.

The fireplace girl flung a tangle of dirty auburn hair off her forehead, twirling it around the matted braid against her ear. She raised an eyebrow at Nadine. Her eyes were a different blue than Team Buddha's, more cloudy silver.

All these new blues, Nadine thought nonsensically, still reeling.

"Whoops. We broke her," said the fireplace girl.

The Buddha swung toward Nadine as though just remembering she was there. "Perhaps she's hungry. Are you hungry, young woman?"

"That really is just a myth," Nadine heard herself mumble. "About the ship."

If the Buddah didn't quite rock back on his heels, he definitely tilted. *Satisfying*, Nadine thought, and the satisfaction settled her, some. Re-rooted her inside herself. Letting her new companions wait a few seconds longer, she moved to the fire and sat down for the first time since leaving the bus. The fireplace girl joined her immediately. The carpet felt scratchy and stiff when she splayed her fingers in it, like dead grass.

"You know what we are discussing?" the fireplace girl said.

"I mean, it isn't likely, is it? A ship full of books—because book boats just rolled up and down the Seine every day in the 1500's—"

"Fourteen," the Buddha murmured.

"Is that an argument you are making?" snapped the fireplace girl. "You are saying this because 1400's are *more* likely? Because already I am seeing sense in my surprising new colleen friend."

The girl giggled as she brushed the back of Nadine's hand with her own. She was just a teenager, Nadine realized. Not twenty, possibly not even eighteen.

"—And then one of those ships," Nadine continued, "just happens to sink close enough to Notre Dame and the bridges that the crew can all swim ashore? A fine and committed crew they must have been, too, because they rescued the books, and of course, books were light and uniform size in those days, easy to stack and carry and swim with. Then, having gotten ashore, our resourceful sailors realize they've saved the library—which didn't belong to them—but lost whatever money they had that did. So," she snapped her fingers, "*voila*! It's Paris. They set up a sort of Dark Ages lemonade stand? Maybe they used wreckage from their ship! And they found so much demand for their damaged reading material—all presumably written in languages other than French—among all those passersby in pre-Renaissance Paris who could actually *read* that they thought, well, now." With a jolt, Nadine realized she was sounding a whole lot like her mother. Like her mother trying to wean Nadine off Kieran. Even more surprising was the comfort that realization brought her.

"So they perhaps got more driftwood," the fireplace girl joined in. "Built the first of the *bouquiniste* bins. And created the world's first second-hands book fair!"

"Hand," the Buddah murmured.

"One-hand book fair?"

"Do you know what wreckers were?" Nadine asked, offering her new friend what she hoped was a saucy smile of her own.

The girl shook her head but clapped in anticipation.

"For God's sake," said the Buddha.

"Maybe they became wreckers," Nadine said. "Got themselves some more discarded wood or dried driftwood, waited until the next time a book-boat drifted into town in the dark of night, lit fires, and lured the ship into crashing on rocks and sinking in the deep and roiling Seine. Then they fished up the cargo, dried it, and, again, *voila*! Instant stock replenishment ."

The Buddha's expression had changed slightly. *Melted* some, sagging at the corners of his eyes and mouth. He wasn't laughing or clapping. He didn't even seem to be thinking much. His eyes flicked back and forth from the fireplace girl to Nadine, then settled on Nadine.

Apple cake, she thought crazily. That was the missing ingredient here, and the reason she felt like she was being mean. When her ma did this to people, she also gave them apple cake.

"You were all talking about the old bookstall," she said, sans sauciness. "Right? The one they're opening for the first time in 150 years tomorrow?"

"Doo-wang," said the fireplace girl. Two syllables Nadine had never heard together before, their meaning nevertheless unmistakable even before the girl clunked the palm of her hand off her forehead and dropped her mouth open in mock-amazement.

The Buddha leaned back, folding his hands on his folded legs. "Remarkable, your wandering in here. Almost as though…" His smile came slowly but felt sudden. "…you saw our fire."

"Like *we're* wreckers," said the boy, and his father sighed.

"That was indeed the implication."

"I thought there'd be more buzz about it," Nadine said. She was talking to the fireplace girl, smiling at Buddha junior. She made herself meet the Buddha's gaze. "Not that I've had many conversations, I just got here. To

Paris. But…a century and a half-old mystery bin, just hanging there by the Seine, opening tomorrow. You'd think…"

"But you wouldn't," murmured the Buddha. "The more conversations you have with other human beings, the less you'll think that." His expression stayed serene, half-melted. "You're hungry, aren't you?"

It took Nadine a second to realize he meant that literally. She hadn't been hungry. Or she had been, but forgotten. Now she was ravenous.

Half-patting, half-nudging his son off the couch, the Buddha nodded. "Get this young woman a crepe."

At the door, the boy turned. "What kind?"

Amazingly, that was the first question—the first moment—since arriving in France that made Nadine feel west-coast Irish. Provincial despite all the reading and researching she'd loved doing in every library she could walk or bike or bus to since she'd learned to read.

What kind were *there? Where did one get crepes at this hour? Seen my faery anywhaery?* Her smile felt helpless, defensive. She shrugged. "The crepe kind?"

The boy left.

With a sort of jerky unfolding, as though raising a sail, the Buddha lumbered to his feet. He wasn't actually so big, standing up. Nowhere near six feet, not even very heavy. Just a bald middle-aged guy in a blue shirt. He stayed across the room from Nadine and the fireplace girl, and his gaze floated over their heads toward the fire.

"There's another bed in your room, isn't there?"

"Two," said the fireplace girl, spinning toward Nadine with her hand extended. "Binna."

Nadine shook Binna's hand, which was warm, nubby, and dry. "Colleen," she said.

Binna blinked, clutched Nadine's hand. Then she burst out laughing. "Not actually."

"Nadine."

"We will be getting along."

"That does seem to be happening."

"In the hall," said the Buddha—again to the air, as though the girls were no longer present—"I believe I saw…" Off he went.

Dragging Nadine to her feet, Binna took her shoulder bag and led her to a small, nearly-triangular room, posterless and windowless, lined with three military-style cots. The only one with sheets had been wedged back where the walls came to a point. Nadine remembered her notion about this whole building having elbowed into the alley. Having arrived late.

"Right or left bunk?" Binna said. "It is a personality test."

Nadine dropped onto the right-hand cot. What she wanted to do was prostrate herself and close her eyes. She was at least as tired as she was hungry now that she knew where she'd be sleeping. Instead, she studied the mussed sheets on Binna's bed. The balled-up sweater she'd apparently used for a pillow.

"What does your cot choice reveal about you, then?"

"Far from the door," Binna said.

Before Nadine could even weigh whether she was still kidding, the Buddha appeared with an armful of thin, gray sheets. Actually, they were more no-color. The color of sheets washed ten thousand times. A question occurred to her as she stood, and she started to ask right as the Buddha said, "I'd be curious to know—" and the front door burst open.

"Cheese and mushroom," called the Buddha's son. "All they had left."

Binna had stayed standing. The Buddha glanced her way, now. "Tea," he said. "When you're ready."

The boy had brought crepes for everyone, but only he and Nadine ate them. Conversation seemed to have dwindled with the fire, which every now and then twitched and reared like something dreaming, but mostly just sank into itself. Nadine could feel its intermittent heat on her back, the oily cheese slicking her tongue, the crepe skin warm against her own through its wrapper. Dead-grass carpet scratched at her ankles when she moved. So much sensation, none of it Lissycasey chill or dampness. Buddha and son returned to the couch, and Binna stood over Nadine with her arms folded. Shadows filled the room as though creeping out of hiding.

Like the Frank family, Nadine found herself thinking, dreaming, as she automatically lifted her tea, lowered it, lifted it again. *Like little Anne, after the Nazis had probably gone for the night. Slipping out to whisper hello.*

Appalling thought. Bizarre. She shook her head. Sipped more tea. "I'm tired," she said to no one in particular. She put the plain ceramic mug in front of her, in the center of the empty crepe wrapper, and forced her tingling, weirdly unresponsive hands into the carpet to push to her feet.

"One moment," the Buddha said from his perch. Not harshly or even insistently. "I want to know yours."

Mine? *Know*? The room tilted, rocked back toward level. Nadine rubbed her palms against her cheeks.

"You don't seem to think it's books," the Buddha continued. "Or at least, not the *bouquinistes'* ur-books, rescued from the Seine. I agree. I don't think you think it's a dead cat, either."

"Why not?" The boy bounced once in his seat.

"Because she is not like you two." Glancing at Binna, the Buddha laid a hand on his son's head and sighed. Possibly, that constituted tousling. Fatherly affection. It looked like more pushing a jack-in-the-box back in its container. "She's like me."

Binna snorted. "I am very one hundred percent certain she—"

"Egg," Nadine said, startling even herself. She hadn't realized she'd been thinking that, or thinking anything, for that matter. Certainly, she hadn't been settling on any theory.

"Cat egg?" Binna chirped. "Wait, do cats have eggs?"

"Auk."

Something new surfaced on the Buddha's face, surprising only in its ordinary older adult-ness: plain old disgust. Bored disgust, for all three of them.

Then that look split open, revealing something even more familiar, and surprising in a whole new way. Because she'd so rarely seen it on someone else's face.

She is like me...

He leaned forward, now. His mouth wriggled. Not exactly smiling. Better than smiling. Trying not to.

Nadine's head cleared. Another brand-new sensation quivered over her. Or awoke. She had something to share and knew it. That wasn't new. But this time—for the first time in her life—she had someone to share it with.

"Auk," said the Buddha said. "You mean great auk, don't you?"

Where had this idea even come from, Nadine marveled, even as she started to explain it. *When had she thought of it? Just now, as she was saying it. And yet it seemed plausible. Fully formed. Maybe even* right.

She told them all about the very last great auks—two, a mated pair—strangled together on an island near Iceland over 150 years ago.

"In the middle of a storm," said the Buddha. "The sailors who'd found them thought the birds were causing it."

"English sailors, then," Binna said, rolling her eyes. She finally took a sip of her tea, then another.

Nadine shook her head. "That's another myth. Made up. The sailors who found them were looking for them, on behalf of a collector. But their eggs..."

"Smashed with a boot, just in case they were witches."

Clearly, the Buddha had heard other versions of this story. But he hadn't conceived of the possibility Nadine had. Also, he was teasing her. Or testing.

She held up a weirdly unsteady finger. She appeared to be even more exhausted than she felt. "Not smashed. Smuggled. To France, so the story goes. Whole, and carefully preserved. Then they vanished, right around... what year did you say that locked *bouquiniste* stall appeared?"

The Buddha stared at her. "No one knows. Not exactly."

"No one who will say, anyway," Binna murmured over Nadine's head.

The Buddha was wrong, Nadine realized. Binna was like them, too. Curious to the point of hunger. And he could choke back that grin all he wanted; she could still see it on his face. She let hers loose, settling back against the warm bricks that ringed the fire. For no good reason, she thought of the Causeway. No faeries anywaerrrries. No giants.

But great auks? Oh, yes. Auk-ghosts. Auk-memories. There for anyone who looked and listened. Her theory could be right, she realized. She also wouldn't mind if it wasn't. Because tonight, there was the possibility that tomorrow morning, she'd be present at the opening of a bookstall that had hung locked beside the Seine for 150 years, and inside it, there would be great auk eggs, with the last auks that could ever have existed on Earth still curled up inside them.

Binna had sagged down beside her, now. Nadine felt the girl leaning into her, even warmer than the bricks. Her head brushed Nadine's shoulder as she tilted sideways.

"Auks," she said, sounding almost as tired as Nadine felt.

"And to think," said the Buddha, genuinely marveling. "Somehow, as if out of thin air, you just happened to wander into this room..."

So satisfying, his amazement. Or it would have been. Should have been. Except he wasn't just talking about her theory, or even their shared interest in the bookstall. He kept glancing around at the walls, the carpet, the dying fire. As if they were all as new to him as to her.

Because they are, Nadine thought, struggling to straighten up, clear her head again, make sense of whatever had just occurred to her.

But she was too tired. She almost fell asleep right there. Binna definitely did, at least for a minute or two. Somehow, Nadine got to her feet, pulled Binna to hers, and moved them off toward their room. She thought about asking the Buddha where the washroom was so she could brush her teeth, then forgot, then figured she'd find it on her own. How big could this little wedged-in world possibly be, anyway?

Sprawled moments later atop the single sheet on her cot—she could still taste crepe, and she'd wriggled half out of her sweatshirt and unbuttoned her jeans but that's it, and the light was still on—she remembered something else she'd meant to ask: she had no idea how much this bed was costing her. The Buddha hadn't said, and he hadn't asked for money.

In the cot wedged into the corner, Binna stirred, flipped her fraying braid off her face.

"Binna," Nadine tried to say, through what felt like a mask of gum. Or crepe cheese. She flicked at her face, felt nothing but her face. "Binna."

"...na?" said the girl, half-rising off her pillow.

"Is this their house?"

Possibly, Binna's answer wasn't even to that question. It came from far away. It also might have come much later, as Nadine kept winking in and out of sleep. And it might have been a joke.

"Is now," she said.

The next time Nadine woke, the room was pitch black, and there was someone else in it. Someone standing. Not Binna, whose breath whistled in her sleep like slow-speed birdsong. Locking herself still, holding her own breath, Nadine fought the weight on her eyelids, got them open.

But all she saw was blackness, total and complete. Impossible, surely, in the City of Light, in a room with a window. *Where was the window*?

She couldn't find it, twisted her neck, heard the cot groan beneath, caught a gasp as it hurtled toward her open lips.

Almost caught.

Like a vault, she thought crazily. *Like we're locked in a bin.*

The idea electrified her, helped her keep her eyelids pinned back. The crepe taste had soured in her mouth, sunk mostly away, but the gumminess remained. As though she'd swallowed a cobweb. Speaking, she realized, somewhere in the tiny not-asleep part of her brain, might be a terrible idea. She did it anyway. Thought she did.

"Hello?"

Had she said that? She said it again.

The dark whistled when Binna breathed. Eddied when the other person in here moved. Whoever it was didn't answer. Was over by Binna, Nadine decided, which triggered another lightning-charge, and jolted her up on her elbows.

Rape, she thought, trying to get breath under her voice. *He's going to rape us.*

But she'd been wrong. He wasn't by Binna. He was right beside her.

He didn't touch. If she reached out, if she so much as twitched, she knew she would feel him. But she didn't dare. She held her breath, clutched at her open pants. There was a smell. Actually more a sensation. That prickling of skin as something else living passes. Centipede-awareness of something dangerous, nearby, and watching.

Whoever it was moved. Knelt, Nadine thought, and shuddered back toward the wall, or tried to, or thought she did. Her brain, this room, everything somehow went darker, still. The sound, when it came, was a relief, at first. At least she could identify it.

Swish of fabric across barely carpeted floor. Her bag sliding out from half-under her cot where she'd stowed it. Lifting away.

The dark emptied. Maybe even lightened. It was still too dark, but just dark. Whatever that meant. "Binna," Nadine managed to whisper, got whistling for answer. She made to get up. Fell asleep again.

When she opened her eyes next, it was morning. Dawn, anyway. Some time with an hour attached, bringing trickling gray light that seemed to burst in that space, after that vault-deep darkness, like fireworks.

"Binna," Nadine snapped, sitting up too fast. The room pitched around her, and crepe rose all the way up her throat and hung suspended in the back of her mouth. Risking vomiting, she swung her head over the edge of the bed and checked her bag.

It was where she'd left it. Almost where. *Possibly* where. She'd never been one to leave a zipper open. But she'd been so tired. Unbelievably, impossibly tired. Because of Kieran, leaving home, having nowhere, finding here.

Or else she'd been drugged.

Staggering to her feet, Nadine slapped herself in the face, did it again. Her head didn't clear. She also didn't vomit or fall over. Her pants, she was relieved to find, seemed exactly as she'd left them. Half-unbuttoned. Sleep-rumpled, nothing more. She wasn't hurt. Nothing ached, hardly even her head. She stumbled toward Binna's bed, but Binna was already stirring.

"Nnnh?" she mumbled, wedging up on one elbow. "Buh." She sat all the way up. She took in Nadine, then whirled. Saw the window. The dawn light. "*Andstokans helviti fjandans djofull!* We're late."

Fumbling at her slim gray sneakers, batting her braid off her shoulder, Binna pulled herself together and leapt to her feet. She grabbed Nadine's wrist and yanked her out of the bedroom, through the living room—which was empty, the whole place empty, Nadine could feel it—and out the door into the alley.

"Late?" Nadine called, tripping behind her.

Binna's laugh was the one from last night, tickle-light and teasing. "'*She is like me*,'" she intoned, in remarkably precise Buddha-ese. "Clown"

The morning was colder than the previous night had been, the air stinging their faces like a snapped towel. Cooing broke out over their heads, and from farther away came a surprisingly familiar, barely-there squeak and trill.

Treecreepers, Nadine marveled. *Here? Had they followed her from Lissycasey?*

Not until they burst from the alley did morning Paris rise fully to meet them. Taxi horns, bicycle bells, a groaning waste truck, a woman shouting across the street from the window where she was hanging long johns. Binna hadn't let go of Nadine's wrist, hadn't slowed, and that seemed grand, better than grand. With every sprinting, pounding step, Nadine felt herself hammered back into her bones, her memories re-tacked to the walls of her brain, as though they'd been shaken loose in a quake but undamaged. Not lost.

The Burren in misting rain. Her mother. The Shannon, in misting rain.. Apple-caramel cake. Treecreepers. The Tipperary-Kilkenny barbed wire showdown at Croke Park. The Giant's Causeway. In rain. Auks. Kieran. Mothersodding Kieran. The kissing boys in the Jardin des Luxembourg last night. In Paris, where she was.

All present and correct.

Right as a grin broke wide on her face, Binna slowed, pulling Nadine to a standstill.

"What?" Nadine said, freeing her wrist of Binna's grip, and right as she asked, she thought she saw. *What had she seen*? A billow of blue half a block back, across the street. Which was ridiculous, how could she have seen that, she hadn't even glanced that way?

Even if he really was trailing them.

"But why would he?" Nadine asked, studying the street, the passing Parisians in their chattering, jostling dozens, baguettes waving before them like bayonets. "I mean, what possible interest could—"

"Forgot," Binna chirped, stopping Nadine mid-question. The girl wasn't looking behind them or across the street. Hadn't been at any point, Nadine realized. Was reacting to something else. "They can't start without me, can they?"

Right there in the middle of the sidewalk, Binna unzipped her jeans and reached into her pants. A taxi, turning left, honked, and someone in the just-opening *brasserie* on the corner whistled. Out came Binna's fingers, dangling a key on a plain wire ring.

To Nadine, it might as well have been a mesmerist's pocket watch suspended there over the Paris street. The key was made of some kind of mottled, not-quite-golden metal that caught light but turned it old. Nadine glimpsed herself in it, and the city around her, as though in a daguerreotype. As though this whole morning had happened a hundred years ago, and *today* was the memory.

Except for that cab horn honking. The waiter whistling.

"*Et toi*," Binna called, curtsied, zipped her pants, shook her keys, and reclaimed Nadine's hand.

At the next corner, they crossed, and as they stepped onto the far curb, Nadine smelled the Seine again on the whooshes of air stirred by cars and passing people. A big city river, bored and sleepy, sliding into town to do some book browsing.

"Hungry?" Binna asked.

They got baguettes and cigarettes at a just-opened market and set off again at a stroll. They'd gone another few blocks when Nadine got her first glimpse of Notre Dame moored like a ship among its surrounding buildings, then of the bridges, then the walled banks of the river along which the *bouquinistes* were already taking their places. Suddenly, finally, Nadine stopped, tugging Binna around to face her.

"They can't start without *you*?"

Chewing bread, cigarette perched in the corner of her mouth, Binna shrugged. The weak March sunlight seemed to twist itself into the braid of her hair. The key dangled from her wrist like a bangle.

"It's *your* stall," Nadine said.

Binna grinned. "My family's. My father sent me to do this. You are only now figuring this out? I took you for smart."

Nadine tongued bits of crust against the inside of her cheek, felt their surprising sharp edges. "More dogged than smart, I think," she murmured. Then, abruptly, "Who's your father, then?"

"Dead. I hardly knew him." Shaking the keys like maracas, Binna shimmied a hip. "But he left instructions."

She was moving again, flicking the butt of her cigarette into a gutter, but Nadine stopped her again. "Binna. Doesn't it seem weird to you?"

"My dead father leaving dated instructions and secret money in an envelope for me to come to Paris when I am eighteen to open a 150 year-old bookstall he never opened? What is weird about this?"

"Not that," Nadine snapped, tasting last night's crepe, and also the tea the Buddha had poured them both and watched them drink. Feeling the weight of that vault-like dark, utterly empty except for the presence she'd felt ghosting through it. Hovering over her. "Us. All of us just happening to wind up in the same place?"

Eyes narrowed, Binna pursed her lips, started her own question. Then she shrugged again. "Does it matter?" She jangled the key, set it swinging. "I must go."

Nadine followed barely half a step behind, though Binna's gait quickened as the river neared. They traversed a long city block, took a quick jog up an alcove, a right turn back into full morning light, and suddenly, there they were. Nadine and her new Icelandic friend, on the actual Left Bank.

For a few moments, Nadine let herself stand still, try to take it in. More, she tried to fit *herself* in. She was gazing down a long, wide sidewalk overhung with linden trees, their leaves yellowing at the tips like thousands of lit candles. Beneath them, umbrellas unfurled over circular iron tables outside *brasseries*, and people—hundreds, thousands of people already—strolled or shouldered or bicycled by, as rhythmic in their movements and remote from her as horses on a carousel. Nothing she could talk to or touch or ride.

And yet.

On impulse, as one tall, gray-haired woman with shopping bags in her arms and an actual, flowered hat on her head edged past, Nadine leaned left, bumping her lightly on the shoulder. The woman didn't slow or look up as Nadine said, "Sorry. *Excusez-moi.*" But that had been an actual shoulder, all right, attached to a real person. The woman's hair and open coat both smelled of coffee.

No Giant's Causeway faery. No carved carousel figure. Just a woman in Paris. *Like me*, Nadine thought. She glanced ahead to where Binna had gone, and saw them.

Saw him, immediately.

Mothersodding Kieran.

His showing up here, of course, wasn't weird at all. Was, in fact, entirely predictable, given the gorgeous redhead laughing as she picked lint off his coat. Nadine could imagine—could practically see—the whole banal progression.

Sometime in the months since his letter, Kieran, lowlight bug-zapper that he was, had accidentally caught that woman's attention as he brooded on a bench or in one of these *brasseries* or bent over a bridge railing as though he just might, not tonight but soon, climb on over. Once he had her, he'd have to come up with things to fascinate her, wouldn't he? Fortunately, he'd already spotted that *bouquiniste* thing, the article he'd sent to that lithesome, ludicrous Lissycasey lass who'd trailed after him for years, now. If dogged little Nadine liked things like *bouquinistes*, why not gorgeous, laughing redheads?

It wasn't only the woman's laughter that pricked Nadine, though; Kieran was laughing, too.

It happened so easily, when it did. Nadine felt her eyes simply slide away from and then past him, like light off a rock. Her attention returned to the street, the trees, the crowded sidewalk, Binna moving easily through the small crowd clustered in an ad hoc semi-circle around that lone, green shuttered stall. It was maybe four feet tall, wooden of course, the sloping lid warped but the wood itself pristine, clean of bird shit and rain streaks. If anything, it looked newer than the stalls around it. Better cared for.

Someone bumped Nadine from behind, then someone else, not hard. Then the Buddha and his son were past her. Which meant they *had been* behind her. Which wasn't the same thing as following. Necessarily. What was even strange about it, except that neither father nor son bothered with "Excuse me", let alone "Hello"?

Hardly strange at all. Especially in comparison to the four of them winding up together in that hostel—if it had been one—on Marathon night. She watched Buddha and son slice through the crowd, settling in the front row of onlookers maybe five feet to the left of the stall. There they stood, twitching in rhythm, pulling at their billowy shirts, wiping their faces. Nothing about Buddha-senior, especially, suggested serenity today. Finally, with a quick glance over his shoulder at nothing Nadine could detect, he stepped forward, grabbed the combination padlock that dangled over the keyhole like the lid of an eye, and gave it a pull. Another. Turning, he pushed out a laugh, returned to his place, tousled his son's hair.

Binna had seen that, all right. She was a few rows behind them, and now she glanced toward Nadine, gestured with her chin at Team Buddha, and winked. Then she went back to turning slowly in place, taking it all in.

A good thirty people had gathered now, maybe more. Nadine stepped closer to the edge of the semicircle, smelling the river. Binna lit another cigarette. Every now and then she caught Nadine's eye and mouthed, *Wow.*

One of the watchers seemed to be a journalist, maybe even the guy from the *Herald-Tribune.* He kept scratching away at a notepad. He'd brought a photographer, who unslung a pair of cameras from his shoulder now and knelt and started snapping off shots of the stall and the crowd, though not of Binna. Not yet. If it were Nadine, she'd be shooting the Seine. Paris in morning light. She'd be doing that even if she saw Paris in morning light every single day.

Eventually, she supposed she'd get some shots of that bookstall, too. Bookstall and river together. Daughter and mother.

Two older men, across the semicircle from Nadine, had brought milk crates on wheels. They weren't together, but they'd seen each other, all right.

Knew each other, Nadine was pretty sure. One had a scuzzy white beard, filthy coat, and could have been a vagrant except for the way he kept surveilling the other guy with a crate. Tweedy, that one, elbow patches and a pipe, no less. Eventually, he acknowledged the first man by lifting a corner of his lip in a half-sneer. Then he opened his coat, flashed a white envelope in an inside pocket, and smiled wider.

Booksellers, Nadine decided. Book *acquirers*, anyway. Serious ones, both of them. For the Bodleian, maybe, or even Charlie Byrne's, the beautiful new bookshop in Galway that she'd practically lived in this past term, decided she was going to be visiting weekly forever.

Way back last week, when she still lived in that country and figured she might always.

Years later, leafing through her files and glancing just once at the only photo she'd ever found of this morning—taken, no doubt, by the reporter's companion, right as Binna stepped forward, bowed to the assembled, and lifted her key like a conductor's baton—Nadine finally noticed the three elegantly suited men in the back. She hadn't seen them at the time.

Pinstripes. Pocket squares.

Squad. House guys, anyway. Sotheyby's representatives, or Christie's. Whichever's dress code been in its Dandified G-Man epoch.

There was a lone cop, bored, at the far edge of the semicircle. To Nadine's amazement, he leaned over at one point and said something to Kieran. Whatever it was, it made the redhead laugh even more. As far as Nadine had seen, that girl never stopped laughing.

Binna was still milking her moment, tapping that beautiful, rust-red key against her arm, when Nadine finally noticed the man in the middle of it all. He stood in a little halo of open space he didn't seem to have created. That is, he wasn't glaring at anyone or muttering to himself or flashing a knife or asking questions. He just stood, tall in his too-thin windbreaker, glasses less falling down than clinging to his nose. Spine too straight for comfort. *Tensed without tensing*, Nadine thought. Like a weathervane tilting one way, then the other in the faint spring wind. Or a tent pole to which everything and everyone else in sight had been attached and suspended.

Several more seconds passed before Nadine realized why she'd noticed him at all: he was facing the wrong way. Turned toward the street and the people around him. Not once did he glance back at Binna's shuttered stall. He just kept scanning faces.

Who's this, now? Nadine wondered.

Right that moment, he caught her watching. Or maybe realized *he'd* been caught. To Nadine's amusement, he blushed, seemed finally to remember his glasses, and rescued them from their precipice. With a nod she for some reason interpreted as collegial, he resumed his surveillance. Or...browsing. Which is really what it looked like. She found herself doing that, too. Right up until the moment Binna bent to the padlock, twirled its combination, and stepped back as the lock snapped open and clunked to the pavement.

All eyes—even the Weathervane's—swung toward the river wall. Binna hunched over the green wood, fiddling with that beautiful, magical key. Even at this distance, Nadine thought she glimpsed its strange not-color amid Binna's fingers. The whole crowd captured in it, nestled in her palm.

The Buddha had crept forward, leaning farther in than that gut should have allowed. Abruptly, Nadine remembered the worst moment from the night before. The one she half-decided she'd dreamed:

The sound—*feel*—of snuffling. Right by her exposed hand.

Kieran, naturally, was the only person paying no attention to the big event. He was way too busy throwing a casual arm around the redhead. Draping those nicotined fingers down the formidable slope of her breast.

So much time I wasted on you, Nadine thought, but felt nothing. Even recrimination felt irrelevant. Not worth the brain space. Not even the most interesting sensation in the instant she experienced it.

In the center of the group, the Weathervane spun slowly, searching faces. He caught Nadine's eye, let go.

"Uhh," Binna grunted, into a silence Nadine only then realized had settled over everything. She looked up just in time to see her key slipping—*getting sucked*?—into the keyhole at the top of the stall. It vanished entirely, and for a second, Nadine thought Binna had dropped it inside, wouldn't ever be able to get the lid off.

All in one movement, like some 19th century automaton, the sides of the stall slipped their hinges, dropping with a thud to the sidewalk as Binna flung back the lid. Everyone—Buddha, his kid, bookbuyers, Kieran, journalists, even Weathervane—squeezed forward, and the automaton sensation intensified. Except this time Nadine felt almost *part* of it. They all were. Locked in their grooves, moving where they must. In the only ways they ever could. Toward...*into...*

Discussing it later, Nadine would swear there was a *whoosh.* A warping in the light, like a wind through grass. Like a wave underwater. There wasn't any sound—the *whoosh* was a feeling—but there might have been a smell.

New fire in old ashes. Closest she could get.

There was a burst, a blink, or maybe her eyes had snapped shut and now they opened, and what she saw was *that room. The same room. Brick fireplace, yellow couch, then orange light unfolding in the air, exploding like a firecracker except silent, and behind the light was yawning, sky-wide dark streaked with color, the color swirling, surging, sucking the whole street toward it as though rushing everything over a falls but into nothing. Nothing streaked with not-color.*

The whole assembled crowd shuddered, rippled, elongated, slipping toward the mouth of Binna's stall or the vastness overhead, stretching as though along the rim of a black hole.

In one instant, everything—smell, whoosh, room, color, dark—winked out. Nadine did hear something, right at the end: a keening whistle, the echo of a shriek banking over the city and back toward the Seine, downriver out of Paris into the world.

Then tires squealed as Nadine slammed back into herself. Behind her, she heard the crunch of car into car, followed by voices shouting at each other in French. She hadn't realized she'd shut her eyes again—or else she hadn't done that, and ordinary Paris had just snapped back into place in front of her as though on a projected slide—and what she saw now stunned her. She couldn't figure out why, even before she took in everyone else in the crowd. She glanced at the Seine, the bridges, Notre Dame pink in the midmorning sun, her skin pink in the midmorning sun.

The midmorning sun.

What time was it? How long had she stood there?

The whole world—that projected slide—lurched into motion. She saw Kieran collapse to his knees, face giving way to the soul-deep hopelessness Nadine's ma read as a style choice and Nadine had believed for so long she could soothe. Could dam or even drain one day. She saw his new girl with her red head thrown back and her mouth positively splitting open with her laughter. She saw the silver pocketknife the tweedy bookbuyer flipped open a split second before he plunged it into the scruffy one's bearded neck and ripped sideways. She saw the Weathervane in the midst of everything with one hand stretched to catch or steady Kieran, the other flung out toward the booksellers as though to staunch spurting blood, but he had his head back, too, aimed straight up in the air—*at what Nadine was so sure she'd glimpsed in the air*—so that he looked less weathervane than antenna. Capable of conducting signal, or at least capturing it.

Finally, Nadine wrenched her gaze toward the riverbank, the open bookstall, and saw Binna. Saw the Buddha behind her, having just rifled the empty bin, as he turned, threw one arm around her neck while the other pinned her hands to her back and his son...his son...

Yanked Binna's pants to her knees. Yanked her panties to her knees while his father screamed directions. Orders. Nadine couldn't hear the actual words, wasn't sure of the language. Knew those were orders, anyway.

She lurched toward them as the kid's hands fumbled in Binna's panties, pulled them toward him as though rummaging in a drawer, stared down into them, then up at his dad. With a snarl, The Buddha shoved Binna sprawling half-naked into her bookstall, which splintered beneath her and dropped her to the pavement. He was on his knees now, patting around with his hands and paying no attention whatsoever to her, his son, or Nadine flying towards him. He didn't see the Weathervane until the Weathervane kneed him in the face.

Almost, Nadine stopped to kick the Buddha, too. Instead, she continued to Binna's side, helped her roll over, pull her pants back to her waist. In his fury—or rush—the Buddha had popped the button completely off Binna's jeans and broken the zipper. Nadine found herself holding the pants closed, holding Binna's hand, shouting her name for no good reason since the girl was clearly conscious and barely even bruised.

"*Kukalabbi*," Binna screeched. "What is wrong with..."

But her words trailed to nothing. Following her gaze, Nadine glanced up just in time to see the Buddha and his son fleeing across the nearest bridge. As they ran, the Buddha grabbed the kid under his shoulders, hoisted him off his feet. Nadine thought he might just chuck him in the Seine. Instead, he lofted him over his head, caught him, swung him in a wild circle so that the kid's feet crashed into multiple startled passersby.

Like Limerick fans after winning League. That was the only thing Nadine could compare it to. She watched until they disappeared, dancing, into the Latin Quarter.

After that, there were police. Paramedics, too, who had to wrestle the wounded bookseller out of the arms of the guy who'd stabbed him. That one had his bloody hands pressed deep into the wound he'd made, and his mouth wide open. Tears poured down his face as though from a burst street pipe. The police didn't even bother handcuffing him, just led him, finally, to a car and lowered him gently inside. Then they questioned everyone who'd seen what had happened—or seen *something* that happened, since nothing Nadine heard or even said made sense to her—for hours, well into the afternoon, which warmed, turned golden, set the Seine sparkling. Nearby *bouquinistes* watched from folding chairs or perches along the river wall, munching sandwiches, gossiping.

The police took names. At some point, without meaning to, Nadine found herself next to Kieran, who was still weeping and kept tottering every time he tried to stand up. The redhead knelt when he knelt, held him against her hip when he staggered upright.

"I'm sorry," he said to Nadine. "Hello." Then he apologized to the redhead. Eventually, they left. Nadine watched them go. She hoped the redhead really had as much light in her as she seemed to. Or that she got away faster than Nadine had managed.

Finally, she wound up on a bench beside Binna, munching apples the Weathervane had given them. Shivering fits kept seizing Binna, letting her go, like gusts of wind. Each one was just a little less violent.

The Weathervane reappeared with more apples and a wheel of cheese. He gestured at the bench on the other side of Nadine from Binna, raising his eyebrows. He was trying not to spook Binna, she supposed, though the way he just stood there in the sun was unsettling enough.

"Christ's sake, sit," she said.

He sat. Another shiver swept over Binna but barely rippled her. "*That* was his plan?" she snapped abruptly. She straightened, accepting a wedge of soft cheese. When she spoke again, her voice was almost her own. "Have his demon child rape me in the middle of the street?"

"I don't think—" Nadine started, at the exact moment the Weathervane said, "He didn't want—", and then they eyed each other. Slowly—shyly, Nadine was pretty sure—he smiled.

"Who's you, then?" she asked, her hand finding Binna's and squeezing.

"Normal," said the Weathervane.

Nadine's laugh was at least as much release as amusement. "I don't think so. No."

And there's him blushing.

"Norm. Normal, believe it or not. My actual given name. But Norm." As though remembering, he reached into the pocket of his blue-checked, fraying button-down shirt and pulled out a card. He handed it to Nadine.

There was his name, all right. Then more words, **Fossilist. Finder. Resource.** Under those came what Nadine supposed was a slogan.

I might help.

"We might have to work on your marketing materials," she muttered, starting to hand the card back. Then she pocketed it instead, flashing a grin. Just to watch his flush spread all over again. "Mr. Fossilist.

Beside her, Binna cleared her throat, peering around Nadine's shoulder. "Oh, hi. Don't mind me. The rape victim."

Nadine put an arm around her, felt tremors still wiggling around inside her. This fierce Icelandic girl. Her new friend. "He didn't rape you. Thank God."

"Did he find it?" Normal asked, startling them both. This time, he was blushing before Nadine even turned around. But he went on. "Do you still have it? I can give you 15,000 francs for it if you do. Probably more, I'd have to check."

"For what?" Binna asked.

"What you kept...there..." said the Weathervane. He did not actually look at Binna's pants.

"It looked to me like *they* found it, in the end," Nadine murmured.

The Weathervane glanced up, met her gaze. "To me, too."

No blush, this time. But something else. She'd seen it there before, all morning, as he'd scanned the crowd: awareness. More than that, actually. *Curiosity.* More antenna than weathervane all along.

Not a fossilist, no matter what his card said; he was too interested in the living things in front of him. But a cataloguer, for sure.

Collector, maybe.

"It's just a stupid key," Binna continued. "It opens that one lock on that one box. Which just got smashed apart, in case you have not noticed. And had fuck-nothing inside it anyway."

Nadine and the Weathervane watched each other. Almost, she just up and asked what he'd seen—heard, felt—at the moment that lid swung back. But she couldn't. Not yet. She didn't have the words.

He'd seen it, too, though. Or something, too. She could read it in his wide open, curious face.

"I have a new slogan for you," Nadine said. "For your card."

The Weathervane startled. Whether at what she'd said, or the fact that she was now blushing, she had no idea.

"'*I pay attention.*'"

"Clearly," the Weathervane whispered.

"No. I mean, yes. But that's your new slogan. For your card. My gift. No charge."

Now they were both doing it. The blushing. Also the grinning.

"What would you even want that stupid key for?" Binna asked.

The Weathervane—Collector—finally broke eye-contact with Nadine. He looked at the bridge where the Buddha and his son had vanished. "I don't. But I know a guy." Bending over, he picked the busted lock and a hinge—both that same strange, rusted no-color as the bin key—off the pavement, jiggled them in his hands like dice. "Hmm."

Later, when they'd devoured the whole wheel of cheese and the police had gone and the crowd scattered, they got up together and went to pick up the bags Nadine and Binna had left in their room. They found the alley, okay. At least, they found the alley with the gouged payphone at its mouth (unless all Paris payphones had gouges in them, some sort of subtly avant-garde French design flourish). Certainly—almost certainly—this was the street Nadine had been walking last night, and that they'd emerged into this morning.

But the buildings down that alley were all the same height, the same gray stone. Two of them had fire escapes zigging up them.

None had a door.

HOME

"Mmm. Paris night crepes," murmurs the Rev, zooming right past neck stabbings, father-son tag team assault artists, great auk eggs, and disappearing youth hostels.

"Best night food in the world," Nadine hears herself agree.

The Rev fondles his tea spoon, ticks it lightly against his cup as though testing a bell. He has one hand on his pointy chin and his eyes on the floor. He shakes his head. "Oh, I don't know. *Mqilia* by the train station in Casablanca..."

"*Char kway teow* in Singapore? Bao in Shanghai!"

"Red bean or meat?"

"Red bean isn't night food."

The Rev grins. "It's barely food. Just testing you."

"Hot dogs on Houston."

"Kosher ones!" This time, the Rev gives his cup a whack and he rings it. Then he winces and glances down, checking for cracks. "Sorry."

"Kosher ones," Nadine agrees. By the time he looks up, she's grinning, too.

He picks up the uneaten half a Rich Tea on his plate, puts it down. "Fish and chips in Devonport by Auckland."

"Fish and chips in *Galway*, Mister. In a proper midnight downpour." Her grin fades, not unpleasantly, as memory of taste gets washed away by memory of rain.

There's an unexpected moment. The two of them just sitting, Nadine with her legs tucked under her and her sweater sleeves over her hands, the Rev tapping his spoon in the air. Neither of them quite looking at each other or tasting what they're remembering, taste being one of those rare, marvelous things that can't be collected, like most of the most marvelous things. Like *anything*, Nadine thinks abruptly, works that idea out in her head the way she might have once, out loud, to Normal. Still might have, if they were alone. *Collecting is the hoarding of signifiers of memories of moments, most of them not even the collector's own. Which makes collecting a collective experience? The act of people acknowledging, remembering, or discovering that they really are people?*

"Great day," the Rev whispers, staring down into his spoon. Into his own face upside down in his spoon.

The comment jars Nadine from her reverie. Instinctively, she folds her arms across her chest, sits up straighter. But the Rev is still smiling, just as she was until a few seconds ago.

"Are you meaning today?" she says, after a pause that feels too long and shouldn't.

Idly—or else not idly at all—the Rev lifts his saucer, turns it in his hands, checks underneath as though expecting to find some maker's mark, china artist's signature. Nadine's just hoping there's no Target sticker. *$4.99-for-12.*

Plate back on tabletop, the Rev again swings his eyes around the room, from glass front doors to floor-to-ceiling windows filled with evening mist to mostly bare walls to dark hallway to kitchen to wishing tree clock. His hands are in the couch cushions, and they're not still, either. They're flexing. Probing. As though he's lost his keys. Or he's cold. Or...

"Could I see your catalog?" he asks.

For a second, Nadine is confused. Out of habit—a fading one, she only thinks to do it right before she speaks—she glances toward the hall, hoping for a glimpse of Normal's face. A glimpse of Normal *in* his face. Right on cue, he appears, as though she's summoned him. But he's not looking her way, not looking at anything as far as she can tell. He comes three steps into the room, his eyes toward the mist but not exactly seeing that either. He turns, half- turns back, looks at the floor, disappears again. It's like watching a sturgeon in a murky aquarium tank, something strange and wondrous and lost, still conscious but not of her. Not of here. No longer itself.

Then she remembers who she's dealing with today. Which is to say *not* dealing with. The last remembered tastes flee her. "We don't sell," she says.

"Ever? That's some business model you've got."

Nadine shrugs, starts to qualify, realizes she is not obliged to. She really needs to get out more, she thinks. Hit some neighborhood yard sales, preferably prowled by the local gaggle of octogenarian haggling champions. Get her dulled skills sharpened. She raises one shoulder, lowers it. "Pretty much never. Certainly never to you."

The surprise isn't that the Rev is annoyed, but that he's offended. He rocks back, cups his cheek as though she's slapped him. "Why not?"

"It's not personal," Nadine says, hand up, as though she's calming a child. Maybe *he* needs to get out and joust with the octogenarians. "You're just not where the Collector and I would deal. If we dealt."

For another long moment, he just sits, bristling and hunched. Then he shakes his head and laughs. "Oh. Right. The House." He laughs, murmurs something to himself. It sounds like "Me either."

Nadine lowers her hand, feels a sort of smile on her own face, automatic, reflexive. There because his is. Primed response as opposed to personal one. Unless primed *is* personal, our social mode the natural order, and the sense of some internal, private world of one's own construct. The human fallacy of believing in one's self as a self. This time, she doesn't glance toward the back of her house. But she hears her man back there shuffling around. Haunting the private world he has constructed. Sealed up in himself like a boy in a hyperbaric bubble. Or a caterpillar dissolving into its cocoon.

Or a crazy man.

Tears, then. Primed response. Ordinary, social, human interaction.

"How about a client list?" says the Rev, leaning forward, hands laced in his lap. Clenched, actually. No cocooned caterpillar, he. More puppy at window.

Barking puppy, Nadine realizes. Demanding an answer. She doesn't wipe at the tears in her eyes because she doesn't want to call attention to them. "Client list."

"Could I see that? Look, I'm not stealing your business. Assuming you do any. Ha." He snaps his fingers. "Can I see your list? I'm just trying to get a sense—"

"You're joking," Nadine says, cool and low. Properly herself at last. There, so. "You cannot possibly imagine—"

The bang comes like gunfire, like the earth cracking open, which is exactly what Nadine thinks it is before realizing the room isn't shaking, the windows aren't rattling. She leaps to her feet and scurries down the hall, checks the bedroom, which is dark and empty, swings to the den, and spots him immediately.

He's perched on his rolling green file cabinet, kicking his legs out. Every third kick or so, at least one sneakered heel slams into the cabinet. Hence, bang. When he sees her, he starts singing. Or he had already started, nothing to do with her at all. The chorus from *Clare to Here* again, except to the wrong tune. To *Sullivan's John.* Another song there's no reason in the world he should know, even through knowing her. When has she ever sang or played him that?

Once or twice. Surely. Sometime. An old favorite of her da's. One of the only things she has ever remembered or known about him.

Another far from home song, too, not that she's reading much meaning or intention into that. Anything Irish or Irish-themed would fit that description, after all. And Irish was pretty clearly the binding thread for today's inside-the-walled-off-castle-of-Normal playlist.

"Goddamn it," she says, and finally lets herself wipe at her eyes. No one here to notice, after all.

The Collector sits and kicks and grins like a babe in a high chair. Who has just flung peas in her hair.

Me either, she thinks. *Was* that *what the Rev had said*? He had, she decides. Right after she said she and Normal didn't sell to the Houses.

But that would mean…

She's tiptoeing as she returns to the room. At the lip of the hall, still hidden in shadows, she pauses. The Rev is up again, tapping a finger against the back of Tony's chair, and not idly, either. More like he's sounding a mango or melon. Getting a ripeness reading. His eyes flick to the wishing tree clock when it blows, hold there a second too long, return to the chair. He senses her watching, she can see that happen. But instead of glancing her way, he returns to the couch, lifts his empty cup and tilts it—reading tea leaves, now?—and holds up the remaining half of Rich Tea biscuit and scowls.

The banging behind her stops. She whirls, expecting the Collector over her shoulder. He's there, all right, but not coming her way. He retreats again into the dark bedroom without turning on lights.

Sighing, Nadine steps back into the living room. The Rev watches. It's jarring, that chilly blue gaze. Not unfriendly, not invasive.

Something else, though.

"I was out of line," he says. "Sorry."

With a shrug, Nadine moves back to the couch, though she doesn't sit. "Don't even know what you mean."

"When I asked for your client list."

"Oh." She waves a hand. "That was more barmy than out of line." She tries for a smile, but it won't quite come.

"What's barmy," says the Rev, holding up his saucer, "is serving anyone you don't actively hate one of these cookies. What on earth is this?"

This time, her grin comes without any thought at all. "Well. I could offer you a better one, but…"

HEXENHAUS

"Now, see?" the Collector half-shouted while Terry Riley music tumbled through the sunlit room like leaves in a spring wind. "This is the secret to sustained happiness. Right here." Then he took a slurp of whatever it was he'd brewed that morning, leaned even closer to whichever of his thousand blogs and private web-boards had momentarily drawn his attention, and forgot he'd been speaking.

For her own purposes, Nadine let him forget for a bit. Despite the pulsing music and the chatter from the radio the Collector also had blaring this morning, their A-frame retained its stillness. It was like a forest burrow, somewhere they inhabited rather than owned even though they owned it. A proper place, in other words.

Setting her own mug on the countertop, she glanced at the correspondence that needed answering, and the separate piles of research materials strewn across coffee table and kitchen table and living room floor. Rather than tackle any of that, she decided to badger the Collector some more. She walked up behind him, leaned over, and let a twist of her dark hair dance down his cheek.

"What's that, then?" she murmured.

Ignoring—no, not even feeling—her hair or her breath, the Collector gestured at his screen. "Remember that woman and her gun shell casings who—"

"The secret of sustained happiness," Nadine said. "Not the website."

Around them, music whirred and spun. From the radio, the "Morning Edition" theme melted into the clamor. And against Nadine's breast, the Collector thrummed with the heat of his thoughts.

"Oh," he said. "Wanting to work."

Nadine sighed. "And here, I thought it was giving the love of your life the rogering of her dreams before you're even properly awake."

He did glance up then, at least, bumping her chin with his head. "What? No. That...that's waking up, period. That's a given. A necessity. Not even momentary happiness possible without—"

Laughing while he floundered, Nadine started to hug him, and he pushed her out of the way.

"Hang on, listen." He turned up the radio.

The *Morning Edition* theme faded. Rachel or Noel or one of the other genial hosts was in the midst of offering yet another gently ironic intro to the new half-hour, in that tone that made every one of them sound clever, professional, and knowing. And also, oddly, unlike anyone she'd met or would care to know better.

"Just how good are *the delicacies at the Hexenhaus Bakery in Oak Park, Michigan? Last night, a determined thief smashed through the shop's front window with an aluminum bat. The thief left the cash register and safe untouched. But he cleaned out every last crumb from both pastry cases. No word on whether he got to the milk in the refrigerator. It's Morning Edition."*

"Well, thanks for kaboshing our morning flirtation, I wouldn't want to have missed that news right there," Nadine started. But she was speaking to an empty chair.

Moments later, the Collector reemerged from the back bedroom fully dressed, untied sneaker-laces flapping, balled up green windbreaker under his arm. He stopped when he saw her.

"Aren't you coming?"

Their drive took them over the Donner Pass into Nevada. On the slopes of the mountains, poppies and popcorn flower and lupine unfurled in the new grass and old snow like flags from obscure nations. As usual in the spring, the Collector left his side of the Jeep unzipped, which meant that every now and then, whiffs of pine resin surfaced in the soup of diesel smoke belching from the logging trucks in front of them.

Sighing, closer to content than she would have expected, Nadine opened her laptop. "Want to give me something to start on, then?"

"Don't want to spoil your appetite," said the Collector.

"Care to whet it?"

This was the moment, generally, when he dropped a hint, or asked her to look something up. He also usually grinned at her right about now, or at least in her general direction. Today, though, he kept his eyes on the road.

"Just tell me what you see, Nadine. I'll tell you when."

She didn't bother asking when what, or what she was meant to be looking for. An hour later, they were on the outskirts of Reno, bumping down a sandy road past two trailer parks, then a long stretch of Nevada nothing, until they came to a surprisingly homey cabin tucked back amid the mesquite bushes. The cabin had shingle walls and a flat roof and solar panels that flashed, blinding, in the mid-morning sun. It was bigger than Nadine initially thought, burrowing back into the rocky hillside behind it.

Expecting desert silence, Nadine emerged from the Jeep into the buzz of generators tucked against both sides of the cabin. There was nothing else but sand and dead yucca stalks and desert shrub for miles around. In the wide blue sky, a single winged thing circled.

"Is this place completely off-grid?" she asked. "Is that why you didn't call whoever this is first, or—"

The cry that filled the air had so little breath in it, so little human tone, that Nadine first thought it came from the bird overhead. But the scuttling, quick and clumsy, came from the cabin. The front door flew open, and an old man stumbled out.

Stopping a few feet away, the man stared at them out of watery blue eyes. He looked spindly in his too-long shorts. His gray T-shirt sagged off him like skin coming loose. Fine gray hairs covered his actual skin like a tarantula's. Fumbling in his pockets, he withdrew a pair of scratched spectacles and jammed them onto his face.

"It *is* you," he said.

Not hairs, Nadine realized, but distortions in the air caused by the man's constant twitching. The Collector stayed quiet. When Nadine glanced toward him, she found him looking at the sky, the house, her face, but not the old man. She couldn't read his expression.

The trembling man burst into tears. "It *is* you. You've found them, after all these years. I'd given up hope."

Only then did the Collector smile, and only vaguely. "I promised my colleague here a reward for coming all the way out here."

"You did?" Nadine murmured.

"Reward?" said the old man. Tremors wracked him.

"A little hint of what you're looking for."

For a second, Nadine thought the old man was literally going to shudder to pieces. She turned on the Collector, started to snap at him. But he stood absolutely still, hands in his pockets.

"What I'm..." the old man mumbled. Then he straightened, got partial control of his shakes, pushed his glasses even harder against his face. And smiled. His teeth flashed startlingly white, glinting in the sunlight. "Of course. Come in, come in. I'm so very glad you have come." Waving them to follow, he disappeared back into the cabin.

The interior proved dim and cool, cave-like. The air hung heavy, hushed as opposed to still, and Nadine found herself moving slowly, then more slowly. The old man directed them to tall, wooden chairs drawn up to a table laid with a pristine white tablecloth. The edges of the tablecloth hung so precisely, the corners cut so sharply, that at first Nadine thought it was some sort of enamel design-feature. But it rippled as she drew back a chair. In the exact center of the table, a crystal vase housed three stalks of pink flowers, their petals folding together like filigreed cake frosting. Mozart music didn't so much fill the air as infuse it. Nadine realized she wasn't even sure whether it had been playing when they came in or switched on afterward.

"Did we just teleport somewhere?" she whispered as the Collector settled into the chair nearest hers.

The old man returned bearing a silver salver laden with flower-patterned china tea cups and saucers and a single, covered china plate. The effect was marred only by the way the flatware rattled in the old man's hands as he laid each piece, just so, before his guests. "Let me..." the old man murmured. "Allow me to..."

Nadine started to get up to help, but the Collector squeezed her wrist beneath the table.

"Allow him," he said.

Nadine studied his face, waiting for the smile that always accompanied these moments. His invitations to new experiences. Instead, he squeezed her wrist again. Whatever that was meant to convey, Nadine didn't get it.

The old man continued laying the table until he had everything where he wanted. Finally, he lifted the covered plate and set it precisely between Nadine and the Collector.

He lifted the cover.

The room's low light helped Nadine hide her disappointment. She wasn't sure exactly what she'd expected. But given the tablecloth, the flowers, the music, the fact that she and Normal had dropped off yet another map together...

On the plate sat two tiny loaves, dull brown in color. They'd once been rectangular, but now had broken edges and crumbling bits that made them look like woodchips. Several silent seconds passed, long enough for Nadine to feel the old man's anticipation. She leaned forward to mumble something vague and appreciative, and both loaves winked.

Winked?

They did it again, in different places along their crumbling tops. Nadine leaned in closer. Tiny red flecks dotted the tops like stardust. As soon as she'd noticed the flecks, she became aware of the snowflakes, faint dustings of sugar-smoke so lacey and delicate that they seemed to be sifting down from the air.

"Taste," the old man said. Commanded, actually.

Both she and the Collector moved hands toward the plate at exactly the same slow, cautious speed, as though wary of scaring something off. Her loaf, when she touched it, proved warm; not hot, not even toasted, the heat organic somehow, radiating out rather than baked in. However delicate the sugar snowflakes looked, not a one so much as moved when she lifted the loaf between thumb and forefinger. The taste of it began to seep into her senses—all of them, registering through skin and eyes as well as nose—long before her fingers reached her mouth.

"Forbidden?" the Collector asked. Then his loaf reached his lips, and he stopped talking.

The old man said nothing, just watched and shook until both Nadine and the Collector had taken their first bites. Then—with a flat-lipped expression Nadine read initially as a suppressed smile, then realized might be impatience bordering on fury—he nodded.

"Forbidden. *Ja.* Probably. I have...made adjustments. But they would of course still say so."

"They?" Nadine murmured eventually, the loaf long gone but the tastes still trickling into each other on her tongue, combining, swirling, recombining. *Pepper, maybe? Mint, certainly. Cinnamon. Some ghost-fruit something. Ginger.* It would be a long time before she touched the tea. If she ever did. This taste would have to leave her of its own accord.

"The Guild," said the old man.

"Guild?"

The Collector sighed, eyes still closed, empty fingers by his nose so he could smell residue as well as taste it. That seemed such a good idea that Nadine followed suit.

"*Lebkuchen* Guild," the Collector murmured. "Nuremburg branch. One of them."

"There is only one," the old man said. "One that matters."

At that, the Collector did grin. Nadine, too, without even knowing yet what this guy meant. That was simply the sort of comment their clients always made.

The old man did not grin.

"The only one," the Collector corrected himself. "Technically, Nadine, these...cookies, I guess we should call them, though that hardly seems apt... are not allowed to be made outside of Nuremberg. By anyone. Not even privately, for honored guests. Our man here could be held accountable."

Abruptly, the old man unfolded, smacked his trembling hands on the table, and whimpered at them. "You will tell me? Is it today? I will see them today?" Shuddering there amid his perfect flowers and *lebkuchen* smells and Mozart music, he burst into tears. "Will I have them today?"

Lowering his sugar snowflake-dusted fingers with a sigh, the Collector shrugged. "I had to make sure you were still out here, didn't I? Had to make sure you were still interested."

The old man's breath came out hissing. "You don't even know for certain? You came to me, and you are not sure?"

The Collector met his client's gaze and held it. The old man was shuddering so hard, Nadine could hear his teeth.

"Normal," she whispered. "What the hell are you doing?"

"I'll know tonight," the Collector said flatly, to the old man. "At least, I'll know if this is a real lead. The second I've confirmed, I'll be back in touch." Without so much as a nod or thank you, he stood. "Come on, Nadine. We have a long drive to the airport, then a long flight."

But Nadine wasn't ready to go. Or rather, she wasn't ready to plunk herself into the Jeep beside the Collector. Not until she understood his current mood. She'd never seen him like...whatever the hell this was.

"May I use the bathroom?" she asked the old man. Not even looking at Normal, she followed the direction of her host's shaking hand into a dim, surprisingly long back hallway. She passed a single bedroom with a half-closed door, and then a tall, unlatched linen closet on her way to the very rear of the house.

When she'd finished, she stood a little longer by the mirror, in this tiny space lit only by a single-bulbed, bent-necked metal lamp that made her think, incongruously, of interrogation rooms in 1940's gangster films. The lamp might have made her sad except for the shine on it. Everything this man owned winked, shone, infused. On the countertop, centered perfectly in the glow of the lamp—as though the old man stood right where she was, and only there, to read it—lay a spiral-bound packet of papers covered in translucent vellum. The vellum looked markless, either handled never or only with gloves. In the center of the cover, a single, flowering tree had been stamped, its roots burrowing down the page. Above the tree rose a single word: *Lebensspuren*. The word tingled on Nadine's tongue as she mouthed it, lit a fuse buried somewhere in the back of her brain. She stood still, let the fuse run. But no revelations burst through her.

Gently—using a tissue to keep from leaving blots—she flipped through the papers. But all the words were German. Closing the packet and switching off the light, she realized she didn't even know what she and the Collector were hunting this time. Bent-necked metal lamps or fingerprint-resistant vellum for all she knew. From down the hall, Mozart music ghosted, twinkling and ephemeral as the sugar on the old man's cookie-loaves. And still, that taste—those tastes—floated on her tongue.

In the hall, lit only by the glow from the dining room at the far end, Nadine passed back in front of a single row of pictures she hadn't noticed before. All of them were black and white. The first showed a cottage in snow, somewhere sleepy, far away, European, and old, with a young woman out front. The woman had a snow shovel in her hands and a sort of smile playing on her thin lips through the steam of her breath. Her eyes were the clear gray of blue eyes in colorless prints, and they seemed trained on something far from wherever she was. The second frame held a framed certificate of some kind. Then more photos, one of a soldier on a train platform, another of a child racing through long grass along the lip of a sloping pine forest that was nowhere in this country or on this continent, trailing something—*a kite?*—behind him.

Only in the old Irish north had Nadine seen forest remotely like that. Bonagher Glen, near Dungiven. Thick, silent, shadowed. Ancient. But no Irish forests sloped that way, or grew that dense. These were mountain trees. *And that isn't a kite*, she realized. She leaned closer, felt the prickle in her skin long before understanding hit her brain.

Little boy, hurtling past dark trees. Black flag flapping behind like the wings of something swooping down on him. Except that he was holding it. Flying it. Next to that picture was another, of row upon row of little boys. Five or six years-old, maybe. Their formation perfect. Their hands outstretched in identical perpendiculars from their shoulders.

Straightening, Nadine felt her back brush the door of the linen closet. Turning as though in a trance, she opened it.

To find towels. More tablecloths, their folds crisp, tight, perfect. And there. on the third shelf, two perfect, folded flags. One of them almost certainly the very flag she'd mistaken for a kite in the photo behind her. Which she suddenly didn't like having behind her. She whirled.

The photo hung where she'd left it.

Returning her attention to the closet, Nadine stared at the flags. Red and black. She didn't need to unfold them to know their insignia, and she didn't want to touch them. But she did anyway, and that was how she discovered the box underneath. Before she could stop herself, she'd pushed the flags back, withdrawn the box. Then she stared down in disbelief.

An actual copy. The real thing. The box edges just a little rounded but the colors still bright, even in these shadows. Nadine had read about this game, but hadn't quite believed it was real, somehow. Certainly not played. Not by actual children. Her right hand lifted all on its own, floating across the top of the box as though over an open flame, still trailing faint, twinkling *lebkuchen* smells.

JUDEN RAUCH! the box proclaimed. *Wenn Sie erreichen, weg von 6 Juden zu sehen…*

Shoving the box back under its covering flags, Nadine swung the door shut and turned, half-expecting to find the old man blocking her way, trembling. Instead, she saw empty hall, empty dining room beyond that. The Collector and the old man had gone outside, apparently. Left her alone in here.

She was almost sprinting by the time she reached the front door of the cabin—*bunker, really;* That's *what this place was*—and emerged, blinking, into the sunlight. The Collector had not just climbed into the Jeep but zipped its side and started the engine. With a mumbled "Bye," Nadine moved fast past the old man, who stood as if rooted in the sand, spiky and parched as a mesquite bush, arms juddering crookedly at his sides.

She waited until she had herself zipped in, until the Collector had turned the Jeep and they were safely back on paved highway and headed for plain old ugly, pitiful Reno, before turning on him. "*Lebensborn*," she said.

The Collector looked blank. Then he nodded. "Ah. I knew it was something."

After that, they drove in silence. And because of the fading tastes in her mouth, the ghost-scents on her fingers, that photograph of boy and flag and forest still hovering under her eyelids, Nadine only registered the speed at which they moved—the lack, thereof—at the moment the Collector finally stirred. He looked at the dashboard, glanced at her, grunted, and drove the gas pedal into its accustomed depression in the floorboards. The Jeep rocketed forward.

"Right, then. Good morning," Nadine murmured. It really did feel as though they'd both been drugged, and were only now stirring.

"*Lebensborn*," said the Collector, turning the steering wheel slightly left, slightly right, the way he always did on open straightaways, like a little boy playing a video game. One who couldn't bear the straight sections even for a second. "Hitler Youth? Is that right?"

"Not quite." Nadine opened her laptop, confirming what she'd already dredged from her memory. "More Hitler Youth-in-Training. Kidnapped Hitler Youth-in-Training."

"Kidnapped? All of them?"

Nadine shook her head, thought of the old man's metal-backed lamp. His Mozart music and white tablecloths and winking cookies. *How was she supposed to feel about all of that?* That was the question of the day, of course. The reason the Collector had told her nothing about this particular client beforehand. He'd wanted her to sort this out for him.

"No," she said. "I don't think so. Actually, wait, I think it started as an anti-abortion campaign? Maybe? I'll check. But some of them were kidnapped. From villages, mostly from Poland? They'd take the wee ones—babies, little kids up to five year-olds, I suppose—and set them in Nazi foster homes or training institutes or whatever."

Like monsters out of myth. They really were. Come away, human children…

"To fight? To become soldiers?"

"Hold on." She tapped at her keyboard. "No. I mean, eventually, probably. But they were too young for the war. They were raised instead as the next True Aryans. Master Race, Mach Whatever. The war ended before almost any of them came of age. And these kids…" She looked up from the computer, stared straight ahead of her. "I think they just got sent home afterward. As in, to their old villages. Or just…deposited somewhere."

"Not retrained or de-programmed?"

Returning to her laptop keys, Nadine stayed silent. Hunting. Trying to trace the word that had triggered her revelation. *Lebenspuren.*

"Not then." She stared at the translation of the page she'd found, then at the desert rolling by outside her window. Cactus and casino billboards. A McDonalds. Oil derricks. Two hitchhiking Hispanics so covered in sand that they looked more like dust devils than people. *The new Lebensborn*, she thought. *Not kidnapped but lured. Abandoned all the same and left to wander the American wasteland. Which was no one's Fatherland.* "Not ever, really. There are organizations, now. Some international support groups. Even those only formed recently, it looks like. Kind of…Nearly-Nazis Anonymous? Now that all these people are too old for any support or deprogramming to matter. Whatever sense they have made of their lives, they've made it themselves. Are you listening?"

"Always," said the Collector.

From long experience, Nadine knew that was true. Today, he seemed unusually distracted even for him, though. His eyes kept flicking from road to mirror to desert, but they didn't seem to be looking for or even noting anything.

He did locate Reno-Tahoe International Airport without any guidance. Once he'd parked and switched off the Jeep, he pulled a pack of licorice gum from his pocket, started to offer her some, then grimaced and put the gum back.

"I don't want to pollute my taste buds," he said.

"Ever again," said Nadine.

"What if we get hungry?"

She smiled. "It's a problem."

"So you're saying we *should* help him. The old man. Right?"

Surprised more by the directness of the question than the question itself, Nadine pursed her lips. She didn't even know what Herr Shuddering Man wanted the Collector to do. She thought of those flags folded in their linen closet in that dark hallway, then of the board game they shrouded. *Wenn Sie erreichen, weg von 6 Juden zu sehen...*

"You know him better than I do," she finally said.

"I very much doubt that," said the Collector. He took her hand, held it, and looked at her. He was taller than she was, and yet his gaze seemed aimed upward, like a five year-old's.

She looked at their entwined hands. "You haven't told me enough. I can't weigh this for you. For us. That's not fair."

"I got you a cookie, didn't I?"

He was smiling. But not kidding. A while passed before Nadine smiled back. Her words came out in a whisper. "It was a really, really good cookie..."

Somewhere over the Dakotas—the country a Candyland gameboard below, all Mr. Mint-green grass under a Princess Snowflake sky, blue and whipped cream-white—Nadine succumbed to the inevitable and opened the pretzels the airplane attendant had insisted she accept. At the first pallid *crack* between her teeth, the last echo of *lebkuchen* vanished off her tongue. Not just the taste, but the sense-memory of it. The exact, exquisite texture, the way it gave just so under her bite. For a moment, she had to clench her jaw closed to keep from spitting pretzels into the seat back in front of her;

she held on only by convincing herself—by *knowing*—that the damage was already done. The taste lost. The loss irreversible.

Once she'd swallowed, she was angry. Hungry, but angry. She poured the rest of the pretzel packet into her mouth, gulped it down, turned from the window to the Collector and woke him with a hard jab to the ribs. "So it does matter to you," she snapped.

"What?"

He sounded dreamy, still. *Because he hadn't eaten again, yet. Knowing him, he wouldn't for days, partially to savor every last taste of the cookie, partially because he often forgot about eating anyway until she reminded him.*

"Our clients. You always say it's about what they're looking for, not who they are. That we are instruments of the hunt. Bloodhounds-for-hire, nothing more. So how come—"

"Nadine," he interrupted, struggling upright in his seat. "Once we land... when we get there. I want you on full alert. Okay?"

"What? What do you mean?" After a second, with increasing annoyance, she added, "Get where, by the way?"

"The bakery," said the Collector. As though she were being willfully dense.

"Bakery?"

"The Hexenhaus. Hexenhaus."

"Hexen... The one on the radio? From this morning? You can't be..." But of course he was. He always was. "Norm. Normal. Is this you full mental, now? Are you telling me we're looking for a cookie?"

"Nadine, I mean it. I want that intuition of yours cranked into the red, okay? There's something—"

"Feck away off. It's a really scary cookie we're seeking? What makes you even think that bakery has anything to do with—"

"The radio story, Nadine." He'd gone completely upright in his seat, straining against his seatbelt like a balloon stretching for release. His hands waved as words rushed out of him, magicking her aggravation right out of her in the process.

"Okay. What about it?"

"It's wrong. It has to be."

"Define *wrong*."

"It has things wrong with it. It can't be right."

Even as she slapped him on the arm, the Collector's chatter burbled in her ears like a fountain, settling her, drawing her back to the moment upon which he wanted her to focus. He was still prattling, but what she heard now was the radio broadcast, which she'd barely even registered at the time. This was a skill he'd taught her, or discovered in her. One she treasured. A condition of their relationship, and a foundation for it: her ability to stay that awake at all times. Absorb moments as she lived them.

"You're right," she interrupted a few moments later. "It's all kinds of wrong."

Instantly, the Collector stopped babbling. He tilted onto the armrest between them, crowding her in his eagerness. Warming her with it.

"They didn't say the burglar didn't *get into* the cash register, did they? They said he didn't *touch* it. He never even tried."

The Collector stroked her arm. "That's good. I hadn't even noticed that."

"Also. What kind of serious bakery closes up for the night and leaves pastries in the case?"

"*There* you go," said the Collector. "That's the one."

Nadine pursed her lips, shook her head. "It's like leaving out a food dish for stray cats."

"Except behind glass. And a locked door."

"Which would make it more like...bait?"

Surprising her with a quick, soft kiss on the mouth, the Collector settled back into his seat, folded his arms as though suddenly cold, and, frowned. "I hope so. I really hope that's it." Then he went quiet, and he stayed that way until they landed.

Detroit surprised her.

From everything she'd heard, she expected gray ruin, crumbling buildings, shot out streetlamps, corpses of the homeless curled in the sprung trunks of abandoned Torinos. What she saw instead, as they spun their rented Chevy through the all but empty streets toward the Woodward Corridor, reminded her of Ireland. The late spring sun, still out even after eight o'clock in the evening, glowed warm on her forearms through the windshield, and golden on the green, green grass that rolled over boundary-less lots and through tenantless structures, flowing up to and over the edges of sidewalks and roads like an incoming tide. Like a sea reforming. Fireflies and bright yellow butterflies wheeled above bright yellow flowers. Some of those were dandelions, but some were daffodils.

A lost land, to be sure. Like her own home, except with no one to sing for it. She leaned her head against the vibrating window.

"We're here," said the Collector, after some time. "We're almost here. Nadine, I need you to wake up."

"I'm awake. Just…sad? Am I sad?"

"It's the cookie."

Nadine laughed.

"I'm not joking."

"That's why I'm laughing," Nadine said, and brushed his arm with her fingertips.

As they slowed, the sun finally disappeared over the low rooftops. Shadows rose from the sidewalks, inhabiting the sad little storefronts and tiny brick houses like ghosts of customers or residents. Echoes of them. The Collector counted down addresses. "8864…8862…"

"There," Nadine said, gesturing across the empty street.

On the cracked sidewalk, broken glass twinkled in the twilight. Caution tape marked off half the block, stretching across the entrance to the bakery and between tilting NO PARKING signs. Just to the right of the bakery's door stood a crooked statue, a wooden woman fully five feet tall, her skirts melting into their shadows. Her carefully carved dark shawl obscured her shoulders and eyes, but the beak nose and O of her mouth were plainly visible. No broom, no pointed hat, no green tint to the wooden skin, nothing whatsoever to identify the figure as a witch. She just *was* one.

"Hexenhaus," Nadine murmured.

The Collector eased the Chevy to the curb and parked. Then he turned, studying not only the bakery but the whole block, and for quite some time. "Witch House," he said. "Right? That's what it means."

"Very specific witch, I think. The one in 'Hansel and Gretel.'"

"Huh." He was looking behind them again. From somewhere up the residential street behind the bakery, children screamed. Happy screams. The Collector shot her a glance. "Well, that's pretty perfect, you have to admit."

"The screaming?"

"There he is," said the Collector, popped the locks, and left the car.

"What...?" Nadine started, fumbling to unbuckle herself. When she glanced up, she discovered that the witch had a companion, now. A living one.

Scrambling from her seat, Nadine joined the Collector, who'd stopped by the hood of the car.

"Thanks for waiting for me," she said.

"I wasn't wai—"

"I know." Her smile was fleeting, completely for herself, and not without sadness even after all these years. The Collector was lovely, and also who he was. He would never be anything else.

The man beside the witch was a hunchback, tipped forward so far that his torso nearly paralleled the sidewalk. He had white stubble along the line of his chin and startlingly large blue eyes. Because of their size, their forward position, and the fact that they didn't blink, they made him look like a fish. He had his hand on the witch's elbow as if she'd escorted him out here. Quasimodo the fish-husband and his hand-carved witch-wife, with the very ground twinkling around them.

"You do take me the most amazing places," she whispered.

"Remember what I told you," said the Collector, barely moving his mouth, as though worried the fish-guy could read lips.

"Which thing?"

"I doubt he'll offer. Even assuming I'm right. But if he does—"

"Offer? Normal—"

"Remember our client. Mr. *Lebensborn*."

He started forward, but she pulled him around. "What about him?"

The Collector held up a hand in front of her face. For an astonished second, she thought he was going to slap her. Instead, he set the hand shaking.

"His...Parkinson's?" Nadine said slowly.

"It's not Parkinson's. I don't think"

"*Why* don't you think? What is it?"

Now he was watching his own hand shake, as if he'd only just discovered it could do that. A long moment passed before he shook his head. "Not Parkinson's." Slipping free of her grasp, he crossed the street.

Nadine watched, her mind whirling. Just as he ducked under the Caution tape, the new moonlight caught him, dancing along his hairline and down his back, as though he were exiting this time, or this plane. Disappearing into the Wardrobe or through the Looking Glass. Again.

Wait for me, she thought, already moving. She didn't bother calling out. He wouldn't wait.

Because he knew she was coming.

She was close enough, by the time the fish-man spoke, to hear what he said. His voice came out thin and constricted, as if something was strangling him.

"You are him? Herr Collector?"

"You're the proprietor? The man I spoke to? I didn't get your name, Herr—"

"Your question," said the fish-man. "When you called this morning. It intrigued me. Ask it again? *Bitte*?" The voice could have been a grandfather's, really. A dying one, perhaps, but threaded with light. Soft as spun sugar. The German accent faint, its serrated edges blunted by years of American English use.

Nadine had seen her man curious and excited almost every single day. But she'd rarely seen him hesitant.

Eventually, he nodded. "I asked, did your burglar get what he came for?"

Lifting his fingers from the witch's elbow, the old man burst into a grin. When he clapped his hands, grains of flour dust flew up, winking on moonbeams like fireflies. Or the shoemaker's elves. "*Gut.* Marvelous. I will answer this question. But before, you must answer just one from me. Okay?"

And then you will have cookies. And perhaps milk. The baker didn't say that, but his tone suggested it. Oh, how Nadine hoped that was true. Given the experience she'd had earlier, she thought this could well turn out to be a landmark—nay, historic— cookie day.

As long as she forgot about the folded flags. That board game. Her trusty internal alarm, which would not shut up.

"The person who sent you," said the baker of Hexenhaus, smiling, straightening, to the extent that he could. "You will tell me his name."

If Nadine hadn't known better, she would have suspected the Collector was bargaining. Withholding. Playing poker. But more likely, he really didn't know. Names simply weren't one of the ten thousand things he tracked. For his work—for him—they just weren't relevant or necessary, most of the time.

But then he shrugged. "Nathanael Ho—"

"We're From the Guild," Nadine overrode him. Acting on instinct, plain and simple.

The Collector knew better than to correct her. He did glance sidelong at her, though.

Somehow, the baker's eyes got even wider, seemed almost to inflate. "Guild?" His smile slipped. "*Nurnberger Lebkuchen*? Again?"

"Well, we have made ourselves clear," the Collector said. Nadine tried elbowing him to shut up, but of course, he was into it, now, already embellishing. "We did warn you. And yet our agents confirm that you continue to produce authentic *lebkuchen* five thousand miles from—"

Laughter bubbled out of the baker. Once again, he clapped his hands. "*Nein*," he said, flour-mote elves twinkling around him. "*Nein*. That is not true."

"It could have been true," Nadine mumbled, glaring at the Collector's back.

"You are thinking..." Laughter overtook him again. He actually had to hold up a hand and pause for breath. "You imagine *Nurnberger Lebkuchen* has...like *The Sopranos*? That they send out squads of..." Those blue eyes poured over them, subsumed them. "...clever Irish brunettes and less clever walking sticks to keep the Secret of the Cookie inside city limits?"

"I always hoped it was more about luring people to go there," the Collector mumbled, eyes downcast. "So they actually get to have singular experiences, make memories, and leave with stories to tell."

The baker stopped laughing. This time, he did manage to straighten some. At least he stood taller than the wooden witch, now.

The Collector met his gaze. "I know people who have done a lot worse things to protect a lot less."

"*Ja*," said the baker, softly. "I have, also."

"I think your burglar got what he came for," the Collector said, shooting a look at Nadine. In it was the same question he'd been asking all day. But she had no answer for him, yet, and he knew it. Not enough data. Down the block, a metal trash can rattled in place as though someone had pinged it with a rock. The Collector returned his attention to the baker. "I also think it won't help him. Am I right?"

Instead of clapping his hands again, the baker drew a slow, tired breath. His smile slipped the rest of the way off his face. "I think you are a man in a thousand. A million, maybe. And also, I am old."

He said something else, but his voice got buried in the clatter of the garbage can as it crashed to the street, revealing the trembling man from Nevada as he lurched from behind it. From his mouth came the same bird-shriek Nadine had heard outside his bunker this morning, and in his eagerness he almost sprawled headlong onto the pavement. If he had, maybe he would have dropped the gun.

Had the Collector known, Nadine thought frantically? And then, *All day?* Had that pathetic, shuddering person somehow managed to stay close enough to follow them through this whole impossible day? From his cabin to the airport to the plane to this place?

Then she turned and saw the baker of Hexenhaus. His grin glittered on his face.

"I thought so," the baker said.

"It's you," said the trembling man, upright again, pointing the gun straight into the baker's fishy stare. His hands vibrated so hard that if he pulled the trigger, Nadine figured he would most likely hit the Collector or her. Or a passing car. "*Tier.*"

For the third time, the baker clapped his hands.

"*Teuful*," spit the trembling man. "*Damon.*"

"You have had a long trip?" the baker wheedled. Unless that was cooing. "They have been…*hard* years?"

The trembling man flung up the gun, and Nadine and the Collector both ducked in opposite directions. But instead of shooting, the trembling man sobbed. Viciously, savagely, snot bubbling from his nose and saliva from his mouth as though he were a pot boiling over. "You destroyed my life," he said, shaking so hard that Nadine thought he might shatter.

"Come," said the baker. "Your life was destroyed long before we ever met. And I had nothing to do with it."

"My whole life."

The baker's teeth glinted. "You're here now, aren't you?"

Somehow, the trembling man stopped shaking. He got the gun steady and pointed directly into the baker's face.

Not Parkinson's, Nadine thought. *Withdrawal.*

"Sweet Jesus," she said, "it really *is* the cookie." It did occur to her, even as he turned, that she was looking away from her potential murderer so she could stare at her partner. But frankly—as always—her partner was more interesting. "This is all about a cookie."

The Collector had turned to her, too, and away from the gun. So they could discuss further. So he could see her reaction. One of them, she thought, really could have used a Watson.

"But not the one we ate," she said.

"At his house, you mean?" The Collector gestured at the baker, then their client. "To these guys? That hardly even qualifies as—"

The gun exploded, shattering the wooden witch's beak-nose and sending Nadine and the Collector diving to the sidewalk. Nadine's knee scraped cement, and something sharp stabbed into the open wound. She gasped as tears filled her eyes.

When she looked up, though, the baker hadn't moved. Hadn't even stopped smiling. "Think, now, *mein Herr*. What will happen if you shoot me?"

"I'll find them," snarled the trembling man.

At that, the baker tilted back his head and laughed outright. "Yes. Of course. I have a tin in there with your name on it, and the recipe labeled in my files." He snapped his fingers, and the trembling man deflated, collapsing into himself like a fallen soufflé. The gun sank to his side. Mucus and saliva mingled as they streamed down his face.

"Please. You have ruined my whole life. Have mercy."

"Of course," said the baker. Suddenly, his voice was full of music. "Don't you realize that all you had to do, all these years, was ask? Put away your little toy. It can't help you anyway."

Shuddering, sniveling, their client hesitated one moment longer. Then, to Nadine's amazement, he shuffled forward. His arm lifted again, but he was offering the gun, not aiming it. As though paying homage. Or trading.

Until the Collector said, "Don't."

Hands on her bleeding leg—she wasn't pressing for fear of grinding glass bits into the wound, just holding the shredded skin closed—Nadine stared at her partner, got her brain quiet. Processed. Turned to the trembling man. "Give the gun to *him*," she said. "To the Collector."

"Ah," said Normal. "That's even better. That's perfect."

The trembling man trembled, gun half-raised. Whatever he was thinking, he was still thinking it when the baker pulled his own gun from the folds of his apron and shot him in the kneecap. The trembling man went down screaming. His gun flew from him as the Collector lunged forward, ripped the baker's weapon away, and stepped back. He didn't lift or aim it, but he didn't toss it aside, either.

The baker ignored him. He just watched the trembling man roll back and forth over the shards of glass on the pavement, clutching his shattered knee and weeping. Eventually, he nodded. "*Ja.* Okay. Excuse me, please, while I call the police."

"Why?" the Collector snapped.

Cell phone in hand, the baker quirked an amused eyebrow. "*Why?* Last night, the robbery. Today a crazy man appears, waves a gun in my face and—"

"Why bother, I mean?"

"Ah," said the baker. "One moment, *bitte.*" He dialed 911, spoke into the phone, returned the phone to his pocket.

"Two possible reasons," Nadine said. Her skin stung and her ears rang. Gently, carefully, she pushed to her feet. The blood in her scrape was coagulating, at least; it felt cool on her leg in the sweet spring evening. Which she sometimes thought was the only real sweet thing on this planet. She gestured toward the wounded man. "Either this really is a Guild matter—"

The baker glanced back and forth between the Collector and Nadine. Once more, his eyes got old. "Only Americans, or people who have associated too long with Americans, would shoot a man on a sidewalk over a…a cookie violation."

"—or else this is about the *Lebensborn,*" Nadine finished.

The baker stopped grinning. His eyes riveted themselves to Nadine's. It really was like locking gazes with a squid. Something alive, yet utterly alien. Not like her at all.

"Then you know," he said. "So you understand."

"But I don't. Not really. I mean, are you Jewish?"

The baker said nothing.

Nadine had no idea how to read that. "Or…you're German secret service? Erasing the past? Enforcing judgment? Or—Oh!—are you also *Lebensborn?*"

"Does that matter?" whispered the baker.

Which meant that was probably it. Though as to why that would trigger whatever had happened here…

The baker might have said more, but the trembling man humped up suddenly, scuttling forward on his shattered kneecap, screaming as he came but coming anyway.

"No," snapped the Collector, snatching the second gun off the ground. Then he stepped directly between his client and the baker. The trembling man sobbed, sagging to stillness at the feet of the wooden witch.

For a moment longer, the baker watched. Finally, he sighed. "There, there. Perhaps it really is enough." Ignoring the half-raised gun in the Collector's hands, he vanished into the shadows of his shop.

"What do you think?" the Collector murmured as soon as he was gone. "Nadine, tell me what to do. Tell me what you know. What are these people? What do they believe?"

But this time, Nadine's instincts failed her. She thought of the booklet in the trembling man's bathroom. The boardgame and flags in his closet. The unimaginable, baffling life he must have led. "I don't know. I don't know how *they* could know what they believe."

The baker returned carrying a tray of something draped in a single, white napkin. Seeing it, the trembling man whimpered, stretched out a hand, then shrank back into a ball on the sidewalk. Little hums percolated from him, seemingly involuntary. The purr a cat makes when it has been run over, right before it dies.

Instead of kneeling, the baker stood just out of his reach and watched.

"She asked you what you were," the Collector said, settling the gun in his palm. Not quite raising it. "I think you should answer."

"*Bitte*," the man on the ground managed.

The baker glanced at the Collector, at Nadine. He shrugged. "I am the Angel of Mercy." He knelt but didn't remove the napkin from the plate, nor place the plate within reach of the trembling man.

"Mercy?" Nadine snapped. "Look at this man you shot."

"You cannot understand."

"*PLEASE*!" shrieked the trembling man.

For one moment, the baker's fish-eyes seemed to darken. In that instant, they looked almost human, and not unkind. Not entirely.

Police arrived. Four of them. They took statements, confiscated the weapons, did police things. An ambulance appeared. The trembling man shrieked only once more as he was unfolded and strapped to a gurney.

"Come on," the Collector said, grabbing the baker's arm. The baker still held his covered plate. "What can it possibly matter? Give him one."

"Would you believe me," the baker said quietly, "if I said it would only make him worse?"

An hour later, the police had gone, and the baker and Nadine and the Collector stood alone once more, in an evening that had gone cold, now, moonless, disconcertingly dark.

"Tell me what you did to him," the Collector said.

"Did to him?" The baker sighed. "I gave him the single most exquisite sensory experience he will ever have. I let him know such experience was possible. I gave a demon from hell a taste of heaven. That is all."

"So you did wreck his life."

"Or I gave it purpose. Filled his mind with obsessions other than the monstrous ones he'd already been given. Maybe I saved other lives in the process. Many of them. Have you considered this? Is that so cruel? Am I a cruel man, do you think?"

Nadine heard the danger before Normal did, because she was listening to the man's voice, not just what he was saying.

"Don't answer that," she said. Fast. "There's no answer to any of that."

"I'll tell you what," said the baker.

"No, you won't. Come on, Normal. We have a plane to catch." But she was too late. The baker had the Collector's arm. Had ignited that light in the Collector's eyes.

The baker nodded toward his shop. "Come inside with me. I'll let you judge for yourself exactly how cruel I have been."

"Don't do it," Nadine said. "For God's sake."

Of course her protests were useless. The Collector went into the bakery.

He came out barely a minute later. For a moment, she took the sparkle in his eyes for reflected broken glass off the sidewalk. Then she realized it was tears. She took his arm and led him to the rental car, eased him into the passenger seat, drove them back toward the airport and home. He said nothing the whole trip, and he didn't even try to wipe the tears away.

But whether he was crying because he had tasted cookies made by the baker of Hexenhaus, or because he hadn't, she never asked, and he never said.

HOME

As if the word itself—*Hexenhaus*—has summoned him, the Collector emerges from the hallway, headed straight for the kitchen. Her story finished, Nadine watches as he takes a pan lid out of the cabinet, puts it on a burner, puts it in the cupboard with the water glasses and somehow manages not to knock anything over. He opens the refrigerator and takes out a butter stick and puts that back. He's whistling like a tea kettle, moving his mouth. Possibly, he has been listening, and now he's remembering. Hunting that taste (assuming he actually tasted it). But when he does discover the most recent tin from the Hamtramck baker on the counter, he doesn't open it; instead, he takes a fork from the flatware drawer and bangs it off the top as though smacking a crash cymbal. Then he drops the fork to the floor and returns to the living room, headed straight for the wishing tree clock.

"He's got a knack," the Rev murmurs, massaging his temples as though soothing a headache.

Nadine has no idea if the Rev means for discovering, remembering, confusing, or what. Doesn't matter. Her answer retort would be the same for each or any. "Always has." Her smile is for Normal, and it still has affection in it. Even more, it has the memory of affection. Affection just starting its slide toward duty, the way she suspects a caretaker's must, sooner or later, as days drain into years.

The Collector snatches out a hand as though to stop the clock's pendulum, hold it—and time—still. But all he does is brush that not-gold metal with his fingers. He spins around and walks right between Nadine and the

Rev. He has resumed singing. No more Irish folk tunes, nothing to do with Nadine now, though she recognizes the song. This one is his own talisman from back in his just-dropped-out-of-San-Francisco-State years, which he says he spent lurking on the walls of dark SOMA clubs in dark clothes with other lovely lurkers Nadine wishes she had known or at least seen. All of them, even now, so unimaginable to her, so far from even the worlds she imagined from her bedroom in Lissycasey. All of them bumping into and off one another, speak-singing mantras just like this one at or past each other over dulled electronic beats that barely rippled the air, let alone the floor. The lyrics cryptic as Morse Code, repeated like Morse Code. This one something about jinxes and cages, buying rounds for dark companions.

Before she was his light one.

He keeps cutting back and forth across the room, moving from clock to window to clock. He barely stops chanting long enough to breathe. Finally, Nadine gets up to try to stop or slow or comfort him. As she does, she glances at the Rev, who still has his head in his hands. "Sorry," she says, but the Rev doesn't respond. She raises her voice to say it again, and only then realizes—by the set of his shoulders, the fingers steepled in front of his mouth—that her guest doesn't mind the Collector's racket one bit, because he isn't paying any attention to it.

Isn't paying attention to the Collector, period. Has barely looked at him since he came into this house. Hasn't tried to speak to him. Has not asked Nadine what's wrong with him.

Not even once.

"Excuse me a sec?" she says.

He hears that, okay. Waves a hand without looking at her, returns to raking his eyes over her walls.

As batshit as Normal, she thinks. *Maybe they could have a throwdown.*

Instead of intercepting the Collector, she brushes the back of his hand with hers as he passes, then leaves him wander-humming and the Rev wall-gazing and ducks down the hall. It takes her a minute to remember where she last saw her phone, in the pocket of a sweatshirt. Miraculously, it still has charge. Seven percent. Last used three days ago to respond to the text from the agitator in the living room and confirm today's appointment.

Her speed dial has four numbers in it. One is her ma's, one Binna's, and both of them are thousands of miles away. Another is the Collector's. He's even farther. The fourth is Spook's. She's about to punch that when she realizes she can't see the living room from where she's standing.

Which matters why, exactly?

If this is a robbery, she hopes the Rev enjoys his cookies. If it's a fishing expedition for rare finds to sell, fair play to him and good luck with that. If it's attempted rape, what has this whole afternoon and evening been? Foreplay?

And yet. When has the feeling she has right now ever been wrong? Misdirected, yes, occasionally. Once or twice. But wrong?

Instead of calling Spook, she texts him.

Something's happening. Someone's here. Come?

Her index finger hovers over SEND. In the end, she decides she has the text right. It's accurate. It's the extent of what she knows. And it's exactly coded enough to trip Spook's spy-wire, get him off his houseboat and racing up the Avenue of the Giants toward here.

It would take him hours. But at least now her own and Normal's corpses will be found. If this is murder.

The front door slams.

That was fast is her first absurd thought. Her second is that the Rev has found what he came for, grabbed what's left of the 12-for-$4.99 china from Target, and fled. And her third…

Hurtling from the hallway, she takes in the tableaux: the removed seat leaning against Tony's chair; the papers she'd been working on this afternoon out of their file jackets and scattered across the tabletop; the Rev standing where the Collector so often does these days, staring into the wishing tree clock as though it's a mirror or the ocean; the front door flung open, not closed, as though the Collector just raced out to meet the new rain rolling down the hillside.

"Are you *completely* rat-arsed?" she shouts as she passes. The Rev does glance toward her, but not with concern. Barely even comprehension. He looks like he just woke up.

Then she's out front, the rain in her hair and all down her sweatshirt and face, the smack and spatter everywhere as the hills waver and the long grass leans into the downpour as though holding on for dear life.

"*Normal*!" she shouts, because he's nowhere. The Jeep is there, that's something, and his shoes are by the door, she noted them as she passed, not that bare feet would stop him. Would ever have stopped him, even when he was in his right mind.

Relatively speaking, of course.

She's mid-call again when she hears the *thunk* behind her, too heavy for rain. She whirls, and there he is, staring at the wood shingles the way he does at his clock, inside the arc of waterfall gushing from their leaf-choked gutters. He's not even one bit wet. Like a cat that got out but then spotted the rain, or one of those old wind-up trains that still runs but not straight, and so inevitably turns into walls. Keeps moving, goes nowhere.

"You're going to leg it now?" she says, stepping forward, pulling him gently around to her. He shivers at the wetness of her touch. "Oh, that bothers you? Well." She shakes her head hard, flinging drops all over him.

"CLARE FROM HERE," he shouts. Not at her. Still singing, as if he's got his own private pub in there, where she can't come. The only place he's ever gone where she can't come.

"Eejit," she murmurs, and pulls him back inside. Only as she shuts the door and flips the bolt does she realize:

Not one time in these past eighteen months has he done this. Gone out. He hasn't even tried. Until this second, she'd have sworn he didn't remember how.

"Get me a towel?" she calls to the Rev.

He's coming back from the bathroom, towel over his arm, when she pins him with her stare. Apparently, whatever else she's lost, she can still do that. For the first time all evening, the guy looks guilty.

Like a kid. Caught kid, sent on an errand.

Like...

"You let him out," Nadine says, dead low, ice-hard.

Whatever she saw or thought she saw, it's gone. The Rev is his insouciant self again. He shrugs.

Fecking shrugs.

"Why would you let him out?"

"He had places to go. I wanted to see where they were."

"You will *never* see where they are." She's all reared up without even moving. To calm herself, she looks away, guides the Collector to a chair.

"How about Jolene?" the Rev says. And pins *her*.

She has her arm through the Collector's. Rain runs from her skin onto his. One of them, she thinks, is dissolving.

"You've..." she starts, then remembers. She glances toward her papers spread over the table. "Oh. You read the name. Congratulations. Ever heard the song? It'll kill ya."

"Done more than read. And heard more than that."

What's happening here? What are they even talking about? Tingly-spidery-sense, why have ye forsaken me?

She eases the Collector onto Tony's chair. He goes placidly enough, tucks his feet under himself and pulls up the blanket.

"What is it you're thinking?" she murmurs.

"I think it's a hotbed. The caldera of a volcano. Maybe getting ready to blow."

Straightening, Nadine meets the Rev's stare. "You've been to Jolene." She purses her lips. Shakes her head. "I don't believe you."

That smile. Insolent as fuck. "I didn't claim anything."

Abruptly, he's across the space between them. But he only drapes the towel around her, pats it once against her back. For one freakish second, she thinks they're going to embrace.

That that might feel good.

He lets go, stands right on the edge of too close, but not over it. "You keep acting like I'm trying to steal from you. You're acting like any of this is something you two own. Like it's your territory."

"Jolene isn't mine. Or the Collector's. Or yours, either. It's a place. People live there. I wouldn't tell...and even if I wanted to, I'd ..."

Her smile comes from nowhere, catches her by surprise, as it has her whole life: her mom far; her dad gone; the Collector here but nowhere; the places they've been and the paths she's found or made down a Giant's Causeway stranger and less solitary than her childhood self could possibly have dreamed or would have dared to ask. And yet.

That was Kieran's problem, she thinks, marveling at the leaps even as she takes them. *Her homeland's, too. Not knowing what to do with the sorrow. The Irish revel in it. Americans fight it. Whereas she and Normal...*

It's a full-on grin she's wearing now. Tears-in-her-eyes grin. "Anyway. I'd have to find it again first."

He's grinning back. This bastard kid. This fearsome thing. "I could help."

"Oh, you think so?"

"I'm good at finding."

"Me, too," Nadine whispers.

It's almost prayers they're doing, now. Call and response.

Replacing the cushion, he settles into Tony's chair "Tell me what you found there," he says. Almost as if he knows.

She tells him.

PITHOS

From across the room, on the still-warm couch with the white counterpane pulled to her shoulders, Nadine watched the Collector picking shells out of the egg he'd just cracked. She could practically hear those long, bony fingers ticking as they worked like grasshopper wings. Outside, through the wall of window, the drizzle that had crept down their hillside with the morning fog fell straight and steady, connecting the grass they rarely mowed to the gray sky overhead like strings on a loom.

"Uch," the Collector muttered, shaking egg from his skin in the general vicinity of the sink.

"Nothing but sticky on those fingers all morning long," Nadine said. "Poor you."

She waited. Waited.

He looked up. "Ha," he said.

So their session had been good for him, too, today. One he'd been most of the way present in his body for, at the same moment she'd mostly inhabited hers, with fog for a cocoon and rain on the shingle roof for company. A sweet, misty morning all around.

Except, of course, for his plans for the rest of it. *Fly, meet ointment...*

She sat up, and her curls fell over her right eye, bobbing like beaded curtains through which something had passed. That was the first thing he'd loved about her face, he'd told her once, on one of the rare occasions he said such things: the hidden place. Person-cave to explore. He loved it still, she knew, at the moments he remembered. Didn't seem to care that those curtains of curl were cookies-and-cream, now, not proper Irish full-black. Actually, he didn't even seem to notice the change, which was close to the same thing. Almost as good.

"Normal," she called, and let the blanket slide nearly—not quite—off her breasts. Another vista he liked exploring when he remembered it was there. "Stay home. Don't go."

"You just don't want me seeing Tony." Now he was hunched over the stove, watching the poaching pan do its thing. He had a weirdly enduring fascination for eggs rounding and cohering, so that he could collect them.

"Tony's a twollocks."

"It's important and healthy that we have different friends."

Nadine burst out laughing. It wasn't just that he was quoting her. He was also parroting a pricklier tone she knew had once been hers. In her proper Irish full-black days.

"That's true for regular people," she said.

He went on hovering over the pot as though awaiting the exact moment *poach* happened. His hand swooped, came up with pot lid, and steam swarmed him, startling him back.

Again, Nadine laughed. "You, however, should let me pick your friends."

"I'm a pretty good judge most of the time."

"You have blind spots. Tony's one."

"I picked you."

"I worry about that every single day."

Sliding from the couch, Nadine threw on jeans and her favorite tatty white sweater with the hole blooming like a flower over the left shoulder. Her Sunday best. She let her hair bob where it would, catching sight of herself only in the screen of her laptop as she tapped it awake.

There she was, in the split second between blankness and overflowing in-box: Star of the County Clare, wild hag of the misty, moisty California North. Researcher-demon the Collector had saved from academia or imprisoned in arcana or both. Most days, she still thought of herself as all those things and a thousand more. It was part of what she loved about her life: there was room for almost all of her in it, because she'd chosen a partner who had no interest in constraining or even knowing everything there was to know.

Which had its downsides, of course. Depending on which Nadine awoke each morning, and which mist rolled in off the dunes, through the redwoods, and down the grass.

Apart from the usual yearning weekend missive from her mom, across the world in a colder mist in Lissycasey—*oh, if you were only home, Nadine, I'd boil up a stew so rich and sour that you'd never, not ever, go roam with that rounder you married (or, right, didn't) again. Oh and did you see about Limerick in the feckking all-Ireland, can you Youtube?? It's now been 4383 days since you last watched hurling with me* —there was only the daily deluge of collecting group threads and rumor gathering and inter-library responses to her latest obscure queries. A couple new requests for the Collector's help from addresses she didn't recognize. And, at the bottom of the first page—sent at 1:42 this morning, so probably toward the rank, ashy end of fatty number three of his Saturday night—two sentences from Tony.

The first read, *This is for him obviously.*

Did he copy and paste that, Nadine wondered, or type it new every single time, like she was sure her mom did with her days-since-hurling-viewing count?

"Dear?" Nadine called.

He waved a plate of eggs in her direction. "Perfect. Nadine, these eggs are *perfect.*"

"That's mine you made, then? You're not just displaying your achievement?"

"*Perfect,*" he said again. Which wasn't an answer. But there did appear to be a second plate on the raised countertop, so he had remembered that he lived with someone else today.

All told, a satisfying morning all around.

Hoisting her laptop, she moved to the counter. The egg on the plate he slid in front of her wobbled just slightly atop its toasted sourdough like a *panna cotta.* The Collector had even conjured arugula from somewhere—good god, had he gone *shopping* at some recent point??—and a bright orange slice of tomato. The spice sprinkles on top were dill, not basil, but hey, he'd remembered that whatever it was she liked on her egg was green and got sprinkled, so…

Not just satisfying. Edging towards remarkable.

Except.

"What's Tony's e-mail say?" He'd gotten most of the way through the sentence before shoving his egg in his mouth and bursting it with his teeth.

"Stop grinning," Nadine said. "You look like a vampire. With Irish teeth."

For answer, he pursed his lips and slurped. "Tony wrote, right? What's the plan?"

"For God's sake. Here's your man." She read the words one at a time, with exaggerated stops, as though decoding a child's scrawl. "'*Got. A. Feeling. Big. Guy. I. SMELL. Something.*' He's included, hold on, one, two, three, that's four exclamation points after 'something.'"

"He's rarely wrong when he smells something. You have to admit."

"I admit he smells."

"Cheap. Beneath you, Nadine."

"There's a postscript. Were you wanting that read as well?" She looked up, then took pity.

He was staring at his empty plate, already mopped free of all trace of egg except for one faint and fading yellow smear.

"He says to bring the Jeep. His truck—here's a shock—is in the shop again. Where it lives. That's my addition, incidentally, not his. Oh, he also says I can tag along."

"See? He goes out of his way to be nice to you."

"Because that's a thing I do, right? Tag along?"

The nuance, the delicate sting, was wasted. He had turned his back, shuffling sadly to the sink to wipe away the last, forlorn trace of yolk. Here it was, Nadine realized. The one thing the self-proclaimed Collector actually would collect if he could: poached-egg breakfasts.

In the Jeep a half-hour later, weaving down the coast past Eureka, they kept getting glimpses of ocean through the drizzle and mist. It should have looked gray but glowed green, as though the sun that was nowhere overhead had taken refuge underwater.

"One day," Nadine sighed, "if you're very, very good, I'll take you on a pilgrimage to a proper coast. I'll show you a Causeway so Giant and magical, it will teach you to love what's lost for being lost." She tried smiling at her own ghostly reflection in her window, remembering walking the Giant's Causeway with her Mum—actually leaving her Mum far behind as she sprinted from the cliffs to weave among those pillars of rock leading off the edge of Ireland into an unimaginable, watery nowhere—and calling out. Not to anything or anyone, exactly. To the mystery. To being there.

Abruptly, she shifted in her seat and eyed her partner of more than twenty years. "Did you really just say, '*Oh, egg*?'"

The Collector blinked. "Did I?"

"Were you still thinking about your breakfast?"

"I'm thinking about it now," he murmured, gazing into the mist. Calling out to the mystery.

She sighed. "Right. So. What's our *craic* for the rest of the morning, then? Good estate sale or five? Preferably with bereaved, weeping family members in the corners or at the checkout tables? Isn't that your Tony's *métier*?"

The Collector edged the Jeep off the freeway and down a scraggy street of sawed-off tree stumps. Amid the shadows of the trees still standing stood rusted trailers with beer bottle shards and discarded tires for lawns. "You'd be surprised. Actually, you should know better. That's not what he's after."

"That's *exactly* what he's after."

The Collector turned right, pointing the Jeep up a hill, past a series of tilting shed-like structures that had never actually been sheds but didn't qualify as houses. Former temporary lumberjack barracks, maybe, and now squatters' cabins, desperation meth-labs for when the rent on the crack house got too high. Places the homeless disappeared into when the coastal city councils routed them from their streets.

"Actually, in a way, you're right, Nadine. That is what he's after. But not in the way you paint it. And estate sales…that isn't where he finds it. "

"No?"

"The stuff at estate sales is what got *kept*."

Sequoias vaulted up from the ground. Through the Jeep's vents, all at once, came the smell of pine, of cool and clean river water instantly spiriting the shacks and squalor through which they'd just passed further into memory than they should have been able to go. Tony's immaculate, two-story white shingle house appeared through the trees, and Nadine shuddered.

"You don't see it, do you? That makes it even worse."

The Collector either didn't hear or had no answer. Or he was still mid egg-reverie.

"So, a good foreclosure auction then? With the evicted family up on the podium waving goodbye to their lives?"

Not until he'd parked in Tony's flower and fern-lined circular drive did the Collector respond. His glance might have been pleading if pleading was something he did. That he even bothered to argue was a sign of rare respect.

"In foreclosures or repo auctions, the goods have been *seized.* Once again, completely different, and not what he's after."

"*JAYsus* Christ," she whispered. "Do you even hear yourself?"

He ducked forward like a chicken to seed and kissed her cheek. "Nadine, I don't have many colleagues."

The loneliness in his voice startled her, kept her quiet as he left the Jeep to call on his friend. The words themselves were even more surprising than the tone, verging on outright self-awareness. She felt a sudden, almost overwhelming affection, and more than affection, comfort. Security, even. Because the fact that the Collector had thought about what Tony meant to him implied that he'd also...which she knew he had, she'd always known, but...

She was smiling as she unzipped the canvas siding and stepped out to wait in the open air. The drizzle had evaporated, and even these few miles inland, the mist had thinned. Kneeling, she took in the arc of flowers Tony had seemed not so much to have laid as herded here, penned in their beds but then left to roam and intermingle as they would. Whites and reds and red-blues bloomed atop one another. Milkmaids, two-eyed violets. She reached for an especially vivid red-striped, lolling petal.

The front door opened, and Tony emerged in a cloud of gray smoke. Yet another genie the Collector had loosed from its bottle. Pot stench sweetened and sickened the air. Nadine started to stand, remembered the petal at her fingertips, waited. She watched Tony actually clap the Collector on the back as they moved toward her. As though clapping was something one did with the Collector's back.

"Look, love," she called sweetly when they were close enough, lifting the petal just a little toward Normal. "Fetid adder's tongue."

If the Collector understood or felt the poke, he didn't let on.

"That's its name, don't wear it out," said Tony.

The verbal equivalent of clapping her on the back, too. With a sigh, Nadine stood and climbed into the rumble seat in back so the boys could jabber.

Which they proceeded to do. About other guys—almost always guys—they'd encountered separately, online or in person, in their separate solitary, necessarily secret traverses of Collecting-land. If Nadine had felt like listening, she might have enjoyed the chatter. If she'd felt like participating, she could have. She definitely recognized most of the people they named, had had her own experiences with several, and not only in the Collector's company. More than once, in that next hour, she got close to jumping in.

But Tony's skin was like a steaming marijuana sponge strapped into the front seat, fouling the cab even when he wasn't opening his mouth, which was stuffed with Dentine, which masked absolutely nothing. It wasn't even *for* masking, in Tony's case. He just enjoyed the pot/chemical-cinnamon flavor profile.

She kept her own mouth closed. At least until she realized that she genuinely didn't know where they were going, and that they'd been going quite a while. Past Trinidad, various Eel River fishing roads, the Ferndale turnoff. *Just how long a morning had she let herself in for?*

"Right, what's our target, then?"

Tony jumped as though he'd forgotten she was there, and turned. His gaze was shameless. He had deep brown eyes, distant but surprisingly alert or at least awake. Maybe she'd been a little wrong about him.

"Up the ass of the Eel, baby!" he crowed. "Wooooo-ooo!"

Or else less wrong than she'd ever been about anything in her entire life, ever.

"Your area of particular expertise then," she muttered.

"You know it. Back in the trees, amid the trailers and compounds and secret retreats where people with little to hold onto hold onto what matters."

"Christ, you're speaking in slogans."

"Hey, you're right. That'd be a good one, wouldn't it?"

He fished a notepad from a pocket and flipped through coffee- (or ash)-stained page after page, looking for a splotch-free spot. Upon locating one, he patted around his body, opened and closed the Collector's glove box (*which wasn't at all like rooting through a friend's underwear drawer, just felt that way when Tony did it. Or else Tony was simply the walking, talking embodiment of root-in-your-underwear-drawer).*

He turned around again. "Pencil? Pen? Lipstick? Come on Nadine, you carry some even if you don't wear it, right?"

"Living embodiment," she said, and handed him a Pilot G2 from the stash in the front flap of her laptop case. "Just…what is it you do, then, Tone? Define it for me. What's that slogan I just found you for, exactly?"

In the mirror, the Collector lifted his eyes. He didn't say anything or even register an expression. Possibly, he was asking her to leave his friend alone. Possibly, though, he was as interested in Tony's answer as she was.

But Tony just looked surprised. He raised one millipede eyebrow and tongued the Dentine wad all the way into his cheek. Clearing a path.

"What *you* do," he said, chinning first at her, then the Collector.

That spark in his eye was spark, not twinkle. He wasn't playing or flattering her by including her, and he sure as fuck wasn't flirting. But the Collector's colleagues, such as they were, rarely recognized her contribution, let alone saw her as full partner.

Therefore, what he'd said deserved consideration. A good minute went by. The Collector exited the 101, turned them left onto a two-lane, empty road running straight into the towering trees.

"No," she said quietly. "I don't think so. All right, where are we going? And when did we decide, by the way, did I miss that?"

"What does *he* say I do?" Tony asked.

That brought on the most delightful moment of the morning: the Collector eying Nadine in the mirror, Tony in the passenger seat, then settling back in his own seat and sighing. Like a man with cats on his lap, or a Saturday morning dad—the kind Nadine had had for just long enough to remember and treasure and fear and miss—with his family around him.

"He doesn't know either, does he?" Tony grinned so wide she could see the gum curled in his cheek like a second tongue. As though he'd planted fetid adders in there, too. "He's certainly never asked."

"He doesn't do *ask*."

So easily it happened: ganging up on the Collector. Even with Tony. She was practically hissing in her own head, now. Disgusted with herself. As though he'd planted fetid adders in *her*.

What was it about this guy? Not his grin. Not that spark, even if it wasn't twinkle. She'd always preferred spark to twinkle, trusted it more.

"Fortunately for both of you," Tony said, "I will tell you, whether you ask or not."

"I did ask."

Ignoring her, Tony snapped his fingers—a magician's flourish—and produced a business card seemingly out of the air. He extended it to Nadine.

The physical revulsion she had to overcome as she accidentally brushed his hand made her still more annoyed with herself, until she realized it wasn't Tony's skin that provoked the reaction. It was the way he had her slip the card from between his extended index and middle fingers, which made her feel like she was bumming a smoke.

She was going to pocket it without looking at it as a show of defiance. But she accidentally caught a glimpse. Then she held the card up. The syllable she emitted got free of her lips before she'd even realized they could form it.

"Awww," she heard herself say. Like a fecking five year-old with a baby chick.

"Right?" said Tony.

"This still the road?" the Collector asked. "We're going past Miranda, Tone?"

Across the top of the card, in tawny, block lionskin letters, each sporting little tufts of mane, was the name L O U I S A. For just that first second, Nadine's thoughts went spun out of control. *Lost daughter? Dead sister? Had Tony once* been *a Louisa, and undergone change? Did he* aspire *to be Louisa*?

But no. Louisa was the business name; the url at the bottom, Louisassentimentalvalue.net, made that clear. It was also, without question, the name of the stuffed animal whose photo dominated the card. A little lizard, tan and darker tan, with tiny black pin-eyes, one of them hanging just a little out, not dangling, not even bulging, just no longer set in its pinhole socket. One front foot had a tear in its fabric-skin, but no stuffing spilled from the opening. The lizard had no mouth to smile with, no trying-too-hard bow or fairy-bunny ears. Its stains were kid-finger stains, including one incongruous, thumb-shaped green splat across its back. It was stuffed-animal cute, all right, but only because it was so, so clearly someone's friend.

Or had been.

"Sick fucker," Nadine spat.

"What?" Tony swiveled all the way around. "Why?"

"We're at Miranda," the Collector said, fast. "Where to, Tone?"

Tony kept staring at her.

"I'm sor..." Nadine started, but let the sentence trail away.

He wasn't glaring. Wasn't offended at what she'd said. He was genuinely asking.

With a shudder she couldn't have explained, she tucked away the card and nudged her laptop awake. The GPS screen told her the same thing the Collector had: they'd reached Miranda, were already passing through it. She saw log cabins set back in giant tree shadows, general store-style buildings housing the Redwood Palace & Trading Co. and The Jail, which according to its sign was now an arcade. Whatever that currently meant in Miranda. Sequoias loomed over all of it, making the town seem even smaller than it was.

"Tone?"

"Oh," said Tony, popping back up behind his own eyes, as though the inside of him was one of those blowy, inflatable yard-phantom things. He returned his attention to his friend. "Keep going."

"We're not stopping here?"

"Past here. To Jolene. I'm not sure there'll be signs."

"I'm not sure that's a place," Nadine murmured, studying her screen. A surprising sprawl—you couldn't call it a network—of unnamed roads or maybe-roads or trails spoked in all directions off the thruway they traveled, vanishing into the woods like roots the trees themselves had sprouted, leading to hidden summer cabins, abandoned hobo camps, survivalist compounds, artist retreats, pot farms, ranger stations, meth labs. The Lost City of Z, maybe.

Every time they passed a turnoff, Nadine felt her eyes drawn down it, felt the Giant's Causeway fairy she'd always either been or housed—the thing inside that had led her across the world to these men and this car and this misty morning—peeping over her bottom eyelids like a little girl over a banister. Just to see.

There was mist out there, all right, flowing under and between trees. Within it, little ponds of filtered sunlight pooled. Along the ground were grays and deep-forest greens, dirt and moss, but also winking patches of inexplicable fire-reds and yellows. Flowers and animals you thought you glimpsed out the corner of your eyes, remembered always, named never.

"Slow down," Tony said. "I think."

"You think," said the Collector. Enjoying himself.

Miranda. Louisa. Jolene.

"Is it a person we're looking for?" Nadine asked. She held up her laptop. "Because this is pretty much a Here Be Dragons-free map. And there's no Jolene on it."

She only saw the edge of Tony's grin, and only because he grinned so widely.

"Now, really. Would I take the great Nadine and Normal somewhere marked on a map?"

He sounded gleeful. Almost sweet. *Respectful*, even. Even so, she shuddered again, thinking of Louisa the Lizard now warm in her pocket. Tony's perfect goddamn familiar. Or closest friend.

"So how did you find it, then?"

The Collector shot her another rearview squint, one she damn well deserved. In their community (if such a thing existed), that question more than any other deserved contempt. It was akin to demanding trade secrets or secret formulae. More importantly—much more importantly— it was a killjoy.

But Tony's only response was "Ha." He fished in another pocket and came up with his phone. "Hold on, I'll put it on speaker. Slow down, dude, you're going to miss it. Know what, just pull over. Listen."

There wasn't really a shoulder, just cracked pavement dissolving into rutted dirt, but the Collector eased the Jeep onto that and slowed. Tony held up his phone, finger hovering over the keypad, but he kept waiting even after they'd glided to a stop.

"Oh," the Collector said, understanding, and shut off the car.

"Listen." Tony closed his eyes and hit play.

Silence for a few seconds. Then shifting or rustling. Then a woman's voice. Old, Nadine thought at first, then thought not. More *crumpled*. A wadded-up tissue of a voice.

"Yes. Hi. Mr… Sorry, I don't remember your name, it doesn't say on your card. Mr. Louisa?" More rustling. A cough. "A few years ago…you probably don't remember, why would you? But you bought a…" *Cough… then a laugh? A little laugh?* "…pocket watch hunter casing. The bottom half of one. At my jumble sale. That my… my daughter made. It had a left hand on it, raised? Silly thing she designed and made herself. So the hand looks like it's pressing the watch closed? I even called you a few days afterward offering to buy it back. Remember?"

The laugh again. Not much actual laughter in it. Not much anything else, either, as far as Nadine could tell.

"Anyway," the voice went on. "I found the other one, the top. I thought you might want it. If you can find your way back to Jolene."

A long pause, a sniffle. Or else just rustling. "I thought it might...I thought the other one might want company. In your heaven." The woman finished in a rush.

"Anyway, this Sunday only. Early, please, we'll be done before ten."

If she hung up, Nadine didn't hear it. Tony either, apparently, because he stayed leaning over the phone, head turned halfway between the Collector and Nadine. His eyes shimmered, but whether with amusement, tears, or just wispy forest light, Nadine had no idea.

"God, do you hear that?" he whispered.

"What did she mean, 'in your heaven?'" Nadine snapped. She couldn't take her eyes off his face.

"It's like a symphony." He straightened, wiping at whatever his eyes had in them. "Like Mahler's 5th. That is what God hears, if he hears. Don't you think?"

"I think I don't know what you're on about."

"I do," said the Collector. But not as if he did, Nadine thought. More as if he wanted to.

"Of course you do." Tony clapped his friend's forearm. "All that loss. Love. Regret. Thoughtfulness. It's what we're all about, isn't it? It's what we do. It's the hum in human."

"Ah, Christ, you've practiced that one."

"I considered it as a slogan. You asked what I do. What I collect. You just heard it."

"Sick. Fuck."

He laughed.

As the Collector started the Jeep again, Nadine pulled out Tony's business card and stared into the little lizard's not-quite-hanging eye. In the weak, misty light, it looked more deep-forest green than black. She half-imagined she could see herself in it, a miniature Nadine being appraised. Greeted, almost.

Hello, she felt herself mouth. Very nearly say.

"Slow down, slow down," Tony told the Collector. "Wait, I remember... no, not this one. Next one! Next right. I recognize that stump."

Replacing the card gently in her laptop pouch, Nadine shook her head, which didn't clear it. Not entirely.

"Nope," she said. "I still don't get it. Why did she call you?"

"Your clients don't call you? *Here*, dude, right there." He was laughing, pointing, almost grabbing the wheel. "I told you, next right."

"That wasn't a right," said the Collector, sounding remarkably like Nadine for once, which relaxed and even relieved her more than she would have expected. It also gave her permission.

The Collector had his arm over the back of Tony's seat to see behind them as he reversed the Jeep, so he was looking right at her as she finally up and blurted it out.

"What is your business, Tony? Why would anyone call you?"

"Same reason your clients call you."

"No. A, we don't give out our number. Strange species, our clientele. You might not have noticed."

"This?" The Collector, gestured into the woods. Nadine looked where he did. Possibly—if she squinted—there was a path between trees. An open space, anyway, relatively straight, sort of smooth.

"I think," said Tony. "Yeah. I do think."

"And B," said Nadine, "that wasn't a client."

"You're right, there. It was a source. A supplier."

"A person."

The most surprising reaction wasn't Tony's—he snorted, right on cue—but the Collector's: he laughed, the way he did over his eggs. Except this time, she knew, over her.

Her and Tony, actually. Probably.

"Your sources aren't people?" Tony asked.

The Collector, still laughing, edged the Jeep off the road and onto the floor of the forest.

Nadine's smile felt rueful even to her. "Not usually. Not in the classical, fully formed sense."

"Which is why they don't actually call *me* when they call Louisa's Sentimental Value, my dear. They call my *hotline*!"

Jiggling the phone over the seat at her with one hand, Tony pointed through the windshield with the other. "I'm sure, now. It's a ways. Mile or two, maybe. There's a… it's kind of a town. You'll hit it."

"One way or another," said the Collector, but now his smile wasn't for her or his friend. That was his hunting grin.

Off-road, the daylight dimmed, but not toward dark. It was like light beneath the surface of a lake, seemingly carried on the mist or in it. As though the mist itself were floating light. Pockets of it hovered all around them like the flashlights of villagers fanning out to find a lost child. The trees loomed so tall overhead that they barely registered as trees, especially from the car. More like pillars. Dock pilings. The ones that held up the world.

Quiet permeated the car. Roots rose from the earth, bumped and shook them, never too hard. It was Tony, not Nadine, who said, "Okay, sorry, I'm a little less sure. This might be wro—"

But the Collector slid forward in his seat. On fucking point. "That?" he said. Not like a question.

Ahead, seemingly cohering out of dirt and groundcover in their headlight beams, cabins appeared. Five, maybe six of those, a couple A-frames, a double-length log structure along the right side of the path. The log structure had picnic tables out front, was clearly some sort of general store or diner or communal shed.

"That's her!" said Tony. "*Jo*-lene."

No wonder maps didn't mark it, Nadine thought. Was it even a place? How did one categorize and name this? It wasn't a town, certainly not a development. More of a compound.

In her hips, belly, fingertips, tingling started where it always did, and it spread fast. Her fairy-sense. Giant's Causeway radar, ringing her awake.

"Huh," she said, not even trying to keep the thrill from her voice.

"Told you he was one of us," the Collector said.

She couldn't quite bring herself to pat Tony's shoulder. But she patted Normal's. "Aye. You surely…"

It was forest shadows, the lack of light, that made the people at those picnic tables seem to cohere, too, sliding all together into solidity. And if it wasn't shadows—and those really were will-o'-the-wisps out there—Nadine would have been even more delighted.

As the Collector eased the Jeep into town, everyone at those tables rose, moving in different directions. Not scattering, not scurrying, but all at once. More people she hadn't initially noticed—a surprising number, at least twenty, plus a few kids, even—poured off the porches of cabins or out from front doors. They began—continued?—milling around blankets and folding tables spread willy-nilly across the dirt yards and along the lip of the road.

"It's like a giant communal lemonade stand," she said.

But what it really resembled, she realized later, was a set. As though she was watching the opening of a play. Or maybe nothing so formal or practiced. A couple dozen shadows slipping into position, having received the signal that the birthday boy was coming.

"You know, you're right," Tony said. "This place! I should buy the whole town. This should be Louisa's Sentimental Value fucking headquarters! Jolene, you are *beautiful.*"

"Where do we park?" the Collector murmured.

Tony thought he was kidding and laughed. Nadine knew he wasn't, reached quietly around the door side of the front seat, and stroked the Collector's arm. There, again, was the difference between her man and his friend. Normal never assumed a welcome.

"When I relocate here, I'mma build the whole town a metered lot. Right there. Raise Jolene some *capital.*" He pointed to a flattish space steeped in shadow that ran unbroken behind the general store, fading into the forest on either side of town. "Pay this place back for being itself." He clapped his hands.

The Collector eased the Jeep into a sort of turnout a few hundred feet past the last cabin. Nadine let her eyes trail over the eerily barren forest floor. So strange, these stretches of the redwoods. The smell of life, the *feel* of it everywhere, but almost no sound, and so little to see, especially on the ground. Just this silty inland ocean of decomposing dead things, with occasional patches of living fern or moss floating in it.

Like Jolene, she thought. *And us. And everyone.*

"Hotline," she said, stopping Tony with one foot already out of the Jeep.

He turned. Grinning. "Want to hear it?"

She hadn't even been speaking to him; the word had just resurfaced in her mouth, oily and crude. But Tony was already tapping his phone. There was his voice, tiny in the speaker but as wrong in this giant-tree quiet as a chainsaw.

"You loved it once. You're letting it go. Doesn't it deserve a heaven? Let Louisa's Sentimental Value remove, lovingly restore, and find new homes for the things that made your home home. Generous terms. Thoughtful consultation. Of course we do house calls."

They stood together next to the Jeep now, half-turned toward town but taking a moment. Settling into that forest stillness, or letting the stillness they'd disturbed settle. Nadine searched groundcover and tree trunks for anything moving or cheeping. She thought she glimpsed a glint of yellow way off to her left, sliding silently into the earth. One of those glistening things, banana slugs. Or else stray sunlight filtered through mist and the canopy far overhead.

"So, you're like the Pound," she said, though half-heartedly. At least partly teasing, now. The forest had her, and Tony didn't trouble her much. "You're the stray dog collector of collecting."

"That could be any of us," said Normal. It was hard to tell from the direction of his gaze whether the forest or Jolene affected him most.

Tony pocketed his phone, took a deep gulp of piney air, and launched into motion. "More Humane Society, I like to think. Rescue shelter. I don't kill my strays, or recycle them. I don't even refurbish, usually, because whatever damage or scars they've incurred enhances their value. *Is* their value. My paying clients understand that. It is in fact what they're paying for."

Trailing behind Tony and the Collector, eyes still combing the woods for movement or color, Nadine felt a sudden, sharp pang.

For the lizard, she realized. For pin-eyed Louisa.

Ridiculous.

"And the items your clients don't snap up? The 'rescues' consigned to your 'heaven'? What happens to those? Into boxes with foam and bubble lining? Photographed for catalog and stored somewhere dark and temperature controlled? Or do they get little coffins?"

She didn't realize Tony had stopped, would have bumped into him if he hadn't dropped a hand on her shoulder. As soon as she glanced at the hand, he dropped it.

"What do I *do* with them? I treasure them."

With that, he left Nadine and the Collector and sidled off into a little crowd of people that parted and admitted him, as though through a curtain.

Nadine watched him kneel beside a dad and daughter in matching Russian River fishing caps. He began perusing pots and picture frames, then a box of old View-Master reels. Nadine knew she would be having a flip through those once Tony moved on. She'd always liked the feel of them. Oversized communion wafer-wheels of white plastic embedded with dark squares that glinted with the colors buried in them. She'd found a set, dinosaurs and marine animals, at a jumble sale when she was young. Forever afterward, they'd reminded her of church-window cookies, the sugar-marshmallow Sundays where she'd learned to love collecting.

As in the act, not the things collected.

Was that what bothered her so much, and maybe so unfairly, about Tony? Did he like the actual things too much? But what kind of sense did that make?

Russian River daughter was laughing with her father and Tony, now, holding up some sort of felt toad. Unless it was a Pokémon.

"This isn't so bad a Sunday," Nadine murmured to the Collector beside her.

But of course he wasn't beside her anymore. He'd wandered toward the tables in front of the general store, where more items—flatware, candelabras—had been spread almost like place settings, except clearly for sale. These weren't Normal's types of items, and Jolene wasn't his domain. But everything here unfolded in his rhythm. All these conversations and poses were ones he knew. All these people picnicking peacefully on the banks of a manmade river of goods rolling gently, relentlessly through the world, carrying the remnants and record of lives lived to the sea.

Nadine spent longer than she expected at the View-Master box. She slid reels from their paper sleeves, turned each in the light to catch the colors. This whole collection actually *was* a collection, not just some random attic assortment. All of them were souvenirs of travel or imagined travel. All had come from surprisingly specific places that had somehow, for some reason, at some point, produced View-Master reels to sell alongside postcards and T-shirts and plastic spoons. *Sunken Gardens, FLA. Greenfield Village. Storybookland. The Temple of Thought.* Nowhere Nadine had been. Nowhere she'd even heard of except, amusingly, *Mt. Olympus* and *Valhalla.* One day, she was going to have to find an actual View-Master and look at those reels. She picked up the whole box, checking around for someone with a money can or fanny pack. But she didn't see a likely candidate, and no one moved toward or motioned at her.

For a long minute, she observed everyone milling. Browsing. Not silent, but not really looking at each other. Definitely not looking at her. Not a single one of them buying.

On the porch of the cabin next door to the yard in which she stood, Nadine finally located a woman who seemed to be watching. She had a cable knit, loam-green shawl around her shoulders, and her stringy black hair in a half-hearted bun at the side of her neck. She was smiling. Maybe. Her lips flat but curving in the right direction, anyway. A fat, orange tabby perched on the railing in front of her. Every time the woman petted it, the cat lifted its tail, then its whole hind end, as if being drawn skyward on a string.

Nadine held up the box.

"Huh?" she saw more than heard the woman say. Then, "Oh." Her laugh carried across the open space, over the heads of the browsers. The quiet browsers.

"How much?" Nadine called.

"What's it worth to you?"

Moving around pods of people toward the porch, Nadine started to smile, too. Her shoulders, which she hadn't realized were up, relaxed. Her words, even her cadence settled into that so-familiar rhythm. Garage sale patois. Parry-riposte, touches scored on both sides and no one judging. The most consistently pleasant—or at least most authentic—human language she knew.

Across the street, the Collector sat next to some old guy in a surprisingly spiffy rust-red leather jacket, making circles with his hands and explaining God knows what. Tony had edged a little farther away. He seemed to be stopping at every blanket, checking everyone around him but not engaging. Smiling but not laughing.

Even as she held up the View-Master box, pursing her lips as though weighing exactly how much it *was* worth, Nadine felt a chill slide over her, gentle and fleeting as forest mist. Tony had turned back, crept another blanket closer, holding what looked like—what clearly was—a garden trowel. He wasn't looking at it, or at any of the other goods the people of Jolene had laid out.

He was studying faces. Not just looking, but practically shoving that hairy hound's nose toward everyone he passed as though sniffing.

Actually, not toward everyone. Just the women.

Because he doesn't remember, Nadine realized. The chill sharpened even as it faded, leaving a residue like dew on her arms and cheeks.

It wasn't so strange. Yes, she and the Collector remembered everyone they had ever dealt with in person, but they dealt almost exclusively with the most rarified corners of their rarified little world. Whereas Tony, like most dealers, just went out hunting stuff. He'd remembered the *thing,* the pocket watch-casing, not the woman who sold it to him.

The one who'd called his hotline, sounding like *that.*

Given his area of expertise, though, he probably got dozens of those calls. Seller's remorse calls. Even the Collector got them, sometimes. Why should Tony remember her face?

Three things—or not-things—happened at once.

Standing from his bench, the Collector moved her way, calling, "Whatcha got?" An homage to *Deterctorists*, the only television show they'd ever shared.

And Nadine, turning, realized she'd stood silent for a long time in front of the View-Master woman's porch, but the woman hadn't stepped down to meet her. Wasn't even looking at her.

And two blankets away, right at the edge of this yard, Tony bobbed on his heels, hand sailing halfway up for a wave but stopping. As though he was almost sure.

There was an instant of preternatural quiet. The mist, the road, the people of Jolene and their possessions, the whole morning seemingly subsumed into giant tree time. An absurdly elongated moment through which a thousand more ephemeral moments—lives—flickered, flared, and vanished.

Then a voice billowed out the open screen window behind the woman on the porch. Fuller, more flush with overtones than the voice on Tony's hotline, but unmistakable all the same.

"*There* you are."

Out she stepped. She was smaller and rounder than her sister, her eyes sparkling green against the pallor of her cheeks, which wasn't unnatural or even that pale. The color of life lived in shade. It had spread to her lips, though. Her red and white hair spilled in curls over her right shoulder and down her light blue cable knit sweater.

Did the sisters knit together, Nadine wondered? Right there on that porch in the giant tree quiet? Did they have knitting races? Or un-races, the winner the one who knitted slowest? She watched the shawl-woman reach out, poke her sister's side.

In that moment—encased in amber even as it happened—Nadine decided they did have races of one kind or the other. Momentarily, she loved them.

No. Envied them.

"Hel*lo*!" Tony said, dropping the trowel Nadine was sure he hadn't bought and hustling to the porch, wiping his hands on his jeans as though he'd just finished washing dishes. As if he'd known whom he was looking for all along. "Thanks so much for calling."

"Thanks for coming."

"Don't be ridiculous, ma'am." Abruptly, he jabbed a finger in the air. "*Denise*!"

The Collector reached Nadine's side. To her surprise, he touched her arm. "Where do you think he pulled that out of?"

"I just hope he got it right," she said.

The women let Tony dangle long enough that he started to squirm, conjure pre-apology sounds in his throat. Then the redhead, Denise, manufactured a pale-lipped smile.

"Mr. Louisa, in the flesh. "Wait right there."

What was it that made Nadine flinch, glance behind her? What did she think she'd seen, just for a second. Before it changed?

Everyone standing. Not watching. Not quite. Not even looking at each other.

That was it, she realized. *They all know each other.*

So what?

The Collector hadn't turned. He hardly seemed to be paying attention, except maybe to the trees.

"Here you go," said Denise, reemerging with a black clamshell box cupped in her pale hands like a butterfly. She was looking at her palms, not Tony. At the box nestled there.

Tony bobbed once more, glanced briefly at the Collector and Nadine. But he was a pro, versed in these exchanges, practiced and efficient. He mounted the first step toward the porch but no more, kept his hands at his waist, never held them out. He even bowed his head, but not too much. A vassal receiving a gift valuable enough to be painful to part with.

"I'm so glad you called," he said. "I'm honored."

Blue-shawl sister touched Denise as she started forward. Gently, on the hand, with the back of her own. Barely a touch at all, possibly accidental. A branch stirring in wind.

Did Denise's step hitch? If so, momentum carried her forward. She moved down two steps and held out the box toward Tony.

"You're the place for it." Her voice caught on *place*, right as she smiled again. "With its companion piece. You still have that, don't you? Or did you sell it?"

"Oh, I have it." Now, Tony had a hand out, palm up, barely belly-high. So patient. "Haven't even listed it, actually. It..." Abruptly, his cadence shifted out of professional haggler into everyday-Tony. Actual Tony. If there was such a person. "It didn't want to go. I mean, I didn't even know about its partner, here. And yet..."

"You're a sensitive man." Denise smiled back. She hesitated, then pried up the lid of the box. Her green eyes glinted forest-creature bright.

Was she crying?

The Collector edged forward, hands in his pockets. But Nadine noted that hunch in his spine that always startled and woke her. Except today, she'd been awake first.

"Tony," he said. "Leave it be."

But Tony was already leaning over the open box, emitting an appreciative whistle. He gave a respectful shake of his head. After a few seconds—longer than business acumen or even courtesy suggested—he murmured, "Ma'am. Are you sure?"

With a *smack*, the woman snapped the box shut, all but shoving it into Tony's chest. "It's no good to me. Not without..."

She was definitely crying, now. She didn't actually say the word *her*, barely even mouthed it.

Bastard, Nadine thought. *Predator.*

If Tony asked how much, Nadine neither saw nor heard. Money changed hands. There were twenties involved. The box disappeared into Tony's pocket as he retreated. Denise trembled, lifted a foot as though to start after him, then replanted it and swayed, arms folded hard across her chest and tears on her cheeks.

"Bye," she whisper-croaked.

"I'll take good care of it," Tony said, turning slowly, pulling Nadine and the Collector with him. "I'll treat it the way it deserves."

Denise didn't so much wipe her face as smack it. On the porch, her sister made no move whatsoever. But she did say, "Come on, hon."

"Like the treasure it is," Tony said, on autopilot now, easing past the people who'd stopped even pretending not to be looking. "Like *she* would have—"

"I don't give a shit," Denise snapped. "Do what you want." With a single, vicious kick at the step where she'd stood, she turned and disappeared into the house.

Just like that, everyone else started milling again. Yardsaling. Paying their visitors no mind.

Letting them go? Or just acceding to the end of the spectacle, like neighbors everywhere?

"So beautiful," Tony whispered, fervently enough that Nadine half-expected tears on *his* face.

There were none, of course. He'd slipped the box from his pocket again, though, started to push back the lid, but the Collector stayed him with a low, flat wave.

"Hang on," he said.

He said it again when they were already clear of Jolene, past Miranda, the edge of the forest plainly visible through the Jeep's windshield, the mist evaporating as they carved through it. The sudden sunlight on the service road that returned them to the freeway glittered on the still-wet asphalt. Through the canvas flap Tony had left a little unzipped, Nadine caught a whiff of diesel, sharp and stinging, and sucked it into her lungs.

Life smell, she thought, recognizing the perversion. Inversion. She gulped more anyway.

Five miles up the 101, Tony twitched, glanced sidelong at the Collector, then snatched up his box and opened it.

"Oh," he murmured. For a while, he did nothing else. Finally, lifting the circle of tarnished silver from its velvet cushion, he turned and extended it toward Nadine. "My god, look." But before she could, he snatched it to his ear and held it there like a shell. "*Listen.*"

Nadine couldn't tell if the Collector was eying her or Tony. Not road, that was for sure.

"Listen?" she said.

"This thing mattered. It *mattered*, Nadine."

The hum in human, she thought. The next time Tony held the watch casing over the back of the seat, Nadine took it.

It seemed to nuzzle into her palm. It wasn't silver. Copper, plus probably nickel. Scrap. Tony had handed it to her empty-side up. She almost didn't want to turn it over to see the design. The curve of the carving, the raised ridges, felt friendly and firm against her skin. Almost warm. Practically pulsing.

Like holding a hand, she thought, flipped the casing, and saw.

The clumsiness of the cutting, after Tony's buildup and Denise's tears, disappointed Nadine, but only momentarily. It was the clumsiness, after all, that made this what it was. Something made by someone.

A little girl? Grown daughter? Dead now? Just lost or estranged?

The fingers etched into the metal were too long, distinctly feminine but bumpy, more like roots. The space between pointer and middle fingers was too wide, and the ring finger and pinkie almost folded over each other, which made them look gnarled. Like roots, again.

Undeniably, though, these were girl's fingers. A specific girl's, pressing this case closed. Or reaching to pop it open. Fascinated, Nadine ran her own fingers along the rim.

"Hmm. How does this even click together?" She couldn't feel any grooves, no little tongue or catch.

Right as Nadine passed it back, at the instant it left her hand, she almost thought she *could* hear it. More whistle than hum. But something. Almost.

"I've got to admit, it's magical, Tony. It's a great get."

Laying the casing carefully in its box, Tony closed the lid. "I've got to get it home."

The Collector hadn't asked to see the watch and barely seemed to be listening. But Nadine noticed his smile. He didn't care about Tony's acquisition.

Today, he was just enjoying being out with his friend and her. Almost like an actual person.

Or the person he actually was. One of the two. The mystery had kept her engaged and exasperated and sometimes in love for more than twenty years. Apparently, it still did. And when he realized Tony had mentioned getting home—which meant his playdate was about to be over—and swung his head around, Nadine could have kissed him. He looked bereft, five years old. Younger, actually. The world's smartest, strangest newborn.

"No lunch?" he said.

Nadine laughed.

"Lunch?" Tony snapped. "Dude." He waved the box. "But hey. You can drop me at my warehouse."

"Drop… You mean we can come in? You're letting us see it?"

Nadine stared at the back of her man's head. "You've never seen his warehouse?"

"I'll let *you* in," Tony told the Collector. "Not so sure about her."

"Really? Never? How long have you two…" She was about to say *known each other*. But this was the Collector and one of his very few friends. *Known* didn't seem the word. *Friend,* either.

Glancing over his hairy arm, Tony winked.

"I go where he goes," she said.

"Guess you're both going to heaven, then."

Box clutched to his chest, he turned away. He didn't make another sound for a long time, except to grunt when the Collector said, "Ferndale, right?"

By the time they exited the freeway, more streaks of color had spread through the mist still clinging to the grassy hillsides, as though the sun were squeezing day into the world from tubes. Preparing to paint. At some point, desultory, Nadine had opened her laptop, started tapping around in databases and catalogs, looking at paired hands, pocket watch-casings, Sunken Gardens, Mt. Olympus, the Temple of Thought. The shredding-soul lyrics to "Jolene." Bespoke containers and their lids.

Lids.

"Hey, fellas?" she started, but Tony cut her off, pointing.

"Dude, dude. Right, turn right. Ach. You just missed it."

Braking, pulling to the shoulder, the Collector glanced out the window.

Nadine looked, too. Rows of semi-detached, cement-block garages, swathed in mist, stretched at least half a mile away from the road, all the way to the long grass at the base of the hills. Weirdly, momentarily, the site reminded her of Ireland. Of council estates after the garda had swung by and the kids had fled.

"U Stor," she read from the orange and black billboard towering over the front-most garage.

"Another surprising place to find heaven," said the Collector. Nadine couldn't resist sliding forward, slipping an arm around him. Tony still had his box imprisoned in his lap as though he worried it might open wings, flutter free.

"Why don't you just go on and put that *in* your pants?" Nadine teased. Couldn't help it.

"Are you two done?" Tony snapped. "Can we go?"

"I thought smoking pot makes you patient."

He didn't even turn around. "I'm not sure heaven's letting you in."

Beyond the storage garages, on the green slopes of the hills, cattle roamed. They looked half-formed at this distance, brown and white dots with legs. Animated backdrop.

The Collector gave a disappointed sigh. "I always pictured Louisa's Sentimental Value in a Butterfat Palace. One of those big, beautiful caramel-colored ones right in the heart of Ferndale."

"Well, I'm honored by that, Normal," Tony said. "Maybe someday one of us in this car will be able to afford one of those."

"Not likely," Nadine and the Collector said together.

They laughed. Tony, too. The Jeep moved off as Tony directed down the third row of garages. On the hillsides, the cows solidified but also stilled as though settling into slots in a pop-up children's book. *Big Red Barn* moved from its bucolic, imaginary American Midwest to the misty, mucky valley of the Eel.

"Thought it would at least be across Ferndale Bridge," said the Collector. But he'd slid forward again, now. So had she. Goddamnit. Because no matter what she thought of Tony, or whether she was right about that, his place was going to be a place. Somewhere to see.

Tony's eyes stayed in his lap. "Next right," he told the Collector without looking up. "Then quick left." He pointed only with his chin. "That one."

In the scope of this morning—in their world, in their lives—Tony's next comment didn't seem so strange. Even if he really was talking to the watch-casing.

"You feel it. Don't you?"

The second the Collector shut off the engine, Nadine heard whistling. A high electric sizzle, almost certainly emanating from the cell tower directly behind the garage in which Tony housed his heaven. A hundred thousand conversations captured and compressed and released again, streaming on a hundred thousand invisible, individual virtual wires. Nadine knew it didn't work like that, actually had little idea how the technology worked. But that's what she imagined.

Voices in the air. The hum in human.

In the distance, atop a taller rise behind the hills where cattle grazed, a power plant pumped white steam into the blue overhead. Tony had come around the Jeep now, hands cupped and held out in front. He looked less like a boy with a butterfly and more like a disheveled drunk surfacing from a binge. In handcuffs, even, because of the way he kept his arms out even as he stumbled toward his garage door. As if the box were leading him.

"Keys," he muttered. "Normal, hurry up. In my pocket."

But when he turned, he was again flashing that unabashed, blissful Tony smile Nadine had always taken for stoned. Probably, it was. That didn't make it less irresistible, though. Not in person.

"Want to hold it again?" he asked Nadine, extending his hands as though offering his baby.

She almost said no but didn't. Accepting the box, she cupped her own hands without even thinking.

"I can't wait to show you," Tony said. "I've been waiting for the right day."

"For twenty years?" The Collector sounded neither annoyed nor amused, but delighted.

"You'll see."

With a last glance at Nadine's hands, Tony bent to the padlock on the garage door. Getting it open took a surprisingly long time. Nadine noticed his wrists shaking. His shoulders, too, as though his whole body was a fault line juddering against itself, grinding toward separation.

Unsettled, oddly embarrassed, she glanced down the row of padlocked sheds, orderly as tombstones. Her own fingers curled around the box Tony had given her. The sizzle in her ears seemed to get harsher, alive and spitting words. Against the empty sky, the cell tower looked like a giant candelabra. Not an offering to heaven. Just another pitiful human prayer for one.

The padlock didn't so much click as crack, then drop heavily into Tony's hands.

"Can you feel the grace?" he said.

"Oh, boy," said the Collector. Teasing.

"You're about to."

He yanked open the door.

"Oh, Tony," the Collector murmured, even before his friend had gotten the lights switched on, and long before Nadine made sense of what she was seeing.

Despite the way Tony always referred to this place, and everything this morning should have suggested, Nadine had expected his shed to be a garage. Boxes, shelving, packing supplies scattered about. A broken bong or two. Possibly glass cases, although Tony didn't deal in glass-case merchandise.

What she saw instead was a raised wooden circular platform in the center of the shadowed space before her. A dais.

It wasn't just the platform creating that effect, but the chair. It was turned away from the outside world, facing the room, not the road. Some kind of soft leather La-Z Boy, definitely old, riven with cracks but glowing wherever light hit it. The cracks were less suggestive of wear than use, and the glow seemed internal, organic, the cumulative effect of decades of care. A lacy purple antimacassar, hand-crocheted, draped the headrest. Down the right-hand side, a single purple strand dangled like a curl escaping from a perfect pony-tail.

"Hang on, hang on," Tony was saying, scurrying into the shadows at the back of the shed. "Okay. Now look." More lights clicked on.

Already, the Collector had crossed the threshold out of the sunlight, but Nadine hung back, staring A floor-to-ceiling wooden shelving unit blanketed the back wall. Hand-built, probably by Tony, the shelves warped with weight and years, the spacing between them not quite uniform, the whole thing not simply alluding to but seemingly lifted from someone's childhood basement bedroom. Maybe even Tony's.

And on those shelves…

Faces. Stuffed rabbits, weasels, elephants, cats. A red felt, three-eyed puppet- dragon folded down onto itself, head tilted sideways so it seemed to be leaning on its gap-toothed grin. Bears, of course, threadbare or positively bursting with fur as though they'd sprouted like Chia Pets. Dead center—fourth shelf from the top, right in the middle, on a handmade miniature wooden throne of its own—sat Louisa herself. Little pin-eyed lizard. Queen of Heaven.

The Collector had stopped a few steps into the space. He was nodding, making low, appreciative noises. So was she, Nadine realized. At least, she was emitting sound, although it didn't feel like it came from inside her. More like she was being pinged. As though *she* were cell tower, now, reflecting sound back at the beings that made it.

There were other things on those shelves, between and among the animals: old and jacketless hardback books and junky airport paperbacks, marked as part of this collection only by their bent corners, water-damaged covers, and general shabbiness. Their *used*ness; a velvet smoking jacket; some shirts carefully though not neatly folded; cufflinks; tie pins; rings on little display pedestals or leaning from half-open boxes; some kind of dulled-brass horn curled around itself into no configuration Nadine immediately recognized. The shelves themselves had shiny bits strewn across their surfaces like pennies. Some of those *were* pennies, or coins, anyway.

But not most. A new sound escaped Nadine's mouth, this one definitely from her. Almost birdlike. Chirrup, mating call, warbled hello to the sun-streaked, heartbroken morning. All those things and none. *Truly birdcall,* she thought crazily. *The sound of being alive and making sound.*

Dog tags. Most of the shiny things on those shelves were dog tags.

Sentimental value.

"Coming in?" Tony said, startlingly near, half-in half-out of his storehouse, paradise, whatever this was. He had one hand on the Collector's shoulder and the other extended toward Nadine, and he was glowing. Bathing in his borrowed light.

The word that filled her mouth was *no.*

It's a trap, she would remember thinking.

Run.

But she said none of those things. In fact, she stopped feeling them almost before she articulated them to herself. Already, instead, she was experiencing something else. She didn't have a word for it. But it made her want to drop to her knees. Fold down on herself like that puppet dragon and cock her head and try, with the only face she had, to make other faces brighter.

Tony's extended hand twitched, the fingers spasming like upside-down crab legs, and Nadine realized he wasn't reaching for her at all. He wanted his prize. Involuntarily, Nadine glanced at it. Another noise popped free of her mouth.

The box was open. When had that happened? And when, exactly, had her fingers slipped inside it, caressing the watch casing, the velvet around it?

For one moment, she froze, arm half-raised, her weight forward but her eyes riveted on her own thumb stroking the ridges of that clumsy, carved hand. The hollows between the metal fingers felt warm. *Were* warm.

From the sun. Because you opened the stupid box.

But she could feel that hand flattening under hers, stretching like a cat being petted.

Unless it was reaching.

Right as she snapped the box closed, in the instant before she passed it to Tony, she noticed the letters engraved at the base of the carving, barely visible at the point where half-wrist melted into formless metal.

Pit? But there was more, fading into scuffs and scratches. Pithos?

She all but flung the box, earning a "Hey—careful!" from Tony. He caught it, closed his own palms around it, and glared.

"Fucking Gollum."

Blinking, stretching her arms wide to the warming air, Nadine blew out a breath. "What?"

"My *preciousss*," Tony said, in a falsetto Nadine realized was meant to sound like her. Her, possessed. "*Nasty hobbit collectorses. Preciousss.*" He stroked the box, leaning over as though murmuring to it.

"Shut up," said Nadine. She made herself laugh.

But only until he turned his back, and then she had to check herself from stumbling after him, and also will her arms back to her sides.

He'd been wrong, though. She didn't want the box. Or the watch-casing inside it.

She'd wanted to keep them from Tony.

"Normal," she called.

Of course, he'd already seen or sensed. Maybe he had all along. Maybe that's why they'd come along this morning in the first place. Now he stepped into his friend's path, blocking it artfully, as if by accident.

"Dude," he said. "Let's cross the Eel. Get us some Poppa Joe's. Hang with the poker players."

Poppa Joe's. Their favorite local breakfast. Framed old photos of unnamed, clearly loved faces between the antlers. Old guys in the back seemingly molted into their booths, playing poker for pennies over hash browns. Actual Collector heaven, she thought. A place with history—sentimental value— accruing to the salt shakers, the polyester of the waitress uniforms, the very walls.

All borrowed or imagined history, of course. All someone else's, nothing to do with Nadine and the Collector, and therefore not so different from Tony's shed. Not different at all, really. Except…

"No can do, brother," Tony said.

"Au contraire."

"Don't patter with me, bud." Like an eel, so slippery, Tony slid around the Collector toward his shelves. "Patter's not for you."

"Well, we're going to Poppa Joe's."

"Go ahead."

"Put down the box."

"I'm going to. Right now."

"Not up there. I think maybe—"

"Nadine, get Normal out of here. You're both boring me, now. St. Tony-Peter says you're not ready for his Paradise. He repels you from his gates." He knelt before his shelves.

The Collector hunched as though preparing to tackle him. But then he straightened. Nadine watched him not move. Not be sure. Maybe that's what had felt strange all morning. Usually in these moments, the Collector somehow intuited, even understood. Not always what was happening, but what might help.

Today, though, he'd just seemed slow. He watched Tony fumble on the bottom shelf, come up with the other half of the watch casing. Already, he had his new box open. He brought the two casings together slowly, as though introducing stray cats to one another. Or reuniting them.

"Tony," the Collector tried once more.

But Tony just went on pressing the halves of the hunter case together, turning them, trying to make them catch. Nothing rumbled under their feet when the casings touched, and no lights flickered. The shiver rippling up Nadine's back got triggered by the Collector's glance, not anything Tony did.

They left him turning those carved hands one way, then another, leaning them together, laying them on top of one another, switching them around.

"Poppa Joe's?" the Collector finally said when they were back in the Jeep.

But he didn't key the ignition until Nadine said, "Okay." And he didn't speak a single word at the restaurant, not even to order, though he ate as much patty melt as he ever did. Nadine always hated hauling out her laptop in places like this—places to be in—but she couldn't help herself today, and once she had it out, she went to work. She wasn't sure what she was searching for, and yet the more she poked around, the more the world tilted under her wooden stool, sliding her down one of those virtual rabbit holes that hurtled her across links and through digitized libraries into deeper databases that led to labyrinths that left her lost, stripped of hours, less than she was.

Olympus. Watch-casings. Jolene, the song and the not-exactly-town. At some point, she clicked on a YouTube rip of the music, expecting Dolly, and got what she took at first for some hipster guy's cover version, a surprisingly good, dirge-y thing that sounded as desperate as the original in its way, meaning pretty fucking desperate. Then she realized it wasn't a cover at all, but a Dolly 45 played at 33. Jolene slow. Defeated sigh instead of pleading wail. *Which causes deeper bitterness*, she wondered as she listened, typed, clicked, searched: *dread of the inevitable or acceptance of it? Please-don't-take* or *here-go-ahead*? She thought of Denise on her porch in her town, with her sister but not her daughter. Knitting things.

Making things.

But no, the daughter had made the watch. Or the casing, at least. Right? The women had said that.

Why did it matter?

While the Collector played with his fries and watched her or the window or the poker guys in the back—searching, too, in his Normal way—she scoured a whole University of Pennsylvania art criticism sub-database about fingers and hands. Then another about *pithos*, which plunged her into a

Hesiod pdf about Pandora and what was left in her box, either because she'd caught it or because it had been secreted there. The Gods' most savage gift of all. The one we got to keep.

Hope.

The hum in human. The sense that if we just reach hard enough for long enough, we really might somehow, one day, attain...discover...accidentally get to experience...

Olympus? Pithos?

Watch-casings emptied of watches, the watches replaced with...what? And by the mother? The daughter?

To comfort, or torment?

"Normal," she murmured, shoving back her stool without any clear sense of what she might say next.

But the Collector was already up. His hand caught hers and held it. *Right hand into left, fingers stretching, catching. Holding, the way we sometimes let ourselves, and can. For all the good holding does.*

"We've got to go back, Nadine."

"We better hurry."

They weren't fast enough. Nadine knew they wouldn't be. That's what had been so strange and wrong about the whole morning, really: the slowness. Nadine-and-the-Collector slow.

Because of Jolene? Because of what Tony had spirited out of Jolene? Or simply because Tony was Normal's friend, which had blinded him just long enough?

Even before they turned into U-Stor, they saw whirling red and blue lights, heard siren-whoop. By the time they reached Tony's garage, the paramedics were already inside, grabbing at Tony's flailing limbs as he writhed and kicked on the ground. Stuffed animals flew from him in all directions, seeming to erupt off his skin like kernels popping. Louisa the lizard was one of the last, launching from Tony's chest as the paramedics finally got him in restraints, strapped him tight to a flat board. That's when he started screaming.

"You his friends?" the burliest of three paramedics asked as they wheeled Tony out of his shed. The guy had a new black eye, and he kept shaking his head and spitting out breath as though he'd inhaled something.

The Collector nodded.

"You the ones that called?"

"No," said the Collector.

Tony screamed again as they loaded him into the ambulance. But the moments between screams were worse. That's when they heard his teeth cracking as he smashed and ground them. Muscles and veins had risen in his neck like furrowed rows. Or carved ridges.

Fingers.

The door slammed shut on Tony's screams. The burly paramedic spit at the ground, touched a palm to his eye. "Fucking Christ." He shook his head. Then he laughed. Sort of. "On the fucking floor. Screaming and gibbering with, like, a thousand stuffed animals pulled up over him. Like his teddy bears jumped him." Another barked laugh, then the guy hurried around to the driver's side of the ambulance and climbed in. The siren's scream drowned out Tony's. But barely.

"Like his teddy bears jumped him," Nadine repeated.

But the Collector shook his head. Looked at her with tears in his eyes. "Pulled up over him. Like a blanket."

Which of course was right. A pathetic defense. Last, hopeless attempt to keep warm. Keep out the desperation—the awareness of loneliness, the hope of somehow, one day, assuaging it—he'd cordoned off his whole life, warehoused in his U-Stor. Until the ladies of Jolene unleashed it.

On the floor in the corner, glinting at the edge of a cone of sunlight, the watch caught Nadine's eye. It had been fitted together at last (*and so activated*?). Now it sat wide open, tilted on its side. An empty shell. The thing it had been created to house gone.

Loosed.

The Collector looked where she did. Then at her.

They drove home silent, holding hands.

HOME

It's the way he's sitting, which isn't the way he sat then. Also that subtle lifting of his chin when he looks at her, that hint of I-already-knowness she'd taken all afternoon for House smug even after she'd realized he wasn't House. Mostly, though, it's the specific blue of his eyes, which she'd swear hadn't been that color when he came in the door. But now, at last, she knows. Sees.

How could she not have seen?

Because he wasn't there. Not all the way.

Ridiculous, obviously, he's been here the whole time. Except he hasn't, not completely. Even now, it's like he's...*loading*. That's the best she can come up with. There, tangible and touchable, but with elements still flickering into place. She can practically see and can definitely imagine her computer's little color-wheel spinning over the Rev's head as he slowly, slowly, takes shape. His own shape.

"It's you," she says, right as he slams both palms down on the table hard enough to ring the glass and also hurt his hands. He flings them out to his sides and shakes them, wincing.

"Waste of time. This whole goddamn day. He doesn't know and couldn't say if he did. Neither of you do. You don't even know what I'm talking about. Look at you. Standing on the lip of the ocean, and proud of yourselves because you've found some sand."

He leaps to his feet. Across the room, where he's been sitting cross-legged under the wishing-tree clock, the Collector leaps up, too. He lurches forward, and the Rev moves in the other direction, toward the windows. When he whirls to come back, Normal does, too, faces the clock, takes a few steps that way. To Nadine, they're like opposite ends of one of those kinetic motion ball sculptures, where the smacking of one sphere sets the sphere at the opposite end arcing into the air.

Actually, it's more like they're on a see-saw, one descending as the other rises. So that they never actually meet.

"It keeps happening. All around you." The Rev waves his hands and rants and never stops moving. "Over and over, you're gifted opportunities, and you *waste* them. A taste that drives men mad. A literal boatload of souls. A centuries-old *bouquiniste* stall full of nothing that drives people to their knees or to stab their friends in the face."

"Neck," Nadine murmurs, mesmerized by the motion but also the way the Rev waves his words in front of her, as though wiping clean a windscreen that has been fogged her whole life, only she didn't know it. Thought the fog was the world, period. All of it that she (or anyone) would ever get to see.

"A pathetic, groveling loneliness that drives a man to hoard talismans—well, okay, that's everyone, isn't it, that's just people—except this guy doesn't just hoard them. He *bathes* in them. He creates a groveling-loneliness *sauna* in a fucking storage shed in the middle of nowhere, plunks himself down in a comfy chair, and just..."

Abruptly, the Rev halts in front of her, shoots out his hands and grabs her wrists. The Collector bangs into the wall feet first and stays there. The Rev isn't shaking her or yanking her anywhere. But he won't let go. Wouldn't, Nadine realizes, even if she tried to jerk free. Which she isn't doing. Yet.

"You keep brushing right up against it. You keep *flushing it out*. You two, so good at finding, I'll give you that. If this were a grouse hunt, you're the bush beaters I'd call. Except every time you roust it, every time it flutters up in front of you all wild and free, instead of realizing or understanding or, God forbid, *harvesting*, you stand there slack-jawed and *let it go*. Let it just evaporate before it can—"

"How's your dad?" Nadine asks, and shuts him up.

For the fiftieth time today, she watches emotions mass and merge and flee across his face. It's the sky-blue in those eyes that makes her think of clouds. He hasn't dropped her wrists, and she still has no idea if he's going to shove her, strangle her, or ask her to marry him. It's the way he glances at the Collector that triggers that last thought. The guilty little twist to his mouth.

Unless that's envy?

In her own mouth, she can taste the crepe he brought her from some Paris nighttime street stand all those years ago. On her skin, she can feel the light from that fire and the scratchiness of that rug. In that room that wasn't there.

More expressions form and fall apart on the Rev's face. His still-young face, unmistakable, now. Impossible not to remember. He drops her wrists, sighs, and glances once more toward the Collector.

"How did it happen?" he asks.

Which, again, seems so much the wrong question. Or the question after the one he hasn't asked. The one about what's wrong. Normal steps back from the wall but stays turned away from them. Bending forward, he puts his hands on his knees, breathes in, holds the breath so long that Nadine finds herself holding hers, until he finally exhales.

She shakes her head. "I don't know. Obviously, he hasn't said."

"What do you know? Were you there? Did you see it?"

"See..." *What, exactly*? "You act like it's an event. A discreet thing that happened."

The Rev watches the Collector lift one leg and turn on it like he's some kind of wind-up ballerina, then glances back at Nadine. "I'm pretty sure a thing happened."

"Like a car crash, you mean? Like one of Tony's animals hid in the back of the Jeep and jumped him, too?" Tears fill her eyes. Jump her. Goddamn it. She wants to grab Normal's hand. Stop him spinning, at least. She wipes away the tears, but new ones well, as though she's cut herself and can't stop bleeding. "Isn't it a whole lot more likely that something in him that was brewing for a long, long while just—"

"Right in front of you," the Rev mutters. Not even to her. "Every single goddamn time."

"What do you think happened, then?"

"Where was he? Can we start with that?"

No, Nadine realizes. Ask her about almost any other morning of Normal's life—even ones from before she met him—and she probably could have said, or at least guessed with considerable confidence. But that one...

"I know what he went to look *at*," she says, blushing, because now, good Christ, on top of everything else, she's embarrassed.

With a clap of his hands, the Rev drops onto the couch, perches on the edge, like a dog on point, told to stay. Knowing he's about to be turned loose. For the first time all day—or that other day, really, way back in Paris, when she was young, too—he looks like his dad.

"I still have the note. Pretty much the only note he ever wrote me."

On her way to the kitchen, she touches Normal right between the shoulder blades. The gesture feels ritualized, almost more genuflection than expression of love. She touches him now in the same way he gazes all the time into his clock.

That clock.

Something pings inside her. Whatever it is, it's going to make her cry more, so she ignores it. Sliding open the drawer by the sink, she digs under the paperclip box and take- out menus for both places that actually deliver here. The piece of paper she pulls out is crumpled, egg yolk-stained, ripped from some pocket notebook she doesn't remember either of them owning and has never seen since. She returns to the living room, hands the paper wordlessly to the Rev, and stays standing while he reads it.

He's disappointed, of course. Sags a little in his seat, presses his lips together. "I think maybe he could have paid more attention in English class."

The smile on Nadine's face feels like a drawn sword. She holds it steady until he looks up and sees it.

"Right in front of you, Rev," she says. "And you just keep missing it."

Sheathing the smile, she steps around behind the couch so she can see the note over his shoulder. Not that she needs to. She could recite or even reprint it from memory. Not just the words but their slant, not just the letters but their exact size and relationship to the lines that don't quite contain them.

Off to get some lost. You know I Love a Mystery.

"I thought what you thought, so," Nadine says. "For maybe two seconds."

He notes the dig, she can tell. But he waits. Which is wise—he really is wise beyond his years, a Rev in more ways than one—because even as she starts to tell him, she discovers something new. Realizes, for the first time in the sixteen months since it happened, why the Collector didn't take her with him on what turned out to be his last outing.

Not because he had an inkling. Not because he was afraid or protecting her. He just didn't think it was going to be interesting. To either one of them.

She points at the words. "Get some lost. Not 'get a bit lost.' Not 'get lost', not like he and I mean."

"Me, too," the Rev murmurs back. Reverently.

"It isn't hipster slang, either, because he wasn't and wouldn't. So. 'Get some lost.' 'Get' as in, '*pick up*.' Pick up some lost."

The Rev understands already. Nods. He's really their sort, after all. Same order, same genus. Not quite the same species, but close. "Like, Pick up some milk," he says.

To her surprise, the Rev laughs. "Pick up some toilet paper."

Even more surprisingly, she laughs, too, in spite of her man behind her, staring at the wall. In spite of everything. "'Get some lost.' Meaning, acquire a lost thing. Something someone else has on a list. Routine, every day collecting and retrieving. Not really of interest to either one of us. Just paying the bills."

The Rev nods a few times. He looks at the note, fondles it. The corners of his lips turn down. "No. I don't see how these words tell you that."

"They don't. The capital letters do." She waits a beat, can't resist clucking her tongue at him. "Ah, ye poor wee chiseler. You're so young." Is it the taunting that annoys him? The fact that he *is* young? Or dawning comprehension that there really are things she understands and he doesn't? Nadine can't tell, doesn't care. Does wonder why she's enjoying it. "He's not saying he loves a mystery."

The Rev glares, now. At the note. "Those seem to be the words."

"And that there? That's called a *capital* L. Capital M. Not he loves a mystery, so. 'I Love a Mystery.'"

Still nothing.

"*I Love a Mystery*. The radio show? The legendary lost episodes everyone's been searching eighty-odd years for? At least 19 of those. Possibly all of them. Turned up at last, just lying around in some old lady's basement like props for the feckin' *Antiques Road Show*, waiting all these decades for her bored great grandkid to open a box in a basement and thread up the first of those unlabeled reel-to-reels and—"

"Reel-to-reels," the Rev says, spine jerking straight as though she stuck a skewer down him. He slaps his hands against his still-crossed legs, seems to flap in place like a staked tent. Nadine thinks he's going to get up, blow away, but he just starts to laugh like his dad and leans back on her couch, which *twitches*, flickers yellow, melts out of shape.

Except it doesn't. She's had her hand on it, and it's her couch, she'd know it anywhere, knows it like her own skin. But for that one instant, it looked like *theirs*. As though that one—along with the light from that fire, even a tinge of its heat—had been teleported here. Or superimposed. Real, completely distinct and tangible, but also ephemeral. Temporary as cloud shadow. As being that young and lonely and free. And in Paris.

"Reel to fucking reel," says the Rev. "Oh, yes. That could work. Brilliant. Even the *process* of that. What even is recording? Collecting in the moment of creation! Say something into the air, and the tape spins. Wraps it up. Like a web, see? Like a cocoon. Simple and safe and natural as…" He glances at the Collector. The whole room tilts with his gaze, sliding down its own walls to make space for—

"Tell me" the Rev snaps, bolting to a standing position. He grabs her wrists again, not in anger but giddy, giggling glee.

Which feels even more dangerous?

"Tell you what?"

"He went out that morning. You didn't even see him go. Then he came back like this. Right?"

Is the Collector listening? Nadine can't tell. He has his hands on the wall on either side of the wishing tree clock, and he's leaning into it as though over steam from a kettle. As though trying to clear his breathing.

"Pretty much," Nadine says. The tremor in her voice is more alarming to her than anything the Rev has done. She hadn't realized, until right this second, how badly this loss has broken her.

"Pretty much or exactly?"

It's his gaze more than his grip she needs to jerk free from. "I don't understand what you're asking."

"I'm asking what I asked. Was he *like this*? Has it gotten worse, or was this already him?"

"By which you mean *in* him?"

He drops her hands so he can clap his. "See? You really do see. Finally. That's *exactly* what I mean." Whirling to the Collector, then the big windows and the reflections of this room and everyone in it floating like phantoms over the deepening dark—like all rooms in all nighttime windows, ephemeral and fluid and always glimpsed in the act of vanishing—the Rev claps his hands again. He laughs and launches once more into his own circle around Tony's chair, the couch, the far wall and back.

"You're not blind. Either of you. I take it back. You're just...willfully small-minded."

If it weren't for Normal—if she thought she could have gotten him to come with her—Nadine would have fled. Out her door to the Jeep, headlong down the Avenue of the Giants until she spotted Spook racing up to meet them. But Normal is still leaning over the clock or into the wall, and he has his eyes closed. Whatever he's listening to, it's inside him.

Web. Cocoon...

"He recognized it. You, too, though I think he'd put it together more. And then he actually got to *touch* it. Again! Everything you've both been hunting for. The *real* world of your dreams."

Nadine doesn't want to answer, instinctively doesn't even want to remind the Rev that she's there. But she can't stop herself. "You don't know my world. Certainly not my dreams. You never will."

If anything, his pacing intensifies, and his laugh edges wilder. "Probably not. The question, my bonny lass, is, *will you*? It's right there. Everything you've sensed and seen and brushed against and yes, goddamnit, *collected*. You have it all. You have what all of us want."

Tears again. Not just welling, but spilling down her face. "I agree. We did."

The Rev practically hurtles Tony's chair to return to her. His face has gone firelight-red, and he's no longer laughing. He's so angry, Nadine realizes, he can hardly keep himself in his skin.

"And what have you done with it? All the treasure there is in the world?"

"Dreamed," Nadine whispers, mesmerized. Unable not to answer, again. "Helped people."

"Helped people!" His laugh is a single bark. "Like your Nazi friend? Is that what he'd say you did?"

"He wasn't—"

"How about all those musicians who left pieces of themselves on that boat? Do they feel *helped*, do you think? Or your man's best friend with the stuffed animal vault? Or the booksellers of Paris? Would you say you and Normal saved the one who got stabbed in the neck, or the one who did the stabbing? Have the famous Collector and Nadine helped or saved even one person?"

"He saved me," Nadine whispers.

The Rev stares. Waits.

She doesn't want to go on. More than that, she knows it's dangerous.

But she can't stop. Because this kid knows something she doesn't. Or because he's drawing something out of her. Or because there's something here, it's been here all day, and it's unfamiliar, brand new, and everything she has ever been and done has trained her not to ignore the unfamiliar when it somehow, miraculously, surfaces.

Or because what the Collector did still, even now, breaks her heart.

PRIDE

Like all their best hunts, this one started as a search for something else, and ended in failure. They'd been days in the hills above Ruidoso in the middle of winter, back and forth across the Mescalero Reservation in a rented Jeep whose sides didn't zip. They never did find the Kiowa trader the Collector had heard—somehow, through that impossible, disorganized scatter of decades-old contacts and anonymous web informants and intuition he'd constructed around himself—was back in the country. They had hoped to fulfill an eight-year-old request from an east coast numismatic by asking the Kiowa to trade or sell at least one of the three pre-Mayan axe-head coins he supposedly kept on his person at all times, reportedly for luck. Luck he actually believed in. Why he would ever consider parting with one, Nadine had no idea.

"These people," Nadine told the Collector as they drove through blowing snow and gray light, across dead, desert hills that seemed to fade with the day from the dull sepia of old photographs to the dissolving sepia of ruined old photographs. She had books open on her lap, her laptop atop those. Doing what she did, what she loved. Filling the Collector's quests—and life—with meaning, the way he filled hers with purpose. "This Mayan tribe? They had so little use for metal—they were so good with shells, and wood, and leaves—that they assigned it the least important function in their entire cultural system."

"Meaning money," the Collector said. Curled forward in his seat with his dark hair uncombed in need of cutting, he still looked weirdly peaceful, like a windblown cypress. He smiled. "Brilliant." Then he swung his head around to look at her some more. As usual, he did that for too long.

"Goddamnit, drive," Nadine said happily, as the Jeep skidded onto gravel and back off it.

With no real hope left of completing their task, they stopped in the dead dark of 4:30 in the afternoon at a reservation bar. Clumps of snow scudded across the empty parking lot like herds of ghost buffalo. The neon sign over the bar's wooden doors read BAR, and the place radiated all the low, windowless charm of an adult bookshop. Inside, instead of the Kiowa, they found Nartana.

Later that night, in the after-storm silence, as they descended from the high desert toward the west Texas waste, Nadine would wonder how Normal had recognized the man, or even remembered they were looking for him. But then, that ability—to keep every active request in his head and accessible at all times, and to seize on the one particular that just might, someday, bring the quest to resolution—was what made him who he was. It was also why, despite Smartphones and linked databases and indelible digital footprints, people still sought him out.

In Nartana's case, the Collector had seized on the sandals. Nadine noticed them too, of course, the second her eyes adjusted to the bar's dim, blue light. The man wearing them had propped them on the table right by the door. The feet they encased looked hairy, bloody, covered in flaps of dead skin, more like a brace of shot squirrels than feet.

"Nadine," the Collector said, gesturing at the sandaled man. "Go to work." He kept one finger in the air, as though testing for wind.

The bartender—a middle-aged Apache woman with a dishrag in her hands and salt-and-pepper hair in a neat bun—watched them without curiosity. On the jukebox, Keith Secola—Nadine recognized the song from an earlier quest—wailed the reservation blues.

Nadine finally got her gaze past the sandaled man's feet, up his long legs and blade-of-grass torso to his face.

"He's sleeping."

"Ask him if he wants a grilled cheese. And a chocolate milk."

"Chocolate milk?"

"Come on. Do your stuff."

"My stuff works better on awake people."

"It works on everyone."

"I *do* want a grilled cheese," said the sandaled man, opening his eyes without lowering his feet from the table. "Yes I do."

Instantly, Nadine felt herself switch on. As though she'd flipped a sign behind her eyes to read OPEN. That's what the Collector always told her it looked like. It wasn't conscious, simply what happened when she caught a scent of something.

Glancing sidelong, she caught her man grinning at her like a little boy. Which made her grin back.

"Am I having my sandwich with you?" said the man.

Dropping her bag to the floor and her coat over the back of the nearest wooden chair, Nadine sat. "See to the sandwiches?" she called to the Collector. "There's a good boy."

He moved off.

The sandaled man removed his feet from the table and sat up, some. His threadbare button-down was too wide but not long enough for him, draping his shoulders more like a saddlebag than a shirt. The twiggy thing between his lips, which Nadine had taken for a cigarette, turned out to be a twig.

"Right, so," she said brightly. "Why do you think we're here?"

The Collector returned, pulled up a chair. "Nartana. Right?" He introduced himself and Nadine.

Nartana blew into his chocolate milk. Bubbles rose to the rim of the glass and seemed to rotate there. For a moment, Nadine thought he was going to launch them like smoke rings, do tricks. They trembled with breath, then sank. When she looked up, Nartana was staring at her.

"You notice," he said. Meaning what he'd done with the bubbles. Which had been a trick, after all.

"I do," she told him. Before they'd even finished their sandwiches, she worked him around to his flutes.

This time, Nartana's eyes widened comically. "You know about those?"

"We've heard about them."

"Are they here?" said the Collector, leaning forward. Up until that moment, he'd displayed no trace of impatience. Actually, he'd displayed the opposite of impatience. That was *his* magic. "You have one with you?"

Shrugging, Nartana reached under the table and pulled up a clinking, canvas Trader Joe's bag.

"Perfect," said the Collector. "Oh, God."

For a second, as Nartana struggled to free a recorder-like mouthpiece from whatever it was tangled with, Nadine thought he was about to play the whole bag, that the bag itself was an instrument. Trader Joe bagpipes. Then Nartana got a flute loose and set it on the table.

It wasn't much to look at: a cylindrical reed, warped almost apart in several places. The colorless feathers glued to the edges of the finger-holes looked caked with salt or gypsum sand, as though they'd been dragged behind a snowplow. The mouthpiece was pinched nearly shut, and bent inward like a crooked finger.

"Can I hold it?" the Collector asked.

"Knock yourself out, man," said Nartana.

The Collector held it, handed it to Nadine. It felt different than she'd expected. Softer, maybe. The feathers like fingernails brushing the bottoms of her wrists. Raising goosebumps there.

Nartana seemed pleased by their reactions. But when the Collector asked whether they could trade for or buy the flute—or commission the creation of a new one—the man raised both eyebrows.

"What do you mean?"

"We know a guy," Nadine said. "He...well, he collects. Instruments. Handmade breath instruments from all over the world. In honor of his wife." And then—unsure not just of why this might convince Nartana but whether she wanted to—"She died."

Nartana considered, then shook his head. "How can I give him my flute?" He sounded utterly sincere, and also as though they'd asked for one of his lungs. He put the instrument away. The Collector didn't argue, just removed a card from his pocket and slid it across the table. "In case you change your mind. Ever." He stood.

"Could you play for us?" Nadine said.

The Collector sat back down.

They still hadn't spoken, fully two hours later, when the Collector turned the Jeep off Route 11 into the parking lot of a Family Pride supermarket that had materialized out of the blowing wisps of snow, lights blazing, like a frontier trading post. "I'm hungry," he said. "Come on."

As she eased into the air, Nadine felt both knees pop. She stretched next to the Jeep, listening to its sides snap in the wind while snowflakes kissed her outstretched wrists. Disconcerting in their dryness. Even precipitation in this endless, greenless space seemed devoid of liquid, as unlike precipitation in her homeland as Nartana's fluteplay was to pennywhistling. No less stirring or beautiful. Emptier, though. Even lonelier.

Theirs was almost the only car in the long, square lot. The new-risen moon poked through a burl of heavy clouds. Far ahead, at the edge of some low hills, a ribbon of light, or maybe lights, stretched the length of the horizon. A town, maybe. From under the front tire of the Jeep—as though it had been there for hours—a tortoiseshell cat crept out, appraised Nadine with narrowed eyes, and scurried away. Two more cats seemed to rise out of the asphalt to join the first, and they glided together toward the store.

"Hello," chirped a tiny, dark-haired girl in a Family Pride apron as she passed in front of the Jeep wheeling a stray shopping cart. Whatever that horizon light was, it flickered in her too-large glasses.

"*Uh-uh-uh OH*!" sang another girl Nadine hadn't noticed, chugging up behind the Jeep, steering a whole line of shopping carts.

The first girl laughed, spun her cart around so she was pushing from the wrong side, and raced toward the oncoming line. The collision produced a strangely disappointing *ping*, but the girls staggered back as though from a car crash, then leapt into the air and butt-bumped each other, scream-singing "*Hello*!"

Nadine smiled. Stopped smiling. Watched a snowcloud blow over the girls. Neither one, she realized, was as young as she'd initially thought. The first had to be in her twenties, dark braid thumping down her back, glasses clearly the cheapest she could find, the prescription probably years out of date judging by her squint. The second was taller, pale-cheeked, round and squishy everywhere like an uncooked loaf of bread. Her eyelids not just heavy but set in their heaviness, like a new mom's.

Nadine had known so many of these girls in Lissycasey. Woman-girls who could have gotten away, gone to school, gone to Dublin or London, meant to, but stayed instead to help parents or wait on a boy. Got stuck without realizing. Without even noticing, sometimes. Spent the rest of their youths wriggling like flies on flypaper.

"Nadine!" called the Collector, standing before the open sliding doors. "They have cactus candy!" He disappeared through another knot of cats into the market.

"It's gross," said the round woman, pushing her carts past Nadine. "Don't do it."

"Tastes like cactus, though," called the woman with the braid. Glasses twinkling.

"And belly lint," said the round woman.

Nadine laughed.

Inside, opening her coat but finding less warmth than she'd hoped, she strolled past closed checkout lanes and a trio of black kittens clustered around a plastic saucer of milk next to the stacked firewood. In the Express Lane, a cashier sat behind the register. Pretty, dusky, Hispanic girl, maybe nineteen, with tired eyes that made her appear almost Asian and a red, glinting mouth, just a touch lopsided. Kisser's mouth, Nadine thought. Homegrown-tomato mouth.

"*Buenas noches,* welcome to Family Pride," the cashier said without looking up from the Pauline Kael paperback she had propped against the vegetable scale beside the register.

Smiling without knowing why, Nadine strolled ahead, searching for the Collector. She passed more wandering cats, a few stray shoppers, a drunk guy in a Stetson picking through boxes of off-brand cereal O's. In the Health and Beauty aisle, she saw another Family Pride employee kneeling to restock tampon boxes along a bottom shelf. This woman actually looked up when Nadine passed. She'd affixed wrapped, taped-together tampons behind each ear, and they bobbed like antennae as she straightened.

"Those," Nadine said, with what she hoped was proper reverence, "are exquisite."

"You should see my spatulas," said the woman, and returned to her stocking.

By the time Nadine located the Collector, he'd paid and was on his way out of the store. She caught up as they traversed the lot, and he offered her a candy out of a bag with a painted cactus on it. She took his elbow instead. They walked in silence back to the Jeep through the spitting snow. He held her flap open for her, as he occasionally thought to, took too long making his way to his own side, then stood with his own flap unzipped. Any heat left in the cabin streamed out, and the chill poured in. A long, gray tabby hopped up, too, sat in the driver's seat as though preparing to take the wheel, then hopped down again.

"Like Scott himself, he looked," Nadine finally intoned, in her best BBC documentary voice. "Frozen to the side of his vehicle. His beautiful, brilliant companion frozen inside. One turn of the key from safety, warmth, civilization..."

The Collector dropped into his seat and turned on the car. Then he turned it off again while wind battered the canvas and the chill chased down their bones.

"What?" Nadine said, following his gaze but seeing only the woman with the braid, hunched as she burrowed to the far corner of the lot to collect a cart that had wandered all the way to the barrier.

"Nothing," said the Collector, not starting the car. He wiped the windshield free of breath.

Nadine waited.

Eventually he turned, his face unreadable but his posture stiff. As though he really had frozen. "It's just that I know a collection when I see one," he said.

Then he slid through the flap and set out across the lot.

She was too surprised to follow, and too cold. So she just watched as he went, popping another cactus candy in his mouth. His clothes whipped around his stick-figure frame. He stopped a few feet from the girl, not helping with the cart. The girl spoke to him. When the conversation showed no signs of abating, Nadine clambered out and started toward them. Airborne snow danced along her scalp and neck like little fingers, tickling and teasing.

The girl was laughing as she removed her glasses and wiped them on the edge of the sweater sticking out from her coat sleeves. The Collector's smile was for show, not his real one. Nowhere near.

"What time do you get off?" Nadine heard him say, and stopped. The question startled her, despite the fact that she knew better.

The girl's answer got swallowed by wind, but the Collector said, "Uh-huh. And what time did you come on?"

The girl started to answer that, too, laughing some more. Then she stopped laughing. Put her glasses on, but not before Nadine saw.

The person in there. The woman-girl. Panicking, without making a sound.

Almost casually, never disengaging his gaze from the girl's, the Collector lifted his foot and kicked the cart toward the edge of the lot. It bumped against the curb.

"Stop," the girl said.

"Hey," said Nadine. "You're freaking her out."

The Collector moved to the cart. Popping it up on two wheels, he shoved it over the curb onto the gravel shoulder of the road on the other side. Then he went over the curb himself and pushed the cart just a little farther away, right to the edge of the asphalt.

When Nadine looked back at the girl, she was stunned to see tears streaming down her cheeks. "I'm from Juarez," she said abruptly.

"Honey, it's alright," said Nadine, moving to her side. "He's...I don't know what he's doing. But he won't hurt you. He's never hurt anyone."

"That isn't true," said the Collector.

Nadine whirled. "What's wrong with you? Stop torturing this poor—"

"Come on," said the Collector to the crying girl, gesturing at the cart. "Go get it."

Wind whistled past, dry as dust, heavy as breath. The girl from Juarez stood and wept.

"Okay," he said. "I guess I better talk to the manager."

"Oh, God, you can't do that," the girl breathed.

"For fuck's sake," said Nadine, "I'll get it." Letting go of the crying girl's arm, she moved for the cart. The sensation didn't seize her until she'd reached the curb, had her foot off the ground and halfway over, and when it hit—like the yank of a leash, but *inside*, around her esophagus and also her hips, not painful, not strangling, but *permanent*, impermeable, inescapable as her own skin—Nadine gasped in surprise. She glanced toward the Collector, who looked even more surprised. Only then did she get scared.

"What is this?" she whispered.

He didn't answer. Her fear intensified. She tried starting over the curb again, realized she'd never make it, stumbled back.

"It's not so bad," said the girl with the braid, stepping forward. She took Nadine's hand. Tears had frozen on her wind-whipped cheeks like the tracks of something that had just raced past. Footprints in desert sand. "Really, it isn't."

Abruptly, the Collector grabbed Nadine around the waist as though he were going to sling her over his shoulder and break for the Jeep.

But the girl clamped tiny fingers around both of their arms, squeezed hard. "Don't," she said. She glanced toward the market, then down at her feet, where the gray tabby who'd jumped into the Jeep twined about her ankles.

Nadine felt the Collector let go. He caught her eyes, but not for long enough that she could see what he was thinking.

"Be right back," he said.

"What?" Nadine snapped.

But he'd already moved away, returning to the Jeep without turning around. And the girl with the braid was pulling Nadine gently across the lot toward the market, where the woman from the cash register had just emerged through the sliding doors. She had her book in one hand, a freshly lit cigarette in the other. Perching against the frost-caked front window, she settled into a cloud of her own breath, staring past Nadine and the braid-girl at the empty road. The pinprick moon.

Nadine felt herself start to panic. Or—no, *not* panic—which frightened her even more, because it made even less sense. "You can't be serious," she shouted to the Collector. "You're *leaving* me here?"

With one last stroke of her arm, the braid-girl left Nadine by the open sliding doors. The warmth from inside and the cold out here met on her skin, shooting shivers through her. In disbelief, she watched the Collector close himself into the Jeep, start the motor, and drive off into the night.

Later, and forever afterward *when she thought of those days—only six, the Collector assured her, and the longest of his life, though sometimes she suspected he was lying, that it had taken him much longer—Nadine would try to remember if she had ever actually seen the Ibis. Certainly, she remembered the cats. Dozens of them, their claws clattering over the linoleum as they chased each other down the aisles. Their head-bumps and purrs whenever any of the women who worked at the market knelt or sat to stock or just sit. Their very occasional, quiet meowing at the front windows, almost always just at dawn. Sometimes, even now, Nadine believed*

she could perfectly recall—could sketch from memory—every single one of their furry faces. Their whisker-twitches. Their eyes that glowed, radiated, overflowed.

Of course she remembered the women, too. Their faces, though she couldn't recall most of their names. Had she ever learned them? Had she told those women hers?

Had she known hers?

The braided girl was right, though. The days weren't bad. In fact—and this the worst, the scariest thing of all—they'd rung with laughter. With broom hockey games played with melting margarine stick-pucks, and tiniest-bubble-blowing contests using FreeAffix, the worst-tasting gum on Earth. With murmured, sleep-away-camp conversations while they all sat with their backs against the dairy cooler, the chill like the shock of diving into a snowdrift moments after fleeing an overheated house. Purifying, somehow. The conversations about nothing: proper ingredients for fry-bread, and how accordions sound from a window in a city; the first times they'd each tasted Yoo-hoo, and the stupidity of Stetsons; their far-away moms.

Did they eat? Sleep? Where had they slept? Nadine didn't know, didn't want to. What she did remember, could not get away from, was that feeling. That sense that every single moment was suffused with a sensation she'd forgotten she'd ever felt, and so hadn't been able to identify at the time. A specific sort of effortlessness. A restlessness so old and familiar and permanent, it felt like peace.

As though she'd been sucked all the way across the Atlantic and landed on her backside in the middle of the Burren, then hitchhiked back to Lissycasey, but this time with her sisters. If she'd had sisters.

As though she'd wandered through the drafty front door of her mother's house with her ma yelling, 'Jaysus, shut it!' and the apple-caramel cake already cut but still warm, just sitting there waiting.

He came back on a Sunday morning, was waiting on the mat when they unlocked the doors, newspaper in one hand and a steaming Styrofoam cup in the other. When he saw Nadine, who'd been stacking Duraflame logs beside the woman with the tampon-antennae, he grinned. His grin did nothing, she thought, to hide his relief. Then thought itself erupted through her, and she dropped the logs she'd been cradling and swayed in place. Tingling. Stinging. As though every inch of her had been asleep.

"Hi," he said. "So, okay. Cactus candy? No." He raised the cup. "But pinon nut coffee? *Yes.*" He took a steaming sip.

Glancing sideways, almost all the way awake, now, Nadine noted that her companion had frozen, too. Her tampon-antennae quivered. Her lower lip, too.

"He's here to help," Nadine said—forcefully, to convince herself, really, or maybe just remind herself, because he *really had fucking left her here*—and slid an arm around the woman's waist. "He's with me."

"With you..." the woman murmured.

"I'd like to see the Ibis, please," said the Collector.

The woman stiffened. Unless that was Nadine's own arm tightening. As far as she knew, she'd never heard that word spoken here, and yet she knew exactly whom he meant.

"You can't," said the woman beside her.

"Don't," said Nadine. And then, "You left me here."

"She's not back there," said her companion. "She's—"

"Back there?" The Collector gestured down the soup aisle toward the stockroom. "Right." He looked at Nadine and winked. Stupidly. Held up his hand, and something gold-ish flashed there, like a coin halfway to disappearing. Somehow, that was the moment Nadine saw what leaving her had cost him. How scared he'd been of what he'd find when he came back.

How scared he still was.

Down the aisle he went. Nadine followed. Her first impulse was to stop him, pull him back, but she couldn't quite catch him. Cats foamed and fled before him like a wake. He was still several feet from the stockroom doors when he slipped the whatever-it-was into his pocket and pulled out an actual, decades-old snub-nosed revolver. Nadine was still gaping at that—and thinking, mostly, that he wouldn't even know how take off the safety, was more likely to gun down the Raisin Bran than any actual person even if he got that thing to shoot—when the doors swung open and the Ibis appeared.

He didn't stop moving. Nadine would always remember that. She saw the impact hit him, his knees half-buckling and his back twitching while cats scattered and Nadine herself flinched and she fought her feet to a standstill, somehow made herself stay where she was.

The Ibis stood in a halo of her own light. Or maybe that was her hair, a shale-and-white cascade that tumbled all the way to her waist. Her tawny skin seemed to glow, too. Lion's skin under feathers.

The Collector stopped, lowered gun in one hand and pinon nut coffee in the other.

"Don't," Nadine whispered, edging closer. "Oh, please."

For a while, the Collector just stood there, took nervous sips of his coffee. He never once turned around.

"Safe's in the back," the Ibis finally told him, her shoulders high.

"You have something of mine," said the Collector. For a second, as he bent, Nadine thought he was going to kneel. Kiss the Ibis's hand. She thought that might be a good idea. Instead, he placed his coffee at his feet and straightened. "Someone."

The Ibis seemed to stretch as she straightened, looming over the Collector like a bobcat in a tree. Her smile flashed blinding-bright. "If she's here, she's not yours. Otherwise, it wouldn't work."

For the second time, the Collector's shoulders twitched. Again, he held his ground. Lifted the gun, though not to point it. "This either, I suppose."

"Oh, that will work. On me. It won't solve your problem, though."

"Thought not," the Collector muttered. He laid the gun atop a stack of soup cans. "Don't know why I brought it. Don't even know where I got it, actually. Do you, Nadine?"

Nadine, she thought dreamily. *Is me. Is* me...

For a time—though she would never know how long, time being lost to her, then—the Ibis and the Collector went on eying each other. Exactly like cats. The Ibis's next smile, when it came, wasn't without pity.

"You men. You grasping, stupid, lonely men." She turned back toward the stockroom. "Do try the cactus candy before you go."

"Tell me how it works," the Collector said.

Pleaded? Was he pleading?

The Ibis turned back, no longer smiling. "Sure," she said.

She told him. Not about herself, but her girls: the braided one, whose sister, cousin, and mother had had their lives ended for them in the alleys of

Ciudad Juarez, the cousin and mother on the same night in different alleys; the checkout-stand woman, who'd left the University of New Mexico to nurse the sick uncle who'd molested her as a child into his grave, then stopped here for string cheese on her way back to Albuquerque; the tampon woman, who'd literally walked off the Reservation because no one would drive her, with no destination in mind except elsewhere; the junkie hooker from El Paso who'd somehow cold-turkied herself one summer night—though not in time to save her hearing or one of her kidneys—and spent her off-shift hours humming to herself in the bakery aisle.

Others. So many others.

"But it's not *all* women," the Collector said, when the Ibis finally stopped. "It doesn't work on every woman."

"No, indeed. On very few, actually. They have to be worth saving. They have to deserve the home I've given them."

"And have left their old one."

"For good. That's right," said the Ibis, clearly surprised.

The Collector's voice came out sadder than Nadine had ever heard it. "And not fully settled in their new one." He didn't look at her then, either. That was another thing Nadine would remember.

"Right again. You are a rare one."

"And with whole worlds inside them."

The Ibis positively swelled, throwing her arms wide and gazing around at where her employees had gathered by the dairy cases, in the produce aisle. All of them watching, same as the cats that crouched under nearby shelving or hunched, submissive, at her feet. "That, most of all."

The Collector started to say something else, but she cut him off. She couldn't help herself, now.

"That's why I'm here. That's why I came."

"To trap. To imprison."

In mid-gesture, she froze. Swayed. "I thought you understood."

"I'm hoping you do," said the Collector. "I'm here to help."

For the first time Nadine could ever remember, the Ibis laughed. "Help. You? Scarecrow man? You already know better, I think. What help can you give, in comparison to mine?"

"I can help you let them go."

"But that's the beauty of it. That's what makes it so powerful. So unbreakable. Don't you see? It's *not me.* It's nothing I've done. I simply created the opportunity. Opened the doors. That's the secret. These women. All these beautiful, marvelous women. They *want* to stay." She raised her arms again, like a faith healer. Like an angel. "They want to."

"Unbreakable, you said?"

The Ibis looked too enraptured to answer or even listen.

The Collector just looked small. "It can never be broken."

"Not by me. Certainly not by you."

"That's what I thought."

There it was again. That undertone of regret. Nadine shuddered. Finally, the Collector did glance at her, then turned back to the Ibis. "That's why I had no choice but to call your brothers."

Silence flooded the market. As though whatever was coming had already happened, its impact pre-determined but not yet felt. Lightning before thunder.

"You did what?" the Ibis whispered. Arms still outstretched.

"I'm sorry," said the Collector. "I know you meant well. They're on their way."

"But...how could you...how did you even learn who..."

"You should go now. You really don't have long. And I have an option. I can..."

The Ibis lowered her arms. From everywhere, cats—dozens of them—crawled from their hiding places, edging nearer, bumping each other, meowing their confusion, if that's what it was. Raising trembling fingers to her lips, the Ibis stared at the Collector. Everything in Nadine screamed, *Run.*

But all the Ibis said was, "Why? Why would you do that? Do you understand what they'll do? Never mind to me. To..." She had her arms out again, but no longer looked like an angel. Too earthbound, somehow, but majestic at the same time. She really did look like a mother bird, trapped in her nest because of the chicks she'd hatched. Flapping her wild, desperate wings at the threat. "Do you know what they'll do to her?" She gestured at the girl with the braid. Then the tampon woman. "And to her? Oh my god, what have you..."

Abruptly, she dropped into a crouch, snapping her fingers at the cats while also waving her women close. "Come. All of you. We have to hide. Hurry."

Even before she realized she was moving toward the Ibis, Nadine experienced a shot of knee-jellying terror. It happened at the moment she saw Normal's face, and realized that whatever he'd planned, it wasn't working.

He shook his head. Turned again to the Ibis, voice more urgent, and said again, "I have a way. I brought—"

"We can't wait, thanks to you." She was pushing cats through the swinging door into the stockroom, waving her employees closer, her whole frame a whirl of motion.

"Please," the Collector said. "Listen. For everyone's sake. If these women really want to stay...what do they need you for?"

Once more, the Ibis stopped moving. From her knees, she looked up. Flapped. Nadine felt herself lean toward her.

"If you're right," said the Collector, "and they want to stay, you can go. Lead your brothers away. That way, they can stay. If they really want."

For a moment, the Ibis actually seemed to consider. Or else she was about to hurl herself at him. Eventually, she shrugged. "I didn't invent it." In the blackness of her pupils, Nadine saw flashes, like fireflies in a cave. A wildness she'd never—no, rarely—glimpsed in another living person. "All I did was set it loose. To save these deserving, beautiful creatures from the world."

"From the Winged," the Collector said.

The word pinged in Nadine's ears like a pebble against ice. Then again, and again, as the ice in her head began to crack, and the cracks multiplied.

Winged. Winged. Winged.

The fucking Winged. The Ibis's brothers were the fucking...

"You contacted the Winged?" she whispered. But neither Normal nor the Ibis was listening.

"Yes, from them," the Ibis hissed. "Jesus, someone has to. And also from themselves. From everything they've been taught to want. And they have learned. They've *learned.* They're free now."

The Collector laughed. At the irony, of course. But Nadine didn't. Because in a way—in a whole lot of ways—it was true.

"Laugh all you want," said the Ibis, arms full of cats, nodding her employees through the doors. "But if you really called my brothers, you will have done nothing for yourself. It won't get you the woman you imagined as your possession back."

"I never imagined that," the Collector murmured. "Not once, ever."

"You might have gotten us all killed, though. It's possible you've achieved that. But it won't return anything to you. Because if she's here, she's already made her choice."

The Collector's shoulders sagged. He glanced at Nadine again.

It wasn't working. Because as the Ibis had said: it wasn't his choice to make. In Nadine's brain, mouth, skin, that word still echoed. *Winged.* Like the ringing after a roadside bomb. Not that she'd ever heard or been near one, though she'd seen aftermath. That burned-out cottage in that Connemeara field where she'd somehow been let loose to play, and where she'd found ashes, and in the ashes bits of what she'd eventually decided were ears. When she was very young, and had two parents, and her country was still sawing itself in half.

Like this one, now?

The words spilled from her mouth—her choice made—before she even realized she was saying them.

"That's why *I* called them."

For the first time—lightning-fast, like a nictitating lid flicking shut and open—the Ibis blinked. Then she set down the cats she was holding. Straightened to her full height. "What?"

"That was the plan all along. Get me in here and under your spell, but with your brothers' details in my pocket. So I could *actually* choose, unlike the rest of your captives. Tell her, hon."

But Normal had gone blank. He looked as baffled as the Ibis. In other circumstances, Nadine might have thought it funny. She had no idea if what she'd done would work, was acting on instincts she wasn't even sure she was feeling. The only thing certain was the threat. Threats. The leash around her neck. The Winged coming.

"You didn't really feel it," the Ibis snarled. "You aren't one of us. Weren't worthy of the choice, and therefore never had one."

"Oh, I felt it. And yeah, right, you're bang on: I'm not one of you. Because I *choose not to be.* So do they." She shot a glance at the woman in the braid. The tampon woman. Her friends.

Sisters.

Suddenly—finally—the Collector nodded. "Exactly right. Yep. Worked like a charm, too. We had to make sure you were who we thought. Make sure we were giving your brothers reliable intel. One doesn't want the Winged thinking you're messing with them."

"Monsters," the Ibis whispered, wild eyes grabbing Nadine's, which set her shaking. "You most of all. Do you realize what you've done? What even are you?"

Somehow, Nadine held herself still. Even though absurdly, she was now crying. "One mama lion chasing off another."

"*Bitch!*" the Ibis shrieked. "Shut your whoring mouth. Monster. Blind, stupid, whoring..." She had her arms out again, striding forward while cats squealed under her feet.

How soon did the Ibis realize what she'd done? Nadine knew only what happened—to all of them—the moment she started shrieking. It really did feel like a leash snapping loose. Hand at her neck releasing. Her throat falling open. The outside world—the vast, ruthless, ordinary world—rushing in.

The spell broken. Not by Nadine, but the Ibis herself.

Not that she knew it, yet. Whirling for the stockroom, she went on spitting and screaming her rage. Also terror, Nadine knew. And damn right. "Forget them," she shrieked toward the rest of her girls. "There's no time. Come on, darlings." She vanished through the double doors.

The Collector turned to Nadine, eyes flickering open and shut as though trying to blink out sunspots. "You're quite brilliant," he said. Then he was talking to the women around him. "Don't be scared. Don't think. Don't worry about the boundary, it's gone. I don't know for how long. Just go."

Even so, not one of them waited. They were all experiencing what Nadine just had. Their old lives engulfing them. As one, they dropped whatever they had in their hands and ran.

Nadine would remember only fragments of those next, hurtling moments. The market's front doors sliding open. The blast of frigid air against her face, seemingly shoving her back. The realization that Normal wasn't with her. The glance behind to see him still at the stockroom doors, shouting through them, waving that coin or whatever it was so that it flashed in the air.

"I have a way. You don't have to stay!"

What was he saying? What did he mean?

Then him racing down the aisle toward her, grabbing her hand. Fleeing across the lot and screaming for the braided girl, telling her to *come on*, jump in the Jeep with them. That exact moment, seconds later, as the Jeep barreled past the exit onto blessed, empty road, when she grabbed the dashboard with both hands and closed her eyes and held tight to the faux-vinyl, sucking in the smell of nowhere, nothing-to-see-here New Mexico.

And the memory, slamming into her moments later, of the instant before she'd thrown herself in the Jeep. The sounds behind her, from everywhere. Audible even over the whistling wind and the engine as it coughed to life.

The cats reaching the curb at the edge of the lot in a pack. Pride. Leaping into the air to cross it. Screaming as they froze, died, cracked to pieces...

"It really was mostly protective," the Collector told her, days later, in the Las Cruces hotel room where they'd holed up since leaving the braided girl— Viviana, a name given right at the moment the girl left them, seemingly as new in her own mouth as it felt in Nadine's ears— across from the pedestrian border checkpoint over the Rio Grande.

He poured her yet another cup of pinon nut coffee. Had already told her he was going to keep making her drink it until she agreed that it was good.

"Protective." She was still cocooned in blankets she could not seem to leave. She'd long since decided she did like the coffee, but she wasn't going to tell Normal that, yet. "But how did you even know she was there? *We* didn't see her until that night. At least, I don't remember seeing her."

"I didn't know," the Collector said. He made like he might touch her, and she shrank back. She was still furious about his leaving her, though she knew she shouldn't be. Probably shouldn't be.

"Nadine, all I knew was what I saw in those girls. and then in you, that first night. I knew that whatever had hold of you, it was powerful. Not something I could break by just carrying you out of there. It had to be powerful, if it was stopping you. Stopping *those* women."

"But..." Nadine stared over the rim of her cup. A new round of shivering rippled up her spine, and yet, somehow, she held the cup straight, the coffee un-spilt. Its cocoa-y smell sweetening the air. "How did you get onto her?"

The Collector shrugged. "Everyone in the area knew she was there. Given who she turned out to be—and the people she escaped from—that's hardly surprising, is it? I mean, the Winged...there are so many more of them than anybody wants to admit. Marching, making pamphlets. Surrounding Navajos every time they venture off the reservation. Pasting *Su casa por alla* stickers on the back of any Hispanic people's trucks or cars they come across. Storing weapons. Getting elected to schoolboards. And your woman's family... I mean, they started it all. They say they're taking New Mexico for New Mexicans, and God help anyone who points out the irony in the name of the place itself, let alone..." He shrugged again.

"The Winged," Nadine said into her coffee, clasping the cup tight as she shivered.

"As in eagles. Winged USA. Yeah."

"Bunch of barse hairs. They don't even know what they're destroying."

"They are thick and manky barse hairs," the Collector said.

Startled, Nadine stared at him. Couldn't help laughing, though the laugh didn't stop her shivering, or make her less angry. "Look at you. Almost like you've listened to me somewhere in our five thousand days together."

"I'm always listening," he said.

"Bollocks."

"The hard part wasn't realizing that woman—your Ibis— was there, or who she had to be. The hard part was understanding that she really believed exactly what she told you. She was out to save you all, from everything and everyone. From families like hers and the monsters they're unleashing. That... thing she did to you...turned loose...it only works in kindness. That was the piece I needed. That's why it broke—why you broke it, and I couldn't—when she got vengeful."

"There was nothing kind about what she did to the cats."

"Ah, but that's just it." He tilted forward, enthusiasm for discovery manifesting even now. "She didn't *do* that. At least, she wouldn't say so. All she did was construct the boundary. Build the wall. A safe haven in a world almost utterly devoid of them. If any of her guests—*daughters,* really—were fool enough to try and leave the paradise she'd created for them...really decided to leave Heaven..." He shrugged.

Nadine shook her head, put the coffee down on the night table as her wrists, then her arms started shaking once more. "Why couldn't they just turn back into whoever they'd been? Why did that have to happen to them once the boundary was broken?"

The Collector watched until her shuddering slowed. It took a long time.

"I don't know. I didn't know that would happen. I didn't even know what the cats were, or *who* they were, until you told me. Maybe, when they... changed... maybe, at that point, they really did become hers. Or the property of whatever she'd conjured up. Maybe they could never go back after that."

"Creatures of Paradise," Nadine said, tears forming. "Members of the Pride."

The Collector stared so long, but so quietly, that the tears never came. Finally, he nodded. "Creatures of Paradise. In a supermarket Eden. Amazing where Edens really can grow."

In spite of herself, Nadine leaned forward, was about to grab and kiss him, when he said, "Unless."

She sat back. "Unless?"

"Unless the transformation energy—cat spell, or whatever—was something else entirely. Something the Ibis created to protect *herself,* from what *she* feared most."

"*Cats*?"

"The women those cats had been. Women who'd tasted all she had to offer—home, Heaven, somewhere free of her brothers and their army, call it what you will—and chose the world anyway."

Nadine thought of Lissycasey, then. And also of the little houses she and the Collector had passed on the Reservation in the hours before they met Nartana. All those leaning walls and flaking roofs. Junked cars in snow. There really is a difference, she thought, between accretion and collecting. The one simply an accumulation of detritus from the life you'd lived. The other a collage of bits scavenged from other people's lives and hung on your wall like a mirror. One accidental, the other willed. The home you were born into, and the one you made. Which was the truer?

Then she thought of the Ibis's home. The one she'd been born into. The family she'd escaped.

"Tell me one thing," she whispered. "You didn't really call them, did you? You didn't tell her brothers where she was. You wouldn't."

The Collector let go of her hands, looked down at the bed, then over her shoulder at the curtained window. "I wasn't going to leave you. But I gave her a way out. Really."

"You *did* call them."

"I left it with her. I hope she took it."

Nadine stared. "Can you go somewhere else for a while, now?"

"Okay," he said. But he stayed where he was, and took her hand again, and held onto it until she held him back.

INFINITY DREAMS

1

Even as she finishes, Nadine feels the prickling these memories always give her. It comes from the soles of her feet, the back of her throat, every hair on her arms and the cilia in her inner ears and the bang of her heart. A sensation sprung directly from that experience that has suffused every other one since, and the ones before it, too. Equal parts guilt, longing, release, relief, loneliness, anguish, amazement, fury, confusion, revelation. Love. She has never gotten comfortable with what it signifies or means, or even to whom. But she has staked her marriage on it.

Except for the actual getting married part.

Why has she told this story to the Rev?

He's just sitting on the edge of Tony's chair, hands clasped around one crossed knee, rocking back and forth and laughing. "He hopes she took it," he says. His laugh gets wilder, also nastier. Sprouts teeth. Releasing his knee, he flops back against the chair and claps his hands. "Oh, wow."

"He saved us." *Has she said that already? She has, more than once.* She does it again, voice rising against that laugh as though shouting into wind. "He saved us all."

Still guffawing, the Rev wipes at his eyes, rocks forward again, waits to speak until he's caught her gaze. *"Meow,"* he says.

"That's not fair. That is not fecking fair. He couldn't have known that. And it wouldn't have mattered if he did."

"As far as you know. You were bewitched. Be-Ibised. You had an excuse. What's his?"

"He saved everyone that could be saved. He helped more people in that one moment than you have or will in your whole skinty life."

His leap catches her off guard, hurling him off the chair as though he's powered by jetpack. He isn't really hovering over the floor, just seems to be, and now Nadine's up, too, eyes darting around the room for the Collector as though she might...*what, exactly*? *Shield him? Put her hands over his ears to keep him from hearing? Whisper 'there, there' while he stares into that goddamn clock*?

The Rev's lunge has carried him past her into the kitchen. He's clapping, barking out laughs, yanking drawers open to rifle the silverware. He opens the cabinet over the range, takes down the bag of powdered sugar and shakes it. Little wisps escape the bag and puff around him as though he's summoning specters, and Nadine remembers at least part of the reason she told him that last story.

To stall. Give Spook time to get his covert ass up here. *Where* is *he*?

The Rev has gotten into the pots, now. He takes out each one, weighs it, slides his fingers up and down handles in a way that's more teenager-playing-air-guitar than obscene, but no less unsettling for that.

"He knows," says the Rev, wrist-deep in the rubber-band-and-bills drawer. Rattling things around, mouth moving but eyes riveted to what he's doing. Not like a teenager at all, Nadine realizes. More one of the old dudes washing mah-jongg tiles at the back tables in Chinatown in the city. Trying to feel for luck and dragons through the wooden flip-sides. "I was wrong about you. I thought you somehow just didn't understand. Couldn't see, even with everything right in front of you. But he *knows*. So he thinks it's his property to parcel out. Or control. He actually thinks he *can* control it, or that he gets a say. Oh, man. He '*hopes she took it*.' I bet he does."

"I think you should go now," Nadine snaps. "I think it is way past time you got out of our house and left us—"

The rubber band drawer slams shut as the Rev whirls. "Did you ever even check?"

Nadine shudders, wants to glance again toward the front door, see if Spook has shown up. But she can't look away.

"You haven't, have you? Nadine, the great rooter-outer. Causeway Quester. Seeker of Knowing. You never even checked to see if the Ibis is alive."

Again, his lunge catches her off guard. But he's still not coming for her or even returning to the living room. He vanishes down the hall toward the den and their bedroom.

Getting moving feels like pulling free of cement, or escaping the Family Pride parking lot. Just so much harder than it should be. "Normal!" she shouts. She considers veering into the kitchen for a knife, but decides that would take too long and also that she'd wield it about as effectively as the Collector did his pistol (which she'd never once seen since that day with the Ibis; was that what he'd left her?). She can hear the Rev pulling books off shelves, shaking things. Kicking things.

"Normal!" she shouts again, lurching toward the hall, and spots him.

The Collector isn't back there, hasn't even left this room. He's sitting cross-legged in the corner, facing the floor-to ceiling window like a little boy being punished. Slowly, rhythmically, like the pendulum of a clock, he rocks back, then forward until his forehead taps the glass. His eyes are open, but god knows what he sees. The ghost of himself out there in the dark.

"You don't even know what he brought, do you?" the Rev calls. He's still in the den, at least.

Kneeling by the Collector, touching his hair, Nadine leans her own forehead into the window. She can feel the vibrations when he bumps the glass.

"Brought," she murmurs.

"Right. I mean, I get it. That is, if either you of were normal or stupid people, I'd get it. I'm not qualified to comment, obviously, but that's got to be one of those marriage minefields, right? Did or didn't my partner sacrifice a desperate woman to the Winged? Have another human being murdered? You're right. Better to narrow your perspective. Another successful mission. Nadine successfully re-collected. Nadine and the Collector reunited, over and out. But hey, he hopes she got away. He prays she realized what he brought her, and used it to..."

Nadine has no idea what the Rev is pawing through back there. But she hears when he stops. Can tell the by sudden, total silence. "Oh, for God's sake," she hears him murmur. "He fucking *wishes*." His laugh, this time, sounds totally different. A little kid's laugh. His own laugh from when he was little. From when he ventured out into the Paris night and found her a street-crepe.

The Collector's forehead bangs window glass so hard that Nadine's bounces off it. She grabs him by the shoulders to still him, checks the glass for cracks, and so sees what happens next in reflection. As though *through* glass, in a crystal ball. The Rev erupting from the hall, making straight for the wishing-tree clock. He reaches it right as it goes off. Blows its kiss.

For a single second, that seems to hold him. Freeze him there in transparent amber, and Nadine has a notion, a full-on spider-sense blast, and staggers to her feet. She still has no plan, still doesn't grab for a knife or anything heavy, but she's moving, now, stumbling toward the Rev until he straightens. His hands toward the clock, wrap around its softly shining not-gold pendulum.

"No," Nadine says, but this time she's the one frozen. Suspended over a chasm of dread she only now realizes has been there since the day the Collector staggered home from his *I Love a Mystery* quest. Since before that, most likely.

Also, she's paralyzed by warring, simultaneous urges: to hurl herself at the Rev and stop him, or to drape herself over the Collector like camouflage netting. As if that would do any good. As if either action could do any good.

Or absolve him from whatever he'd done. And her, from not finding out.

Too late, now. She watches the Rev's fingers slide up the pendulum to the notch at its top, right at the base of the wishing-tree trunk, and curl around the thin part. The neck. As though he's strangling a cat. In one motion, with no visible strain, he rips the rod from its casing.

The whole room—world—goes silent. But it's the same silence that has always been here, Nadine thinks. Wants to think. The clock makes noise only at the quarter hour, and even then, all it does is breathe. The Collector produces sound now only when he's babbling or singing. The perpetual fog makes no noise, ever. For just that last instant, she lets herself believe nothing has changed.

Clutching his prize in both hands, the Rev holds it up. "Look," he says. He turns it one way, the other. The rod catches light, shades it redder. With one finger, he probes the half-inch gouge along its right side. "Hmm. Did he do this, do you think? Save a little piece, because he knew better than to use it all? Or, oh, this is what he gave the Ibis! Once again, he knew so amazingly much! And yet, all he could think to do with what he had and what he knew was *hoard* it."

The light in that rod is mesmerizing, mostly because it seems to sink into the metal instead of reflecting from it. As though the rod is actually a pool, and inside, down at the bottom, is a river, and that river rolls away into some far and soft red-gold ocean.

"He never hoarded anything in his life," Nadine murmurs. "Except eggs." Her smile is unconscious; she barely feels it.

"No. You're right. He's just so arrogant that he decided he could and should *protect* us all from it. Well, your job is done now, sir." Waving the rod once more, he sucks it into his fingers in a gesture almost identical to the one the Collector made as he moved to the back of the Super Pride to meet the Ibis.

See the coin? See the coin vanish?

"You don't know it yet, Nadine," the Rev says, without malice or anger or even contempt, suddenly. "But you're going to thank me. I sure as hell thank you. I mean it. Thank you both."

The Collector has stayed seated. He's no longer banging his head against the glass, just seems to have slumped down onto himself. A Collector marionette with its strings cut. Performance finished. Nadine realizes she is crying. Has been. She has no idea for what. Or rather, for which thing. There are so many.

Every minute, for everyone alive, there are just so many things.

"Thank you?" She sounds angrier than she feels. She has no idea what she actually feels other than heartbreak. "For what?"

The clock rod vanishes into the Rev's pocket. His smile erupts on his face. The found-a-night-crepe smile, times a million.

"Giant's Causeway, ho!" he says, and bolts out the door into the night.

Leaving silence. Stillness. Their house, exactly one clock-rod emptier than it has been. The tears in Nadine's eyes are like a cellophane wrap, sealing away her world. Separating her from it. The fog out there enfolds the house, burying the twenty-plus years she has spent here and the life she loved. Her prime, she supposes. That was it, just there. That blink. Those two decades. Not so bad a prime, even if it has left her home bereft, her most important relationship a memory and a duty, her partner destroyed, her place in the world unclear, her future unimaginable.

Like everyone's, she thinks. Or almost everyone's. When and why had she started to imagine—the way most lucky people imagine—that her prime was going to be different? That it would lead her life somewhere, add up to something, leave residue?

A snarl explodes from her throat, floats out the open door into the mist, dissipates immediately. She snarls again, pounds the back of Tony's chair. This feeling, she is quite sure, is nothing whatsoever like being raped, or even robbed. Viviana and Binna would howl with laughter at the thought, then mock her for melodramatics.

Nevertheless, something has been taken. She should call the police, she guesses.

And tell them what? *Well, yes, I did invite him, Officer. Yeah, yes, I gave him cookies, but only Rich Teas. He stole the tongue from my cuckoo clock.* She opens her mouth to snarl again, whirls for her phone to call off Spook, and smacks elbows first into the Collector.

He's just standing there, hands in pockets, smiling at her.

Smiling at her.

"Better get a coat." He nods toward the windows. "Looks cold."

Nadine gapes. Stands there. He kisses her, then nudges her aside. "Hi," he says. "Come on."

Hi. "Hi?" Nadine says. Sways. The second time she says it feels like firing a gun. *"Hi*? You *feck away off,* cumquat. Turn around!"

He turns around.

"Is that you?"

"Always has been."

"Really, now. Sure it has. Because to me, Normal, you seemed more like—"

"I brought some guests. I didn't mean to."

She stares at him. Just like that, the old feeling—the most familiar one she knows other than longing—rises from wherever she has stored it these last eighteen months.

This tingling, anticipatory bewilderment.

This barbed wonder.

"Guests."

And there's his bewilderment, right on cue. Right there on his wan, weary face. Alongside—no, infusing—his smile. The very source of that smile. "Like I said, I didn't mean to. But I couldn't just turn them out. For everyone's sake. Nadine we have to—"

The front door was already open, but somehow Spook comes crashing through it anyway. He's shaking wetness from his head, calling out, and the white in his beard winks like radio tower lights. His trench coat flaps around him, thudding against the frame as he stumbles to a stop.

"Nadine I'm here, I'm here, are you alright, I came as…got here as soon as…"

One by one, like planks on a wooden bridge in a cartoon, his words give way beneath him. He takes in the tableaux. Spy Santa, wreathed in fog. Bearing no gifts. Wearing two different shoes. One of them galoshes.

So…galosh?

"Oh, good," says the Collector. "You we definitely need. Coming? Hurry. We don't have much time." He's talking to both of them, but it's her hand he grabs. Barely leaving her slack to grab her coat off the hook, he pulls her out into the misty, drizzly night.

2

Every time the windshield wipers flick, Nadine feels her world snap into place, reconstitute itself, then instantly start melting again. She keeps staring at the Collector's face. He keeps sensing that, turning, grinning. The second he does, the grin drains away, sliding back into blankness.

Flick, and he's back.

Flick, he's gone.

Flick. Back.

Flick.

"You're really back," she whispers.

"I never left."

"Grand. You sure fooled me."

"I didn't mean to. I had to…keep my mind where it was."

"Meaning not with me. Meaning you *did* in fact leave."

"Meaning I was busy. I couldn't...I knew where I was. Mostly. I knew you were there. I was so glad you were there, you have no idea how glad. But I really had to… I was distracted. Let's put it that way."

"Distracted."

His smile, this time, is more than a grin, and the wipers can't whisk it away. Too much Normal in it. "Was it really so different than any other days with me?"

Nadine punches him on the shoulder, hard enough that he jerks the Jeep across the meridian, then almost up on two wheels as he straightens them out, which is what finally causes Spook to look up from whatever he has been doing back there. The black, knobby device cradled in his lap has winking yellow lights all over it. Ridiculous puffy headphones balloon from his temples, as though his ears are blowing bubbles.

"Whoa," he says, and the Collector catches his eyes in the mirror. Smiles at him, too.

"Sweet Jesus," Nadine murmurs, watching it happen. The two of them reacquainting themselves with each other, like cats. *How can there be so many of these people,* she wonders? *How does she keep finding them?*

Is she one of them?

"Dude," Spook says. The Spook equivalent of smiling. Or *meow.*

"Hey, man."

Nadine glares at both of them. Spook doesn't even notice, but the Collector tries out a wink. She winces. "I can't decide if I want to climb over there into your lap or kick you off a cliff."

At least he doesn't wink again, or grin either. "I accept your decision either way."

Light rain ghosts over the road, and logging trucks clog the slow lanes. Lighter clouds mark where the moon must be, though Nadine can't see it. She has so many questions, such as where they're going and at what point, exactly, he decided that. But what spills out of her mouth is, "Normal, what *happened*?"

To her surprise—as though it all just occurred, and he just got home and has been waiting to tell her, which in a way *is* what has happened—he answers immediately. "It was this awful house in the hills right outside Chico. Down one of those streets that crosses those little bridges and changes its name ten times, so you can't even say where you are, exactly. You know those streets?"

"So, a totally run of the mill you-and-me house."

She expects a nod. Instead he shudders, shakes his head. "Location, yes. House, not really. Not at all. It was more like a frat house. Or an ex-frat house. Sagging gutters, shingles all warping away from the frame, porch in the process of sliding off the front. Yard full of broken glass."

"Charming."

"Inside was worse. Beer, barf, and spiders, that's what it smelled like."

"Spiders have smells?"

He doesn't smile. "These spiders."

"What were you *doing* there, Normal? More to the point, why wasn't I there?"

For the first time since the moment he resurfaced—since he kissed her gaping mouth in their living room, *less than hour ago*—he reaches for her. Touches her hand without taking it, leaves his fingers there a few seconds, retracts. "My biggest fear, you know? I never want to bore you."

"Bore me?"

"It wasn't a you-and-me trip. This was nothing interesting. Nothing even unusual. It was a pay-the-bills trip. Some run-of-the-mill collector's Holy Grail, not one of ours. You know *I Love a Mystery*?"

"Yes. I am aware of this fact about you. It turns out I, too, love—"

"The show. The radio show. From the forties?"

He glances at her lap, and she realizes he's expecting her to flip up her laptop, get tapping. Instead, she smirks, waits until he sees that. "*If you like high adventure...*" she intones, in her best approximation of that voice. Just one of the voices she'd once imagined as her da's. Or *a* da's. After hers was gone.

From the backseat, Spook pipes up. "*If you like intrigue.*"

"*Stealth* of intrigue," Nadine corrects.

The Collector bursts out laughing and joins them. "*If you like blood and thunder...*"

She waits just long enough to let him doubt her, then makes the thunder noise. All three of them laugh. As though it's wacko-couple's-night again on Spook's boat. As if they just had one last week.

"Actually, technically, that's the wrong show," the Collector says. "That's *Adventures by Morse.* They did that after *I Love a Mystery*. I think *Mystery* just started with a—"

"Right. Well. Are you by any chance remembering the last line of the *Adventures by Morse* opening?"

When he finally figures it out, he doesn't smile. At least that saves him another shoulder-punch. "*Come with me.*"

"Aye. So."

He doesn't apologize. Of course he doesn't. He looks at her, though. At one time, she would have interpreted that as gauging her anger, like a little boy. But it's more just saying hello. Like a cat, again. Telling her he loves her, the best way he knows.

She sighs. "Beer, barf, and spiders…"

Off he goes. "It was a really old house, though. The woman who called, her father apparently knew about us. He'd just died. It was his house, but he was letting his grandson and his friends use it while they were at Chico State, and—"

"I'm remembering that greatest fear you say you have."

He skips ahead. "This woman said she'd found a box in the basement full of reel-to-reel canisters, and a note saying to get in touch with us. A couple of the canisters had Post-its on them. *The Case of the Transplanted Castle. Stairway to the Sun.*"

This time, when he waits, she does open her computer. He keeps his smile to himself, so at least she doesn't have to swat him. Her search takes three seconds.

"The lost episodes."

"Some of them. Maybe all of them."

"The ones the old time radio loons have spent 75 years hunting."

"Those."

"And knowing me, as you claim to, you decided, *ach*, lost stories, adventure, blood and thunder, she'd have no interest in those."

"Hearing them? Sure. In our house, in the fog."

Another glance. She can't help it, meets his smile with hers. "Over custard creams."

"Egg breakfast."

"Goddamn you," she says. Because he's here and enraging her and she's laughing.

"But finding them? Or, in this case, fetching them? A thing everyone already knows was probably *somewhere*? Already knows pretty much what's on them, and that they'll be less interesting, in themselves, than their absence?" He shrugs. "Not exactly Giant's Causeway material."

In the backseat, Spook scoots forward. "Hey. Whoa. Listen."

Unplugging his headphones, he holds up the black box with the knobs. It sits inert in his hands like a flipped-over beetle in its shell. Dead or playing dead.

"Wow," Nadine says.

"Oh. Damn it."

She half expects him to shake the box, thwack the top of it. But he just turns a knob.

"*Seven*," says the box, in that voice Nadine has heard a dozen times on Spook's houseboat. Blank, flat, female murmur, all the more alien because it *is* human. "*Six...nine...three...seven...null...eight...three...null...four...null...*"

"So?" Nadine finally snaps.

"It's your station," the Collector says. "It's your friend there, saying her numbers."

"There are more of them," says Spook. He slides his headphones on again and sits back, closing his eyes.

What is it, right then, that causes Nadine's shiver? Nothing the Collector has said, at least not yet. Not that voice, no matter how many numbers it's saying. Suddenly, though, Nadine has to clench her arms to her sides to keep from whipping around, ripping the headphones off Spook's head, and letting her listen some more. Or else grabbing the box and hurling it out of the Jeep into the woods.

The Collector feels it, too. He's not looking at her anymore, or at the road, either, even though his eyes are aimed that way.

"Normal," she barks, and he snaps out of it. Misting rain and dark billow around the Jeep, settle behind them, as though they're hurtling through some giant phantom wheat field. Something newly sprung from the earth and not quite solid. Yet.

Touching the Collector's arm—to keep him anchored, and to feel skin—Nadine blows out breath. The whole insane day hums inside her. "I assume you found those canisters," she says.

"In the basement. Right where our caller said they'd be." He lifts a hand off the steering wheel, takes hers, squeezes hard. Lets go. "The boxes were disgusting. Wet, rank, falling apart. Full of spiders. But the canisters were perfect. All sealed and weirdly clean. It gave me the strangest feeling when I picked them up. Like this whole thing was a joke. Snipe hunt. You know what it reminded me of?"

"Paris," says Nadine immediately.

Once again, it isn't anything they've said that triggers the shudder. It's the fact that *he* shudders. Then nods. Which means she has it right.

"I didn't like being down there," he continues. "Don't get me wrong, it was just a basement. Lights, rug. Perfectly comfortable. But..."

"Normal," Nadine snaps again.

"Right. Sorry. I pried open a canister, the *Stairway to the Sun* one. I pulled out my trusty portable, unfoldable reel-to-reel player."

"We have a trusty portable unfoldable reel-to-reel player?"

On a regular day, in full command of his faculties, the Collector would have ignored that. But today he can't help himself; he grins. Because he's at least as happy—as relieved—to be here as she is to have him. "I ordered one, long time ago. Seemed like something we should have."

Nadine taps a finger against her teeth. "Baffling construction. Impossible-to-find replacement parts, Profoundly limited use. I agree."

But his grin has gone. Also, his eyes have misted over again. Blurring him.

"Normal," she says.

He shudders. Surfaces. "It took me longer than expected to thread it. That tape was... wet. Except not. Slippery like it was wet, but with no wetness. I got it in the end. And then I just sat there. I didn't...I couldn't get myself to switch the player on. Ridiculous."

"Paris," Nadine whispers.

"Then this giant—I mean giant, like snow globe-sized—daddy longlegs dances up out of that tape onto my machine. The only thing I could think to do to scare him off was hit the switch."

This time, even though he's quiet, he stays behind his eyes. Nadine can see him in there, staring into the dark as though it were a slide on a microfiche machine. Something old, miraculous, half-forgotten. Or never truly seen.

"It took me maybe twenty seconds to realize that the recording wasn't what the canister said. It wasn't those shows. Close, though. Better in a way. Those were Doc's and Reggie's voices, all right. But they were just rehearsing. I recognized the lines. You would, too. They were doing the famous one, 'The Thing That Cries in the Night.' They kept laughing, cracking each other up. It was kind of beautiful. I didn't even notice the hiss. Not at first. Then I figured it was tape noise."

He pauses. Doesn't look at her, doesn't shudder.

"Then I realized I wasn't actually hearing it. I was *feeling* it."

Her usual response—the word *what*, said just so, half-reprimand, half-laugh, all amazement-as-encouragement—forms automatically on Nadine's lips. But what she says, in a voice so small she barely recognizes it as her own, is, "Yeah."

At least that still triggers her favorite response: the sideways glance, brimming with startled, grateful connection. Collector-speak for *I love you*.

"You know what I mean? You've felt it, too?"

"Almost," Nadine says. "I'm pretty sure I'm about to."

"You have. I know you have. In Paris."

Nadine nods. "In Jolene."

"In Detroit. Right after—no, right before the baker shot our *Lebensborn*."

"On Spook's boat. I mean, on that other boat. That night in the fog with Blaine Fury singing."

Somehow, the Collector is nodding, flashing his *I-love-you* look, and shivering all at the same time. "Turns out, those were just whiffs. Gentle breezes. But this..."

Momentarily, she thinks he has gone silent again. She reaches out to shake him but doesn't have to. He's right there. Gathering himself.

"It kept coming, Nadine. I couldn't move. I couldn't shut the damn player off. The noise didn't get louder. It didn't get harsher. It just poured into me. I don't know how else to say it. I could feel my blood fizzing. Like it was...carbonating me. Irradiating me. I can't...I have no idea how long it took, but I finally got my fingers to the Off switch and flicked it. But it jammed. I didn't know what to do."

"Take the headphones off?"

"Too far. For my hands. Which were...glowing. I think. I started getting warm all over, especially down in my pants, and—"

"Right, so, a little T much I even for this story." She's joking because she can see him tensing, shivering so hard she's worried his skin will fly off him like batter from a beater.

But he's still him. Oblivious to everything but what he's talking about. He looks at her like he has no idea what she means, which almost makes her laugh. Even now.

"Hands and pants glowing. Okay. Go on, hon."

"That warmth. The fizz. That's why it took me so long to realize." Digging in his jeans pocket, he pulls out a sliver of not-quite-copper.

Nadine stares. Opens her mouth as memory rushes into or out of her, she can't even tell which. Because she has been blind. Stupid. So blind and stupid she has believed herself smart her whole life. The wishing tree clock, its pendulum, that glint in the Collector's fingers on his way to confront the Ibis, the flicker of reflected sunlight on the Seine.

Beside the Seine. Where there was so much more of it.

"From Binna's key. You had the clock made with metal from Binna's key." It's as though she has kicked over a wall which has toppled into another wall, and now walls she never even knew existed are collapsing everywhere, leaving her naked to the actual air, which she has never before breathed. "You had it all along. You took it that first day. The day we met."

"No. Of course not. They took the key, remember? The dancing fat guy and his son. Binna got the lock. I took the hinge."

"You've had it all this time. You knew what it could do."

"Okay, that's ridic—"

"You *knew*."

His whole being slumps. Except his hands, which grip tight on the wheel. "I knew feck-all, as my beloved has taught me to say. I liked the color."

"Normal, I swear to God, I will marmalade you."

"Have you seen that color? Anywhere else? Anyway, it doesn't matter."

"It matters to me."

"This matters more. Please believe me. I need you."

The magic words, Nadine thinks, not without a flash of self-loathing. Three little words, and her anger's gone. No apple-caramel cake necessary. Really, in the end, how much has she even changed since the Kieran days?

Then all that's gone, too. She unfolds her arms, looks at the Collector's face. At him inhabiting it. "Right," she says, just quietly enough that he can't hear her voice break.

He flashes the sliver of metal at her again. "My lucky charm," he murmurs.

Ironically? Literally?

"It's what attracted them," he says.

"Them?"

"It. Them. I don't know. But I think it's also what saved me. I could feel that fizz all over me. Like a million ferrets scrambling up and down my veins. Except, I don't know, not *sentient.* They weren't trying to get out. They weren't thinking or wanting. In that instant, for them—it, whatever—I think it was just about *being.* Getting loose. Escaping where they'd been. Making noise. Riding the waves from the pump of a heart. It was all just… really distracting, you know?"

With each new utterance, he has pressed down harder on the accelerator. The Jeep is positively flying, now. So fast that even Spook looks up. He starts to say something, catches sight of his friend's face, goes back to his headphones. His extra numbers.

"So. You've swallowed a million ghost-ferrets," Nadine finally says. "And being yourself, your thought is, *Grand. I'll hold them in?*"

The gas pedal has to be flat to the floor. But somehow the Jeep lurches into another gear, like a cartoon car with a rocket booster strapped to the back.

"Not at first," says the Collector. "For a long time, I wasn't thinking anything. Wait, no, I was thinking too many things, all at once. But eventually, yeah. That's exactly what I decided. Letting them loose seemed dangerous beyond belief. Then the whole thing changed. I started feeling less like a ferret cage. More like…" He looks at her. "A cooling rod."

"Normal, I'm sorry, I don't under—"

"Like in a nuclear reactor. The ferrets, the fizzing sensation, that was fission happening. And me—what there was of me, what I could keep calm and still—that's what was preventing it from exploding." He doesn't shudder. But only because he is holding himself rigid again. That's what he has been doing Nadine realizes, with every breath he has taken for a year and a half.

"The part of me that's me," he says. "And the breath from the wishing-tree clock."

In her mind's eye, Nadine sees what she has seen since the day he came home changed: his constant circling; his returning again and again to the clock, right at the quarter hour, to inhale another gust.

Because the clock pendulum had more *bouquiniste* hinge in it.

Has. Except now the Rev has it.

"So does your being here with me mean you've exploded?" she finally asks.

With a visible effort, the Collector relaxes his shoulders. Allows himself a wince. "All I know is, they're not here." He waves a long, thin hand at himself, then the world. The night-trees hurtling past. "They're out there. But maybe not irretrievably? Yet? Maybe they're still heating up. Or melting down. Or just spreading. Running wild toward absolutely nowhere, like they did at first in me."

For a surprisingly long time after that, they just sail south. The rain stops. Ocean unfolds to their right, the furrow of moonlight blazing across it toward the beach like a brush fire erupting. They pass no more cars, not even a truck. Nadine wants to turn on the radio, hear music or headlines or George Noory's call-ins enthusing about UFO clusters over their local Del Tacos. Anything to suggest that the world she and the Collector have always skirted the edges of is still out there.

"Hey," Spook says, leaning right between them like a little kid—the one she and Normal never quite decided not to have, just didn't—waking up after a backseat nap. "Where are we going?"

The Collector can't answer, or doesn't. Nadine starts to for him, then realizes she has no idea what to say.

"Ferret hunting?" she finally tries.

Spook has been their friend a long time. Has spent longer around the two of them together than anyone else. He waits.

The silence extends. But when the Collector breaks it, it's more like he's turned up the volume on a conversation he was already having. "I don't know how yet. But we can't just… I don't know what it does. Will do. It. They. Except we *do* know. We've had a couple tastes. Think about it, Nadine. That boat. The *bouquiniste* stall. The bakery."

"The Family Pride," Nadine whispers, and Normal flinches.

"Tony," he says. She touches his arm, but he flinches again. Keeps going. "All barely even hints. Cap gun fire." Without easing off the accelerator, he looks her full in the face. "This is the mushroom cloud."

Instead of asking any of the thousand questions he has to have, Spook lifts his headphones as though in confirmation. "New numbers," he says.

Normal nods. "It's already started. We have to track it down before it spreads even more. We have to lure it back. But first, we have to find it."

"*Them*," Nadine says. "The Rev, and his father. Maybe we should find them."

Her first flicker of insight since the Collector's return. First moment she has felt like herself. She'd thought it might earn her a smile. An approving nod, anyway. But the Collector just stares ahead, eating miles with his eyes. He hasn't needed her insight or ideas or research, not for this leg. He already knows where they're going. So, abruptly does she.

"We need more wishes," she says.

That earns her a smile. "And a really weird map."

"And a Frosty?" Nadine says.

"I love you very much," says the Collector.

Nadine doesn't even try to control her laugh. Her amazed, relieved laugh. She'd forgotten she had one. "Strip Mall of the Gods it is."

"Those guys?" Spook glances at each of them in turn. Then, with no trace of irony, adds, "Those guys are fucking weird."

Nadine laughs more, even as she catches the look on the Collector's face. The exhaustion that looks baked in, now. Ghostly jags of paler color streak his skin like seams in rock. Mined veins. Her tears come as easily as her laughter, and do nothing to quench it.

"Is it bad that I'm happy?" she whispers.

He doesn't hear or doesn't respond. Or he can't.

She flips open her tablet, then grabs her phone to text Binna.

3

The night cracks open. Red spills everywhere, engulfing everything like lava, and sirens pour out of the dark and down the hillsides.

"Whoa," says the Collector as Nadine whirls to look. "Am I speeding?"

Nadine's laugh is automatic. Also panicky. "There's a feckin' phalanx back there! Pull over, pull over."

He does, too fast, setting wheels skidding on the drizzle-slicked asphalt. Absurdly, Nadine ducks as the cop cars rocket past, grabbing the Collector's wrist with one hand and her seatback with the other. The Jeep shudders in the wind they make, and she holds her breath, waiting for the shriek of skidding tires, the bullhorned orders to *Freeze* as policemen leap from their vehicles, weapons drawn. Then they're gone, all of them. Darkness resettles over the Jeep, and misty silence with it.

When she lifts her head, she finds herself staring at Spook. He never even looked up, she realized. Never grabbed for his seatbelt. *Does he even know we've stopped*?

She, on the other hand, can't seem to release Normal's hand. Unless that's him gripping hers.

"My boat," Spook says.

"What?" It's as though this whole day, or the last year and a half of her life, has plugged her ears. What she really wants to do is climb out of the Jeep and hop around on one foot, shake her head to clear it.

Sliding his headphones down around his neck, Spook taps the top of his black box. "My harbor. Where my boat is. It's on fire."

"Oh, no," the Collector says. "Oh, shit."

"All your notebooks," Nadine says. "No."

His eyes fill with tears, or the moonlight catches the tears that are already there. As much to give him privacy as anything else, she turns to look after the police cars. After a few seconds, she scowls. "Your harbor's 150 miles from here. That can't be where *those* cops were going."

"Nope," says the Collector, quietly. He keys the ignition, straightens them out, starts them rolling again.

"Normal," she says. "We should take him home."

"Home where?"

He doesn't even look at her, just pushes down the accelerator again. Miles fly by. A rest stop appears, empty except for a single RV with three stringy-looking teenagers perched on its roof like ravens. The teenagers shake beer cans and raise middle fingers at the Jeep as it passes. Next comes a gas station, then a gas station with attached In-'N-Out, then houses scattered up hillsides, uniform gray on their uniform rectangular plots, silent and lightless as gravestones.

"Your father," Nadine whispers to the air—to Spook— and thinks of her mother. Of the tears in Spook's eyes through the film over her own, which she is only now realizing has been there since the moment the Collector resurfaced. Came home. *An hour ago*? *Not even*? She turns to say something comforting, touch Spook's hand. But he's under headphones again, hands clasped tight on his box, eyes closed.

As they exit the freeway, red and blue light floods the Jeep again, and Nadine looks up, expecting another phalanx. But the police cars are ahead of them this time. Actually, they're to the left. Dozens of them, fanned out in a snaking line all the way across the giant parking lot of the Russian River Outlet Mall. The cops themselves are out of their vehicles, forming a neater and straighter line from the edge of the mall sidewalk all the way back to the main entrance to the lot, so that they and their vehicles form a sort of cop cross. Or ad hoc fence. Because on either side of them…

"Normal," she says.

"I see." Incongruously—ridiculously—he stops at the bottom of the offramp for the red light.

"It's like that film you like," Nadine whispers after at least three rounds of red, yellow, green from the traffic light. "Like your fucking Warriors."

On either side of the police and their cars—in all four quadrants—people are shouting. They've pooled together, and now they're boiling up and down, brandishing shoes and shopping bags at the pools of people around and across from them. In the back of the quadrant nearest to the road, Nadine sees a grandmother whirling what really could be two hot-dogs-on-sticks like maces.

But when the Collector unzips the top of his side flap, what pours into the cab isn't only yelling. Some of those people—a lot of them—are singing.

Not the same songs. Not any of them, as far as Nadine can tell. But they're throwing their heads back, bellowing straight up into the air. Which is definitely better than shooting into it, or menacing neighbors with Pups-on-Poles.

Still seriously wrong, though.

"Okay, not *The Warriors. West Side Story*?"

"More 'Three Pieces in New England'," Spook says from the back, apparently out from under headphones again. It takes Nadine a second, but then she understands. That crazy classical piece where marching bands collide.

Except in that piece, the racket comes off like celebration. Some of it does. She turns to say so to Spook, but he's already got the phones on again. So instead, to Normal, she says, "Can we please go?"

He waits for the light to turn green again. But then he goes.

Half a mile past the outlets, the road rises. They pass a supermarket strip mall, its lot mercifully empty of everything but open dumpsters. Then another strip mall with a TGIF and a Costco, looking pretty much like a strip mall with a TGIF and a Costco. Then the entry circles to a series of gated communities. A last run of streetlights planted like flares, and then the road rises, dips down and keeps dipping, and the buildings and lights vanish behind them, leaving them safely back in the nowhere-spaces they have always called home. Or believed home might be, if it was anywhere.

"Normal," she says as he stares into the dark. "Is all this you? What was in you, I mean?"

He takes so long to answer that she thinks he isn't going to. She has also decided she's more than okay with that. But eventually, he shrugs.

"Does that mean it might be?"

"I don't know, Nadine. Honestly, I think *they* have most of it, don't you? Your visitor today—"

"The Rev."

As she knew he would, the Collector glances her way, raises an inquiring eyebrow. Can't help it. Instead of asking, though, he nods. "The Rev. And his father."

"But...whatever the fuck is happening right this second...it could be your ferrets, couldn't it? That's what you think."

This time, he keeps his eyes on the dark. "Let's just say that's why we're here."

Then they really are there. Here, at the world's westernmost A&W drive-through. For a second, as Normal turns into the Strip Mall of the Gods—just another strip mall, three storefronts in a low, concrete bunker of a building, plus the A&W at the edge of the parking lot—Nadine thinks he's actually going to drive them through. Get them Frosties.

Then she realizes she's annoyed that he isn't.

"We need Frosties," she murmurs.

That, of all things, earns her an all-the-way head-turn. A full-on stare. "Are you joking?"

"They're comforting. Calming. Also the most amazing thing about this place."

"They're the least amazing—or important—thing about this place. This place has *those* two guys." He gestures at the side-by-side stores as he parks. THE OTHER PATH and CLOCKSHOP. Both with their lights on, apparently open, because why would this hour be different than any other if these are your businesses? What constitutes optimal hours for their sorts of patrons?

Like us, Nadine thinks to herself.

"And what do those two do?" she continues. For some reason, this argument feels crucial right now. "Every single day, or at least every time we come here? They get Frosties, don't they? Or they make you bring them one?"

She can't stop thinking about the outlet mall. The police cars and families seemingly singing their way into battle like reincarnated *clanns* folk. She's also thinking about the last eighteen months of her life. And the last 60 minutes. Banter, is all that's keeping her from breaking down.

That, and the way Normal is looking at her. Plus the fact that he hasn't actually shut off the engine.

"You're right," he says, sounding as grateful as she is for the distraction. And in love with her, still.

"I'm always right. Also, you're a snob. You think Frosties are less special because they're everywhere, and anyone can get them."

He nods.

"Just because everyone likes them doesn't mean there's no magic in them."

"Yes," he says. Almost grins. "You're right. I keep thinking it does."

"You know, if not for Spook back there, and the thousand cop cars breaking up a riot of banshee grandmothers we just passed, I'd climb over there for a proper how's-your-father right this second."

"We can put him out," the Collector says. Nadine laughs, glances over her shoulder, and sees Spook with his mouth wide open, hands pressing the headphones to his ears.

When he sees her looking, he slips off the phones and holds them out, pads up. Like a dead pet. Except she can hear sounds seeping from them. Some sort of string section. Something whistling.

"This music," he says. "It's the most beautiful..."

Instinct—self-preservation—keeps Nadine from taking the headphones. Even from where she sits, that whistling is working toward her ears. She can actually feel it gliding up her, hovering over every pore.

"Normal," she murmurs. "We need those Frosties."

He shuts off the engine, hops out of the Jeep, and for a ridiculous second, Nadine thinks he has listened to her. Then she sees Mr. Map—it's not his name, his name is Bob or Hop or something else cartoon-cowboy—stepping out of The Other Path, and the Collector moving to meet him, hand extended. As always, the gesture looks absurd when her man does it, the angle of the arm the giveaway. Something he has learned to mimic, knows is expected without fully understanding the point or connotations.

"You can't go anywhere," she hears him say.

Every single time, Nadine winds up surprised to see Mr. Map without his Stetson, and then remembers he doesn't actually own one, at least as far as she knows. He does wear scuffed brown cowboy boots, suede vests, a belt with a brass buckle and a holster—a *holster*—with a flare gun wedged in it. The hat is merely implied.

"Really," Normal says. "We need you."

Mr. Map engulfs the Collector's hand. "Just getting my nightcap." He waves toward the A&W.

"Better hurry. No time. It's urgent."

For a second, Mr. Map holds his stoic expression. Then he laughs. "Not a phrase I often get in my line of work. As for time..." He pats Normal on the shoulder. Stoicism restored. "Not my concern." He waves toward Clockshop.

"We need him, too."

"Tell him. He'll like that. Watch out, though, he's in a mood. Thinks he's lactose intolerant, all of a sudden. Make sure you tell him I went to get a Frosty." Whistling, waving at Nadine, he continues across the lot toward the A&W.

"Come on, Spook," Nadine says, climbing out of the Jeep. But Spook has his headphones on again, and his eyes closed. Every time he breathes, he shudders. Maybe, Nadine thinks, he's mourning his lost notebooks. His connection, however tenuous or imaginary it has always been, to his father. She hopes it's that, but can't keep from glancing back the way they've come, across the valley toward the other side of the hills. The rest of the world. Whatever's happening there.

The Collector is holding Clockshop's door for her. But for the first time since he came back—woke up, whatever—he's flashing his impatient face. It's amazing to Nadine how comforting that is.

"Alright, alright," she says, moving past him. The door swings shut behind them, and just like that, they're elsewhere again. In another loon's bespoke, semi-private world, where the air is close but breathable, the light dim. As for time…

Always, the aquarium feeling washes over her. The Clockmaker keeps the units he is currently repairing or displaying or inventing in individual glass cases built in rows up the walls, lit by dimmed, indirect green bulbs that make the cases look like fish tanks. The purpose of the cases is utilitarian, she knows, not decorative; they're soundproofed, amongst other things, to keep any discrepancy or variance in the ticking from driving the Clockmaker out of his fragile, glowering mind. In truth, leaning close to those tanks or putting a hand to them, saying hello or feeling the vibration from any of the marvels caged in those walls, reminds her more of being in an animal shelter than an aquarium. Same sense of wonder. Same flash of sadness she can hardly bear.

"We're closed," growls that voice from the back of the shop. Like a dyspeptic bulldog, less threatening than startled awake.

Both Nadine and Normal have been here enough times to know not to answer. To wait. The Collector is clearly struggling with that now, though. Nadine has to touch his wrist, leave her finger there. He calms again.

Finally, back there at his curtained workbench, the Clockmaker stirs. He emerges through the curtain. Nadine takes an unintended step back, but also starts to laugh. At least she manages to keep the laugh silent.

He's so thin that he looks two-dimensional. As though his shadow is in the process of absorbing him. Screwed into one eye is whatever magnifying or measuring tool he has clearly been using for so many consecutive hours that it has ground part way into his bones. Both his hands sprout long, thin, glinting bits, like extra half-formed digits. The effect is equal parts locust, drunk uncle, and steampunk robot.

"Oh," says the Clockmaker. "You." His scowl deepens. "Don't tell me you broke it."

"Worse," the Collector says. "Burgled."

Wincing, the Clockmaker drops his head toward his hands, remembers the pointy glinting bits just in time, and discards them. They scatter on the counter like iron filings, and he looks at those a while. Whatever meaning he finds there, he keeps it to himself.

"Ransack your whole house, did they?"

"Just your clock," Nadine says.

"Pretty discerning burglar." Glancing over his shoulder at his workbench, the Clockmaker grunts. Sighs.

For a guy whose life's work is the marking and treasuring of time, Nadine had reproached him once, *you're awfully stingy with yours.*

Because I know how little there is, the Clockmaker had answered.

The most efficacious strategy is to outlast him, let him adjust to actual people in his shop. But tonight, the Collector is right: they can't wait.

"Listen," she snaps, "we're sorry, but—"

"That bit you skimmed for yourself," the Collector says, cutting her off before the Clockmaker can. "From the material I brought you."

Even as she spins, startled, Nadine already knows the answer to the question she's about to ask. She knows she will ask it anyway. She knows this will make the Collector feel guilty, and also pleased with himself. Also amazed at her for figuring it out, then for helping him understand why he'd done what he instinctively did in the first place.

The tick of their gears. Machine of their marriage.

"He stole some? And you knew it?"

"Reserved," the Clockmaker grumbles.

Nadine ignores him. A surprising burst of anger erupts inside her, then subsides. "You told him what it could do, too?"

The Collector shakes his head. "I keep telling you, I don't even know what it does now. Do you?"

"I'm learning," she says.

This is the moment where she usually takes his hand. Signals that it's all right. But she can't quite bring herself to do it this time. Partly out of fear that when she does, he'll have vanished back into himself again.

The Clockmaker has been fiddling with his glinting bits. They make a surprisingly rhythmic pinging, like ticking being tuned. The light is so dim in this part of the shop that Nadine only now realizes he's blushing. From embarrassment. "I don't *skim*. I always reserve special material. Out of protection for clients as much as—"

"We don't care," Nadine snaps. "There's no time."

"It just seemed prudent to hold onto a bit. Rare material, clearly."

"Sure," says the Collector. "But you do still have it?"

Naturally, that's the question that jerks up the Clockmaker's head, drops his jaw. He's not just amazed; he's appalled.

"Stupid question," the Collector says. "Sorry."

"I should think so."

"Okay. Well, thank goodness for your forethought, then. Because I brought you the bit I have left. The pin from the hinge. And we really, really need a new clock."

Whatever embarrassment had betrayed itself on the Clockmaker's face, it's gone, now. He scowls. Then suddenly jabs a long middle finger in the air. Not at them, Nadine realizes. At the front door, where Mr. Map is holding four paper cups and doing a sort of slow-motion line dance. With a theatrical grunt, the Clockmaker returns his attention to the Collector. "I can probably manage. Given time."

"Excellent. We'll need it tonight."

If the Clockmaker had accepted a Frosty and had some in his mouth, he would have done a spit take. As is, his eyes widen so comically fast that his eyepiece—monocle, measuring tool, whatever—ejects from his socket with an audible *pop* and splashes down amid the glinty bits. As though the man himself is disassembling.

"Where do you think you are?" he says, not just dour but genuinely angry, now. "Sears?"

From the doorway, Mr. Map sucks in a noisy slurp, swishes liquid around his mouth, gulps it down. "Pretty sure Sears is kaput, my friend."

"McClockRepair?" the Clockmaker sputters. "The mall?"

Always, before, Nadine has felt a peculiar affinity for this man. In his agitation, irrational surliness, and pride, he reminds her of home. Of so many men in the pubs back home.

But tonight, with her own man miraculously returned and the world on fire, he's pissing her off. "*A* mall. Aye. Pretty sure that's precisely where we find ourselves. And yourself."

Mr. Map joins them, hands Nadine and the Collector Frosties. The Clockmaker is ticking toward another response, but Mr. Map shoves the fourth A&W cup into his rigid fingers.

"Drink your root beer," he says.

To Nadine's surprise, the Clockmaker does. Her anger melts away again, leaving only unease. Low-grade panic. In her head, to calm herself, she's chanting Spook's radio-lady numbers for some reason. *Seven. Six. Nine. Null...*

After a second, then a third silent gulp, the Clockmaker looks up. "Tonight? Really?"

"Oh," says the Collector, digging a hand into his other pants pocket. "And we'll need it in this."

Nadine doesn't immediately recognize the open metal clamshell. Not until he holds it out, and she has a flash, sense memory, of those raised metal fingers carved into the other side of it. The ones she can still feel nestling into hers. Lacing through hers.

"Where, and when, did you get that?" she whispers.

What she really wants to do is snatch it away. Hurl it out the door into the night.

But the Clockmaker has it, now. If those carved fingers have any effect on him, he doesn't show it. He stares down into the empty shell, taps around inside it with his index finger, starts to mouth some sort of rote protest. But then he looks up.

"Hmm," he says, and disappears back through his curtain toward his workbench. He comes back for his glinty bits and eyepiece, plus the root beer he'd put down momentarily.

"You're welcome," calls Mr. Map, and takes another rasping slurp.

"Fuck off, Hap." Then he's gone.

Hap. Hop. She'd been close.

Binning his Frosty behind the counter, Mr. Map turns, licks foam off his lips, and gives them a surprisingly rueful smile. "Glad to see you. Haven't had an actual customer in weeks."

It's the wrong moment—there are a few thousand more pressing concerns—but the question Nadine has always meant to ask bubbles out of her. "How do you two even pay rent?"

For one second, as Mr. Map freezes with his napkin over mouth, Nadine thinks she has caught them in something. That's what he looks like, especially when he darts a quick glance toward the Clockmaker's curtain: the little brother about to lay blame on the older one.

Then he grins. "Pay *rent*?"

Now she's the one caught. Embarrassed. At what, and why? She has no idea.

Mopping his lips, Mr. Map lays his napkin on the countertop and hooks his hands through his belt, one thumb curling around the base of the flare gun. Not in any way that would help him draw it, though. "You really are snowflakes. The pair of you. Always thought so."

"You own the mall," she says abruptly.

"This place?" He laughs, gesturing out the door. "Well, sure. But also the *mall*."

The penny drops. "As in, the one by the freeway?"

Mr. Map laughs again. "Wait 'til you hear how we got the money."

But Nadine has already figured that out, just from their ages, their detail-obsessive hobbies, their strange-guy awkwardnesses. This location.

"You're dot-com million—"

The Collector cuts her off. "We need you, too."

"To keep an eye on him, you mean?" Mr. Map pats his flare gun. "Make sure he sticks to your schedule?"

"We need a map."

Just like that, he leans forward, flare gun forgotten as his hands rise to clasp each other. "Map to where? Of where?"

The Collector shakes his head. "I don't know."

It's his helplessness—and Mr. Map's excitement, and her Frosty, and just being here like this again, despite everything—that triggers Nadine's laugh.

Also, she realizes, she does know. "I do." For one moment, she lets them both stare. Bathes in the murky green light of this impossible room. Then says, "Got any Ordnance Survey maps?"

For a second, in his annoyance, she thinks Mr. Map might actually draw his flare gun. But he only nods toward the Clockmaker's curtain. "You realize that's like asking him if he's got anything that ticks."

But Nadine barely bothers looking at him. She's watching the Collector watch her. Reveling in the way he's doing that. "Of Paris," she says.

Oh, the Collector doesn't quite say. Or rather, he says it, but thought-beam style, in her head.

"Ordnance. Survey." Mr. Map punctuates his words with a pointing finger. The gesture would look professorial and pompous, except it also looks like something he picked up on YouTube. "You know those are British. Right? That's a UK organization."

"Yeah, fine, you've exposed my ignorance. Established your mastery."

"Oh, good. Phew." Mr. Map grins.

"Ordnance *type*."

"Now, if you're thinking of the *Institute Geographique National...*"

"Let's assume I am," Nadine snaps.

Mr. Map taps one booted toe on the hardwood floor. "Still like asking him if he's got anything that—"

"We need one with something not there on it," Nadine says. Abruptly, to her alarm, she shudders hard, has a whole-body flash: that cot in that dark in that room; the Buddha looming over her, pawing through her things; the rasp and hitch of Binna's drugged breathing; the still-new shock of being that alone, for the first time in her life. The most alone she has ever been or would be, it turns out. Until this past year. Which ended all of two hours ago.

Mr. Map has stopped tapping, at least. "*Still* like asking..." But then his hands drop back to his belt, and his scowl evaporates. His next words come slowly. "Paris, France. Yes? Things vanish from Paris all the time. Every day. From almost every street in every *arrondissement*."

"I didn't mean not there now. I mean not there then."

One corner of Mr. Map's mouth twists, and his eyebrows narrow. And then...*whoomp*. It's there: the expression flashed by every sort-of friend or meaningful contact she and the Collector have ever made, sooner or later.

Spook, Binna, Viviana, the baker of Hexenhaus, Tony. Even the goddamn *Lebensborn.*

Not excitement, exactly. Not expectation. Not even wonder. The *hope* of wonder. Or not even hope. Longing for it.

"As in, not there when the map was made," Mr. Map says.

Nadine gives her best hopeful, helpless shrug. "I think?"

For one moment more, Mr. Map holds his condescending scowl, until it cracks in half. His smile floods the room, and the clap of his hands seems to startle the clocks in their cages.

"Hey!" shouts the Clockmaker from behind his curtain.

"Shut up," Mr. Map calls. "Drink your root beer." He claps once more, rubs his hands together, turns his full attention to the Collector and Nadine. "I knew I loved you two. I've always loved you two."

She should be grinning back, Nadine knows. But suddenly, as the Collector sidles closer—to Mr. Map, and incidentally her—she's just overwhelmingly tired. "You have a map like that?" she asks.

"Well, you have to understand. The IGN isn't that old. It's only been around since 1940."

"Which means..." Nadine mutters.

She wouldn't have thought it possible, but Mr. Map's smile actually widens. "It means I only have *one full drawer.*" Spinning on his boot heels, Mr. Map heads for the front door. He doesn't wait or look back. He doesn't even stop talking. "You know, you could make a whole new atlas—a whole other Paris—from parks or doorways or alleys or buildings that show up on maps of Paris that disappeared out of Paris. Or were never actually in Paris. Or that not one person can confirm seeing in the place where it's marked, before or after the map in question was made. And I'm just talking about the IGN ones, now. Just the ones from the last 75 years. If you go back further..."

They're outside now, hurrying to keep up, and as they pass the Jeep, Nadine glances that way. Spook is still hunched over in there, headphones mashed to his ears. He doesn't look up. Nadine is fairly sure his eyes aren't open.

"Mark of a great city, don't you think?" Mr. Map unlocks his door and flicks on the lights, which set the off-white walls and varnished hardwood glowing. "Everyone who lives in Paris has their own Paris. And yet they all think it's the same as everyone else's."

The maps in their frames seem to unfold toward the light, the way they always do. If Clockshop recalls a humane society, The Other Path is an art gallery. Pristine, but also welcoming. Somewhere to get lost in. Ironically enough.

Mr. Map really does have a whole drawer of IGN maps—with or without lost things, he doesn't say and Nadine doesn't ask—in the bottom right corner of the unlabeled white cabinet of drawers against the back wall of the shop. Above the cabinet, rows of mounted Civil War-era flare guns climb to the ceiling. The drawer makes a whispering sound on its runners when Mr. Map draws it out, like wind in summer branches.

"That's all Paris?" the Collector mutters, half-amazed, half-alarmed, as Mr. Map lifts a stack of maps, then another. They are all different sizes, some tiny as postcards, others folded and fat as old Bradshaw railway guides. It seems impossible that that drawer could hold them all.

Arranging and squaring piles, Mr. Map snaps on the twin Lightblades mounted to either end of his long, off-white countertop. "A lot of them. Most." He points a gun-finger at Nadine without looking up. "That's actually a whole category you've touched on, you know. Maps of places *someone* says they found, sometime. Probably fifty percent of those concern islands, though. Oceans. There's another twenty percent or so documenting Manhattan. Another ten about the Cotswolds. The Fens. Cornwall. China, obviously. Your old homeland, Nadine, that's probably a third of the category, right there. London, obviously, that's probably another thirty per cent. There's this one Roman road that shows up on maps from every single country that once constituted the Holy Roman Empire, well into the early 19th century, except there's no historical evidence that that road was ever there. So that's probably another five percent."

"You've got some extra percent," the Collector murmurs. He sounds exhausted, too. Also delighted.

Mr. Map looks up. "Appropriate, given the subject, no? Now, then. Where in Paris?"

The words stick in Nadine's mouth. She has to shove them out. "Left Bank. Somewhere maybe halfway between the Jardin du Luxembourg and the *bouquiniste* stalls by the Seine. We're looking for a door."

Whatever organizing system Mr. Map uses, it works for him. Already, he has pulled a Bradshaw-thick map from the left-hand stack. Sliding on gloves, he eases it from its clear, protective plastic. "Going to need additional information," he mutters, looking more like he's conducting than unfolding as he coaxes the map onto the counter.

"In an alley," the Collector says to Nadine. "Right?"

Except for bending closer, Mr. Map has gone still. It's an active sort of stillness, though, like a helicopter hovering. "Keep it coming."

"One building—the building we're looking for—is a little shorter than the others around it. Kind of wedged in. There's a room inside with a circular fireplace..."

"That last part is probably not on the map."

He lowers himself closer to his countertop. Abruptly, he straightens, hands darting into the stack. His new selection comes folded into a little green wallet. The map itself is tiny, hand-scrawled on some sort of journal paper. *Soldier's notebook*, Nadine thinks, without any specific point of reference she's aware of. Mr. Map does his conducting-unfolding thing, revealing four panels collectively the size of a large dinner napkin. With a grunt, he nudges that map aside, runs his finger down the stack again. The Collector reaches for her hand.

All at once Nadine jerks straight. Another shudder wracks her from her head all the way down through her feet.

"Stop," she snaps.

The shudder rubberbands back up her. Action, reaction. The Buddha dances away, the Collector appears. The Collector vanishes into himself, the Rev arrives. Loneliness leading to love. Love to loneliness. Carved watch-case finger to her finger to companion carved finger. Stuffed lizard pin-eye to human eye. Ghost ferret to wishing tree clock breath. The need to move others meeting the need to be moved. Slap of the sea against its own stillness. Curiosity to revelation to cost. Appearance, disappearance. Being, disintegrating.

"Stop?" Normal asks, hand in hers but not squeezing. Not moving. Still as carved fingers, and only slightly warmer.

So she squeezes him. That's all the reassurance she's got. "It doesn't matter."

"It matters, Nadine. You have to trust me. I had it inside me for a year. It—"

"The place." Nadine squeezes again. "Why would the place matter?"

"Nadine, we have to find them. We have to go wherever—"

"—they went. Right. And how are they getting there, do you think?"

"Through places that aren't places. That's what we've both come up with."

"It's all we need. A place that isn't a place. *Any* place."

He's not himself yet. Not all the way. It takes him a good five seconds to catch up. "It doesn't have to be Paris," he finally says.

"It doesn't have to be anywhere."

Now he's with her. There's his smile. "As long as it isn't *actually* anywhere." Of course, now that he's himself, he drops her hand and whirls toward Mr. Map. "What's the *closest* map you've got with someplace marked on it that isn't—"

Nadine's sigh is real enough. Also theatrical and practiced. "Hmm, lover, let's see. Somewhere nearby, but not on a regular map and not on my GPS. Maybe somewhere something sort of happened."

Blank stare.

"Recently. To us."

Still the stare. But not blank anymore. Abruptly, he's humming that song—at Dolly speed, not slow—and he has her hand again, and he kisses it as he spins her, practically dancing, for the door.

"Thank you!" he calls. Not to her, of course. To Mr. Map.

"Don't mention it," Mr. Map mutters. The door swings shut.

Of course, they still have to wait for the Clockmaker. Only once, the Collector sticks his head in there. Even from the Jeep, Nadine hears the wordless bellow he gets in response. They go and get Spook a Frosty, dawdle together over theirs and try to restrain each other from going back into Clockshop.

Finally, after way too long, that door pops open and the Clockmaker emerges. He has ditched his monocle-tool, and nothing glints between his fingers. His white lab coat still swirls around him, though, and from the way he cups his cradled hands, he might have just delivered a baby.

Except if he ever did, hopefully he wouldn't be scowling that way afterward. He extends his palms toward the Collector. "It bit me."

The watch casing is one complete piece now, open so that the carved left-hand fingers point to the sky. It also has a watch in it. Simple white dial, black numbers, nothing fancy. But miraculous somehow in the way of all clocks, never mind ones that tick, breathe, blow, protect. Not just an oyster forming a pearl; a dead shell sprouting an oyster. Stardust triggering movement capable of measuring its own decay.

"It's cheap. A watch I already had constructed that I had to transplant. Be fucking careful how you wind it," the Clockmaker says. Somehow, though, he sounds less dyspeptic than before.

More proud of himself. And also respectful. Of the watch.

"What do I owe you?" Normal asks, cradling the case. Taking just a moment to marvel at it. Nadine does, too, automatically. Both it and the Clockmaker's work deserve nothing less.

The Clockmaker grunts. "A new digestive system? Better workings?"

"Guys?" comes Spook's voice from behind them, and Nadine and the Collector turn and find him leaning out the side of the Jeep, eyes wide, headphones around his neck and tears pouring down his face. From the headphones, they can just hear his number lady, chanting. But faster. "Better hurry."

4

In the parking lot of the Russian River Outlet Mall, red lights still swarm down the sides of buildings and over the hoods of parked vehicles and black pavement. But they're mostly from ambulances, now. The cop cars are gone, and the people have dispersed. Except for the ones on the ground.

Normal stops at the traffic light yet again, but he doesn't linger. Soon, they're shooting north again up the 1. At first, again, they see no other cars in either direction. Then ambulances start screaming past, sirens blaring. They come in bunches, from ahead and behind. After that, the only other vehicles Nadine sees rocket past so fast they barely seem to have substance, flapping the canvas sides of the Jeep as they blur to nothing. Not police, not official. Just assholes, racing. Or panicked people hurtling home. Their headlights leave streaks on the dark like nebulae in space. Flares in the fathomless void.

"Can we turn on the radio?" Spook murmurs from the back. He sounds small, so unlike his seaworthy, competent self that Nadine can't bring herself to face him. She switches on the speakers.

From the Castro, and apparently stretching all the way to the Presidio, an impromptu Naked Bike Ride has broken out. "*There are hundreds, maybe thousands of people out here*," one KQED reporter shouts, breathless, from the roof of a brownstone along Divisidero. Another reporter cuts her off. "*Oh my God, there's a whole pack of people on the roofs across the street. They've got buckets of orange and blue paint, and glitter, and confetti, and they're just pouring it down the sides of the buildings. They're wearing face masks. And no pants. It's...*" The reporter gasps. Or laughs. "*They're making curlicues in the splatter with their fingers. With brushes. Now one's dangling his partner over the side so he can...eww...*"

If they'd been listening on Spook's shortwave, Nadine would have assumed the signal had cut out. But this is local NPR, and the reception is perfect, which makes the sudden silence downright eerie. Terrifying, actually.

When the reporter comes back, she's stage-whispering as though across a table in a library despite the racket around her. "*This whole block just got possessed by Banksy.*"

Unless she said *banshee.*

"*So beautiful*," she breathes.

Meanwhile, on Hunters Point and in the Outer Mission, there are gun battles raging. Or massacres in progress. Or celebrations? The reporters huddling in those places don't seem to know which. But they're holding microphones into the night, and what comes over the airwaves sounds like firecrackers. Also screaming, except that some of that is definitely laughing.

"*It's like the 4th of July!*" one reporter shouts, although it sounds like a question.

"*But...with killing*?" says the baffled studio host.

"Like the 4th of July," mumbles Spook from the back. "Like what it celebrates."

Which is killing, Nadine thinks. *Lots of it. The savage birth of the supposed freest nation in the history of the Earth, which makes her own nation's Troubled, centuries-long birth look like a junior league hurling final by comparison.*

Abruptly, she snaps off the radio. Neither Spook nor the Collector protests. She opens her mouth to urge Normal to go faster, though what she really wants is for him to go slower, or stop. What she finally says is, "Know where you're headed?"

"Off the map," he says.

Nadine nods. "Into the woods."

"Past Miranda, right?"

Nadine glances back at Spook. He hasn't re-donned his headphones, and his black box sits silent in his lap. He keeps one hand atop it, fingers curled as though scratching a cat. She tries smiling at him just to let him know she's there. Or confirm to herself that she is. He doesn't react.

"Normal," she says, facing front again, staring into the dark instead of her partner. "What are we doing?"

He doesn't answer. When he does, she wishes he hadn't.

"We need to put it back."

The silence that comes after that is new. His mouth is still working, as though he has more to say but no words. or has words but has lost his voice. Meanwhile, has his eyes riveted to the road, so fiercely focused that he seems to give off light. For the second time since they've left the Strip Mall of the Gods, Nadine thinks of space. Of stars going nova, or being born. Both at the same time.

Like all of us, every moment we are alive. Going nova. Being born. Going nova by being born.

Her voice barely sounds like hers. She hadn't known she had this much lullaby in her. "Put what back, exactly?"

His mouth keeps working. His hands tighten, relax, and tighten again on the wheel. "The *wildness.*" His expression could be no expression, could be shadow. "Best I've got."

"So it's a feeling, then?" She drums her fingers on her closed laptop. "We're hurtling off the map into the middle of the woods in the middle of night to find a town that might not be there—"

"Might not ever have been there."

"Okay, I'm just going to..." She shakes her head. The breath she sucks in goes down deep, but comes out stuttering. "We're going hunting while the world goes mad in the hopes of finding and vacuuming up a feeling?"

The Collector shakes his head. "I told you before. Ferrets."

"You said it *felt* like ferrets. When they were inside you."

"Emphasis on ferrets."

"That's just really fucking weird, man," Spook says, and for one moment, all three of them laugh. Already, though, his hands have lifted his headphones back into place. Around them, the trees sink deeper into the dark.

"So, they're alive," she murmurs.

"*It.* Or maybe they, I don't know. And no. Or, yes. Alive, but not. Oh *shit.*"

The Jeep skids in the breakdown lane, spitting gravel everywhere as the Collector wrenches it onto the exit ramp they almost hurtled past. They skid all the way to the STOP sign at the bottom of the ramp. Where, of course, the Collector jams the brake to the floor, throwing himself into the canvas flap and Nadine hard into her stiffened seatbelt.

At least this time he doesn't linger at the intersection. He checks Nadine, glances at Spook. Then they're driving again, much more slowly, skirting the woods. Their brights comb the dark for the Miranda turnoff, which they have to assume *will* still be there, Miranda being an actual place. Confirmed on multiple maps, with GPS coordinates that haven't developed half-lives, commenced decay.

"Alive," she says again, eventually. "But not."

Nodding like a bobblehead she's nudged, the Collector sits up straight. He looks excited. Almost himself. "What are those things? You know what I mean? They cause that disease."

"Normal, what in feck's name are you—"

"That sleep disease. The origin for zombies. For zombie stories. You know what I mean, we talked about it for a whole morning. A whole egg breakfast. At Poppa Joe's."

Just like that, she does know. Can taste the eggs, and the words she spoke through them. "Prions."

"Those! Alive but not. They grow and eat. And reproduce."

"Like proteins," she whispers. *Why is she whispering, like that reporter on the radio? Because she doesn't want the proteins to hear*? "The things that are us. In fact, they *are* proteins. So you're saying the ferrets are us?"

"These aren't us. No, that's wrong, they are. Or they can become..."

He doesn't so much stop speaking as turn his voice down, lower, lower, until it stops making sound. As though he, too, worries about being overheard. For once, Nadine doesn't mind. She isn't sure she wants to hear any more. Just for now. Besides, they're both focused, watching for the turn. They almost miss it anyway, have to stop in the middle of the road, back up slightly. Before taking it, the Collector glances at her for confirmation.

Last time, there was a sign. Probably this time, too. But in the dark, through overhanging branches that seem lower and thicker than Nadine remembers, she can't see one. She could, she realizes, flip open her phone or laptop and confirm. But that would involve light. And the thought of light, and then ghost-ferret prions she envisions surging toward it, is just too much.

Absurd. And too much.

She nods. Then they're in the woods.

At least on this road, so close to the Avenue of the Giants, there's no expectation of meeting other vehicles, and the quiet she can feel more than hear out there seems normal, natural. The thousand-year hush of redwood trees. The most life-saturated silence on Earth. As close to the Causeway of her childhood dreams as she has ever come. Quite possibly as close as there is in this world.

Miranda flashes past, leaning up out of the forest floor as through in the midst of being raised. It looks two-dimensional but also like Miranda. Gas station, market, rows of identical houses huddled amid the trees. Another gas station. Burned out meth shack surprisingly close to town, just left there by the side of the road. As a warning, maybe. Or homegrown amusement park for the kids. Crystal Cabin. Crankland.

She has to remind herself to bring her own voice back up to audible volume, because doing that feels dangerous. This is a question that needs asking, though. "Normal. Why are they always where we are?"

He doesn't answer, is too busy combing the woods ahead for Jolene. Or else he won't answer.

Because he's scared? Sorry?

Nadine's thoughts lift from their ledges, scatter through her brain like bats. *Prion-ferrets that came for her at birth. Carried her off, faerie-style. Human child. Come. Or they didn't have to come, because we* are *prions. Proteins that become prions. Perpetually and forever going ghost-ferret. Wanting to.*

"We've gone too far," she says suddenly, loudly, causing the Collector to jump and Spook to stir behind her. "Normal! We're too far."

Instead of slowing, he stirs and resettles. "It's just because you're wanting us to be there. You've forgotten. It was a long way last time."

"We're too far."

"Nadine, I've been watching. There is no way—"

"This is me you're talking to."

Without another word, the Collector pulls off into the dirt and stops. Nadine motions with her hand, and he obeys, switches off the motor, except it's more like he's switched on the forest. The silence around them positively buzzes, but not with anything, or at least nothing audible. It's ridiculous. Impossible to get her mind around. Her thoughts go wild again.

The real *sound of wildness. Not a call that lures, but a silence that engulfs. From within.*

"Nadine?" Normal says, and it's the worry in his voice—the weirdness of her name in it, as though he's said it too many times in a row and it's gone strange, started coming loose from his conception of her—that makes her realize he has been saying it for some time. Long enough to alarm him.

"I'm here," she says.

"You're positive that we're too far? It's just...we need to be right. I don't think we have much time."

Glancing back, half-expecting Jolene to have twitched into place behind her, she sees Spook's face instead. Sad and friendly. Newly homeless. The sight steadies her some. Anchors her, at least temporarily. She makes herself smile at him. Her nod is meant to reassure. "Jolene's back there."

The Collector starts to protest again. Then he keys the Jeep, makes the three-point turn, and aims them back the way they've come. The road under their wheels feels reassuringly like road.

"Go slow," Nadine says.

He does, and all three of them watch out both sides of the Jeep.

They almost miss it again anyway. This deep in the redwoods, this late at night, there are barely even shadows, and the Jeep's headlights don't seem to illuminate or reflect off anything, just drill into darkness that fills with more darkness. Even so, right as she opens her mouth to say *Stop* and realizes the Collector is already braking, Nadine wonders how they could possibly have passed it. Now that they see it, there it is, all visible and solid, the same as before: General Store, picnic tables, houses across the road. The yard where Nadine found the box of View-Master reels. The sisters' house with its porch, and Nadine realizes she doesn't want the Collector to park in front of that, but of course he does. It's where they're headed, after all. The whole reason they've come.

Even he hesitates once he's turned off the engine again, though. He doesn't even turn to catch her eye. Because in doing that, she realizes, he might catch the *house's* eye. That's what he's thinking. She knows this. Knows him.

It's a smart thought. Proper precaution.

"Normal." She's not quite whispering, but only because she won't let herself. She also makes herself turn to the house. In this light—because there *is* light, she realizes, it's just forest light, too subtle to see with daytime-hard, screen-saturated eyes—it looks like a house. "I'm asking again. Please answer if you can. *Why are they always where we are*?"

His expression, when she glances back, is one she knows so well. Brimming with love and self-congratulation and apology and that elusive something else he has always generated, seemingly reflecting something just out of sight, possibly in the woods, possibly inside him. Mysterious and untraceable as the illumination under Rothko colors. Very likely imagined. *But by which one of them*?

"Because we keep looking," he says, unzips his canvas, and steps out of the Jeep.

Once she's out and standing beside him, she takes a long breath of Jolene air. It smells of night resin, decay, mist. There isn't even any actual mist she can see, and yet this place exudes it like a pheromone. The whole woods, not just Jolene. There is nothing special about Jolene, Nadine realizes, except that it's here.

Like everything living. And everything that anything living makes. Special only because it's here.

Whatever the Collector is thinking, it causes him to put his arm around her. Spook has not gotten out of the car. He has even less idea what they're doing here than they do, of course. He's not even watching them, instead settling back under his headphones.

"Hey," she says, letting herself lean momentarily into her man. "Are you really telling me all of this...the fires and naked bike rides and screaming crazies on the freeway and those *do lally* grandmothers back there at the Outlets...it's all them? Your bleeding ghost ferrets?"

Too fast—in that infuriating way of his, as though he's sure of things he can't possibly know, except sometimes he does—the Collector shakes his head. "This is just them running. Leaping around. Being free. Being ferrets.

But by tomorrow, or a week from now, once they start reproducing, and spread…"

It's cold, and what Normal just said has set a clock ticking in Nadine's head, so that she seems to track each second passing. Their usual rhythm dictates that she break the silence. Trigger whatever's next with a question. So both of them are a little surprised when he does it.

"What's our next move, do you think?"

Her lips flatten into a smirk. "Oh, no. This is your show."

"Do we check to see if the house has an address? One that's, you know, like an actual number? That corresponds to any numbering system we recognize?"

"You actually think that house isn't there? It's right there."

"So was your firelit hostel in Paris. At least, you keep telling me it was."

"Maybe we should go up on that porch and knock."

He smiles. "'Excuse me, ladies. Good to see you again. Could I just ask…is your house here?'"

"Well, what was your plan, then?"

"*Your* plan. This is actually *your* show, Nadine. You're the one who thought of Jolene."

"Let's pretend we've done whatever your plan was instead. Fucked off to Paris and located a neighborhood that doesn't exist except when it does. What were you thinking to do there? Offer it a Frosty? Wave a wand? Did the Clockmaker build you one of those?"

He shrugs. "Say 'Open Sesame?'"

Grunting, she glances toward the house. Back to Spook in the Jeep.

In the Jeep. *Something…*

"What now?" Normal asks quietly. Nudging her along. Knowing she's got something. Almost does.

"Now you go home," says the voice beside them.

It isn't as close as it sounds, Nadine knows this even as she whirls with her hands flying up to protect her face.

The voice came from across the street, from all the way across the yard. From those porch steps. But it's the voice from Tony's phone message, the one that lured them here in the first place. Not the sister, the one who'd mostly spoken to them last time, but the griever. More recent griever. The one who'd sold Tony both halves of the watch case.

Nadine watches the woman step into the grass. Solidify as shape. There's her hair, like a mass of leaves piled around her face, which is just a less dark spot in this light. Her eyes are less dark spots within that.

"There's nothing for you, here," says that voice.

Naturally, the Collector steps forward. Practically skips, has to keep from bounding like a chained puppy toward its master. Except this time—as only Nadine could have noticed, and only because she has known and restrained and sometimes out-bounded him for so long—there's just the slightest hesitation. As if the eagerness is a front.

"There's nothing for anyone, here" he says, his voice one note too cheerful. "There's nothing *here*."

On the porch, the sister has emerged. The one Nadine had designated, on their first visit, as the stronger of the two, and so the bigger threat. She comes slowly down the stairs, tugging a shawl around her shoulders, and slides an elbow through her sister's. Locks tight. As though they're all about to play Red Rover. But the women just stand there, spinster siblings from every Victorian gothic ever written. Or Circe and Clone-Circe on their Aeaeae-of-the-Forest.

"Go home," the stronger sister says. She sounds older than Nadine remembered.

For symmetry, Nadine takes the Collector's elbow. Unexpectedly, she has to drag him with her into the yard. But he comes.

At the moment their feet leave road, move into softness just a touch too soft for grass, she has a terrifying moment of vertigo, as though she has stepped into open air, isn't falling but will the second she stops moving. Unless that is exactly what's happening, nothing *as-though* about it. She tightens her arm against the Collector's, feels bones. Hers, his. The vertigo, real or imagined, passes. Almost. She glances down, sees her feet. Whatever they're stepping in is grass-like, wet, and sticks to her sneakers. Quite possibly, it's grass.

The sisters watch. No one seems to know what to say.

"Listen," the Collector finally starts (*but after how long? How wet* are *her feet, all of a sudden, and why does the night feel like it's sweeping past them like floodwater released from a dam?*). "We're not here to..."

Movement stops him, the neighbors to their left not so much materializing at the edge of the yard as cohering. Not there, then there. Nadine recognizes them from last time. The dad with the kid. The dad has a shotgun this time. And the kid—*Christ's sake*—has a rake. Which is taller than he is.

"She said go home," says the father. If not for the shotgun, he'd sound about as menacing as a retiree chasing doorbell ditchers off his porch.

But out here in the trees, with that watch in its newly repaired case ticking in the Collector's pocket, and the world beyond the woods teeming with ghost-ferrets…

The grieving sister bursts into laughter, staccato and bumpy as nightjar call. Not nasty, but in tune with the dark. "Stay if you like." Waving at the neighbors, she turns for her house.

"How about we go where you're going?" says the Collector.

The grieving sister continues to her front door and holds it open, but the older one glances back on her way up the steps. "There's nothing for you here." She's the one who sounds sadder, this time. Her grief is older, Nadine thinks. Has filled every inch of her, hardened like cement. They stare at each other, the woman and Nadine, as though from separate banks of a river just too wide and wild to cross.

Or an ocean, Nadine thinks as her eyes fill with tears and her senses with the memory of slanting Lissycasey rain, apple caramel cake, damp peat smoking instead of burning in the grate. Her mother in a house not so different—not different at all, except for being in a village with a map dot—from this one.

"Nothing for us, either, really," the woman murmurs. Almost kindly. Like a mother, though not Nadine's mother. Nadine's mother's kindness has more cattle prod in it. Deeper serrations.

She takes another step after the sisters, and the shotgun rises in the father's hand.

"Don't bother," says the grieving woman, still holding open her house door. "Leave them be." Then she's gone.

The neighbors, too, melt away into the dark. Nadine wants to leap up onto the porch and kick the door as it smacks shut. She doesn't, mostly because she can't imagine what for, and now she and the Collector are alone again in a yard beside a road in the Redwoods. Arm in arm. Not just in the middle of nowhere, but nowhere.

She can feel the Collector deflating, even as he too glances down at his shoes or the grass. His shoes in the grass. Both clearly where they should be. "I don't know what to do, now," he says.

Inspiration comes only as she's reaching for his hand, which is the only gesture she has ever been sure connects her to anything.

"I do?" She hasn't meant it as a question, but that's what comes out.

Releasing Normal, she lunges for the back of the Jeep. The zipper on the canvas there resists, then pops as she jerks upward. The canvas sags sideways like a lolling tongue. Rooting around in the metallic mini-space that passes for a trunk, she locates the catch on the trapdoor to the tool well, yanks it open.

There it is, right where it has been since the last time they were here. Forgotten in the mania of the morning that followed: Tony's breakdown, the paramedics and police, that awful aftermath-breakfast at Poppa Joe's when they both intuited, for the first time, what it was they kept brushing against. Chasing after.

Articulated for the first time, anyway.

Arms trembling, holding her breath, Nadine lifts out the box. The one she found on a blanket laid almost exactly where the Collector now stands. Inside it, the little plastic View-Master reels stir together like hibernating bats in a breeze in a cave.

Box tight against her chest, Nadine returns to the yard. She starts to lower it, thinks better of setting it in the wetness, and puts it at the edge of the road instead. The Collector, she realizes, has no idea what this is. Probably doesn't even remember that she bought anything here. Possibly never knew. Prying back the lid, she looks down at the dozens of white wheels nestled in protective packing peanuts.

"Right," she says. "Grand. Where to?"

As she riffles the wheels, the Collector stands over her. He doesn't ask, knows he doesn't need to. Also, of course, he's fascinated. By the box and by her in pretty much equal measure. Inquiring too soon would drain mystery from moment. Eject them from this private nowhere they've spent most of their lives working to create and sustain, not escape.

She holds up a wheel and her phone, tilting the plastic into the glow so she can make out the tiny black labeling letters. "Sunken Gardens. Want to try there?" She lays that wheel on her leg, pulls out another. "How about Valhalla? Word is they have a cracking day spa..."

Muttering, she goes on sifting. The Collector kneels. He waits until he can't stand it anymore, then slides his own hands into the box and starts pulling up his own wheels.

"Nod," he says after a few seconds, holding a disc carefully by its edges, squinting into the tiny blackened picture windows.

"The one in the Bible?"

"The land of trembling."

"Hmm," says Nadine, sorting more wheels. "Prefer the Valhalla Day Spa, I think."

"Which you just made up."

"As opposed to the Land of Nod, you mean? Or maybe you don't. Oh, fuck's sake, *get outta my garden.* Come on, now." She stares a second longer at the latest reel she has removed, then extends it toward the Collector.

"I can't see it," he says. "You're blocking the light."

"Then I'll read it to you." She does.

He stares at her. The discs he has stacked on his knees slide sideways, and he lunges to catch them, misses most. They spill into the dirt and lie there, winking every now and then when stray phone-light flicks across them, like flatfish. Land stingrays. Impossible creatures they've dredged from some unimaginable seafloor.

"'*Our Parisian home*,' the Collector repeats. "It really says that?"

"Read it yourself."

"You're blocking the light."

"Shut up. It says it."

His laugh is the sound her current smile would make if it made one. Frustrated. Exasperated. Scared. Exhausted.

Excited.

"So that's where they are?" she finally says. "The Buddha and his son?"

The Collector shrugs. "You seem to think so."

"I think it's where they want to be." She shakes the reel at him. "Their Parisian home."

"But why would their Parisian home be in a box in Jo—"

"I also don't think it matters, Do you?"

"What do you mean? Why not?" Normal asks, but not as though he's challenging her. More like he's catching up, wanting his own reasoning explained to him. His next question is a better one. "I don't suppose there are instructions or directions on the back. Map coordinates, rooms-that-aren't-there schematics, specialist travel agents to contact?"

Turning the wheel over, Nadine shines her phone light on the reverse side. But all she finds is one word. "Sawyers."

"What's that?"

Gnawing the inside of her cheek in frustration, Nadine stands. "Ones who saw?" She opens a web browser on her phone, does a quick check. "Wait a minute. Listen. It's also something sticking up out of water, like part of a tree, that blocks navigation. So maybe I'm wrong! Maybe these discs are *false* trails."

"Like obstacles!" says the Collector. "Things we have to get around."

"Or else it's the toy company," Nadine mutters, and holds up her phone in his face. "Sawyers. They made View-Masters." A dozen different swear words fill her mouth, and she expels them together, as though spitting out a gumball chewed free of flavor.

"*Pffhftack.*"

In the woods—a somewhere more miraculous than anyplace they have been or dreamed—the silence ignores them. Goes about its business.

The Collector stirs. "The point is, it's here,"

It takes effort for Nadine to remember to respond, find words. "What is?"

"That wheel. *Our Parisian home.* It's in a box full of made-up places in this real place that's also a made-up place that you just happened to find one day and take home."

"To our made-up place," Nadine says.

In exactly the way she wanted, for exactly the reason she wanted, he smiles at her. She nods. "Okay. You're right. Let's at least get a better look at it."

Holding the disc in front of her eyes, she fiddles with her phone, turns the brightness all the way up. Light blooms. It still barely penetrates the dimness, and trying to look into those tiny black windows is still like peering through a hedge. But as her eyes adjust, colors surface. Reds and blues. As though she's illuminating an oil spill. She glimpses a shape in there. Possibly.

Several more seconds pass before she realizes she has been holding her breath. As though she had jumped off a high dive into a pool. Except without the pool.

"Shit," she murmurs. Dropping the Collector's hand, she returns to the Jeep. "Where's the flashlight?"

Spook, who has been huddled in the back all this time, finally looks up as she approaches. "What are you trying to do?"

"Have light."

Wordlessly, he slides out the driver's side of the Jeep, reaches around the steering wheel, and flicks on the headlamps.

Hands still jammed under the passenger seat, Nadine swivels. She glances at Spook, then the beams of yellow-white poking into the trees.

"Good on ya," she says, brushing grass from her jeans. "Good man, you. Always have been."

"What have you got?" Spook sounds more like himself than he has in hours. Calm and sad. Content to be with them.

She tries a conspiratorial smile. The one he and she usually share while watching the Collector pore over something, forget they're there. It's not the right one for this moment, but it's all she's got. "Thanks for coming to save me."

"Nadine…" he starts, stops. A flush spreads over his face. She has never once seen it there before. Unless it's the shadow that is always there. Unless *that* has always been a blush. Which makes her blush, she has no idea why.

"Back in a minute," she says.

Then she's laughing, they both are. She has no idea about that, either. She shakes her head, at herself as much as him. Also at her man, Mr. Map and the Clockmaker, this whole stupid year. Always, even in our most intimate moments, we are speaking in code. And even when we've given each other encryption keys—even if we've kept, memorized, and internalized them—we never catch the whole message. Not once. Not ever. About anything.

Beckoning the Collector, she moves into the headlight beams at the front of the Jeep and kneels. He joins her.

"Right," she says. "Let's see where *home* is."

"Right here," he whispers, and for a second, she's so startled she's almost afraid to look up. Look at him. Then she does.

Meaning her? Did he even really speak?

Receiving. Transmitting. Seven. Six. Nine. Null.

"Gobshite," she says, and tilts the View-Master wheel into the light.

It makes a wet popping sound, like a kiss, as it sucks her off her feet and into it.

5

Nadine's first thought, at the instant she catches up to thought, is that she fell off the road into the forest. And it's true, these are leaves she's peering through, long and fat like the bodies of green mandolins. They vibrate when she twitches, tickle her arms while their branches poke into her ribs.

Not redwood leaves, though. No way. So, not Jolene forest.

Also, she appears to be standing, not falling. She's fairly sure she was never falling.

Also, whatever tree this is, she's standing *in* it. On a branch, which tilts beneath her as she glances down and then grabs instinctively for trunk, bigger branch, anything to hold her where she is.

Which is, yep, in a tree. The top of a tree. Which is on the ground.

Not toppled or fallen. *Upside down.* Leaves and branches splayed over earth, the trunk above her, bowing out and up into blank, flat sky, its gnarled roots opening like a hundred upturned hands to the air.

Actually, not like hands. They aren't reaching *for*; they're burrowing *into.* Like, um, roots. The sight triggers something. Reminds Nadine of something.

"Whoops," says the Collector from behind and to her left.

He's on his own branch, hands flung wide for balance; apparently, he hasn't yet noticed the ground six inches beneath him.

"*Whoops*?" she snaps. "Which whoops were you referring to, then? Our mode of transport? Our destination? The evident deterioration in Parisian arboreal care and park design, because this tree..."

...is a horse chestnut. Is perfect, lush, green, and wondrous. Is or was or might as well have been plucked (and then flipped) from the Jardin du Luxembourg.

Which is what she was remembering.

Which makes this Paris, after all?

"Come up!" calls a voice from all the way up at the top—bottom—of the trunk.

There he is, leaning over some sort of wooden balcony rail jutting out from the cracked, gray bark maybe fifty feet over their head. Even without the red smoking jacket or whatever it is he has donned, the Rev would have reminded Nadine of Mr. Toad at that moment. Just because of the glee in his tone. And the fact that he's leaning out of a tree.

He waves and vanishes.

"Does that mean he's sending the lift?" the Collector mutters, still unsteady as he leans from his own branch toward Nadine's.

A good third of the route up to that platform has branches wide enough to step on, at least as thick as the ones currently supporting them. Then comes a stretch of bowed trunk pitched at a comfortable climbing angle. After that, though, they'd need crampons. Pitons. Or a crane.

As the Collector steps across, Nadine drops to her haunches and starts spreading leaves. She knocks on the branch beneath her, studies the trunk ahead, looking for hinges, hints of hidden doorframe. Ignoring the Collector's outstretched hand—which isn't even reaching for her anymore, he sees what she's doing—she stands again, steps forward, then stops, surprised. Stares down at her feet. Abruptly, she laughs.

"Remember the Badlands?" she says, still looking at her shoes. She's a little worried that when she next tries to step, the tree will suck her deeper into it, like quicksand. But it lets her go with just the faintest hint of clutch, like a parent playing monster, allowing a child to escape. She laughs again.

"The ones in South Dakota?"

"Those basalt domes that you can climb because the rock's so soft your feet and fingers sink into it?"

Kneeling, the Collector lays his own hands against their branch, presses down.

"Do you remember?" Nadine says.

"I remember you giggling like a five year-old when you went up them."

Nadine shrugs. "Causeway high. Magical feeling. Come on." Carefully at first, then less carefully, she parts leaves and starts forward. She presses down hard with each step, then realizes she doesn't need to. When she reaches the trunk, she leans into it, settling herself on her hands. She imagines—can *see*—herself there, perched like a lizard mid push-up.

Digging in with her fingertips, kicking her feet into the spongy bark, she launches herself upward. It's even easier than she hoped. The bark depresses to her touch, seems to mold around the tips of her shoes and fingers until she pushes off again, then fills itself back in. Branches almost seem to anticipate her arrival, bend back as she reaches them. She's a good fifteen feet off the ground (or whatever it is underneath the upside-down tree, which she has decided not to think about right this second), and has started laughing like a little kid on a jungle gym or herself at the Badlands, when she realizes the Collector has remained where she left him, staring up. At her, past her. He hasn't so much as put foot to trunk.

"It's easy," she calls.

"Looks easy." He doesn't move.

"Are you actually scared?"

At least he focuses directly on her, now. Then, very slowly, he tilts his head all the way back toward the sky—if it's sky—overhead. Down at the ground. If it's ground. Up the trunk she's climbing and back to her.

Nadine sighs. "Of the tree, you bollocks. The climbing. Are you scared of *that*?"

To her amazement, the Collector shrugs.

"You are? *You*? Jesus, Mary, and Wee Alex Driver, *come* on. You'll climb into the mouth of a dragon to see if its tongue's pink, but you won't climb a couch cushion, which is what this basically is, and come up here with me?"

"I didn't say I wouldn't."

Nadine reaches down a hand, dangles it in the air way over his head. "There, so. Up you come. I always took you for a childhood tree-climber."

"We had saner trees."

Which, weirdly, makes Nadine think of home. Not Ireland, but her current home, with this man, amid sequoias and redwoods.

"No, you didn't," she says softly.

That works, as she knew it would. As it almost always does, though only with him. She can see it in his eyes. In the change to the set of his mouth. He sees what she's seeing, now: their redwoods, silent in slow summer light, in evening mist.

He lays his hands on the trunk.

After that, they climb in silence. Emerging from the highest branches is like coming through a cloud in an airplane: one second, they're surrounded, swaddled, and the next there's nothing. Except here, there's even more nothing, somehow. Nadine can't quite pin down what she means and doesn't want to. She makes herself keep going, study the bark, which is grooved and gray. Not just bark-like, but bark, except beetle-free, birdless. Devoid of knot holes or woodpecker pecks. The grooving and flaking looks appropriately uneven, but also artfully so.

Like a sketch, she can't stop herself from thinking.

Like...

'What temperature is this?" says the Collector, still a good twenty feet below her but climbing steadily now. Not stopping to ask the question. But also, unlike her, not stopping asking, either.

"I know what you mean," Nadine says. Because she does. She's not sweating, is unaware of being warm. She's also not comfortable or cool. Every few seconds—not regularly, not predictably, which is as it should be, surely—susurration occurs around her, and the leaves below and the ground below that stir, maybe even rustle.

But does she actually feel breeze? Or *hear it*?

The whole place has that quality of places in dreams, tangible without exuding anything sensory. Real the way a bubble is in the instant it's a bubble. Essentially ephemeral, though, teetering on the edge of gone.

Like us, Nadine thinks, clutching bark, jamming fingers into the grain and grooves. *Like all the worlds we create in the instant we're us. Gone when we go.* To her surprise, underneath the flaky gray of the trunk, she feels wetness. Sticky, a little heavy.

Sap, she realizes, and her internal alarm tings. Because, right, this tree having sap is the scary bit. Scowling, withdrawing fingers from trunk, she does indeed find liquid glistening there. Not dark, like maple sap. Also not clear. Not any specific color, really, and also...

...not there. Not just evaporated, or sunk into her skin. Gone. Her skin dry. She sticks her fingers into trunk again. Feels the flow in there. Slow, but not steady. It comes in surges.

"You can't stop there," the Collector calls, maybe ten feet beneath her. "Nadine, please, I can't—"

"Yeah, you wee ninny, okay." She considers tasting her fingertips. Also saying something to the Collector. Decides it can wait. Up she goes.

Right near the top—bottom, whatever—the tree tilts back over her, so that she's clinging, climbing with her spine almost parallel to the ground. It dawns on her, just as it did on the Jolene forest road, that she has gone too far, has somehow climbed past the balcony, or worse, the balcony has vanished like the sap and left her clinging to an upside-down impossibility over absolutely nothing. Over void. In desperation she makes herself look up, which has to be better than sideways or down.

Not only has reached the balcony—platform, ridge of roots, whatever it is—from which the Rev shouted at them, but there's a set of steps and handholds cut into the bark, like a pool ladder. No climbing maneuvers or nauseating dangling over inverted space necessary. She can just pull herself over the edge and up.

"It's okay," she calls to the Collector. "We've made it."

"Oh good," he answers. "Then we'll be there."

She considers waiting for him. Realizes that doing that might be not just kind, but prudent. Then she grabs the nearest handhold—the bark sturdy, yielding to her grip but also gripping back—and pulls herself onto flat wooden planking.

Balcony, then.

Or watchtower platform?

Balcony. Because what's out there beyond it, unfurling in all directions, is blankness, all the way to the blank horizon. *Blank* really is the word. It's not just hard to tell where sky meets ground; more like sky and ground haven't been filled in yet. What's overhead is colorless but also cloudless. What's below has neither covering nor slope nor ridges. No features of any kind.

What temperature is this, Nadine thinks, in the Collector's voice, as his head appears over the side of the balcony.

It's not actually flat down there, she realizes. It's *not anything...*

Instinctively, she glances down at her fingertips, where sap isn't. Was. Has left no residue.

But it was there. Not dark. Not colorless, but also not quite any color.

Except that she's seen it before. So often that it has folded into her life, disguised itself as ordinary. Understanding flares momentarily, evaporates before she can hold it.

"Normal," she says as he crawls onto the platform, pushes to his feet, and stares outward.

"Whoa," he murmurs.

The branches below—and the nothing below them and maybe above, too—rustle again in that breeze that isn't there. *Is* there, but isn't breeze.

"Tea?" calls the Buddha.

Whirling, Nadine opens her mouth to swear or cry out but does neither. Doesn't need or want to. In there, at least, through the towering French doors built into the base of the tree, is exactly what she expected to see:

Same room, the one she has dreamed ever since the single night she spent in it. The night her life started. Night before, anyway. The freest, loneliest hours of her life. Possibly the only hours she has ever or will ever have spent when she was simply herself, alone. No part anyone else. Also no one's. Almost no one.

Such a rare, impossible gift. How many people ever get to have those hours?

No rug, this time. Same fireplace, though, with the low brick front with the chipping in its crevices. Same *fire*, Nadine thinks. She's not even sure what she means, she's just sure that it is. Same height of the flames. Same muted, too-regular crackling sounds, which she'd noted then without actually noticing. As if this were a projected fire. Except it throws heat.

Same couch. The Buddha on it, wearing quite possibly the same billowy blue shirt.

The ropes tying him in place are new, though.

"Valhalla," she says abruptly. "Mount Olympus. All those possible inspirations. And you dream this?" She waves at the room, the fireplace.

"Why does everyone assume dreams have to be crazy? That's where the LSD-faddists went wrong." A corner of his mouth curls into a smirk. The look of a man who'd pull your pants down to steal a key. "*Psychedelia*. Purple snow and flying lozenges."

"Whereas you dream bad chipped, unnecessary fire, and tea?" *While playing some kind of bondage game, possibly with your kid*? Nope, she isn't even ready to ask about the ropes, yet.

The Buddha's smirk melts into a tired smile. "In an upside-down tree, to be fair."

"Nadine," the Collector murmurs. He's by the big casement window cut into the other side of the trunk. But he's not looking out it, as there's nothing to see. Instead, he's looking down at his feet. At the hole in the floor.

It's maybe three feet across, with translucent tubes sprouting from it. As though the hole has been disemboweled.

She joins him. They stand together. After a few seconds, she kneels. Instinctively, she doesn't want to get too close. She also keeps wanting to whip her head around, make sure the Buddha's ropes are real and tied tight. So he can't push her in.

Cautiously, she edges forward. It occurs to her that one way or another, she really is about to become the girl in the stories. The one who discovers the body in the well, or becomes it.

The hole dives deep into the trunk of the tree. The tubes, she realizes, aren't part of the trunk, never were. Are less intestines than straws. Sucking up that ephemeral, not-gold, not-clear sap.

Because Buddha and son have tired of street-crepes, and are all about the pancakes, now?

"The clock!" she says abruptly, and stands. *That's* where she's seen that color. Every day, all the time.

In the pendulum of the wishing-tree clock.

In the sliver of something in the Collector's palm, that he brought to the Family Pride.

Flickering in the cassette cases on the pirate radio boat off the Farallons.

In the ridged, raised fingers of Tony's watch.

In Binna's key, and the hinge and lock of her family's *bouquiniste* bin.

This color has, in fact, infused every moment of Nadine's life since that day in Paris. The realization should be reassuring. This material, whatever it is, kept Normal a sort of normal. Helped him fight and briefly restrain his ghost-ferrets. But right this moment, Nadine can't find comfort in it. She's turning toward the couch, gathering breath to ask any one of the thousand questions bubbling in her brain, when she notices the room's other brand-new feature. The one other thing, along with the French doors and giant window, that wasn't in this room when it was in an alley in San-Germain-des-Pres:

the oversized, not-quite-gold spigot mounted halfway up the window on the other side of the fireplace.

Even as she tugs on the Collector's arm, pointing, she realizes there's more to it. It's as if she herself is sketching it all into existence just by noticing. If so, she thinks, she should stop.

Can't.

The translucent tubes—all of them, encircle the fireplace, feed into nozzles connected to the spigot. On the other side of the glass, outside, is what looks at first like some kind of insane miniature Ferris wheel, maybe five feet in diameter: a circle of not-quite-gold spoked rods, with little baskets on the ends.

Except they're not baskets. More...sprinkler heads? With...rotary fans attached? Something? She has no idea what this is, or what it does.

So why does it scare her?

All she knows is the Collector is scared, too. She finds herself thinking about that KQED reporter on the radio, standing on a San Francisco rooftop and watching people pee in paint down the sides of their buildings.

As they watch, the wheel rotates, propelled by whatever's stirring out there. Breathing out there.

"Bird feeder?" she murmurs weakly, trying for lightness. Trying to feel lightness, or generate it.

"Mobile for the grandkids?" says the Collector.

But Nadine is looking at the tubes. The whole thing reminds her of machines in Charlie Chaplin industrial factories that shoot messages up to the boss. Or—yes, this, even more—like one of the mechanisms that spit out thneeds. A holdover from the Once-ler's factory, or his house. *Which was also in a tree, wasn't it? Was that a tree? A dead one?*

She eyes the Buddha. Wonders, suddenly, where the Rev is, turns back fast, sees the wheel turning in whatever's blowing. The sap slowly feeding into it. For no reason, the memory of Tony's screaming reverberates through her, and the taste of apple-caramel cake surfaces on her tongue. Full-blown taste, not memory. The sensation is too strong for memory.

Maybe that should scare her, too. It powers her instead.

"Right," she says, nodding at the Buddha. At the ropes binding him to the couch. "Are you *asking* for tea? Or did you need us to bring you some?"

Glancing down at his ropes, the Buddha sighs. As though he'd forgotten. "I had doubts," he says.

"Doubts?" calls the Rev, actually skipping as he enters from whatever other rooms burrow deeper into the tree trunk. He's not carrying a tea tray. Instead, he's got another length of translucent tubing. Nadine notes the way his fingers sink just a little into its surface, the way hers did into the tree bark.

Because it's the same surface, she realizes, somehow holding in another shudder, clinging to her thoughts as they hurtle through her. *Like everything here.*

Laying the tube next to the hole, the Rev looks at his father and laughs. "You built a *dungeon.* In *our tree.* To put *me* in!"

"It's not your tree," Nadine blurts. Which, right, is hardly the most important revelation she's in the midst of having. Not in the top 10,000, actually. But it's a start.

Kneeling, the Rev drops the tube through the opening, reaches in to do some sort of affixing. The whole process looks mundane, mechanical. As magical as plumbing.

"Whatever do you mean?" he says.

She can't see his face, but knows he's smiling. "Paris," she says. It's an accusation. She's not sure of what, yet, but trusts herself. "That room in the Musee d'Orsay."

"It's hardly a room. Barely a wall. Is it even a permanent exhibit?"

Closing her eyes, Nadine can almost will herself back there. Give her a View-Master reel and a wishing-tree clock pendulum, and she'd be there this instant. As it is, she can almost feel the Collector's hand—brand new for her, then—in hers. And she can see those paintings.

"The Temple of Thought," she murmurs.

"Tomb of a Poet," says the Collector beside her. Then, and now. She hears both, as though in overlay, not quite synched. He knows what she's talking about. Has followed her memory trail before she even left him one.

"City of Tomorrow."

He's right, the Rev. It was just a wall. A few drawings and paintings plus some mostly French text, collectively taking up half a room somewhere upstairs. A bunch of crazy fin-de-siècle architects dreaming impossible spaces and dedicating them to Beethoven or Babel or their dead mothers.

Towers sprouting at ridiculous angles from giant boulders into empty space. Waterfalls of light pouring from the void. Treehouses in upside-down trees.

"All that dreamspace," the Rev says, clucking his tongue. "You know, they really meant to build those structures, those guys."

"You couldn't be bothered to dream your own?"

"This is a placeholder, I admit. I've been busy." He stands, tugging the unattached end of the tube toward the spigot mounted on the window. "Come see."

Partly to buy time—because she has no idea what to do, or to whom, or for what exact reason—and partly because, come on, she's staring at translucent tubes connecting an upside-down tree to a miniature outdoor sprinkler-Ferris-wheel, Nadine follows. She watches him affix the tube to an open nozzle, then step back as she approaches, hands up by his shoulders, palms out. *No threat.*

Or else, *Look ma, no hands…*

She sees what she saw before. Sap-pipelines feeding into that spigot, which, turned on, presumably will pour liquid into those sprinkler heads out there. Which will…spray them into the air. Not air.

To irrigate what? With *what*?

"Right, so." She glances toward the Collector, who's just looking at her. Alarmed and stumped. No help whatsoever. "You're…going to make the ground sticky? No, wait, you'd need ground, first."

The Rev grins. Too wide. Fanatic's grin. "All I need is the air."

Still wearing that helpless look, the Collector slides sideways to the Rev's left. Looking for an attack angle, Nadine realizes.

So, not quite stumped. As sure as she is of the threat, even if neither of them understands what it is, yet.

She makes herself hold the Rev's gaze, runs a hand through her hair. It feels loose and wild on her shoulders and yet reassuringly rooted in her. Sprung from her. Essentially and crucially *of* her.

Why does that matter? It just does.

All he needs is the air.

And some stolen stuff.

"That's our clock pendulum," she snaps, pointing at the spigot.

"It was never yours. It's not mine, either. But I've got a better use for it. Want to see?" With a magician's flourish, he produces Binna's *bouquiniste* box key from his pocket, leans over, and slides it into a slot on the spigot. Then twists.

Whatever's happening, it does it slowly. A slight increase—maybe—in the flow of no-color liquid through no-specific-color tubing. Out into those sprinkler-heads, which tilt, tilt back. They really do look like miniature Ferris wheel baskets suspended over the Earth. Awaiting the kick of the motor. The call to motion.

Which comes on its own, and isn't a motor. A puff of breeze.

The Rev waits and watches. She can practically hear him hopping up and down inside himself, all delira and excira, for reasons she is absolutely sure are no good.

The sort-of-breeze intensifies, tilts the wheel, and the sprinkler heads twitch, whirl, spit sap into the air. Which evaporates almost instantly.

Or goes wheeling off. Like a locust cloud.

Or ghost-ferret pod.

Almost, already, Nadine knows. Understands. *Knows.* Can't quite articulate. Not yet.

It's clearly hopeless, meanwhile—he doesn't have an angle, and the Rev is tracking him—but the Collector tries a feint. The Rev swings his glance that way, bright as a watchtower searchlight. It freezes the Collector where he is. The Rev laughs.

The air, Nadine thinks. *Shootouts, harbor fires, naked bike rides, outlet mall riots. Pandora's box. Ghost ferrets going ferret.*

"*That's* what you turned to thieving for? To build a faucet? You know, IKEA these days, they have—"

"Stop it. I needed more. You know it. A concentration. That's what...I don't understand any more than you do. Well, slightly more, but that's because you're being willfully dense. A little of this stuff sliding down your lungs...tingling on your tongue...humming your ear. You've experienced that already. But take just a little more. Concentrate it. Connect it to itself and *harvest* it. And set it loose in the air."

"To go where?' says the Collector, sounding small again. Because he knows now, too. Is in the process of understanding, same as Nadine.

"Everywhere," says the Rev. Just standing there grinning, as he banjaxes the world. "Typical of you two, and your small-mindedness, to look at this space. Berate me for my lack of imagination. Me, I was thinking location."

"The center of the wind."

"Of all wind. The winds that cover the world." He folds his arms in a gesture so king-of-gorillas, Nadine half expects him to thump his chest.

"So for the culmination of your batshit lifelong dream, you've sent the world breeze-borne syrup. You're the Maple Man."

"I am the fucking liberation."

"Oh, boy," Nadine murmurs.

On the couch, the Buddha stirs. He's not exactly struggling against his ropes, more bumping against them. "Son..." he murmurs.

"That's where my doubts come from, you know. That kind of talk"

"That's why you're tied to our couch."

"Liberator of what?" Nadine snaps. "*From* what? Reality? You've gone completely off your—"

"Wrong question. Again," says the Rev, and for one moment, he sounds again as he did when he arrived at her house this afternoon: like a vibrant, lit-up kid. Like that rarest, most astonishing thing on Earth, and possibly the universe: a human being, alive. "What you mean is *of whom*. And what I answer is...*everyone*."

She has no idea what to say. Not even a set of choices. But he's just getting started.

"Reality. When do you think it was, in the history of human evolution, that we decided to divorce reality from dreaming? When did we start to imagine that was even possible? What have we dedicated all our new technology and science to? *Virtual* reality. *Augmented* reality. Because we've finally—*as a species*—figured it out, even if we haven't admitted it to ourselves yet: we've had it backwards. Since the beginning of human thought."

There's definitely an argument Nadine wants to make, knows she should. Must. But she can't find it yet. Possibly because he hasn't hit the objectionable bit. So far, all he has done is chant the unspoken Nadine-Normal Manifesto.

"Nadine and the legendary Collector. Please, either one of you, tell me: what do you call the places you've been? All those stories you've told me. That *house* you live in. I mean it, take me and my dad completely out of the equation. Is that reality, where you live? Where you have ever wanted to live? *In the redwood trees*! Along the Avenue of the Giants!"

On the Causeway, Nadine thinks. Won't let herself say.

"What's the difference between my treehouse and yours? That mine's in a tree I dreamed? Well, what if we've had the human equation wrong? What if we took the thing inside us that dreams—the thing that is *most us*—and turned it loose? What if we finally admitted that reality *is* dreaming?"

The Collector is listening. But he's also looking at the couch. The Buddha and his ropes. Doing that thing he does, that has pulled them back from so many brinks, brought them home time and again.

And so ejected them from the reality they both keep seeking?

"You're finally understanding, aren't you?" The Rev isn't smirking anymore. He's not even lecturing. He's pleading. Not for the first time, she feels a jarring wave of sympathy. Unmistakable attraction. Most of all, *kinship.* Because it really is lonely—by design, by definition—inside worlds we let ourselves dream.

"Think about it, Nadine. What is it that makes dreams, makes music, makes insanity and wars and wildness, yes, but also the whole idea of freedom? Of being able to experience, of recording and translating and communicating experience? That way of living isn't just there for our taking. It's the *only way there's ever been.*

"That feeling you keep brushing up against...these amazing people you've met and the things they've almost harnessed...it's been bubbling underneath us since long before there *was* us. Like magma, or one of those coal fires that can't be put out and goes on burning right under our feet, no matter what we do. Because the Earth *is fire.* And we've wasted most of human history trying to leap clear of it. Building churches, schools, systems of governance, civilizations to cool and stamp out the very thing that makes us us. To ensure that the fire that made us is dead in our blood before we can crawl or speak."

On the couch, the Buddha is watching his son, mouth open, hands clenched on the ropes that bind him, but not as though he wants to rip free of them. *Like me peering over the edge of the Grand Canyon,* she thinks. *Like the old guy in the back at a Run the Jewels show. Like a Clinton democrat at an Ocasio-Cortez rally. Seeing the future he helped imagine. Dreading the revolution he helped instigate. Believing he should act, could still act, but also knowing revolutions destroy what they create. Along with their creators.*

For the first time—then or now—Nadine is jarred by sympathy for *him*. Worse, she realizes she *is* him. She and Normal both. The old and paralyzed people at the back.

That's when she hears the clink. Or *a* clink.

The Rev is still raving. "And yet. Every now and then, despite all our efforts, it gets loose, and the world goes wild. Christs and Maimonideses and Mohammeds and Beethovens appear and keep appearing. Renaissances happen. Dirt diggers pull a couple of bones out of the Earth and somehow conceive creatures that set the whole planet trembling, gaping, and marveling. Light refracts into paint and suddenly we have Impressionism, and everyone alive goes out to stand on bridges in rain. Electricity and phonographs, Stonehenge and the Temple of Thought, ordnance surveys of the moon, of our own cells.

"And that's on *fumes*, Nadine. On seepage. Can you imagine what's going to happen—what's already started happening—when I get enough sap out of this tree and unleash it?"

Clink. Slide of foot over brick, onto floor. Because of course, what else but the fireplace would Binna have remembered about this room, focused on when she dreamed it?

Don't turn, Nadine commands herself. Begs herself. She makes herself stare right back at the Rev. Hold his gaze.

"I can, yeah," she says. "A whole lot of people are going to die."

The Buddha glances toward the fireplace, stirs in his ropes. But he doesn't say anything.

The Rev is too consumed to notice or care. "As opposed to now? Or every other day? Think about it. Rulers dropping disease bombs on their citizens. On children holed up in hovels. Profiteers lighting the rainforest on fire, along with anyone who happens to live in it or stand in their way. Blood libels, ritual beheadings, lethal injections, trillionaires. Thugs who believe in nothing but seducing or transforming kids all over the world into thugs who believe in *them* with a wave of the internet. A post on a webpage, pixels in a box. Dying for the Dow, running trucks into Christmas markets, convincing people they *like* it this hot, and that any steps to save themselves or their children or their species from a pandemic or catastrophic climate change is an infringement on their personal freedoms or unshakable fantasy beliefs. And you..."

That clenched fist falls open, and his hand flutters to his side like a dropped leaflet. He's still raving, but not really talking at Nadine and the Collector; he's talking to his father. "You're one of them."

There hasn't been any more sound from the other side of the fireplace, but Nadine knows what has happened. Knows that Binna, bless her, read the garbled texts Nadine sent, hadn't just kept the remains—the wood, the *lock*— from her family's *bouquiniste* box but remembered where to find them. And then, being Binna, somehow figured out a View-Master reel equivalent or substitute and got herself here.

Has the Buddha recognized her? Is that why he hasn't cried out? Has the Collector recognized her, for that matter?

While he's at it, has he maybe come up with a plan? Because the one Nadine formulated pretty much stopped at this point. Although she does know one more thing, she realizes.

She knows why Binna's shoes clinked when she materialized at the edge of the fire grate. And where the Buddha must have built his dungeon.

"But unleashing that much of it," she says to the Rev. Stalling. Thinking hard. "You said it yourself. Do you know what's happening out there already? You're going to create unspeakable carnage."

"True. But this time, when the carnage stops—if it stops, and maybe it won't and shouldn't—who'll be left? Not conquerors. Not trillionaires. Not titans of industry or kings of control. Not the rich or the prudent. *Creatives*! Artists, visionaries, ecstatisticians—I made that up, like it?—hedonists, sensualists, fanatics, explorers. People building lives worthy of the word. Human beings finally awake to the miracle of being awake.

"Can you really imagine it, Nadine? Because I can."

Reaching down to the spigot, the Rev twists it off, holds up the *bouquiniste* bin key. The glint in his eye—*in everyone's eye, when eyes glint?*—is the flashing not-color of the metal in his hand, the sap in this tree His smile is more childish than devilish. Wide open in a way every sentient being forgets how to be. Or flees from being. Or curbs, just enough.

Most of all, in that last moment, with the earthquake that will trigger the tsunami that will drown the world as they know it in his hands, the Rev looks hopeful.

His smile widens, and it is at least partly for her. "We are such dreams as stuff is made on," he says, and starts back toward the hole in the floor.

The Collector's action is all one motion, and even as he makes it, Nadine realizes he has no actual idea what he's doing. As usual. If there's understanding to be had in the experiences they have shared, she's the one who finds it. He, on the other hand, is a creature of intuition. Half ghost-ferret by birth, not choice. He responds to everything they have glimpsed and touched like a sea to the moon.

Out of his pocket comes the pocket watch. It's his, now, not Tony's, not the grieving sisters of Jolene's. The case pops open in his hands. "Binna!" he shouts, and flings it.

Binna, of course, is a force of her own. A formidable one. She has been a physical presence in Nadine's life only once, for two days a quarter century ago. She has remained one, radiating from texts and emails and postcards and unscheduled phone calls—from Vanuatu, where she, in her own words, "out-Stevensoned the man himself" and set up her first "dual-school", where teachers learn language and culture from the kids they teach, or from K2, which she summitted solo, or from a middle-of-the-night, middle-of-winter club in Helsinki where she got marooned by a snap-blizzard for two days and wound up jamming with 22-Pistepirkko, her "favorite crazy happy onion-band," whatever an "onion band" is—ever since.

What happens is instinct for her, too. Or luck. Or muscle-memory, from that moment on the banks of the Seine, the last time she touched key to lock—*ghost-ferret to itself, carved watch-casing finger to its mate*—and what those moments afterward, that none of them consciously remember, felt like.

Snatching the watch out of the air, she lays her lock atop it. Presses the lid closed as far it will go, as though connecting a battery.

The whole room bends. *Bows*, Nadine thinks, to the extent that she's thinking. *Like a bow pulled back. Floor rising beneath them, bark walls arching outward as the ceiling closes down and the Rev and the Collector spread in the air, stretch and pinken and thin like Silly Putty, so thin and so wide that they become translucent, the bay windows and nothingness out there visible through all of their skins, or else revealed inside them. In the Rev's hands, the key seems to curl back on itself like a wave forming, and in that instant, Nadine can feel the undertow in the air, the savage, sparking rip of it.*

It is not new. She has felt it all her life.

The pull of the Causeway.

Human child. Come.

With a cry she first thinks comes from the key itself and only later realizes came from the Rev, the room releases. Snaps back.

Does she actually see the key flying through air, slamming into lock and watch-case? Or the Rev, still clutching that key, hurtling behind it? Or Binna tumbling back—or purposely wrenching around like a shot-putter—as she lets go and flings him into the flames?

Eventually, Nadine will decide that she didn't see any of that. Couldn't have. Any more than one could track a lightning strike. But she does remember the room snapping back into shape like a rubber band, the whole tree rocking and shaking around them in the aftermath of impact.

And of course, she hears the screaming. Will never stop hearing the screaming.

Her first impulse, at the instant she recognizes having such a thing, is to lunge for the fire, pull out the Rev, save him.

But even as she reaches the fireplace—processes the blandly crackling flames, always and forever that same height, same den-at-midnight low intensity—she realizes. Hears. That scream isn't agony. It isn't even pain. It's fury.

The Rev isn't in the fireplace. He's underneath. Down in the hollowed-out trunk-top—well, bottom—with his hands gripping the no-color ash-grate that has clanged down over him. The flashing in those bars could be a reflection of the flames, or the material they're made of.

The glint in eyes. Dream that stuff is made on...

Automatically, as she has done so many times when passing the wishing-tree clock in their house, glimpsed that flash in it, Nadine closes her eyes. Makes a wish.

When she opens her eyes, Binna has pulled herself back to her feet, rubbing the back of her skull where she banged it and then shaking out her hands, which she will keep doing for hours, as though cooling a burn. The

Buddha hasn't quite wrestled free of his ropes, but he's all tangled up with the effort, and the Collector is kneeling beside him, working at the knots. Momentarily, Nadine wonders if that's such a good idea.

But then she takes in the Buddha's face. It's an old man's face, now, the skin a different, more pedestrian not-color, one with no flash of infinity in it. Sallow and grooved, it clings to his cheekbones, pools at the base of his neck like rumpled sheets after a night of nightmares. Or life of living.

Freed, he pushes to his feet, presses his hands to his shirt as though tucking himself in. Then he stumbles past her to the fireplace and stares down. The screaming from beneath it stops. It's possible, Nadine decides, that she hears a single whispered word.

"*Dad.*"

It's also possible that that was fire crackle.

Meanwhile, she and Binna and the Collector all seem to be lifting their fingers in front of their eyes, tugging at the skin of their arms, patting themselves down. Making sure they're still sealed. Or rather, ordinary-human porous, wide open to air, sound, light which they can neither repel nor hold. Unless memories count.

"Okay?" the Collector says eventually. He takes a hesitant step, as though afraid he's going to burst apart, or tip the tree.

He does neither, comes the rest of the way to her side. She leans into him.

Binna has been staring around the room, out the window, down the tree trunk, into the fireplace. Finally, she turns to the Collector and Nadine. "Ya," she says. "Okay. Need anything else?"

Nadine starts to laugh, and Binna bursts into tears and joins them, and they hold on to one another for a while.

The Buddha is kneeling, now, but looking at the flames, not down and through them. As Nadine watches, he settles on the carpet, crosses his legs.

"Normal." She gestures toward the floor.

The way the Buddha sits, he could be riding a magic carpet. Or levitating above one.

"Is it safe to leave them here? Is that really the plan?"

"This was a plan?" Binna says. Nadine kicks her.

"Safe for whom?" says the Buddha. Chants, really. The words barely words or even mantra, more birdsong. *Safeforwhom, safeforwhom...*

After a few seconds, the Collector runs a hand through his hair and sighs. "What difference would taking them with us make? Unless you're planning to kill them. And even then." Abruptly, he smiles at her. Exhausted smile, with the whole last stretch of his life in it. His eighteen months in her proximity but not her company. In a prison he made for and of himself. "There'll always be people like them."

"Like us," Nadine whispers.

He nods.

"If your concern," the Buddha says, seemingly from far away, from wherever he imagines he's currently floating, "is that this has all been ruse, and for your benefit...and that the second you leave I am going to free him from the Sycorax-like prison I dreamed up and built myself to keep him from finishing what we'd both dedicated our lives to starting..."

At first, no one responds. Eventually, Nadine stirs, meets his placid gaze. "Wouldn't he be Caliban? And you Sycorax?"

The Buddha's smile might have been beatific if it weren't so lonely. "Not on my island."

"Besides," says the Collector. "We won't leave them the means." Leaning over, he picks up the key from where it has fallen, and Binna's hinge, and the pocket watch, separating them all carefully into separate pockets. Then he studies the spigot on the window. In the end, of course, all he needs to do is slide the wishing-tree clock pendulum down a groove that may or may not have been there in the second before he decided—imagined—it should be, and pluck it from the glass. He slides it into his shirt pocket.

"What good is that going to do?" Nadine says. "They've got a whole tree full of this stuff. An irrigator out there they can redream right after we undream it."

The Collector shrugs. "The power, or at least the nuclear explosion, seems to happen when this stuff touches itself. And at least some of it apparently needs to be stuff that exists—meaning, stuff you find, in the world—not just imagine. Right? I mean...they came for Binna's key. And twenty years later, they were still so stuck that they came for our clock."

There's no precise moment or occurrence that triggers their leave-taking. They move apart and around the room for a while, staring out windows, taking solo turns on the balcony, lurking near the fire. Only the Collector gets close enough to gaze down into it. Meet the glinting eyes of the new denizen beneath. Neither he nor the Rev says anything Nadine can hear.

Then, somehow, she and Binna and Normal are together at the door, and the moment has come. And as though he has been waiting for it—or wants to delay it, wants company on his island for just a little longer—the Buddha clears his throat.

"The one remaining question," he says, "is what you'll do with what you now have in your pockets. And whatever else you find out there." He waves his hand at the window, leaves it suspended in the air a few seconds, which really does make him look like some Olympian God painted into a vase, dangling a devil's choice just to see what his pitiful creations do with it.

"Destroy it?" he continues. "Harvest it and seal it in some sort of Pandora's silo? Or upside-down tree? Are you really content leaving what happens to all that *potential*...to chance?"

If the question disturbs or even intrigues the Collector, he doesn't show it. He looks at her. From his expression—lit-up eyes, faint smile—she would guess he is thinking about poached eggs. Or maybe even her. Sometimes, she knows, he really does.

She takes his hand.

Then they're out in the air that has nothing of air in it except, apparently, whatever allows them to breathe it. Over the edge of the balcony goes Binna, without any prompting or instruction, sinking her feet and fingers into the spongy trunk and clinging. With surprisingly little hesitation, the Collector drops to his hands and knees and prepares to follow.

"Look at you, all bold now," Nadine says.

"Twenty minutes ago, I saw my feet through my arms" he mutters. "Made climbing seem less intimidating." He's still trying to figure out which leg to dangle first, though. How to get his feet into the trunk of the tree.

"And yet you continue look like a bulldog chewing a wasp."

"You're supposed to support me in my endeavors. Cheer me on."

"Got better things in mind for you than support."

"Now see, that's helpful," he says, flat on his stomach, jackknifed over the edge. "That's a good distraction. Was that so hard?"

"Insert obvious next line here," Nadine says.

He doesn't quite grin. But he goes. She follows.

The climb does seem easier getting down. Even so, she keeps stopping to look up, half-expecting to find Rev and Buddha leaning over their balcony, grinning and waving and dangling some unexpected implement that will allow them, at last, to free the whirlwind. Flood the whole world before she and the Collector can even get home.

Get home.

Hmm.

At the bottom, standing on a long, heavy branch, waist-deep in other branches and leaves that spread about them like a giant, unwieldy hoop skirt, she and Normal and Binna gaze around. None of them, Nadine notes, bothers glancing up anymore. There's nothing up there. Not above the bottom-top of the tree, anyway.

There's nothing anywhere except blankness, seemingly stretching forever. Except it doesn't even stretch. Has neither distance nor dimension, isn't denuded or empty. It just *isn't.*

"Right, so," Nadine murmurs. "Home is...?"

The Collector pulls out the clock pendulum. "Got your View-Master reel?"

"Yyyyesss..." She pats her pocket. "But it turns out I left the one we never had made of our actual home in my other pants, though."

He purses his lips. Not like he's exasperated. Not even like he's concentrating.

"Also," she says, "while you're considering that. Assuming we do get home somehow. What *are* we thinking we're doing with all that stuff? What's the safe disposal protocol there, are you thinking?"

Raising an eyebrow, the Collector says, "A little to the Clockmaker, by way of thank you?"

Nadine thinks about Clockshop. Those glowing, green aquarium tanks. The Clockmaker with his eyepiece ballooning from his socket.

"Mmm. Not too much there, I think."

"Sure."

"But how about Nartana? To make another flute?"

"Now you're thinking. We'll figure it out."

"Once we're *home*," Binna snaps. "Could we focus on that?"

But suddenly, to her own surprise, Nadine has gone quiet. Feels herself suffused with a calm that seems to come not from her will, or even from her core, but from the life she has lived. The people she has shared it with, to the extent that sharing is possible.

"Listen," she says.

Is it really there, riding the not-breeze? Right where it has always been, only Spook isn't just homing in on the signal or calling it down this time, but beaming it out? Leaving it playing so they can find it?

"Listen to what?" Binna snaps. "I don't even hear my own—"

"Sssh."

It really is there. Nadine is almost sure. Unless she's imagining it. In which case...*thank you, Imagination. For somewhere to imagine going other than nowhere.*

"*Seven. Six. Eight. Five. Null...*"

"That way." She opens her eyes, points into the void.

Immediately, whether he's heard what she does or not, the Collector nods in agreement. Smiles at her.

"Ready to walk the Causeway?" she says.

Hand in hand, Binna behind, they set out together into nothingness which parts in front of them, closes behind them, is something other than nothing only in the instant they pass through it.

ABOUT THE AUTHOR

Three-time International Horror Guild Award Winner Glen Hirshberg's previous novels include *The Snowman's Children*, *The Book of Bunk*, and the *Motherless Children* trilogy. He is also the author of four widely praised story collections: *The Two Sams*, *American Morons*, *The Janus Tree*, and *The Ones Who Are Waving*. A five-time World Fantasy Award finalist, he has won the Shirley Jackson Award for the novelette, "The Janus Tree". He also publishes new fiction, critical writing, and creative nonfiction in his Substack newsletter, *Happy in Our Own Ways* (https://glenhirshberg.substack.com/). He lives with his family and cats in the Pacific Northwest.

Made in the USA
Middletown, DE
08 December 2021